LAFRAGUA

M. A. Fantoni

*Pour Lise et Irvin,
mes vrais amis,
très affectuesement,*

M. A. Fantoni

Shadow & Harley
Lake Worth, Florida

LAFRAGUA

Published by Shadow & Harley
P.O. Box 383, Lake Worth, FL 33460

Library of Congress Control Number: 2003114225

Printed in the United States of America

First Edition: April, 2004

ISBN 0-9746655-0-9

Lafragua—pronounced with the classical 'a' as in 'Ah' and the accent on the second syllable (la-frá-gwa)—is a surname, that of José María Lafragua, who in 1871 left 2,300 books to the, at that time, *Colegio Carolino* in the city of Puebla, Mexico. The library is now named after him, and is now a library of the *Benemérita Universidad Autónoma de Puebla,* the library which inspired in part this fictional story. Apart from serving as a surname, and as the name of a great library, *la fragua* means "the forge." *Fraguar* means "to forge," the work of a blacksmith. *Fraguar* also means "to scheme" or "to hatch a plot." In English, to forge means to make up, form, devise: forge a treaty. It also means to counterfeit: forge a check, a signature, a document, a painting.

CONTENTS

1

MAGALI'S ADVENTURE

It was the evening of July 5th, a Wednesday, about a half hour before nine, and Magali Smith, on her way home for the night, decided to take one more look at the interior of the Church of the Company. It was not for religion that she entered. She had come to Mexico, to the *Universidad de Puebla de los Angeles,* as a professor to assist in the teaching of English, and as a graduate student from Boston University to do some research on the old churches and convents of Puebla.

The Church of the Company, an old Jesuit church, was located right next door to the main building of the university, so on many occasions Magali dropped into the church after her work. She would just enter the church and sit on one of the benches, close her eyes, and let the unique atmosphere transport her back to ancient times.

Magali was fascinated by the mystery connected with all religions. The shapes, the gold, the darkness; the silence; the memory of rites a thousand times repeated—the muffled voices and the Gregorian chanting still lingering among today's saints and sinners; that particular odor, that air rotten with centuries and with incense, dead flowers and cirios, old wood: the patina of time.

She found a pew near the back and to one side and sat, closed her eyes, and relaxed. After a while she opened her eyes and looked around. Above the high altar, and surrounding the apse of the church, the monumental statues of the twelve apostles seemed to sustain the central dome with their strong backs of marble.

In the course of her research she had visited this and most of the other older churches in Puebla. She began to look about the church, following a routine, to see it again and to check that there were no details she had missed on her other visits. One always sees something new, no matter how many times one visits a church. And for her it was important to get all of the details.

She had visited this particular church many times, studying ornaments and statues, confessionals and altars, and old paintings (those somber oils in whose carmesi and soot was born the Velasquez school), and she had observed that the two small doors on each side of the altar of the Virgin of Lourdes were always so tightly closed that they appeared as if they were only painted on the wall.

The door on the left was partially hidden behind a twelve foot statue of some unknown saint. For how much she had wanted to find out about his name and origin, she had not been able to discover who he was, nor his position as guardian or patron of . . . what? She had called him "the Saint with the Wild Eyes."

This evening she noted that that same door on the left was partially open.

The main lights were suddenly turned out, and then on again. It was getting late, and the church was almost empty. The few worshipping old women that were there—forgotten like piles of old rags on the wooden pews—came to life and began to leave, silently, each in turn half-way genuflecting, making the sign of the cross.

Then the lights went out again. The church was plunged into darkness, the only light now coming from outside, through the huge main door, still open.

Except for the tabernacle light—which was always flickering, always uncertain, but always present. By its light she was barely able to distinguish the pews. The pulpit, in the dim, flickering light, was but a faint and distorted shadow, protruding at the side of the apse like a dragon with its huge mouth open.

While the others were leaving, she, without thinking about it, nor stopping to consider the consequences, found herself propelled by the same spirit of adventure that had caused her to accept the proposal to come to Puebla. She approached the door and covertly pried it open, assuring herself that there was nobody in the surrounding area to observe her.

The door moved easily, opening without a sound. It opened to a small room, too small to be a sacristy or to serve the priests as a room for study or rest (such as there are in the older churches). At her position in the church, except for the yellowish light that came from the tabernacle and that barely permitted her to see, it was completely dark. In a crouch, she eased herself through the opening and into the secret room.

Inside, the air smelled of mold and was somewhat rarified. Connected to a worn electric wire which her head had brushed against as she entered there hung from the ceiling a light socket and a naked, and very ancient appearing, bulb. She turned on the light at a switch which was conveniently placed to one side of the door. Although very weak, probably only twenty watts, the light permitted her to see.

In the middle of the room was a table of thick wood—of that old kind, worm-eaten, that is exported from Puebla with such success to Europe—covered with a thick layer of dust. A wooden chair was to one side of the table. Against the wall to the right was a large bookcase which contained a few old books in a very bad state of conservation. Some of them were open, exposing their worn and yellow pages.

The remaining walls were totally bare, except for a yellowish painting on the facing wall which, covered in places and blackened by mold, appeared to represent a Biblical scene. All the walls had paint peeling away, and their surfaces were marked by large, grey, somewhat circular stains, the product of time and humidity.

The ceiling, unlike those in the old houses of Puebla, was very low; she could almost touch it with her hand. It appeared that this room had not been used for a long time, though the electric light indicated that it had been in use in the not too distant past. After inspecting the room, convinced finally that it was of no real interest, she decided to leave.

At that instant there was a loud bang from the front door of the church being closed, and the resulting gust of air closed the door to her secret room. Push as she would, she could not get it open again.

She began to pound on the door with all her strength, crying for help. But she had little hope that anyone would hear her since, with the front door closed, the church must surely be empty. Finally, tired and her hands hurting, she sat in the chair next to the table and tried to keep from panic.

Think. She had to think.

She was then conscious of her collosal stupidity, trying to explore alone, and at night, a room which had certainly been for a long time unoccupied, and of whose existence probably very few even knew. Nevertheless, she realized that she had to do something—to at least examine the room to see if there were some other exit.

Puebla was at a high altitude and the air was normally thin, but it appeared even thinner inside the room. Her breathing became labored, the breaths becoming deeper and more frequent, and she quickly became conscious of her breathing, and she began to be afraid. She surmised that there probably would not be much oxygen for very long since there were no windows and the only door was almost hermetically sealed, allowing at the most only the smallest amount of air to enter. Maybe not enough for her to last till morning.

Feeling a little claustrophobic, she turned to the wall where the bookcase was, the other walls offering no way of escape. Thinking there might be an extra door behind the bookcase, a possibility she had found common in her study of the old churches and convents of Puebla, she pushed as hard as she could against one side of it, trying to move it sideways along the wall. But it appeared to be fixed in place. She tried again, and again—to no avail. Then she tried in the other direction—also to no avail. Then, using the chair as a lever, she tried to pry the bookcase away from the wall—also without success. Finally, tired and sweating, she stopped, feeling a bit dizzy. She approached the table and sat again on the dusty chair which was to the side of it, resting. Her head was aching, her breathing irregular.

She closed her eyes, blaming herself for her unrestrained curiosity. It was like in her childhood in the convent school in France, always sneaking into places where she was not allowed, just to see what was there. Wondering how she got herself into this current mess, she closed her eyes. In a state of semi-consciousness she started to remember. Back. Back to Springfield, Mass. And Boston. And Boston was, of course, BU. BU and friends. BU and François.

After a while she opened her eyes, got up, slowly, carefully. Had she fallen asleep, or had she been reviewing her life, as they say it happens, when you are facing death? The strain must have been too much for her blood flow. She was facing away from the bookcase, and began to sway. She reached backward to grab onto something for support. Her hand touched a book shelf—just below her reach if she had been standing upright—and she grabbed for it. In grabbing it, reaching backward as she did, she pulled it to her in an effort to steady herself. Normally it would have been a good hold to keep herself upright. In this case, however, it was anything but secure. In fact, as she pulled it toward her, or tried to anchor herself to it, it actually gave a little. It appeared to move upward. It *did* move upward! It and the whole bookcase moved upward—just a little bit. The whole bookcase moved *upward!* She stopped—found it hard to believe what appeared to be happening. Did she still have a grip on her sanity? But it did happen . . . it *did* move . . . *upward!* Just a little.

Suddenly she no longer felt dizzy. Her blood began to rush through her body. She was re-energized. The bookcase had actually moved. She turned to face it. She got in a good position and pushed up on the shelf above the one she had grabbed. Slowly, but evenly, the whole bookcase began to move upward. She continued—pushing harder. It moved. It kept on moving. It moved up several feet and then stopped. And there, facing her, in the wall behind the bookcase, was a door.

She was elated. She was ecstatic! *A door!*

But how? How did that happen? She stopped to collect her thoughts, to make sure she wasn't dreaming or delirious. She had lifted the bookcase upward, without too much effort. She looked around. Then she realized that the ceiling was falling on both sides of the bookcase. But no, the ceiling wasn't falling. Pieces of the ceiling had come down, but each was really the base of a pile of weights connected still to the ceiling.

Now she understood. They were counter-weights. They were just like the ones in the windows in her house back in Massachussets. She remembered her father fixing a window once, and within the frame of the window were pulleys, and ropes going over the pulleys, and iron weights which were connected to each rope, each weighing about ten pounds or so. These, her father explained, came up when the window went down and went down when the window was pushed up. It all made it easy to do. It was then that she got the first lesson in mechanics that she remembered as such, and that she finally understood why it took so little effort to raise the window and usually no more effort to close the window. Both efforts merely shifted the two things on the ends of the ropes: the window and the weights.

It was the same here. Those old monks had rigged a counter-weighted mechanism to gain access to the secret door. The bookcase could not be moved from the wall, or pushed aside, parallel with the wall. It was too heavy. But it could be lifted with ease, thanks to the counter-weights. Anyway, she accidentally discovered how it worked, and now she had access to the secret door.

It was a small door, so small that it could not be more than four feet in height, but that was big enough for her to get through easily.

She immediately pushed against the door to open it. She pushed hard. Nothing. The door remained indifferent and immobile. She pushed again, and again, but try as she would, it would not move. Stuck again!

She sat down for a while, drying herself with her skirt of the sweat which fell along her face, down her neck, into her soaked blouse, clinging to the contour of her breasts. She closed her eyes. Using all her body weight, she banged against it with reconcentrated violence. Finally it opened, with a great noise, and she fell to the floor, skinning her knees.

"Magali, *petite . . . mais qu'est-ce que tu fais?* Playing with the boys again . . . climbing trees. *Mais alors, viens . . .* you skinned your knees again." The sweet voice with the foreign accent of her mother was coming to her, through time and distance.

She raised herself with difficulty and approached the entrance of the dark and not so inviting passageway beyond, which smelled of humidity and rats. Her mother's soft voice had vanished like an ancient aroma.

The passage extended into the distance beyond what little light came from the dim bulb in the room. The walls of stone were humid and coated on the surface with a sticky substance. It smelled of mold and mud, like a cave. And something more . . . it was almost like a being: alive, pulsating, threatening.

"Allons, I've got to curb my imagination," she said to herself.

To assure herself this time that the door to the passageway did not close behind her, she put the chair between the doorway and the door. Then she tried again to open the door that went to the church, pounding on it, in the event that a sacristan or a priest should pass within hearing. Silence. There was no recourse left but to move on into the passageway.

With her legs trembling, groping blindly about the walls, she started her journey inward . . . where? She had neither candles nor lantern. Now nothing mattered but to find a way out, as soon as possible. And she did not want to think of what would happen if, when she found a new exit, it would, also, be closed.

She began to remember what she had read about the Church of the Company and about the secret tunnels in Puebla in which the Jesuits had hidden their treasures and precious parchments when they were expelled from the country by order of the King of Spain.

The air was humid and rarified. The lack of oxygen made her feel dizzy again, but she pressed on, fearful of falling on the slippery floor . . . not wanting to think of rats. She started to feel nauseous, and she tried to reason with herself.

"Calm yourself," she said, "Take it easy. You'll only excite yourself and waste air. Breathe slowly: one, two, three . . . calmly."

When she was a camp counselor summers in Massachusetts, had she not taught her students many times how to avoid panic, breathing into a paper bag? Of course she had no paper bag with her at that time, but she could use her hands, fingers intertwined and curved over her face.

She sensed a tiny sound, like the scratching of the claws of a cat, and she stopped, petrified. What was that at her feet . . . what kind of life . . . crawling, invisible . . . threatened her?

And why, she thought, did she, the intruder of all this warm silence, of this solitude, inviolate for centuries, suddenly feel . . . important? Why did she assume that something or someone should concern itself with her presence in this place, preserved for centuries, like a deep, dark, unfathomable secret?

Her being had no importance now: frightened and transient, she had been converted into someone that, by imprudence, had gotten herself trapped in this tomb, within time—or perhaps out of it? She noted that the passageway commenced to descend, and her fears increased.

She was going down a kind of rampway, covered with mud, and slippery. She had to support herself on the walls so as to not fall into the great darkness below. But she was repelled by the slimey contact of the wall and had to stop again, feeling queasy.

She tried to think of her class, her students; the *Zócalo* filled with *campesinos* dressed in their best Sunday clothes, the girls with colored silk ribbons in their hair, the women in embroidered blouses and long cotton skirts adorned with sequins; the municipal band playing, surrounded by sellers of multicolored balloons, of ices, of yams and sweets; the incongruent McDonald's under the arcade, next to the better restaurants and outdoor cafes; the Mariachis slowly moving among the crowds of tourists.

She continued descending, carefully feeling her way at each step, afraid that there would be . . . what? She continued thus, in slow motion, like in an old black and white Vincent Price movie.

The tunnel continued downward for the longest time, deep into what must be the foundations of the church. She continued moving, feeling her way along the left wall. Suddenly she reached what appeared to be the bottom. There was no more descent, and she now walked along a rough floor, probably a dirt floor because it was so uneven, but now not so slippery.

She came to an end wall and she discovered that the tunnel had taken a turn to the right. She continued following the passageway. She was moving slowly, feeling every step as if she were going to come to a precipice and fall over, or to a hole like in old, medieval castles where they threw victims, never to come out again but to slowly die, abandoned. It must have taken her hours to travel the distance she could have covered in a few minutes in normal walking.

The tunnel then took another turn, to the left, and she continued along a similar rough floor, hanging on for dear life to the wall for guidance. She continued in that way for she knew not how long.

Then she hit something with her foot and almost fell forward, catching herself quickly. She stuck her hand out in front of her, but she could feel no wall. She moved her foot slowly upward, feeling the obstacle in front of her much as a blind man uses his cane to determine what is in front of him. The surface ended, and a level surface continued in front of her. It was a step. She crouched and felt with her hand. It was a stairway. She took a step up, and then another, and another. Slowly, with great caution, using her feet like a blind man's cane, she continued upward.

Then there were no more steps; she was on a level surface again. It was a paved surface, of clean and dry stone. She moved forward again, still cautiously. Ahead there was nothing but darkness, but she continued moving forward. The wall appeared to curve to the right, but she could not be certain of it because it appeared to curve so slowly. She continued moving, for what seemed to be hours.

Suddenly, just when she was about to give up and to turn back, she perceived at the end of the tunnel a very weak light. Imagination? It was a yellowish gleam, a greenish breath, far away, at the end, way at the end—spreading like a fluorescent, oily liquid across the dark floor.

She increased her speed down the passageway—slipping, anxious, trying not to run. After what appeared to her like forever, she came to what she determined by touch to be a door, from under which came a flickering, uncertain light. She started banging on the door, hurting her knuckles.

"Help. Help. Open, in the name of God!"

The door, at last, with great asthmatic difficulty, began to moan, to exhale dust, like an old man waking from his sleep. She stood before the doorway, her body erect with all the force of her desperation, crying and sweating, and then, as it opened, she fell into the arms of a hooded monk, dressed in a brown, woolen habit, his waist tied with a white cord. She could not see his face.

She noted, in an instantaneous glimpse, a candle on a heavy wooden table, a group of old parchments scattered about, a bottle of purple ink and a feathered quill. It was a room with a low roof, a curved vault. The stone walls were covered with wooden bookcases, full of books. As she turned to look at the rest of the room, she suddenly felt dizzy and passed out.

She was awakened by the sound of huge church doors being opened. She was lying on a pew in the Church of the Company, near the altar of the Virgin of Lourdes. A few old women were coming in, genuflecting, entering pews near the center aisle, and kneeling to pray, rapidly fingering their chains of huge black beads.

As more people straggled into the church, Magali got up and quietly went down the side aisle and out. The sun was about to come up; the day looked beautiful. Her watch said half past five. She turned to the right and caught a taxi on *Avenida Camacho* to her home, the small apartment on *12 Oriente*. She was dead tired.

Once inside her apartment she flopped on the bed. Was it all a dream? Had she just fallen asleep in the church and passed the night on a pew? Or was her nocturnal adventure real? And if it was real, to where had she gotten? And what did it all mean? She was too tired to think of it. She thought of home: of Springfield, Mass. And Boston. BU and friends. BU and François. She fell asleep.

2

MAGALI GOES TO BU

Magali's family lived in Springfield, Massachusetts, in a big old house with an attic, a cellar, and a yard. A nice, family-oriented neighborhood. A mixed population of Italian-, Greek-, Irish-Americans. Her own family was French-American. Her father was American, her mother French. And she had been brought up in the best of the two worlds, the two cultures.

Her knowledge of French had helped her to get honors in high school, and when she applied to Boston University, and was accepted, her most cherished dream had come true. The day before she was leaving there was a picnic in her backyard by the big old maple tree, now just starting to turn, with the gold and orange leaves of autumn, It was to wish her good luck and to say goodbye, and all the neighbors came and congratulated her and her family. Even though Springfield was only a couple of hours away from Boston by the turnpike, she had felt, then, the pain of the separation, like the tearing of a bandage from a fresh wound.

And then Boston. The skyscrapers piercing the ocean mist, the big city. The Common and the Public Garden, Quincy Market, the waterfront. The stores, the museums—BU, with its big, old, distinguished, brick buildings, and the tiny quarters of the students. Hers was on the third floor of one of the student housing buildings—just enough space for a bed, a little table with a lamp and a chair, and a closet so shallow that a hanger had to be placed sideways to fit. But it had a big, long, old-fashioned window where she could place her geranium plant.

Her whole family had come to Boston with her, in the old
'69 Buick wagon: her father, mother, and two younger brothers.
They were planning to visit the Science Museum before going
back home.

The car was stuffed with plastic bags containing clothing,
sheets, a pillow (her favorite old goose feather pillow), and some
towels and wash cloths. There were also a cardboard box with a
few kitchen utensils: a small aluminum coffee pot; 2 mugs and a
demi-tasse and saucer; a glass jar with sugar; another with coffee;
2 teaspoons, forks, and table knives; and a sharp kitchen knife.
And, to start her new life on a sweet note, there was a box of
freshly made cinnamon-sugar cookies. A small leather briefcase
rested on her mother's lap, in the front, with all her school papers
and important documents. She sat in the back, holding her
geranium pot on her lap, while two framed pictures (last
Christmas' family portrait, and a collage of several old pictures of
her French side of the family) rested on the floor, protected by
her legs from the movements of the two boys sitting there with
her. This trip to Boston reminded her of one of her favorite
Vittorio de Sica movies, but she didn't mind. Let the other
students think what they may, she had a family, a close one. That
was the only thing that mattered.

She was too busy anticipating her arrival to notice the
turning of the maples on both sides of the highway, or the fine
autumn morning—bright, sunny, and cool. The boys were
counting cars by make and color and having a good time; her
mother was quiet. Magali felt a pang of anxiety and pain, thinking
of her home.

Home!

But there was not much time for regret. Before she knew it,
they had arrived at the red brick, New England-style building, and
after they parked, almost at the entrance (she noticed other cars
there, unloading packages and people), she got out of the car and
ran upstairs, holding the Yale key, and opened, for the first time,
her new dominion. Then she stood at the door, not knowing
what to do, looking at the room, the bed, the walls, the ceiling.
"I've made it," she thought, "I've made it."

Her two younger brothers came running after her, crashing
into the room, jumping on the bed. Her parents followed, each
one carrying part of her luggage.

"Oh," said her mother, *"mais que la chambre est petite!"*

"Never mind," said her father. "I didn't have much more than this when I was at school. And I had to share the room with another student. It will do. Let's bring the stuff in before I get a ticket. It's only a one hour parking space."

They all ran back downstairs. She was about to close the door when another door opened at the right side of her room and a blondish, tall, skinny boy with glasses grinned at her. "First day, eh? Welcome! My name is Stuart. Stuart Wright. I'll be your neighbor. Can I help?" Without waiting for her answer, he went down the stairs, jumping the steps two at a time, and started to bring up some of the parcels.

Soon she was all moved-in, her tiny space covered with parcels and bags.

Her family hurriedly said good-bye, her mother hugged her, and they were gone. She took a box off the mattress and sat on the bed. The boy next door had disappeared. Suddenly, she was alone.

And then school started, the first confusing days, the finding of the faculties and the classrooms, the making of friends, the books, and—yes—the hard nights studying. Never enough sleep, always too much to do.

Stuart had become a good friend. He was, according to his own description, "a professional student." When she asked what was his major, he replied:

"This semester, I'm taking literature. But next semester, who knows?" And then, as she was staring at him: "I already have a B.A. and a B.S. I'm not sure what I want to do a Master's on. I'm debating between an M.B.A. or an M.A., or— "

"But Stuart, you look so young to already have two degrees," she protested.

He laughed—a loud, boyish laugh. "They started me very early at school. My parents, I mean. You see, they travel the world and have no time to take care of a youngster. School seemed the best solution."

"Are you happy here?"

"Of course! I don't have a worry in the world. Besides, I have all kinds of friends—several school terms full of them. One set goes, a new one arrives. Never a dull moment."

Somehow, Magali felt a current of sadness trying to surface from under his apparent lightheartedness.

On Wednesday morning of that first week Stuart knocked on her door a little before eight and she let him into the room. "Hey," he said. "How about going for some cranberry muffins and tea before we go to class? Believe me, we'll need the encouragement. Professor What's-His-Name's classes always bore me to death." Stuart was auditing one of Magali's classes, a Modern Literature one, and he looked forward to their studying together.

They went to "Ye Olde Tea House," where small groups of students were already sitting at the outdoor tables. Stuart went to a table occupied by two young girls—a pretty redhead and a brunette with thick glasses. He introduced Magali to them, pulled up two chairs, and soon they were all discussing that fall's schedule of conferences and concerts at the university, the up-coming book sale of the Coop, and the current gossip about a French professor and one of the female vietnamese students. They continued engrossed in conversation until someone said it was a quarter to nine, and then they all hurriedly got up to pay, said goodbyes, and went to their respective classes.

Magali and Stuart went together to theirs. This was the first meeting of the class, and after listening half an hour to the professor's dry and petulant address to the students, she had to agree with Stuart about his characterization of the professor and his assessment of the class. She wondered if she shouldn't have consulted with him before signing up for it.

That first week-end Stuart proposed to show her the city. She had to admit she hadn't had any time to be a tourist. It was a fine autumn day, a little windy, but perfect for sightseeing, so she took him up on his offer, tidied up her room, put on jeans, a long sleeved shirt, and a windbreaker, and met Stuart at the bottom of the stairs.

They took the train to downtown and walked to the Aquarium. Stuart was acting as a knowledgeable guide ("After all, I live here," he had told her). They looked at the sharks in the process of being fed by a diver, and at the "mutant" fish of Boston Harbor that, because of all the pollution, had changed in color and shape. After looking at a collection of colorful tropical fish, they went outside to look at the dolphins and the seals, sat for a while on the dockside to rest, and finally went to Charley's (a famous place for fish), had a late lunch, and then came back home.

Stuart asked her to his room, to listen to some of his Chopin collection. It was about four by then, and she said she really had a lot of studying to do and had better get to it. He didn't insist, kissed her hand, smiled, and said goodbye.

She went into her room and closed her door. She had had a very good time. But she wondered. About Stuart's invitation, and his feelings toward her. She very much wanted him to be just a friend.

That night, Magali had another instance of her recurrent nightmare. It seemed that she had had it all her life, on and off, since she could remember.

She was walking, in slow motion, in a passageway. It was dark, and smelled of humidity and mold. The walls, as much as she could make them out, were stone, and water was slowly dripping down their uneven surfaces. The floor of the passageway was slippery, like the algae covered rocks at Rocky Neck, in Connecticut, where she used to go swimming in the summer. She was trying desperately to move on, to find a way out. But she couldn't, and her long, white nightgown was floating in the air (or water) around her, as if she were a ghost. The air was getting rarified, and she couldn't breathe. She opened her mouth to cry for help, but no words came out.

Finally, she woke up with the pillow on her face; she was shaking and frightened. "Where?" she thought. "Maybe it's the secret passage between the nuns' convent and the priests, in France, where I was a student, that a friend and I discovered one night by chance?" She always wondered about her discovery, even when she couldn't talk about it.

It was in a 13th century monastery on top of a small hill in a beautiful and romantic spot in Normandie. She was only nine years old when she discovered it. The two girls were caught in the school patio on their way back, by Mere Virginie. "It's a mortal sin," she had said, "to wander at night in the monastery. You shall go to confession and forget all about it." She tried to forget. She tried very hard.

On Friday morning of her second week at the university she was awakened by somebody loudly pounding on her door.

"Magali . . . wake up! Magali! You're late for class!"

The voice of her friend Cathy (Cathy O'Toole, Room 204, Early Education Major) made her jump out of bed. She rushed forward to open the door.

"Come in, Cat. I'll be dressed in a second."

Cathy was a pretty Irish girl: red hair; green, smiling eyes; thin and petite. She had become Magali's friend almost from the beginning, and they shared a warm relationship. Her brother Pat had become interested in Magali, but Magali was always so busy they couldn't really get together. Pat was working in a bank downtown, next to the Common. He was a very attractive young man, with grey eyes and auburn hair, and extremely shy. Cathy was hoping, nevertheless, for the two of them to get together, and was acting as a kind of matchmaker. Magali just laughed at her efforts.

"He is a really nice boy, Cathy, but I have no time—"

"Nonsense," said Cathy. And she continued to try to arrange casual meetings. "Pat is taking us to lunch today," she said.

"Us?" asked Magali from the shower. She came out, hurriedly drying her long hair, dressing for school in a full, printed cotton skirt, a navy blue turtleneck top, and a leather jacket. "Fine," she said. "I'll be hungry. I don't have time for breakfast."

They went to *"La Crêperie"* near Harvard Square. Magali had a spinach crepe, Cathy a ham and cheese one, and Pat a strawberries and cream.

"That's your lunch? It looks more like dessert to me," Cathy said to her brother.

Magali noticed the discomfort of the boy.

"Leave him alone, Cathy. If he feels like something sweet for lunch, good for him!"

The boy looked at her gratefully, and started again to eat.

"How is school?" he asked.

"Hard," said Magali. "They give us so many papers to write, and we have to do so much research at the library. I was there until eleven last night."

"Isn't it dangerous?" he asked, looking at her.

He is so handsome, thought Magali. But such a young boy.

"Well, we actually shouldn't stay so late. But the campus is well patrolled all night. I guess the worse is going back to the dorm."

"You should be careful . . . both of you," said Pat.

They had finished eating in a hurry since the boy only had an hour for lunch and he had to take the train back to the Common.

"Are you going to be free this week-end, Magali?" he asked. "I have tickets for the Red Socks."

"I'd love to go, thank you. But I don't know if—"

"Yes, she will," said Cathy. "Jeremy and I will join you."

Magali was touched and happy to have them as friends. "I wish everything would be so easy," she thought.

After class, she went to the dorm. Lying on the floor by her door there was a long-stem red rose.

The days and the weeks went by, one morning overlapping the other, like a coat of paint that becomes old and needs freshening-up every twenty-four hours.

Nobody claimed responsibility for the rose. She didn't ask. She thought it was Stuart, but she said nothing; she preferred it to remain a mystery. As for Stuart, their friendship was very much alive, but she never let it be more than that. He didn't complain, and he remained her faithful companion and protector. She had no intention of getting involved. She wanted her B.A. And her Master's. She wanted to succeed. She had a goal, and she meant to realize her dream of being a graduate of one of the most prestigious universities in the U.S.

When Thanksgiving came, everyone went to their respective homes. It was a necessary break—not only from school. A time to sort things out. Magali went with Pat and Cathy back to Springfield the Wednesday before Thanksgiving, along with three other male students she didn't know—a car full. Everybody was tired; the new boys, in the back seat, went to sleep as soon as the car got on the highway and headed westward into the late afternoon sun; Cathy and Magali, in the front seat with Pat, who was doing the driving, talked together softly, resting, dreaming of roasted turkeys and stuffing, pumpkin pies, and Moms.

Magali's mother made breakfast for her that first morning home again—*crêpes*, home-made strawberry jam, good coffee, and plenty of orange juice and milk.

The holiday week-end went by too fast. She was suddenly again at school, and the sunrise and the sunset were just one big red ball of fire in between her books and her dreams.

After her B.A. she went for her Master's, taking summer courses in a non-stop effort that left little time for herself or her friends. Most of them went home in the summer, except, of course, Stuart. Faithful, always-present Stuart. He was like a part of her room, of her furniture; and sometimes she regretted that he was not really a part of her life.

When she obtained her Master's Degree the following May, her whole family came to the solemn graduation. They watched her walking in the procession to the slow rhythm of "Pomp and Circumstance" in a formal and very impressive ceremony. After the ceremony she told her family that she was not coming back home, but somehow it was not a surprise to them.

Soon after graduation she approached the Department of Foreign Languages and Literature to apply for admission to the doctoral program. She had to choose an advisor that would help her prepare and present a program of study, as well as a dissertation proposal. She wanted it to be on the Spanish language as related to architecture and the living environment. The program was to be one year of courses in continuous residence, and two or three years of courses and research, which could include study abroad. She had to pick a preliminary examination committee, composed of five members, two not from the department, that would admit her to candidacy, and she hoped that this same committee could serve for the final oral exam for her dissertation defense. She knew the professors quite well now, and she thought that deciding on the members, and getting them to sign on, would not be too difficult. But that, at least, did not have to be done immediately. First, she had to get admitted and then get a good advisor.

She felt a little dismayed looking up the requirements. All that time! All that work! Her head was spinning. But in the end she would be a *real Doctor*, a *Ph.D.* Not a "bachelor's level" M.D., as they are in the U.S., nor the made-up "Doctor of Education," or of "Communication," or "Basket-Weaving."

She went home, leaving her door open, and sat by the window. It was a lovely summer afternoon, and a rich light was descending like liquid gold over the glass and spilling onto her geranium plant, making it look almost fluorescent with life. The seagulls were noisily cruising the blue sky, and the noises of the street below were brought up by the wind in subdued murmurs of a confusing language. Suddenly she realized, with that strange feeling that one has on the back of the neck of being watched, that there was someone at the door. It was Stuart, just standing there, looking at her.

"Oh, Stuart! You startled me!"

"Sorry. You were so quiet, I didn't want to interrupt."

"You never do. I just came from the Department—finding out about the requirements for the Ph.D."

"Ah," he smiled. "Overwhelming, aren't they?"

"Scary," said the girl.

"Let's go for a Cappuccino. You'll feel better. And we can talk."

She was so grateful to him—her one, close, always present friend. She felt the impulse of kissing him, but changed her mind immediately. She had to keep the relationship as it was: friendly.

They went down to the street, took the train for Harvard Square, sat in an outdoor cafe. He let her talk, waiting patiently for her confidences.

"I need an advisor," she said. "Someone I can trust, who would understand my background and my goals."

He remained silent while the waiter served the coffee.

"It just so happens that I might know the very person," he said.

"You do? You're just too wonderful!"

"Am I? Then . . . will you marry me?"

She looked at him, startled. He laughed. "See? I got you back to reality." She relaxed a little, but wondered. She wondered very much.

"My French prof is one of the good guys. Very sharp, but very down-to-earth. None of the pomposity of the older pains-in-the-you-know-what."

"Stuart!"

"OK! But I have to warn you. He is young, and the girls don't leave him alone. A regular Louis Jourdan—of the old movies, of course."

"You think I may try to seduce him?"

"Well . . . I suppose even you have a heart hidden among all those books and those dreams."

"Is this a reprimand?"

"In a way. Of course, I am only a friend."

"Not 'only.' You are the one and best friend I have."

"Shouldn't you take some time . . . for other stuff? Like men . . . romance . . . or me?"

"Now, Stuart. You sound like Mom. But, you see . . . I have to follow my dream. I can't give myself to anyone, not just yet. Not until I have accomplished what I came to Boston to do."

"Oh well. In that case, I guess you'll be safe from his charms. His name is François Deviliers. I'll set up a meeting for you for some time next week."

"Thanks. And, Stuart, no matter what, or who, or when . . . you will always be my very best friend. Always."

He smiled at her, but his eyes were sad, like a little kid that had just been deprived of dessert.

3

FRANÇOIS

A meeting with François had been set by Stuart for the following Thursday. It was to be at 5:00 p.m., in one of the study rooms at the University. Magali had been in the city and the train she had planned to take was so crowded that she had to wait for the next one, and, being late and in a hurry, she was almost sorry she had agreed to the meeting at this hour. She finally arrived at the building, went down the hall, and opened the door of the study room.

It was one of the larger ones, in the west wing, next to the library. The atmosphere was severe, like most other places at BU. The walls were painted in a greenish color, and there were wooden shelves full of reference books along the walls. The lights were old-fashioned and produced a yellow glare that surrounded the furniture and people with an aura.

There were several students in the room, arranged at chairs and tables, mostly reading, some talking quietly among themselves or writing. He was sitting at a table near the entrance, reading, when she entered. She stood at the door and looked at him. "I should've asked for a description of the guy," she thought. But she was sure he was the one.

He was a man in his early 30's: tall; very much the stereotype of the intellectual, but a little nonchalant, which gave him an air of casual elegance; high forehead; long, sandy hair; honey colored eyes; nose slightly aquiline; and thin lips. He had arrived from the Sorbonne of Paris to BU in the post of Professor of Foreign Languages and with a contract for two years.

"Oh, Hell," Magali was thinking. "Another snobbish Frenchman." And then their eyes met, and the room disappeared.

Magali fell into a trance. She was holding her briefcase so hard that her fingers hurt. Her whole being was attracted toward the man like a meteorite in the gravity field of a sun.

She was unable to fight it. "Is he the one?" she thought. "Oh, God; make him be the one!"

It was *un coup de foudre*. She remembered her conversation with Stuart: "Do you think I may try to seduce him?"

He got up, and his book fell on the floor. He didn't bother to pick it up. He went toward the girl. *"Bonjour,"* he said in French.

"Excuse me, but when something is very important . . . really important, French comes out first."

"Mais non," she said. *"Ma mère est Française . . . aussi."*

He felt stupid. Of course, he knew he was supposed to help some girl organizing her dissertation program, a girl that should have shown up ten minutes earlier. Was this that girl? She must be the one! He had read her dossier carefully. He knew everything that had to be known about her. Except, of course, that she was beautiful.

He just looked at her, then, taking her gently by the arm, led her to a chair next to his.

"Excuse me, my name is François. I am here to help you," he said. And then stopped. Suddenly he started to laugh. *"Mon Dieu, que je suis con!* I expected you. *C'est à dire,* not exactly. Somebody. When you entered the room, I thought you were the most lovely thing—"

"I hadn't thought you would be as you are . . . either. I mean . . . It was such a surprise."

He laughed some more—a soft, young laughter. "I know, you expected somebody much more . . . *Voyons* . . . old? With a white beard and a big tummy?"

"Well, as a matter of fact—" she was laughing now, too.

"Why don't we postpone the business meeting and go out to a cafe? To tell you the truth, I was hoping the person would not show up. I'm bushed."

"Okay. It's the best offer I've had all day. And, believe me, it's been a long day, *pour moi aussi.*"

They went to one of the many outdoor cafes near the University. Most were full, but they finally found a table in one of the less popular ones.

"This is fine," she said. "The others are too noisy, anyway."

They asked for Cappuccinos and sat quietly, in silence. When the coffee came with its frothy top laced with cinnamon, he lighted a cigarette. They started to talk. And talk. And talk.

It began to get late; there were now couples walking by, and groups of students going back to their rooms or apartments for the night. François offered to see her back to her dorm.

They met every day after that. They worked together, they ate together, they walked to and from school, they took long strolls in the Public Garden.

They kissed. Everything seemed so . . . pre-ordained, so meant-to-be, so normal. So when he asked her to come to his room one evening, she accepted. And they made love like an old couple: passionately, but tenderly.

François had made her life at school exciting and bright, even during the hard winter days with the snow when the wind would go through her coat like icy needles, and her eyes fill with tears, and her nose become red. He was always making fun of her, calling her *mon petit nez-rouge,* and she would get mad at him. Then he would kiss her gently on the lips, and she would forgive him.

When François found a small old-fashioned apartment in a brownstone on Charles Street (that had been occupied by a colleague of his who was returning to France after his contract with BU expired), they decided to move in together.

The apartment was located in one of their favorite parts of the city, with its classy, old-fashioned buildings; its bohemian cafes and specialty shops; and its crowd of intellectuals, artists, and students. It was next to the Common, and close to the downtown area.

He had been living in University quarters, like Magali, and they didn't have as much freedom to meet as they wished to.

Magali could never stay overnight with her lover, nor he with her. So they were both delighted with the opportunity. It was a prime apartment in a wonderful location, very accessible to BU by train.

Once the lease had been signed, Magali told Stuart.

"I'm moving out of the dorm, Stuart."

She had waited for him, the familiar tennis-shoe muffled sound on the steps; the short walk that hesitated, ever so slightly, by her door before he went on to his own; the key in the lock.

The boy came into her room and sat on her bed, as he had done so many times in the past, saying nothing. He was looking out the window, his eyes wet and silent.

"It's he, isn't it?" he said after several minutes. "Everybody at BU is talking about the great romance of the season." He paused. "It's my fault. I should never have introduced you to him."

The sun was setting, like so many other times. But now, instead of a theatrical, red-orange satin curtain scenario, gaudy and bright, the color was a dull purple over a deep gray.

She took his hand, tenderly.

"Remember what I said to you: no matter what, or who, or when . . . you will always be my very best friend. Always."

The boy finally got up. He seemed to have aged, deep inside. Magali felt a cold, invisible aura around him.

"I'm so sorry . . . But, look! You have to come and see us! And, of course, I fully expect your helping me to move out, the same way you helped me to move in . . . ages ago!" She was trying to sound cheerful, but not succeeding at it. Stuart let go of her hand, and slowly turned his back to her and left the room.

She felt all dressed in black and turned the knob of the heater on, even though it was August, and outside it was almost 80 degrees.

They didn't have any furniture, and it was great fun to go to the antique stores and the garage sales. They picked up a big full-size bed and mattress, a desk, a couple of director's chairs, and a wooden table and four wooden chairs for the kitchen. The apartment had two large rooms with wood floors, a large kitchen

with a big window overlooking a small patio with plants and a
tree, and a bathroom with a large, old tub. The shower curtain
and a few kitchen utensils were bought at the Crate and Barrel.

Magali brought her books and her geranium plant, and
François brought five boxes containing French text books and
poetry. A futon was placed in the living room, and they made a
bookcase with some bricks and old wood taken from a tall piece
of furniture that didn't fit in the apartment.

It took them several weeks of intense labor (which they did
in the little spare time that they had) to finish furnishing the
apartment to their satisfaction, and when they were done, they
decided to give a wine and cheese party as a house-warming.
François prepared a Quiche Lorraine and Magali made cream-
puffs and *Crêpes Suzette.*

Magali called Stuart. The boy seemed to have recovered from
his puppy love and was starting to date. "Stuart, will you come to
our wine and cheese party? And bring . . . that gorgeous brunette
you're dating these days."

He laughed at the other end of the line. "You mean the cute
little blonde I'm going out with these days."

"Mon Dieu! You change girls faster that I can keep up with!"
she laughed. "Of course, bring her. Bring them all, but come."

Cathy, who had graduated two years before and was working
in one of the local schools as a teacher, came with her new
boyfriend (a very quiet, very tall young man, who held her hand
in a possessive way). Stuart (who continued, sporadically, to
accumulate minor degrees) arrived accompanied by a very pretty,
very petite, German exchange student. François' friends, mostly
professors from his faculty, and a few other students filled up the
apartment, admired the location and the "academic" decoration,
and sat on chairs and pillows around the floor. Magali had also
invited their immediate neighbors, a retired professor and his
wife, who brought some *canapés* that disappeared immediately
among the young people.

There were French wines; an assortment of French, Italian,
and American cheeses; and crackers. François had some Bossa
Nova records that produced a relaxed, sensual atmosphere.

The party was very successful, and when everybody left, the couple sat on the futon with the last glass of Chablis. François turned the lights off but left one candle still lit, spreading its soft, warm luminosity around them, and the couple remained in silence, perfectly happy in their own company and in their very own new home.

They had started their life together.

The regular school year was in full swing and Magali's dissertation program, with François' help, was coming along—slowly, but without major problems. She had to do a lot of research and spend many hours at the library. But now when she was late, François would come to pick her up and they would both go home together. His professorial duties included some tutoring and a few seminars, but he would always find time to be with her, and she was grateful.

They would dine in little French restaurants and have coffee in outdoor cafes, and attend lectures and concerts. They visited the Museum of Art at least once a week and shared the same love for classical music and Monet.

Life was wonderful. She was in love.

And then, in the summer, an offer came to her. It was through a friend that worked at the Mexican Consulate in Boston: to teach in Mexico for a year, with time for her own research, in a city called Puebla, famous for its many colonial churches and monasteries, and just two hours from Mexico City.

She spoke Spanish fluently, and the chance to examine old manuscripts, visit ancient libraries, and write a monograph on the old churches presented itself as the realization of a very old, very cherished dream.

And there was, of course, that feeling of adventure, of exotic places, of a different culture.

She went home to François that evening full of excitement and joy.

"François!" she called from the door. She was holding a baguette, a roasted chicken (still warm), and a bottle of Chablis. "François!"

He came to the door, kissed her, and took from her hands the dinner items. She started, excited like a kid, and in a not-very-coherent fashion, to tell him about the trip. When he didn't say a word, she looked at his eyes and stopped. Only then, suddenly, she thought of separation. Only then did she realize that François would not be with her.

Of course, he was wonderful about it. He encouraged her to take the job, and told her he would come to spend his Christmas vacation in Mexico.

"I have never been to Mexico," he said. "And I've always wanted to visit that country. Now, I have a good excuse." He tried to sound enthusiastic about it, but, somehow, he failed.

"I am going to miss you, *chèrie* . . . very much." He grabbed her face and kissed her eyes, her nose, her lips.

"Moi aussi," she said. *"Moi aussi."*

"In a way," her mother told her when Magali called her family with the news, "maybe this separation would make François realize the value of your relationship, and consider whether this relationship is serious enough to become something more permanent."

She agreed with her mother, but didn't want to put their love to a test. Her mother and father had been very understanding towards her affair with François, but they wished a more permanent arrangement for their daughter: marriage, children.

After many days of indecision and anguish François put an end to it by handing her a ticket for Mexico. And she was grateful to him because at that point she didn't feel strong enough to take that step.

Getting together the documents required by the Mexican Consulate had been a bother for her, but she systematically got them, one by one, and finally was rewarded with a 3M Visa that permitted her to work in that country. She took off from Logan Airport at 9:05 on the morning of Saturday, July 30.

Her family had come to Boston early to say goodbye to her. They and friends, including Stuart, came to the airport to see her off. They all waited for the time for her flight to board, and then, in the company of François, she kissed her parents and hugged her brothers and friends and went through "security" to her gate. François went with her and waited with her in silence until the airline official called, "We are ready to begin boarding our flight to Mexico City. We will start now boarding first class passengers and those passengers with small children and those in need of special assistance." Then: "We are ready now to board rows 20 to 36." The girl was trying hard not to cry, but her eyes filled up with tears.

"François—" she said, and her voice broke like a fine Murano vase into a thousand fragments. He kissed her, caressed her hair, and helped her out of the seat. "It will be fine, you'll see. *Au revoir, petite. Je t'aime.*"

4

ARRIVING IN PUEBLA

Magali left Boston at 9:05 in the morning, changed planes in Miami, and arrived in Mexico City at about 4:00 in the afternoon, Mexico City time, for a total trip time of eight hours. Their approach was gray and dark; heavy clouds of pollution hung over the capital like dirty rags, and rain clouds were forming. Through the few breaks in the cloud cover she got some fleeting glimpses of the largest city in the world. The tall, modern skyscrapers were surrounded by what appeared to be little Spanish or mediterranean-style doll houses painted in bright colors. The whole arrangement lacking in symmetry and order, as if they had all been toys left scattered on the floor. She could see the cars and people, thousands of them, moving in all directions, coming and going.

Out of the plane and up the access ramp, she entered the airport and followed the other passengers through the maze of waiting areas and walkways. The directional signs, showing the way to immigration, customs, and baggage, were in three languages, but everyone around her was talking in Spanish, and she became just a little bit afraid. Fortunately, her friend in the consulate in Boston had given her explicit instructions on what to do on arriving in Mexico, how to get through customs, catch a bus to Puebla, even the name of a hotel to stay at in Puebla and how to get there. That gave her something to buoy up her spirits.

She came into a large room where the passengers in front of her were getting into lines for going through immigration. She got into the long line where passengers who were non-Mexicans were waiting for a little old man in uniform and glasses to examine their papers. When it was her turn, he looked at her passport and visa, and then looked at her, and then, suddenly, he said to her:

"*Te olvidaste de firmar aquí, niña!*"

She was so startled by the flood of Spanish that she couldn't understand what he was saying. "You didn't sign here, girl," the old man repeated in English, with a very strong accent.

Suddenly, she felt like laughing. These people were human, after all. She smiled back at him.

"*Lo siento,*" she said in perfect Spanish. She followed the others to the baggage claim area, grabbed one of the carts that were available to the people (free) for moving their luggage, reclaimed her two large suitcases from the carrousel, and moved on to the customs area.

There she faced the "lottery," a pole with red and green lights like a traffic semaphore signal, and below them a large button to push. She pushed the button and the green light went on. Relieved, she proceeded on, unrestrained, through the customs area. If she had gotten the red light, they would have had to thoroughly search all her luggage.

She left the cart within the customs area and went through the posts separating the arriving passengers from the throng of people waiting for them. Almost in front of her was a bank office which served as an *oficina de cambio*, and there she exchanged a hundred dollars for pesos. She was given 330 pesos, which was close enough to the expected rate of exchange.

Her friend's instructions were that waiting outside the Airport there would be a bus of the *Estrella Roja* company which went to Puebla. She dragged her two heavy suitcases, which fortunately had wheels, her carry-on hanging from one side (the strap around her neck and supported by her shoulder on the other side), asked for directions to the *Estrella Roja* bus stop, found it outside on a sideway of a street passing by the airport terminal, and joined the line of other people waiting for the bus. After a wait of almost half an hour the bus finally came. When her turn in the line came, she put her luggage in the luggage compartment and got on. She paid 35 pesos to the driver (or the conductor?) and got on the bus.

They started off down streets that led away from the airport. It was by then past five in the afternoon and it had started to rain. She couldn't see much of the city with its yellowish-liquid street lights, or of the road once they got on the super-highway which led to Puebla. There were several Germans on the bus and many Mexicans, all talking in low voices, some of them sleeping.

The trip to Puebla took a little over two hours. They left the super-highway and quickly wound their way through a few blocks of commercial and industrial type buildings and into the grounds of the CAPU, the consolidated bus station in Puebla. There she had to wheel her suitcases up a long, steep ramp to a second story, and then down a long corridor, and then down another steep ramp, back to the ground level of the bus station. Down the last ramp she came out into the main hall of the station, counters of the many bus lines served there aligned along either side of the long quonset style hall. Facing her as she touched bottom coming down the ramp was a kiosk which served the *Taxis Autorizados*. At its window she bought a ticket, giving the hotel recommended by her friend at the consulate as her destination. She was given a ticket for Zone 3. She was directed to an exitway at about the middle of the right side of the hall to where, outside the station building, but still within the grounds, she joined a line of people waiting for the taxis. It was along the side of the station building, under a small porch protecting them from the rain, and on one side of a walled-in square where taxis entered on the far side, proceeded along a driveway around the square, to where they waited, loaded up, in turn, with passengers, and left. In the center of the square there were parking stations for some busses, which also used this area, most of which were small and in rather poor condition and looked like they provided a commuter service to surrounding towns or suburbs. It was raining hard now.

So far, the directions from her friend in the consulate in Boston had proven perfect for guiding her through the otherwise complicated procedure for getting from the airport in Mexico City to Puebla. She eventually got to the front of the line and handed her ticket to a girl behind another ticket window. It was duly stamped and the number of the taxi she would take (which was waiting in its own line) was marked on it, on the back of each of its three parts, and one part was torn from it and kept. The other two parts were returned to her and she waited for those in front of her to board their taxi. When it was her turn to get into a taxi, she said to the driver, *"Hotel Hidalgo,"* and handed her ticket to the man, who, without looking at her, said, *"Sí, señorita,"* tore off one part of the ticket for himself, returned the third part to her, and started on the road.

The streets leaving the bus station area were occupied by crude vendors' stands along the curb, which appeared to be no more than temporary shelters of plastic and two-by-fours. Anyone wanting to use the sidewalk had to pass between them and the stores on the other side. It appeared to her like running the gauntlet. The streets were littered with piles of trash, especially near the corners. Her first impression of Puebla was of a very dirty, very messy city, crowded with cars, smoke, and people. She closed her eyes. She wished she had never come.

But in about fifteen minutes she arrived at the Hotel Hidalgo. Actually, her taxi came down a street to a place where the street in front of her had been closed and a sort of plaza occupied the space. The street to the right was also replaced by a plaza. The driver wheeled into a position along the curb between the two plazas, rather at the elbow of the curve, and stopped. She got out. The rain had stopped by then. The driver unloaded her suitcases from the trunk and directed her to the hotel entrance, which was a short distance from the corner.

She wheeled her suitcases over the stones of the plaza and through the entranceway of the hotel. There was a small counter to the right, and she reported there, saying she had a reservation. Her reservation was found, and she signed the register. The woman behind the counter was most pleasant and called a boy to help her with her bags.

The Hotel Hidalgo was an old building from the same historical time of the first *Colegio del Espíritu Santo,* and one of the properties acquired by the Jesuits in the XVI Century. It had more recently been converted into an old-fashioned style hotel and was used mostly by tourists and visitors to the University. It was on one corner of the plaza, and the main entrance to the University was half-way down on the facing side.

The rooms were of good size and furnished with heavy, old-Spanish style furniture. Each room had the modern convenience of a private bathroom—even when the water situation deprived its guests from taking a shower at certain hours of the day. There was a big restaurant on the first floor which had once been part of a refectory of the parish, and there they served the typical meals of the region, specializing in three or four different *mole*s (special sauces made with hot peppers, other spices, and almonds, and sometimes chocolate, which was served spread over chicken or other kinds of meat).

It was past seven-thirty when Magali arrived at the hotel, and there were a few tourists dining there under a yellowish light. She was not hungry, so she asked the young bellboy to bring up her suitcases. They climbed a wide, old-fashioned staircase with large stone steps to the second floor, and the boy opened a dark, wooden door with a large, old-fashioned key. She had the impression of being back at her convent in France, and the impression grew stronger when she looked at the little room with the big window, the single bed covered with white sheets and a white-cotton spread, a night table with a small electric lamp, and a crucifix on the wall over the bed.

"*Le traigo agua de botella, señorita?*" inquired the boy. "*Y,*" he added, "*me llamo Pedro.*"

"*Gracias, Pedro. Sí, por favor. Tráeme una botella grande de agua.*" She knew about the problem with the water and didn't want to start her stay in Mexico by getting sick. She could see that a bottle of good water would become an essential in Mexico.

She unpacked and hung up some clothes she would wear in the morning when she reported for her new job. After the boy had brought her a 12 oz. bottle of "*Agua Pura*" and had left, she drank a little of it, got undressed, and took a shower with luke-warm water, and then got dressed in some clean clothes for the rest of the evening.

She was beginning to feel hungry now, but she didn't want to start with a Mexican meal—not after her long journey. She would prefer something closer to what she was used to.

She went down to the lobby and looked around. Then she asked the woman at the desk if there were some other place to eat, not too far away, where she could get something more American. The woman discreetly stopped a smile and then said that near the *Zócalo* (in Mexico, the main plaza or central square) of the city there were several restaurants, including a McDonald's. It was just outside, to the left down the plaza, then left and down the street to the end of the block.

Magali thanked her and proceeded to the door. Outside and left down the plaza, then left and down the street to the end of the block. Nearing the end of the block, she could see more light ahead, and hear more noise. At the corner, to the left, was an outdoor cafe of tables and chairs, under an arcade which stretched to the next street. There were too many men there, so she crossed the street to the *Zócalo* itself, and then to the right side of the main square, where there was another arcade. She went down that arcade to half-way, where there was another cafe, but it appeared too small. Beyond that there was a gallery to the right which went through to the other street. She crossed the entrance to that and continued down the arcade, past another cafe, and the next cafe (or rather grouping of tables and chairs on the sidewalk) turned out to be a McDonald's.

She went in and to the counter. It was just like in the States, but everything was in Spanish. Young boys and girls, the Mexican equivalent of American teenagers, were serving behind the counter and cleaning the tables and mopping the floor. Everything was clean and spotless. At her turn at the counter she asked for a hamburger, fries, and a vanilla shake. Quickly served, she took her tray of food and went outside. At least she was going to eat in a foreign way, like on the Champs Elysées or the Via Venetto, though it was just in Puebla, Mexico.

Outside she found a table and sat down. In front of her was the *Zócalo*. People were walking by, music was playing, lights were shining. To her right was a more upscale restaurant, where tourists and locals were having full meals. But she was content with her food. The city was alive. She never expected this.

When she had finished eating, she took her tray back inside like a good American, deposited her papers and such in the trash bin, and placed her tray in the place provided for it on top. Then she walked back outside and to the right, on down the arcade. At

the end, to the right, was a street closed to auto traffic and lined
with stores of all kinds and filled with people shopping, meeting
and talking, or just walking along, looking at the windows and the
other people walking by. She had never seen such life, not even in
the more crowded malls in the States. She was overwhelmed. And
there were more cafes under the arcade that occupied the third
side of the *Zócalo,* along the street to the south.

But she was tired. It had been a long trip. Now it was time
to get some rest, so she turned around and walked back to the
hotel. She got her key at the desk and went upstairs. She went in
and got undressed. The air in the room was cool. *"Clima de sierra,"*
she thought. She opened the large window to let some night air
in. She got under the covers, noticing a faint smell of sewage. The
distant noises of the street, still alive with people, invaded the
dark little room, but she felt comforted by them and very soon
fell asleep.

One of the many and beautiful legends of the city of Puebla
is that which refers to the choice of a place for its foundation,
and its author, without doubt, is the P. Francisco Florencia who
made it known and propagated in 1692 in his work *"Narración de
la maravillosa aparición . . . ,"* in which it is written:

*"Dicen, pues, que entregado a la quietud del sueño el Señor Obispo
Don Julián Garcés, una noche, que asientan haber sido vísperas del Arcángel
San Miguel, en su festividad, que celebra la Iglesia el 29 de Setiembre con el
título de Dedicación, le fué mostrado un hermoso y dilatado campo, por medio
del cual corría un cristalino rio, y estaba rodeado de otros dos que lo ceñían y
circunvalaban, poblado de variedad de yerbas y flores, cuya amenidad
fomentaban y entretenían diferentes ojos o manatiales de agua que brotaban
esparcidos en todo su terreno, haciendo entender al Venerable Prelado que
aquél era el lugar que tenía el Señor preparado para la fundación que se
pretendía, a cuyo tiempo vió descender de los cielos algunos ángeles que,
echando los cordeles, planteaban y delineaban la nueva población. Despertó
muy de madrugada y la primera diligencia que hizo fué celebrar el Santo
Sacrificio de la Misa, con mucha devoción y recogimiento y haciendo llamar
después a los Religiosos Franciscanos que se hallaban en Tlaxcala (entre los*

cuales fué uno el Padre Fr. Toribio de Benavente, que algunos afirman estaba de Guardián) y otras personas distinguidas y de su confianza, así españoles como indios, les refirió el sueño y les dijo que estaba resuelto a salir en persona a reconocer la tierra por si en élla hallaba el sitio que se le había mostrado en el sueño para cuyo efecto quería que lo acompañasen. Salió, pues, con esa comitiva, dirigiéndose no sin superior impulso, hacia la parte sur y habiendo andado como cinco leguas, llegando al paraje que hoy es la ciudad, suspendió su marcha, haciendo alto en él y teniendo a la vista por uno y otro lado, conocía ser el mismo que se le había manifestado en el sueño, y volviendo a los que le acompañaban les dijo estas palabras: 'Este es el lugar que me mostró el Señor y en donde quiere que se funde nuestra Ciudad.' A todos agradó mucho el sitio y, reflejadas después todas las circunstancias, creyeron desde luego que la asignación que de él hizo el Señor Obispo fué por Superior ilustración."

But, in the *Historia de la Ciudad de la Puebla*, by Antonio Carrión it is reported:

"La fundación de 'La Puebla de Los Angeles' fué el 16 de Abril del año de 1531, Domingo de Pascua de Resurrección, ésto está plenamente comprobado en un libro que existe en el archivo del Ayuntamiento de esta Ciudad que se titula, 'Establecimiento y dilatación de la nobilísima ciudad de Puebla,' y tiene el número 2, a fojas una consta una lista de fecha 2 de Mayo de 1531, en la que se menciona que se repartieron a varios conquistadores españoles que mencionaré después, una o más caballerías de tierra como primeros pobladores y además por otros documentos públicos auténticos que se conservan por fortuna. Las causas que determinan la fundación en ese lugar son varias, pero antes de mencionarlas es necesario para mejor inteligencia dar una idea de los sucesos de la época de élla, y es concisamente lo siguiente:

"Los enemigos de Hernán Cortés, conquistador de México, lograron con sus intrigas influir en el ánimo del emperador Carlos V, rey de España, primero de este nombre, quién dominado por los informes que recibía contra el conquistador, decidió quitarle el mando y encomendar el gobierno del reino de la Nueva España a un cuerpo de magistrados que se llamó 'Real Audiencia,' esto sucedía el año de 1528 . . .

"Estos oidores se aliaron con los tiranos de los indios y se manifestaron enemigos acérrimos de los frailes misioneros, cometieron muchos desórdenes y atentados. Sabedora de esto la corte de España mandó entonces formar una

segunda 'Real Audiencia,' que se compuso del obispo de Cuenca Fray Sebastián Ramírez de Fuén-Leal, presidente de élla . . .

"Esta 'Real Audiencia', a moción de Fray Sebastián Ramírez de Fuén-Leal, aceptó la idea de fundar una colonia de españoles en las márgenes del Río Atoyac, en la llanura que los indios llamaban Cuetlaxcoapan, cosa que solicitó al padre Franciscano Fray Toribio Benavente . . .

"Este religioso pidió 'que se congregaran algunos españoles en la llanura antes de Huejocingo, y camino que es para la Veracruz,' y formaron una Puebla . . . "

5

FIRST SUNDAY

Sunday morning, in a foreign country. The sun was already shining through the window when Magali awoke. She got up and showered, dressed, and went downstairs. It was only eight o'clock, but she acted like it was late, not wanting to miss any part of the day. A day which was all hers, before she had to report for work on Monday.

The restaurant was quite busy, many of its patrons appearing to be professors or tourists. She went in, was ushered to a table, and ordered a Mexican breakfast. She was going to get into the spirit of the country. They brought her a big ceramic cup of coffee—Mexican coffee, made in a big pot in the kitchen by boiling whole coffee beans and lots of sugar. She also had *quesadillas* (tortillas stuffed with cheese), *huevos rancheros* (fried eggs with a green hot sauce on top), and a big glass of fresh papaya juice. There was a dish with hot sauce on the table (both a green and a red one), but Magali decided that any more was a little too adventurous. She enjoyed her meal.

When she finished breakfast, she went to the hotel desk to inquire about places to go and things to do. They gave her several brochures indicating different tours in the city and vicinity. They also gave her a pamphlet of a walking tour prepared by the Tourist Office. She sat on a sofa in the lobby and began to look over the booty she had obtained.

A small map of the central part of Puebla was included in one of the brochures from the Tourist Office, as well as a general scheme of the street naming system. Everything appeared to be oriented from the central plaza. The streets were in a rectangular grid in the central part of the city, and though they were not aligned in a perfect north-south, east-west, direction, they were more or less that way, and if one thought of how they were planned, and one ignored the position of the sun at any time of the day or season and the true directions of north-south and east-west, the system was quite usable. On the "north" side of the *Zócalo* was the *Avenida Avila Camacho*, which went eastward from the northwest corner, from its intersection with the street *Cinco de Mayo* (Fifth of May). This street went from the intersection northward. Southward, on the west side of the *Zócalo*, it was called *16 de Setiembre*. Westward of the northwest corner of the *Zócalo* the *Avenida Avila Camacho* was called *Avenida Reforma*. These four streets formed the axes for the street naming and house numbering system of Puebla.

In the north part of the system the east-west streets were given even numbers: 2, 4, 6, etc. They were called west or east relative to the street *Cinco de Mayo*. So there was *4 Poniente* and *4 Oriente*. In the south part the east-west streets were given odd numbers. In the east part the north-south streets were given even numbers, while in the west part the north-south streets were given odd numbers. In the latter case they were called, therefore, *7 Norte* or *7 Sur*.

It was all very confusing to Magali, but it was all very logical, and she was sure she could master it after a while. She made a mental note to be aware of the street names and to learn from this where she was relative to the *Zócalo*. That would be a good practice for learning the system and for not getting lost.

For now she thought she had better concentrate on what was on the map of the central part of the city for her touring. It was a small enough area to explore for a first day, and she could

walk to wherever on it she wanted to go. She put the Tourist
Office brochure in her pocket and took the others up to her
room.

It was past nine o'clock now. The day was already well along,
so after washing her hands and face, and checking to see that she
looked presentable, she prepared to launch her tour. As a
precaution against an afternoon rain she picked up a small folding
umbrella to take along with her. She also took a small purse
which she could secure in a pocket. She left the room and went
downstairs and turned in her key at the desk, and then proceeded
out of the hotel.

The first destination for the day would be the *Callejón de Los
Sapos,* which was the closest item of interest on the small map she
had.

As her friend in the Mexican Consulate in Boston had told
her, the main building of the University was just across the plaza
from the hotel. The "plaza" was actually called a *"pasaje,"* the
"Pasaje Carolino," which was really a closed street, only one block
long, making a small plaza with the hotel on one side and the
main building of the University on the other.

The street on the north end of the plaza was the *Avenida
Avila Camacho,* which led westward to the *Zócalo.* On the south
end, running along the side of the hotel, was the street *3 Oriente,*
which led westward to the south side of the *Zócalo,* where the
Cathedral of Puebla was. Continuing southward from the plaza
was the street *4 Sur.* East of this intersection *3 Oriente* was
blocked by a plaza which ran along the side of the University
building, a block in length. Behind the University building was
another small plaza, something like that in front of the hotel.
Running southward from that plaza was the *Callejón de Los Sapos*
(Alley of the Toads).

Though it was called an alley, it looked more like a narrow
street with very narrow sidewalks (about a foot and a half wide)
on both sides, like a street in a medieval town in Europe. The
street had just enough width for one lane of traffic and one
parked car, if it could be parked tightly against the curb—or with

two wheels up on the curb, as was often done. *Los Sapos,* as the area is called, is an antique district from long ago. There were many shops located along the *Callejón,* but Magali kept to looking in the windows only, since the day was still early by Mexican standards, and many of the shops were closed.

Continuing on southward down the *Callejón,* she came to a crossing street, *5 Oriente,* and found herself facing, on the other side, an extension of the antique trade into another plaza, called *El Jardín de Los Sapos* (Garden of Toads). Various antique shops lined both sides of the plaza. There were some trees in the plaza, which gave it some shade, and there was an old fountain almost in the center. The plaza was really on two levels, the west side being slightly higher than the east side. The plaza was of the same level at the two ends, so one could walk around it easily, but towards the center one had to go down some steps to go from the western part to the eastern.

The interesting thing about the plaza, which is what people refer to when they speak of *Los Sapos,* is that on Sundays it is the site of a combination antique and flea market, sometimes called the *Fiesta de los Domingos.*

It was still early, and there were few buyers, or sellers. People were still bringing things to be sold at the various stands which had been erected in the central part of the plaza. And those from the shops were busy arranging some pieces in front of their doors.

Magali made a quick tour around the plaza. In addition to the antique shops there were several art galleries, and on one corner, on *5 Oriente,* there was a cafe-bar with an area of outdoor tables: wrought iron tables and plastic tablecloths, under a red canvas awning. It was called *Café Los Gatos.* Inside was a small bar, several shelves full of bottles and ceramic cats (black and of various colors), and a radio turned on low which played Mexican music.

The cafe was open for business, so Magali sat at a table and asked the waiter who rushed over to her for a Sidral (an apple flavored soft drink). There she sat and rested, waiting for the time to pass and people to gather and the fair to get under way. She sat watching the preparations for the fair being made and the great variety of people going by or pondering the merchandise being arranged for sale.

Soon a number of people began to appear in the plaza and in the street *5 Oriente,* and in and around the bar on the other side of the street, on the corner of the *Callejón de Los Sapos*—which she later learned had a specialty of traditional drinks and liquors. New people even began to sit at the tables of the cafe, and soon there were no free tables left. She later observed that the cafe and its outdoor tables was a place of reunion on Sundays for many intellectuals and artists of the city.

Presently Magali got up, freeing her table to the gathering people waiting to grab it, and passed among the vendors of the fair in the plaza—or rather in the *"Garden of Los Sapos"*—which were in greater number now, it getting near to eleven o'clock. Many had tables set up, but many others displayed their merchandise on the tops of cardboard boxes or on blankets or plastic sheets spread on the pavement of the plaza. She started with those closest to the cafe and the street and proceeded first around the west side of the plaza.

There, under the glass eyes of a strange deformed store mannequin from the 20's, were offered for sale old furniture, pottery, tools. There were somber religious oil paintings and gay water colors, framed in gold leaf, or in frames of antique wood; statues of plaster and of bronze; and all kinds of *bric-à-brac* and other objects of assorted value. And wandering among the displays were strolling vendors of seeds, peanuts, potato chips, balloons, and ice cream.

Over to the east side, under the trees, there were tables for eating, and charcoal stoves where a small group of older women, looking very native Mexican, tended their fires and their huge pots. These women, well encamped, obviously long standing regulars at the plaza, made the famous *gorditas* and *chalupas* and other fantastic things to eat. Their pots produced the most appetizing odors, which one could smell from anywhere in the plaza, and their wares were not only eaten at the tables but were also taken to the cafe on the request of patrons there. Magali hadn't tried any as yet, but she intended to get up the courage to try them someday.

It was indeed a festival, the *Fiesta de los Domingos*, under a beautiful blue sky and warm sun that made the antique mirrors and the blue-green, red, or transparent crystal glassware shine, along with the Talavera ceramic with its blue and white designs and its multiple chinese-spanish-arabic personality for which Puebla was famous. A multitude of people: tourists and local Sunday strollers; *gringos* with big hats and safari attire; student helpers with long hindu skirts and long black hair who entered and left the plaza carrying diverse objects—antique biscuit statues, dolls, toy furniture, cases and chests, and paintings—and who added their charm, their exotic beauty, and their mystery to the scene.

There were two Germans at a table at which they sold medals and antique coins of bronze. They were very tall and lean, very well built, even powerful in appearance, like two captains from the Africa Korps. If they had been selling guns instead of old coins, it would have looked more appropriate. An old man had a long table covered with used books under a plastic awning. There were more books scattered on the floor behind the table, up against the wall of the nearby building behind him. He spent a good deal of time moving quickly from the table to the area behind, following eagerly every potential customer, like a nervous squirrel.

There was a Peruvian who sold beautiful mirrors and small boxes and ponchos and small copper churches and brass figures of llamas.

It was a moving and resplendent market. One could almost see Federico Fellini walking through the middle of this, dancing his dance of life and death—a *Dolce Vita* that, at its root, was hard and bitter, but that had its day in the sun.

Along about twelve Magali was satisfied with the fair and decided it was time to get something to eat. She didn't feel like Mexican food just yet. She thought she had probably better work into it gradually. In the end she felt like McDonald's again. For one thing, the food was familiar, which was probably a factor making it digestible. Another point in favor of McDonald's, at least here in Mexico, was that the food was actually good. The meat was like good meat, not like plastic or paper, as in the States. And the potatoes were not greasy; actually they were delicious. She could make a meal of the potatoes alone, probably with a shake or coke to slake her thirst. So off she headed to the *Zócalo* and McDonald's.

In the daylight she had a better view of the *Zócalo*. The streets which surrounded it on three sides were lined with arcades, along which were stores and cafes or restaurants. On the north side, toward the northeast corner, was the *Municipalidad;* on the corner was a bank. On the east side, on the corner of *Avila Camacho,* was a hotel and a first floor restaurant. The area of the arcade southward from the hotel was not too frequented. There one found a shoe store, an office supply store, and a store selling religious goods. There was also a pizza restaurant there, but altogether the area on that side of the plaza was not so inviting. The west side had a variety of retail stores and cafes and restaurants, but it had more traffic—probably because there were more retail stores southward from the *Zócalo* on that street, and probably because in that direction lay the entrance to the cathedral.

The fourth side of the *Zócalo* was occupied by the Cathedral of Puebla—a famous tourist site, of course. Its entrance was from *16 de Setiembre,* on its west side. An iron fence enclosed the cathedral yard. The north side was along the *Zócalo*. On the side of the street that passed there, *3 Oriente,* there were parked a number of tourist busses.

It being Sunday, there was a Mass held every hour, and groups of people were going in and out of the cathedral, wearing their Sunday-best clothes: the women with long, bright, and hand-embroidered cotton skirts, lace blouses, and veils on their heads; the men dressed in dark trousers and the long cotton shirts typical of the region, holding straw hats in their hands. The children were *endomingados* with their special Sunday clothing—the boys wearing dark suits, shiny leather shoes, white shirts, and ties; the girls, like pretty dolls, wearing many colorful ribbons in their braided hair and long dresses or bright, ample skirts covering but not concealing their laced-rim petticoats. An occasional tourist in loud shorts and T-shirt would stick out in the crowd, but he usually would be isolated from the rest of the people, who would cast amused glances at him when they could not be seen. In the atrium of the church and in the yard in the front and to the side, near the side entrance, there were vendors of balloons, newspapers, religious articles, and *nieves* (something similar to "Italian ice"), and these were stretched out all along the sidewalks on the way to the *Zócalo,* where other vendors of Mexican crafts and souvenirs, sweet bread, and lottery tickets were hawking their merchandise among the people there.

The *Zócalo* itself was a square plaza with a fountain in the center. Walkways went from the four corners to a circular area around the fountain, and there were two adjoining circular areas surrounded by typical park benches on the east and west sides of the fountain area. In the circular area to the west of the fountain was a band, performing a Sunday concert. A broad walkway went from the center of the south side of the square to the fountain area and from there to the north side. All around the plaza was a broad sidewalk, also lined with park benches. In the space not occupied by fountain or walkways were beds of a variety of beautiful flowers, and tall trees of various species, many with their name-tags on the trunks.

Magali was fascinated by the whole scene, taking in all the colors, the voices, the buildings, the people—all under a brilliant blue sky. It was truly a people's plaza, in the real sense of the word.

After walking for a while among the vendors and the people in the *Zócalo,* including stopping to admire the band, she directed her steps toward McDonald's, where she hoped to find a chair and table outside from which she could watch the Sunday show in comfort.

She got a chicken sandwich, some fries, and a shake, and was lucky to find a table outside which had just been vacated. Sitting in an outdoor cafe and watching the world go by was always a special treat for her, and it appeared that not too many knew of it or took advantage of the opportunity when it was afforded.

McDonald's in Puebla was in a special class in the world precisely because of that location on the *Zócalo* and the outdoor tables and chairs it provided.

She sat facing the *Zócalo,* watching the people in the plaza across the street and the parade of people passing by under the arcade, enjoying the happy holiday atmosphere of the city. A group of German tourists were sitting almost next to her in the area of the adjoining restaurant—called the Royal something, from what she could see of the sign—laughing and joking, taking pictures, and chatting animatedly in German. Of course they were drinking beer and enjoying huge meals.

When she was about finished with her meal, a very polite Mexican boy wearing a McDonald's uniform came to her table and asked her if this was her first trip to Puebla.

She answered, "Yes."

"Have you seen *Los Sapos,* the antique market?"

"Yes, I've just come from there," she replied.

"Oh," he said. "Then, have you seen *El Parián,* the market for souvenirs and native crafts?" he asked in remarkably good English.

"No, at least not yet. Where is it?" responded Magali.

"Is very close, *señorita.* You just go to that corner," he said, pointing toward the University, "turn left and walk north one block, and then to the east a few blocks and you come to it."

"And just north of *El Parián,* across the street, is the *Barrio del Artista,* where the artists display and sell their paintings," he added.

"Gracias," said Magali. *"Hablas Inglés muy bién. Donde lo aprendiste?"*

"En la universidad, señorita," said the boy, smiling broadly. "Thank you."

When she finished her meal, she threw away her papers, replaced the tray, and went to the bathroom to wash her hands and face. When she came out, she asked for a glass of cold water, *purificada,* before venturing toward *El Parián.*

* * *

True to the boy's directions, one block north and a few blocks east took her to *El Parián*. It was at the corner of *2 Oriente* and *6 Norte*, but actually its main part was a "way" between *2 Oriente* and *4 Oriente*, which had shops facing on it and (backing?) on *6 Norte*. There were similar shops on the other side of the "way" which faced on it and backed on another "way" behind it. On the other side of this second "way" were buildings, some of which had storefronts facing that second "way."

The main action was in the first "way" which had a crude but picturesque paving of rounded stones painted with various bright colors but difficult to walk on. In the center of the "way" was what appeared to be a fountain, though it had no water.

El Parián was a market of craft products, if such they could be called. It had many very small shops, each displaying its wares within the shop and on counters in front of the shop, and hanging above and around the entrance to the shop. There were items of clothing such as vests, sweaters, and hats, and a host of accessories: necklaces, small purses, and such. Some shops sold Talavera pottery; others sold items made from onyx, a stone from an area near to Puebla. Sweets of various kinds were for sale, and a host of plastic toys and other goods imported from Korea and China and other places in the Orient. Most of the goods for sale were as souvenirs. Magali really wasn't interested in such things at that time, having just arrived in Puebla, so after she had made the round of the shops, she moved northward out of *El Parián* and out of the crowd, across the street and into the area of the *Barrio del Artista*.

This was an area similar to *El Parián*, in that it was a "way" rather than a street. It was almost aligned with *El Parián* as a northward extension, so it easily attracted tourists from *El Parián* into *El Barrio del Artista*. For a short distance back from the street, *4 Oriente*, it was just a paved area, paved with large squares of dark stone which appeared to be volcanic in origin, a stone of which most of the sidewalks in the central area of Puebla were paved. Then there was a row of small shops along the west side. They were very small, large enough for a desk and chair and a little space to move around. Each appeared to be used as the office of an individual artist, and for storing his tools and materials. Each had the name of the artist above the door. Some were closed, but in front of some the artist was installed with a chair and easel, either painting or displaying a painting for sale.

Magali strolled down the row of shops, looking at the paintings hanging in front or displayed on easels. Most were of small patios and stairways, covered with sunlight and flowers. Others were of the large windows of Mexican houses, the old style ones, some with balconies, all with flowers. They were all very well done, but they didn't display very much action, so they consequently lacked any power.

About at the end of the row of shops, a little more than halfway, the paved area widened into a small square, near the center of which were some huge sculptures. On the buildings facing the square from the other side one could see a stairway leading to the second story and signs indicating that up there there was a cafe. A few benches were available under some huge trees near the entrance to the square, and Magali found a seat on which to rest for a while and watch the people.

It was getting into the hotter part of the afternoon and the sun was very heavy on Magali's head. Not only was it getting hot, but she was also getting tired. Too much time on her feet. She decided she had better go back to the hotel and rest there, maybe even take a *siesta*.

She slept the rest of the afternoon. She got up about seven-thirty, washed up, and went down to the restaurant for a light meal. She then went back to her room to get ready for the next day; and when that chore was done, really all in, she called it a night, showered, and went to bed.

6

UPA

When she got up the next morning, Monday, she showered with some difficulty because the water pressure was so low that there was barely enough water flowing to rinse the shampoo from her long hair. She dressed in a tan skirt and white cotton blouse, and went down to the restaurant for breakfast. She felt good but a little apprehensive. Her excitement was enhanced as she began to notice her surroundings: the candelabras, the dark paintings of the old Spanish school hanging on the walls (one a painting of Cortés, the *Conquistador*). This was the day she reported to work—at a professional job in a foreign country.

The few occupants that were there with her in the restaurant appeared to be tourists rather than visiting foreign professors, but she could have been mistaken on that. There was a German couple sitting at one table. Four women who were teachers from Iowa—as she learned from overhearing their loud conversation—were sitting at another.

A tall, handsome waiter who reminded her of an old movie star came to take her order, quite openly admiring her beauty. She asked for a big cup of *café con leche* and a basketfull of *pan dulce* like that dispersing an aroma of fresh-baked dough from the table of the Iowa teachers. The waiter suggested also a *jugo de papaya,* which she accepted; but she refused the rest of the Mexican breakfast, *chilaquiles* and *quesadillas,* that he tried to persuade her to add to an already large breakfast compared with what she was accustomed to. She was not up to a full Mexican diet yet.

When breakfast was over, she went to her room, got her briefcase with her papers, and went down the stairs and out of the hotel.

She stood a moment outside the entrance to the hotel, under the small shade trees which were in front, looking at the huge two-story building on the other side of the plaza. She looked up at a pristine clear sky—no clouds, and a blue so deep and so pure that it made her feel dizzy.

The University building looked more like a convent than a school: a majestic, old, Spanish building, with massive walls, two tall stories high, painted in a now dull yellow; and high on the side of it was painted *"Universidad de Puebla de Los Angeles,"* locally referred to as "UPA." Two huge wooden doors like those of the old churches in Mexico, one with its own smaller wicket door within it which could be used when the larger doors were closed, guarded its entrance. Next to the University, to its right, was the original Jesuit church of Puebla, the Church of the Company.

The small plaza between the hotel and the University was already filled with a crowd of mainly young people, chatting noisily, kissing and embracing, laughing, or running to their classes. She walked out onto the plaza, and as she did, a dozen pigeons flew up from in front of the trees, marking the blue with grey, moving spots.

A few steps took her across the plaza and through the huge doors, now open, that were the main entrance to the University. She stopped at a reception office to the right within the entranceway to ask for directions to the office of the Director of the Institute of Foreign Languages (*Instituto de Lenguas Extranjeras,* or ILE). She was directed to another building. It was two blocks away on *4 Oriente,* and just over half a block east of *4 Norte.*

Cuatro Norte was the street running north from the *Avenida Camacho,* in line with the axis of the plaza between the University and the Hotel Hidalgo. So she thanked the girl at the reception office and walked out of the University entranceway and into the plaza again. It was a beautiful day and she looked forward to what appeared to be the short walk northward for two blocks to *4 Oriente*, then east to the ILE.

She had a time crossing Camacho because of the fast traffic on that street. In spite of the number of students waiting to cross, and in spite of a traffic light which was supposed to stop the traffic from time to time so the students could cross, the cars paid no heed to the encroaching pedestrians nor to the semaphore but came as fast or faster. Many cars turned at the corner to head northward on *4 Norte,* so Magali chose to cross to the northeast corner, which she finally managed to do by dashing between cars when at last the traffic had thinned for a moment.

The walk was enjoyable, and she found herself in a short time at the building she was looking for. She noticed that she was only a half block from *El Parián,* so that would make it easier to find her way back on succeeding days.

The building was an old Spanish-style mansion, with an interior court open to the sky. It was two stories high. There was a second court, which one entered through a passageway under the second story and on the right of the far side of the first court. This second court was where formerly the carriages and horses were kept, and where the quarters for the domestics were. The owners, in the olden times, had lived on the second floor. The building still had that romantic attraction of old Spain, and Magali felt an atmosphere that was somehow familiar. At the present time the building had been converted for and was in use by several university departments.

The office of the *Instituto de Lenguas Extranjeras,* was to the left within the entranceway. It consisted of the *antesala,* where the secretary desks and the file cabinets took much of the space, and the Director's private office.

One of the secretaries took Magali's name and had her sit in a desk chair on one side of the room where she could see through a half open door into the office of the Director. She noted the curiosity she had aroused and the giggling of the women. She also noted that they were very dressed up, as if for going to a dance: elaborate silk dresses in gaudy colors, too much hair spray on their hairdos, high heels, lots of makeup. And the perfume they were using was strong and sweet, which, mixed with the cigarette smoke (they were all smoking), made the air nauseating.

Magali also began to notice a general lack of oxygen in the air, a consequence of the high altitude of the city, which added to her discomfort. After a while the intercom rang and one of the women made a gesture to Magali to go in.

The Director's private office was furnished with a huge mahogany desk, several plush, leather chairs, a desk to one side for the Director's personal assistant, a shelve with books, and four telephones (two on top of his desk, one on the wall, and another at the assistant's desk). The phones were constantly ringing.

The interview was short and not very amiable. It was evident that the Director was not interested in foreign professors.

"I have too much trouble with my staff," he told her without looking up from the papers he was reading. "They don't like the fact that we hire American professors and pay them twice as much as they themselves receive."

Magali said nothing. She had laid on the top of the desk a dossier with her documents and was looking at a large photo of Lenin, in a wooden frame, on the wall in back of the Director's desk. Now she examined the man facing her. He had a dark complexion, regular features, straight nose, full lips, and mustache. His hair was wavy and carefully combed to one side. He wore a blue linen suit, a white starched shirt, and a Pierre Cardin tie. His hands were carefully manicured. He might have been considered attractive, by Latin standards. But his eyes were red and his cheeks puffy. He looked as though he had a bad hangover. The telephone rang and he grabbed it, talking to his secretary in a very fast Spanish. *"Celia, no quiero que se me interrumpa más."* And he hung up. He was examining Magali's documents, visa, and school records. Finally, he looked at her.

"Don't expect any privileges," he told her. "You will work in the same conditions as the other Mexican teachers."

Magali felt like laughing. She hadn't expected a red carpet. But this "welcome" was so unusual she didn't know what to think. And then her rebellious, fighting side came out.

"I was hired by the Rector of the University. Maybe you would be kind enough to arrange an appointment for me to see him. Evidently, there must be some kind of misunderstanding. I was told the University would be happy to have me."

The man looked at her, in disbelief. He was used to the servile behavior of his employees. Then he dropped his act.

"Perdone," he said, smiling. "I see you are an intelligent young person. I am required to discourage the foreign intrusions—by my staff and by the Unions. But, at the same time, it is the Rector's wish to upgrade the standards of the University. Coffee?"

"No, gracias," she said.

"You will have to teach at least one class per term. The rest of the time you will have free for your own research. And, I am informed, there may be required of you, from time to time, certain duties for the Rector."

He then asked his assistant—a tall, good-looking, young boy—to take her to the language school and to introduce her to the other teachers.

"They will assist you in the organization of your class and with the acquisition of whatever materials you might require."

Magali voiced her farewell and followed the young man out, passing through the antesala without looking at the secretaries.

"Voilá," she thought. "I won my first battle. This is indeed going to be a challenge." Boston was now just a distant city in a very distant, foreign country. Her adventure was becoming a reality.

The old colonial building was arranged in a series of large rooms around the court. A stairway to the left as they entered the court led to the second floor, where other rooms were located. Another stairway on the right of the court led up to rooms on the second floor of that side of the building. The passageway to the rear court, on the other side from the entranceway and to the right, must have given access to other rooms on the ground level.

The first thing she noticed, while admiring the thickness of the walls and the old Spanish architecture of the building, was the smell. A sewage smell: pungent, powerful, nauseating.

The young man led Magali across the court to a room to the left of the rear passageway, a room which was for the teaching staff: a dirty wooden table in the middle, still containing the greasy crumbs from an earlier breakfast and partially covered with books and papers; a few chairs; and a big bottle of purified water in a corner. One of the walls was covered with lockers, the other with several announcements of classes and events, hand-written. There were five people in the room: a man in his thirties—athletic, dark hair, and brown eyes; two older Mexican women in a corner, with glasses, who were examining papers and correcting them in silence; a fat, balding, short man, reading out loud; and a tall, rather good looking man, who looked American. They all stopped talking and looked up when Magali came in.

"Disculpen," said the young man. "We have a new teacher for you," he continued in English. "Miss Magali Smith, from the U.S.A."

The athletic-looking man jumped up to take her briefcase. He set that on the table and offered her his chair. "Pleased to meet you. My name is Paul García," he said. At that, the Director's assistant went back to the Director's Office.

"I'm pleased to meet you," said Magali, who remained standing.

Paul introduced her to the women first, whose English was not so good. They remained seated, just barely lifting their heads to look at her; and she recognized that look, the same that she had sometimes seen in the streets of Puebla and in the hotel: a mixture of envy, apprehension, and contempt—"another *gringa*, another foreigner to take our jobs."

The men of Puebla, on the other hand, openly admired her beauty—a bit too openly—and a few even followed her in the streets to her hotel; but no one ever made open advances to her, and she never felt threatened.

Paul then presented her to the fat man.

"I am very happy to meet you," he said, with a pronounced German accent. "My name is Hans Leverkühn. When did you arrive?"

"Last night. I'm staying at the Hotel Hidalgo, but I shall be looking for an apartment as soon as possible. I can't afford the $60 a day rooms there."

"We'll be happy to help you find something," said Paul. "I have a cousin who is renting a big room—what you would call an efficiency room—on *12 Oriente*. I'll be glad to take you there to see it. After classes . . . after noon . . . here. If that's all right with you. I have a Vocho."

"Vocho?"

"V.W. bug."

"Your English is native, I see."

"Yes, I was born in San Diego and raised between here and there. My parents are Mexican, living in the States."

Paul then introduced Magali to the tall man—who *was* American. "Hi," he said. "My name is Charles Johnson, but you can call me Charley."

"You're early," Paul continued. "The term doesn't start until the fifteenth. We're still not finished with the summer courses until next week. But that should give you some time to get yourself organized.

"We've sort of picked a class for you to start with: Modern English Literature. Normally we teach American writers, since the English are rather has-beens in the world now. It goes from 11:00 to 12:00, upstairs. I don't know this term what room it will be in, but we can find out at the office. You can pick your own authors and rather run the class as you wish. You're from Boston University, so that puts you at a high level of standing —particularly here."

"Thank you," said Magali. "I hope I can live up to your expectations."

Just then an older man came into the room. He was in his fifties, with greying, neatly cut, short hair; blue eyes; tall (at least 6'2"), with broad shoulders and a deep brown tan. He was dressed rather casually in jeans, a white T-shirt, and one of those hunting vests with so many pockets. He was quite handsome.

"Ah," said Paul. "You're just in time, Father. Magali, this is Father Flynn, Father James Flynn, a Canadian, but really an Irishman."

"Irish by blood, but born in Canada," interjected the newcomer.

"He teaches French," Paul continued. "Father, this is Magali Smith, from Boston University; here for a year."

"Pleased to make your acquaintance, I'm sure," he said, smiling, with a broad, boyish smile.

"And I to make yours," said Magali. "I hope I can look forward to talking with you in French, just to keep in practice."

"*Bien sûr! Ça sera un plaisir pour moi aussi.*"

"*Merci, mon père,*" responded Magali.

"*Mais non!* Call me James."

Paul suggested he and Magali should go to the offices to find out in which room her class was to be taught. It was to be upstairs in room 1C, and the time was 11:00 to 12:00 on Monday, Wednesday, and Friday. Paul led her up the stairs and along the second floor walkway to the room. There he left her to look over her new home, said very politely, "*Hasta luego; nos encontraremos después del mediodía,*" and proceeded back to the stairway and down.

She looked at the man as he emerged below and made his way across to the building's entrance, jumped over some large *mangueras* connected to a water tank truck which was parked in front, unloading water, and was accosted in the entranceway by three female students: pretty, young, and very nicely built—in the sensuous Latin way. "*Il est beau,*" she thought. "And I'm so very far from home."

Magali went back into the room. It looked dilapidated. The paint was faded and there were big water stains on the walls. The blackboards were not clean, and there were no erasers. Even the floor was unswept, and the students' chairs were all in disorder.

She went back downstairs to the teachers' room, where she met Father Flynn, sitting alone at the table, going over some papers. The others had all gone, probably to classes.

"Father Flynn," she said, "could you help me with some problems with my class."

"Certainly," he responded, looking up. "What are the problems?"

"I don't know just how to put it, but no one has given me any information on the basics of teaching here. Are there any forms I have to fill out, such as student attendance. There are no erasers in my room for the blackboard, and the room is a dirty mess. Where and how do I get books? There are a million details such as these that I must address, so to whom do I go for assistance?"

"Whoa," said Father Flynn. "Have you ever heard of that great Irishman, Murphy, and his Law?"

"Murphy's Law? Yes, of course."

"Well, here we have a comparable Law, or at least a suitable excuse for what goes wrong. *Es un país tropical.* Here in the tropics one must expect anything to happen and not be surprised when it does. It is indeed a miracle if anything does work out right, or, more likely, a lucky chance if it does."

"But where do I get erasers? And books?"

"I'm trying to tell you! Nothing works right! I was here almost a year before a wise Mexican friend set me straight on how things work—they don't. The first thing you must learn is that. Then, if you want something to work, you have to make it work yourself; no one else will."

"So, what do I do?"

"To start: everyone brings his own eraser and his own chalk. You have to supply the books. Rather, I should say, you have to pick the books you want to use. We have a small library at the right of the entranceway, and you can take out some books from there that you want your students to read. Form some committees among your students to make photo copies and to distribute the copies to the other students. There is no money available from the University, and the students have very limited funds. Most of them are poor. But they have to pay for the copies; that's the only way they can have books to read.

"As to cleaning, someone does clean up in the evening, but by the time you have your class—which I assume is later in the day—the room will be somewhat in disorder and will by that time have accumulated its share of trash. That's the way it is. You'll have to get used to living with it.

"Keep your own records as best you can. At the end of the course they will give you an official form to fill out with the students' grades. How you keep a record of the grades you will finally give is your own affair.

"Anytime you run into something you can't handle, you can ask me and I'll try to do what I can to help. Try to get with the flow here, which is very slow, partly because of the altitude. It's not the States. *Es un país tropical.* And remember this: Everyone will be watching to see you fail. That's also how it is.

"Now, it's about ten o'clock, and I have a class that starts at eleven. That gives us an hour to have some coffee. Come with me."

He got up, put his books and papers in an old briefcase, and started out of the room, allowing Magali to go first. They walked across the court toward the entranceway, and Father Flynn said, "We'll go to *La Villa Rica.* It's a small restaurant across the street which serves lunches. It got its name *La Villa Rica* from its owner having come from Veracruz. The real name of Veracruz is *'La Villa Rica de la Vera Cruz.'* Like the real name of Los Angeles was *'El Pueblo de Nuestra Señora la Reina de Los Angeles.'* 'The Town of Our Lady the Queen of the Angels.' Quite a different thing from 'City of the Angels.' You'll find yourself going out for coffee on many occasions in Mexico. Its one of the good traditions of the country." Magali went with him in silence, like following a teacher-priest when she was a little girl. But she was glad he offered himself as a mentor.

The restaurant was a small one, just four tables and a small kitchen in the back separated from the eating area by a partition. The owner came out to personally see to their finding seats. It was modestly decorated with framed carvings on the wall of some wood figures of people dancing, probably something typical from Veracruz. Some Mexican music was playing softly.

"Dos cafés Americanos," called out Father Flynn as they came into the restaurant. They grabbed a table near the door and the good Father set his briefcase against the wall. Magali placed hers by her chair, but on the side near the wall.

"Well," said Magali, "tell me what an Irish-Canadian is doing in Puebla; surely you're not here just to teach French."

"No," said Father Flynn. "I'm really here much for the same reason you are. I'm a Jesuit, and I'm here for two years to do some research on the early Jesuit presence in Mexico. You no doubt know something of the Order's history in Puebla?"

"Not really," responded Magali. "My coming to Puebla was rather sudden. I got an offer through a friend in the Mexican Consulate in Boston and grabbed it. I'm almost unprepared for the experience. But I hope to study the churches and convents in Puebla to discover an architectural link with the Spanish language as it developed in Mexico. Of Jesuits, I know very little so far."

"Well, my Order is paying for me, but they have worked out a kind of exchange with the University so the cost will not be too great. I get paid by the University for teaching French, and that helps to cover some of my expenses. I'm really looking at the tunnel system between the churches and convents and other terminals. It's quite interesting, but hard to discover. Much of the system has been destroyed over time, and much was secret and still remains so."

"That sounds much more interesting than my work. I don't even know how to begin my research. I guess I'll just look over all the churches and convents first, then see where I go from there. But, tell me, how is it that you're Irish and from Canada."

"Well, I was born there, in Canada. My father was Irish—from Ireland. Michael Flynn, from Galway. He emigrated to Canada, to Montreal, and met there a girl from Quebec, Annette Maurois, whom he married. I was born in Montreal, took Orders, and joined the Jesuits. I was teaching at McGill when I got the opportunity to come to Puebla instead of taking a sabbatical. I can still take the sabbatical later."

"And how do you like Puebla."

"I'm under orders," he said. "But seriously, I rather like it here. It's a new experience. But to really enjoy it you have to sort of 'go native.' Things move slowly here. You can't do like in the States. Things will not be hurried. And you'll just feel frustrated when they go wrong, which they will do. Even in Quebec one must do it the French way. And they are as Latin as the Spanish and the Italians. But, Mexico: *Es un país tropical.* Really."

They talked some more, until Father Flynn saw that it was nearing eleven and said he had better get to his class. Magali said she had things to do, too, and so they both paid their separate checks and went back to the ILE—Father James Flynn to his class, Magali to the library.

7

THE APARTMENT

Magali came out of the library just one minute after noon and found Paul waiting for her in the patio to take her to see the room his cousin had for rent. They walked out of the big entranceway, into the street, followed by the curiosity of the students.

They walked to the corner where diagonally across the street was *El Parián*. On the corner itself was a museum of some sort, called the *Casa del Alfeñique*. It was another large colonial mansion, made of red tiles and blue and white tiles, which together were laid in the wall to form a geometrical pattern. It was another landmark for Magali and she made a mental note to visit it when she got a chance.

Paul had parked his car around the corner, on *6 Norte*, but back a few cars from the intersection and thereby away from all the pedestrian traffic of *El Parián*. They got in and Paul started off.

The building on *12 Oriente*, just west of *4 Norte*, was not too far from the ILE. It was a large colonial building, but not a real mansion, or, if it was, it was not of the quality of those nearer the

University. It was one of those old buildings with a central patio which had been converted like most of that type into several apartments. She could walk to work. The distance would be only about five blocks.

The room was on the second floor. One got to it by going up a stairway to the right after the entrance and around a walkway, one similar to that in the ILE building. The room, or apartment, had a high ceiling, with worm-eaten wood beams that crossed it. The walls were papered in the old style. They showed here and there stains of mold and humidity, and the paper had commenced, in a few spots, to peel off. The floor was wood, though not very well finished. The room had two high windows (of more than two meters) with wooden frames painted white. They stood about a foot above the floor. They gave onto the street and allowed abundant daylight to enter the room. The windows had wide sills, to correspond to the thick building walls. Magali would put pots of flowers on them to brighten the room still further. The windows were at that time covered by chiffon curtains with lace edges, and they opened onto a tiny balcony of wrought iron. The room was a very large one (almost a loft).

What a difference from her apartment in Boston! Although both were old, this house was from the 1700's, while that in Boston dated only from the end of the 1800's. And the styles were completely different. The architecture in Puebla, and in most of Mexico, had a marked influence of the Spanish; that of Boston was definitely Victorian, and it came with all the conveniences of modern living: complete kitchen (with even a microwave), private bath, hot water.

In one corner of this "apartment" there was a very small gas stove next to an enormous tiled sink with a brass faucet. There was no refrigerator (in Puebla, the apartments were almost always rented completely empty). The "kitchen" was furnished with a small, rustic, wood table and two chairs, and a wood shelf on the wall that was painted white.

The "bathroom" was in another corner of the room, and consisted of a WC surrounded by a curtain of opaque plastic, and an old shower perched over a concrete base which was rectangular in shape and had a raised edge which caught the water and guided it to a drainage hole. There was a small sink nearby.

Against the wall opposite the windows there was an old full-size bed, a *matrimonial*, with a headboard of old wood, and to the left of it a small night table. Against the wall, to the right of the bed, was an old wardrobe, very tall, with a large rectangular mirror on the inside of its door. There was an old circular table, about five feet in diameter, with two chairs in the middle of the room, perfect for spreading her papers and books for study. Two standing bookshelves, about three feet wide, stood against the wall where the entrance door was.

The rent was quite low, so Magali agreed to take it. Paul's cousin, a rather rotund but happy fellow, gave her the keys and promised all sorts of assistance should she require it. The papers could be arranged later for the transfer of utility accounts. She could move in the next day. She thought this place would at least do while she got acquainted with the city.

Magali spent the rest of the week getting to know her way around the city, preparing for her class, and buying things for her new apartment.

For the kitchen she had to get an Italian *espresso* coffee pot (her only luxury), and some traditional blue and white Talavera cups and saucers. She quickly learned that she needed some jars to contain sugar and coffee because of the numerous tiny red ants that invaded everything and everywhere.

For the bathroom she got a new curtain for the WC and one for the shower. Of course it was all one room, but she thought of each area as separate, and she tried to make them physically separated as best she could, first, by leaving a space for an imaginary wall between each area, and further, by setting up furniture on the other side of the "walls" so one was guided to a definite path from one area to another.

She bought an old metal desk lamp with a goose neck for the bedroom, and a small table lamp for the living room. She painted the desk lamp bright red and the night table glossy black.

For the living room she also got an old wine bottle, placed a candle in it, and put it on the table next to the new lamp she would use for study. Then, if the light went out because of a power failure—which was not uncommon—she could light the candle and continue with her reading or studying.

And, like every good American girl, she arranged for a telephone, and as soon as it was installed, she called her mother, and she called François.

Slowly she began to build up a library in the bookshelves: English-Spanish and Spanish-English dictionaries; various books about ESL; some books by Agatha Christie, Robert Frost, Paul Elouard, Saint John Perse, Salinger, and Cervantes; some magazines (some academic journals she had brought with her, and an *Elle* and a *Marie Claire* she had bought in Puebla); several old books on the history of Puebla; and some tourist pamphlets of Puebla and Mexico.

On her first Sunday in the new apartment she went again to the antique and flea market at *Los Sapos,* this time to do some serious shopping. There she found some more Talavera pieces at good prices, and some old books that looked interesting. Going eastward on *5 Oriente,* looking into the small antique shops located along that street, she came to the *Boulevard Héroes del Cinco de Mayo,* which was called *Cinco de Mayo* by everyone, and across the street, on the other side of a small, empty triangle of street pavement, was a square or park which hosted a market of flowers and some crafts. Mostly it was a flower market, and it had a variety of beautiful tropical plants. There were roses of all colors—bright red, dark purple, yellow, peach, coral, white, white with a red center, white with red edges, and a beautiful magenta which was called *Rosa Mexicana.* There was bougainvillaea in four different colors. She saw orchids and other strange plants that she would have loved to have, but she didn't know at that time how to care for them, and they were a bit expensive, anyway. She found some geraniums of a really bright red color and bought three of the plants, already in pots. She hailed a taxi to take the plants home, and she made a note to add the flower market to her Sunday outings at *Los Sapos.*

On Monday, early, Magali dropped into the ILE to visit the library again and to see if there were any activities or developments she should know about. Some of the teachers were in the "faculty lounge" and had wondered where Magali was since the teachers usually checked into the lounge every Monday early. She hadn't known that, and she offered her apologies for her ignorance of the custom, promising to be there on future Mondays.

The bulletin board held nothing new, but she did discover that there were videos in the audio-visual office, right next door to the lounge, that she could see, and even check out—but she didn't have a VCR or even a TV, so that didn't help her much. She could, however, see the VCR movies in English or other languages there in the ILE. In a room on the north side of the patio there were students watching such a movie, an old one in English with Spanish subtitles. The sound and the image were both of terrible quality. It looked like they had a copy of a copy of a copy. So much for that, too.

Not feeling much like the library, she decided to go for some coffee and headed out of the ILE and across the street toward the Villa Rica.

There were Fr. Flynn, Paul, and Hans Leverkühn, going fast and furious in a debate about something. Magali asked to join them and sat down, ordering a *café Americano.*

Fr. Flynn stopped everyone from talking long enough to bring Magali into it, giving her a synopsis of what had transpired thus far. It seemed that Paul had challenged the Catholic—and with it the whole Christian—view of cosmology, alleging that God was gold, or that gold was God. It was taken "tongue in cheek," as it was probably meant, and Fr. Flynn was prepared to apply his considerable training in logic and argument to the task of rebutting him.

So far Paul had alleged that God manifested himself to man in the material form of gold, choosing that matter which best represented his attributes. Gold was yellow—like the sun, a deity for many peoples. It was metal, but soft—gentle. It was clean and pure, could never be tarnished or adulterated. In its basic form as in its essence it was always true. Paul put in that in Spanish gold was *"oro,"* which also means "I pray." But Hans countered with that not being so in either English or German.

Paul added that gold blesses him who receives it. It enables greatness in one who has it. It can produce great works. It comforts and soothes, and gives security in the world. It is both beautiful and beautifies. Many of the greatest works of art have been crafted in gold. Hans countered that gold also corrupts its owners and gives rise to struggles and all manner of crimes for its possession. Paul just now came up with "Yes, but if you take the 'ell out of gold you have God." Hans then countered with—not sticking within one language—"But if you take the 'ell out of *gelt*, you have get." And there they were.

Magali: It's too bad you don't have someone from an Eastern religion; he could say God is not just gold, but water and flesh and air and action too.

Fr. Flynn: I'm happy with my Christian, loving God, who has created us and who cares about us, and who has given us the Commandments to guide our life here on this Earth. If we obey these Commandments, we shall be rewarded on our death with eternal bliss in Heaven. We must recognize that we did not bring ourselves into existence, and He that did create us has His own purpose for our lives. We should obey His laws. Even gold, being matter, must obey laws—the Laws of Nature.

Magali: The good Father is right in one thing. Little children need a "father," or a "mother," to set them right in how to behave. And they do this through "commandments," like: Do it because I say so. If you don't you'll be punished. And bigger children, like those that think gold is God, probably need more of the same teaching. But . . . "Laws of Nature?" Such a law is not imposed by some authority as: Thou shalt, or Thou shalt not. It is simply a description of how things are in reality.

Hans [interrupting]: She's right, Father. In science it is a descriptive statement, an *enunciado* in Spanish. Or an argument comprised of several related statements, describing how things work. Like Boyle's law, describing the relations between temperature and the mass and pressure of a gas—or the laws of thermodynamics, describing the relations between heat and work.

Magali: More than that, it is a statement—or an argument—that is always true, and can be relied on to guide action. If at any time it proves to be not true, it is no longer accepted as a law. So, laws change along with our developing understanding of reality.

Paul: Yes. And gold is ALWAYS true.

Fr. Flynn: But is gold God?

Paul [peevishly]: Even if it's not God, it's good. And God wants man to have it, else he would not have created it.

Magali: *If* there is such a thing as God. How do you know such a thing even exists? And how do you know that He even cares about you? All you can really say is that gold exists, and it may be good for some people and for some purposes. When I was very young, educated by nuns, I felt that science and religion did not mix well, and so I learned science in one part of my mind, separated from religion, and my catechism in another part. And now you see what mixing the two gets you.

Hans: Well put, Magali! Science is truth, and religion is religion. Gold may be good, but it is not God.

Magali: Maybe the most pragmatic thing to do is to serve two masters: get all the gold you can, but don't commit any crimes or do anything bad in getting it.

Fr. Flynn: A good way out—but I never said it! You see, Magali, we can debate anything, even something as ridiculous as gold being God (no offense, Paul). Even that argument is good mental exercise. In deference to Paul I should say that I, myself, am also constantly challenging my own religious beliefs—within my own mind, that is, not with my superiors. One must at least retain the appearance of a true believer.

Hans: Speaking of true believers, did you see that the Russians are coming to Puebla. "Stars of the Russian Ballet"—coming to the Auditorium, up at the Forts, in a couple of weeks.

Paul: Yes! And I trust you're all saving your *gelt* to go there. We should make a group and make an evening of it. Hans, you and your wife. I can bring Sue. And since, Magali, you're still unattached here, maybe you could come with our good Father as an escort, he also being unattached. He could be your knight errant—brave, strong, and . . . chaste (no offense, Father).

Fr. Flynn: None taken. I think it's a great idea. I like to enjoy an evening out now and then. Magali?

Magali: I'm game.

Hans: [to Paul] Okay by me. I'll check with you in a couple of days. You can be the organizer of this. Now I've got to run; [rising] I have a class in about half an hour.

And so they all collected their things, paid their checks, and went out their various ways.

Magali returned with Hans to the ILE and upon entering through the main door said her goodbye to Hans and turned right and into the library.

She was looking over the shelves, seeing if she could find a book for herself, for some recreational reading, when the librarian, actually a young student serving as a part-time librarian, came over to her and asked if she knew of the other University libraries. It appeared that most departments had their own small libraries, and some faculties had libraries. Social Sciences had a really good library, she was told, as did Architecture. She made a small list of the suggestions, noting where appropriate the appraisals of her new guide. This was really a great break for her. She would never have imagined that the University had no large main library.

Since the Social Sciences Library was only over on *4 Oriente* near *11 Norte,* near her apartment, she thought she'd check that out and then have some lunch somewhere.

The Social Sciences Library was located in an old building with an interior patio. It had tall windows and some windowed doors looking out onto the patio which provided abundant light into the study areas of the library. The librarian was a handsome, elderly man, and he immediately came up to Magali to ask if there was some way he could help her. She explained who she was and what she was doing at the University, and he offered to help her find what he could for her on the history of Puebla and its early settlement, and especially on the many old churches and convents in the city. He also told her of the architecture faculty library, down near the *Ciudad Universitaria* (which was where most of the undergraduate classes were offered). In the meantime, he said, she could look at some of the reference works he had there until he could get a list of works which she could choose from for her research. That, of course, would take a few days to get together.

So Magali accepted a few books which he got out for her and sat down at one of the tables to begin the research for which she had come to Puebla.

After two hours she had had enough and brought the books back to the librarian, promising she would come back in the next few days to continue consulting those same books, until he got together the list of other books which might further her research. And, since she was so near her apartment, she decided to go there and scrounge something for lunch and then take a *siesta* before venturing out to the streets again later in the afternoon.

That Sunday Magali arose early to have a quick breakfast at home and get over early to *Los Sapos.* She made her usual round of the antique market and then stopped at the cafe for some refreshment. Then she went over to the park where the plant sales were, thinking this day she would look at the non-plant things there.

She soon saw that most such things were crude and primitive, pitiful to look at. But then she realized that this was the view of the American tourist, and it was hindering her appreciation. Relaxing, trying to keep her mind and senses open to what was really there, she was rewarded by at times coming across something wonderful, or beautiful, that she could appreciate in a pure way, without regard to artistic talent or skill, without regard to any already set standards.

Such was a little boat that she came to call the "taca, taca." It was made out of tin cans: literally, cut up tin cans. It must have been very cheap to make. It was like a speed boat, with a little man as pilot. It was painted in pretty colors and looked rather nice. She didn't really understand just how it worked. It had a pair of metal tubes coming out the back. The pilot was a folded, flat piece of tin can metal attached at where his feet would be to a bottle cap—from a soft drink bottle—which was filled with wax and a small wick, forming a kind of candle. You lit the candle and inserted the little man into the boat's cockpit. This put the candle under a flatish, round container in the boat which was attached to the tubes coming down and along the base of the cockpit and out the back of the boat. After a while, when it got hot enough, it would begin to puff through the tubes and the little boat would begin to move with the sound, "taca, taca, taca," all around the vendor's old fashion metal wash basin filled with water.

It was really wondrous to behold. But then, she thought, "How sad! No American boy or girl could ever play with this wondrous toy. There would be 'do-gooders,' prohibitionists, who would say, 'This is dangerous.' Who knows? Someday they might discover that life was dangerous and try to prohibit it."

8

TEACHING ENGLISH

On Monday, the 15th, Magali arrived at 9:00 in the morning at the ILE faculty room, ready to begin her first day at teaching. She wanted to have plenty of time to get everything ready for her class. Making sure the "ladies" noticed she was there, checking the bulletin board for any important notices, she decided she had better repair to the library for some privacy and quiet in getting ready for her class. But leaving the faculty room, she ran into Paul.

"Magali," he said, "just the person I was looking for. I've got just the thing for you. Come with me." And grabbing her by the arm, he proceeded to lead her out of the faculty room and toward the main entrance of the building.

"Wait a minute," she almost shouted. "I've got to get ready for my class."

"Of course," he replied. "That's what it's all about."

And she found herself accompanying him out of the ILE, but not altogether sure that she was doing the right thing.

"We're going to the Carolo," said Paul. "Wait till your see it." And they continued walking toward the main building of the University, the Carolino.

When they arrived at the *Avenida Camacho*, they crossed to the *Pasaje* and then turned right, heading westward on the avenue, toward the *Zócalo*. On the corner of the *Pasaje* was a book store, and west of it was the Carolo.

It was a cafe, actually two cafes—next to each other. He led her to the second doorway and they entered, looked for a table, found the second one inside of the entrance free, and sat down. Looking around, Magali could see that there were three tables along the east wall just inside the entrance, and facing it, on the other side of the room, was a glass display case exhibiting several deserts. To the left of the case was a serving counter, and behind that and the display case, on top of some low cabinets against the wall, were coffee machines, juicers, and mixers for *batidas*. There was a short wall sticking out to the left of the serving counter, leaving a more or less shielded entranceway to the area behind the counter. There was another such short wall on the other side of the room, the two of these separating the first three tables and the serving area from the back part of the cafe. Also separating the back part was a single step on the floor, between the two short walls jutting out on either side, leading down to a back room which held several additional tables and chairs. In the far right corner of this room was a stairway leading up to a small mezzanine which extended half way out above the back room.

Even at that early hour the cafe was filled with patrons. Most were students, but a number were older—more than likely faculty like Paul and herself. A waitress came over and Paul ordered two coffees. He then asked Magali if she would like a pastry, and she accepted. Paul added two pastries to his order. When the girl had gone, Paul turned to Magali and asked her, "Well, how do you like it?"

"It's nice," she replied, "but why did you bring me here when you know I have to prepare for my class?"

"We *are* preparing for your class," he said. "What is most important for you at this time is to relax. You have to get into the mood that it doesn't matter. You have to develop a pride fitting to your qualifications. The students you will face know almost nothing, though they are intelligent. They look to you for instruction. It is said that Winston Churchill, before he began a speech, would look over the audience and say to himself, 'What a mass of stupid sheep.' With that feeling of superiority he felt he could say almost anything and be a great orator to his audience. You have to get that same attitude of pride. Besides, this is a great cafe and you should get to know it. It's where many of the faculty go for coffee, as well as the better students. Foreign professors, especially, come here since the FALE, the *Facultad de Lenguas Extranjeras*—the Department of Foreign Languages to you—is just down the street. That gives it a certain cosmopolitan ambience. The FALE is our compatriot in the teaching of foreign languages at the University. They try to teach as if the students already know the language and are learning the finer points of expression. We are relegated to teaching how to actually speak and read the language. No matter, there are good people on the faculties of both institutions."

Magali looked around and began to appraise the cafe, realizing that what he said was probably very true. It did look like a nice cafe, full of students and professors, where much of the social life of the University must take place, or at least get organized. She smiled at Paul—and turned to her pastry.

Paul managed to get her back to the ILE shortly before eleven, just in time for her first class. And, suprisingly, she did feel enough prepared for it.

This was a big day for her. No one knew it was her first class "ever," and she tried to make it appear that she was an old hand at it. There were thirty-four young people waiting for her in the classroom. When she entered, their talking ceased and they all sat down in their seats and became attentive. She introduced herself in English and wrote her name in chalk on the blackboard. The girls (heavily made up) looked at her from time to time, giggling quietly, shyly. The boys, dressed mostly in jeans, T-shirts, and "combat" shoes—the previous year's fashion in the States—were near the back of the room, making comments to one another in subdued voice: *"Oye, que linda teacher tenemos!" "Pues sí, habra que checarla!"* There was one boy, actually a young man in appearance, who sat quietly in the very back corner of the room, and whose face and appearance she could not place at the moment, but he reminded her of someone.

She waited until the talking in the back had stopped, and then she began to read off the names of her students, taking attendance. When she had all the students' names noted in position on a plan of the seating that she had made up prior to the class, she announced a test to determine their level of language proficiency. The written part was comprised of ten simple questions to determine their comprehension of the language and grammar. Added was a short translation to do from English to Spanish, and another from Spanish to English. When everyone had completed the written part, she gave each student an oral test, asking short, simple questions—some of a personal nature so as to get to know them and to establish a human relation with them.

Things were getting off to a good start and Magali was beginning to enjoy her class. It was a cultural shock to find that there were no text books, but rather that every teacher had to provide his or her own from which the students would make photocopies. It would be difficult getting used to the physical condition of the classroom and bearing up with the lack of materials and supporting equipment, but she found the human element to be interesting. She was happy to see that even though the oral English proficiency level of her students was pathetically low, they were behaving like good students and responding to her in a very earnest and polite way. The students appeared committed to the requirements of study and were very eager to learn.

She then had the students divide into five groups of seven students each (but one group had only six) and appoint leaders of each group from among themselves. One young man, named Luis, immediately took over student control of the class, and everyone seemed to accept it without question. He knew most of the students and chose the leaders of the groups. Magali later learned that he had been around the University for several years—too often unable to make a passing grade or to finish the term. The idea was that each class day one group would be assigned to present a critique of the reading for that day to the class and then respond to questions from the members of the other groups. They all had to do the same reading, but only one group would report on it. The assignment to report would rotate so that on another day another group would present their critique of the assigned reading. Thus, they all would present critiques in turn, which would provide good training in the language, and maybe some fun.

It would be the job of the students to make copies of the books Magali had chosen for readings, and to distribute them to everyone and collect the costs. She had selected only three books: Hemingway's *Old Man and the Sea*, a book of poems of Robert Frost, and *The Great Gatsby*, by Fitzgerald.

She chose these authors because, though none of them were really great writers or produced great literature, they were all very popular. Both Hemingway and Fitzgerald wrote really bad stories, but they wrote them well and they and their stories were with the spirit of their times. And some of Hemingway's stories were turned into really great movies (although the producers had to almost totally change the stories to get good movie scripts).

Magali offered the books to the class to arrange for the copying, and Luis came up to accept them. He immediately assigned two students to help him to make the copies, and they would give the copies to the group leaders, who would in turn distribute them to their members. Magali was somewhat bewildered by all the action, but it all worked out so smoothly that it was obvious that the students had done this many times before.

That first day was really rather easy, consisting as it did mostly in housekeeping: checking attendance, preliminary testing, getting the books copied, and assigning readings. When she finished assigning the first reading, *The Great Gatsby*, and the reporting group, she dismissed the class so they could get the copying completed in good time.

On Tuesday Magali was asked by the Director to take over an evening class in business English, which met at 7:00 p.m. on Tuesday and Thursday in a classroom on the second floor of the

ILE. The regular teacher had suddenly left the faculty, so the class
was left without a teacher. Magali couldn't really refuse, so she
prepared as best she could for the class, which had no syllabus or
text book.

Magali took over the business English class that evening.
There were only five students, all adults. They were all beginners
in English, though they had some experience in business. That is,
all except one, a woman of thirty something, very pretty, who
spoke English fairly well. Magali was immediately attracted to her,
for her fine appearance as well as for her courtesy in the class.
She had a soft voice, and when she spoke Spanish, she spoke a
very clear and correct Spanish.

The class went well, and Magali decided she would continue
as they had started, discussing aspects of business as practiced in
the U.S. and in the English language: business organization,
documents, laws, and customs.

Wednesday in her regular class things began to go wrong.
The copying had not yet been completed, but Luis warned her of
this on Tuesday, promising the copying for the following
Monday. So Magali decided to do some readings from some of
her own books by the selected authors. Because of the students'
low level of English proficiency—though they were supposed to
be already *pasantes* at the University and in their second year at the
Institute of Foreign Languages—Magali had to translate a lot of
the readings for them before they could begin to comprehend
what was going on. She would never forget that first Wednesday
and the bewildered look in the students' eyes when she read a
page from a chapter of *Tender is the Night* and then started to ask
questions in English about its contents, literary quality, and
meaning.

It was Luis who responded to her, shyly, and said, *"No
entendemos, Maestra."*

"No entienden? You don't understand the meaning of this
chapter?"

Magali proceeded, first reading in English, then translating
into Spanish, and then explaining in Spanish the meaning of the

different paragraphs and phrases. It soon became clear that the students could read the books adequately, but they did not understand what she said. They had only advanced in the reading of English, but they had no ear for the language. But Magali had to develop an ear for Spanish, too, so she understood their problem and modified her teaching to develop oral comprehension. She would speak to them more slowly and in simple sentences, or ask simple questions. It was evident that they were not stupid, nor were they without at least a reading comprehension of English; they just hadn't had experience with real conversation in the language. She thought as time passed they would gain control over oral use of the language, as she would gain similar skills with Spanish, which was a foreign language to her. And she would determine their reading comprehension easily not only from what they said but also from a few written quizzes she would throw in from time to time.

That Friday, after her regular class at noon, Magali reflected on her first week's performance, and she concluded it was not ideal, but adequate. With her regular class, she would now have to wait for the books to be copied and distributed and then she could start giving reading and reporting assignments and the class would really be under way. Until then, she could continue talking to the class about the books and the authors, developing their ear for English and, hopefully, some thinking in English.

She did not know the students well yet, but some of them stood out and she was sure she would get to know at least these rather well and rather quickly. Luis, of course, was in the forefront and she would have to get to know him very well. He was like a teaching assistant at the universities in the States. And there was the young man in the back corner of the room: Roberto. He was definitely adult, very interesting in appearance, and rather reserved when it came to class participation. Where he sat and how he appeared seemed to indicate that he felt himself superior to the other students. And finally there was the very pretty girl that Magali had seen around the ILE office on several occasions: Carmelita. She was very well mannered and helpful, and Magali thought she should keep an eye on her. Not that she represented any danger. Rather, that she might probably deserve some special help if she should ever need it.

With her business class, Magali knew she would form a special friendship with her pretty student whose name was Amanda and who lived in Cholula. She had a daughter of 16, another of 12, and a son of 8. She was of medium height, with a rather good figure, a beautiful face of delicate features, and light brown hair. Her husband, Victor, was employed in business, but he worked in Mexico City and only came home on the weekends, a situation which left Amanda with a lot of time on her hands. She was not content to simply play the roll of "housewife," but wanted to continue her studies.

On the next Thursday, the 25th, Amanda invited Magali to come to her home in Cholula for Sunday lunch.

"Cholula is a tourist spot," Amanda said. "And I look forward to giving you a tour of the city and showing you *la Pirámide de Tepanapa,* the church on top, and the museum. But most of all I want you to meet my husband and my family. And I will make for you some *mole.*" Magali accepted happily.

9

AMANDA

The Russian State Ballet was coming to Puebla for performances on Friday and Saturday. Magali's group had tickets for the Saturday show. This turned out to be lucky because the company was detained by a bus breakdown on the highway from Mexico City on Friday and arrived late, the performance being delayed for almost two hours. To make matters worse they were separated from their costumes, which remained on the disabled bus, and had to give their performance in the few practice costumes that some had with them, some of them having to perform in street clothes. But they nevertheless put on a great performance, and the word quickly got around about their being late and the high quality of their dancing in spite of adverse circumstances. For Saturday they had their costumes and the show went off on time.

Hans was there with his wife, a husky blonde—not fat, but solid, though at the same time rather soft, almost like what was called in the States, "pleasingly plump." She looked like she was a real beauty when he married her. Hans himself was in a dark suit, looking like a typical German *Bürger*. They both had the happy look of Germany before the First World War, the time of German *gemütlichkeit.*

Fr. Flynn was in a black suit and black shoes and socks, as well as a black turtleneck. With his greying hair he looked very distinguished, while at the same time mysterious. Magali wore a black, calf-length, cocktail dress which was strapless. The bottom was a full skirt falling loosely; the top appeared to be wrapped around her, softly, probably fixed by a hidden safety pin. Actually, it was so arranged, and it was an outfit she had put together herself quickly from some cloth she had bought at the market. Around her waste the same material formed a broad cummerbund. She wore a beautiful string of *faux* pearls that looked so real they appeared to be at least a paste of a string of the finest. Her dark brown hair was gathered at the back into a French twist. The pair looked not so much like a gangster and his moll, but like a rich and powerful arms dealer, or such, and his beautiful, and very expensive, mistress.

Paul was in a dark suit, white shirt, and blue paisley tie. Sue, his date, was in a dark blue gown, also calf-length, but not nearly so elegant as Magali's. She had light brown, long hair, and looked to Magali like an east-coast rich girl graduate student at Brown or Wellesley.

The three pairs made an interesting sight among the many students and older people at the concert.

The performance was first class. The company was small, comprised probably of only the stars of the Russian State Ballet. Many classical numbers were done, and many of the dancers were in more than one number, sometimes one and sometimes the other dancing the major role. The best number was a duo in flesh-colored tights, doing a slow, classical performance. The music was from an American popular song, played on a flute. Both the music and the dance stole the show. It was slow, kind of sad, and very classical. It didn't seem possible for the Russians to do such with an American popular song, but they did, and it was beautiful. Altogether, an unforgettable evening in every way.

Magali arose early that Sunday, but instead of going to *Los Sapos,* she left her apartment just after eight and took a *pesero* to the CAPU and went in and to the back lot of the terminal where the *taxis autorizados* were. There she looked for the red and white buses that went to Cholula. There were concrete boarding zones in the central part of the square, one of which was for the Cholula busses. There were several busses waiting to board passengers, one due to leave every twenty minutes. There was already a line of passengers forming for the next one to leave. In the line were a few American tourists, and what appeared to be a Canadian couple who looked like retired teachers, man and wife with rosy cheeks and blue eyes, dressed in khaki slacks and jackets. There was also a German man in his sixties, tall and unfriendly looking, with gray hair showing under a large hat, clean shaven, wearing the typical "safari" outfit designed to be used on a hunting expedition in Africa. He was holding an unlit pipe between his teeth, and fidgeting. There were two British kids in their twenties, a boy and a girl, very white, very blond, shabbily dressed in shorts and T-shirts, who were probably students on holiday. The rest of the passengers were about ten to twelve Mexicans, some children (probably families out for the weekend). They were carrying bags, baskets with food, and bottles of cola. Magali noticed that the Mexican children spoke softly and were very well behaved—girls dressed up in silk dresses and multicolored ribbons, boys in suits like miniature grown-ups.

The exhaust from the running motors of the waiting busses began to make Magali cough. Turning her head away and looking into the distance, she noticed a thick, white *fumarola* from the Popocatépetl volcano floating upward into the blue sky of the early morning. When they finally began to load, she got onto the bus, took a window seat, and sat holding her bag, looking out at the others coming on board. Her bag contained a bottle of fresh water, and a small purse with copies of her passport and documents (the originals stayed at home because picking pockets was the great occupation, or sport, of the area), several bills of twenty pesos, a list of phone numbers, and a card on which was her own address and the University's, with the name of the Director of the Institute in case of emergency.

She also brought an Agatha Christie book in Spanish which she had read previously in English. She noted with amusement how in the translation the plot and characters sounded so different. *La Señorita* Marple and *El Señor* Inspector didn't have much in common with the Miss Marple and Inspector Slack that she knew.

It was a twelve kilometer ride that took about 45 minutes, mostly because of the heavy traffic of Puebla, especially along the *Blvd. Norte,* by the market. She was always fascinated by the number of people that were about at all hours; and because Sunday was also a big market day, now there was also a lot of large trucks, pick-ups, and old cars—many of the vehicles in very bad condition. Most of them were filled to the brim with vegetables, flowers, chickens, and wooden furniture, all trying to find a parking place close to the market. When the bus finally got onto the highway to Cholula, she could see the whole range of mountains resplendent against a backdrop of deep blue sky.

She arrived in Cholula at 9:45. Amanda was waiting for her at the terminal, which was dusty and full of vehicles, people, and trash.

"I'm so happy you came!" she said, hugging Magali. "Come, we'll walk home. Did you have a good ride?" She took Magali by the arm, and conducted her through a milling crowd of people, out of the terminal, and toward the end of the next street.

"Yes, thank you," responded Magali. She liked Amanda very much, with her open and friendly, direct way of talking.

The sun was hot now, and Magali took a sip from her water bottle.

"I see you have your *mamila* with you," smiled Amanda.

"*Mamila?*"

"Yes. Bottle . . . baby bottle."

"I'm not used to the climate, and my throat gets very dry," responded Magali, laughing. She felt that she and Amanda could become great friends. "And," she thought, "when you are in a foreign country, that's what you need more than anything else: a good friend."

Amanda's home was the typical Spanish looking, middle class, Mexican home, with thick walls, with doors and window frames in heavy wood, yellow in color, and with a cement driveway in front. Several plants, purple and pink bougainvillaea and roses, were standing in large, heavy, ceramic pots along the walls on both sides of the entrance door.

The house was half a block from a market, and there, too, there was a constant traffic of people; of urban minibuses, cars, and other vehicles, filling the streets with the noise of their horns and smoke from their exhausts; and of trucks and other vehicles loading or unloading goods, veggies, and miscellaneous merchandise.

Amanda's husband, Victor, was working at a water pump, located in a corner of the front garden, next to the house. He was about six feet tall, lean, with brown hair, clean shaven, in his forties, and quite handsome. He was wearing jeans, a short sleeve shirt, and tennis shoes. He gave Magali a big, friendly smile, and, wiping his hands with a rag, came to her. "So nice to meet you," he said in very good English. "Please excuse my appearance. I was fixing again the water pump."

"You have your own water?" inquired Magali (most of the people in her area, in downtown Puebla, had to get the water from the city, or from trucks when they had used up the city water that had been stored by them in underground tanks).

"No. We get water from the city. It goes into our cistern, and from there it is pumped by my little pump up to our tank on the roof. When it works, it is good, but when it doesn't—" He laughed, pointing to the small electric water pump. "But, please, come in, you might want some nice, cold lemonade."

"*Angélica!*" he called.

A pretty teenaged girl came running to open the door, and then stood shyly to one side. She also wore jeans, with a pink blouse.

He allowed the two women to proceed him through the door, and then followed them.

"Magali," said Amanda. "This is *Angélica,* my eldest daughter."

"*Hola, Angélica,*" said Magali. "*Cómo estás?*" Then, to Amanda: "She's beautiful!"

Amanda smiled.

Victor quietly said aside to Angélica, "*Trae una limonada para la señorita!*"

Angélica ran to the kitchen and came back with a pitcher full of lemonade and a tray with three glasses.

Magali looked around her. She was in the living room. There was a big, comfortable sofa, two chairs, an antique desk, a floor lamp, and several paintings on the walls. At one side, on the wall, there were portraits of the family, wedding pictures, baby pictures, and old grandmother's photos. On a center table in front of the sofa were fresh flowers in a glass jar. "A very pleasant home," thought Magali. "Just like the people that live here."

After talking a while, Amanda took Magali to see some sights of the city.

They started with the mustard-colored San Gabriel Monastery, east of the *Zócalo,* with its three churches and the 16th century *Capilla Real,* topped with 49 Arabic domes.

"We have a bit of interesting history," said Amanda. "The Cholulans prepared to ambush Hernán Cortés when he was leaving the city, but the Spanish discovered it and slaughtered many Cholulans, and then, with the help of the army from Tlaxcala, they ravaged the city. Cortés had his final revenge when he had one church for every day of the year built over the ruins of the city's temples. The most famous one—that you probably have seen already—is *La Iglesia de los Remedios,* which replaced the temple on top of the great Pyramid of Tepanapa . . . there," she said, as she pointed to a church which stood on the top of a nearby hill.

Magali looked up at the church.

"Can we go up there?" she asked. "It looks like we would have an interesting view of the city from there."

"Of course," said Amanda, laughing. "But it's a hard walk up there. We can also go inside the pyramid . . . if you are not claustrophobic."

"No, thank you," said Magali. "I've been inside the basements and corridors of too many old churches. And it's too nice a day to be wasted in the dark!"

The two women walked over to the hill and started to climb up, very slowly and laboriously. The path was very steep, with a surface of dirt and gravel. When they got to the top, they were met with a view which was breathtaking. The city of Cholula was spread out before their eyes like a colorful patchwork of pink and yellow buildings, trees, and flower bushes, with the *Zócalo* and its fountain on one side, and the surrounding country on the opposite side. She could see the streets of the town laid out, and the highway by which she had come. The atmosphere was festive; the sun was hot; and she was breathing hard, but happy.

"I forgot I have to slow down," she said. "The altitude—" She offered some water to Amanda, then took a sip herself from the bottle. She had brought her camera and she asked an American tourist nearby to take a picture of her and Amanda before the church. Then they entered. The church was not as interesting inside as others she had seen in Puebla. They did sit, anyway, in the cool and sombre atmosphere of the place to rest before going down the hill and back to Amanda's home.

Wednesday, the last day of August, Magali's first payday, and she had received pay for the entire month. How great it felt to be paid—her first professional pay. She finished her class from 11 to 12, and faced the whole afternoon free. First to the bank, to deposit what money she didn't immediately need, then to McD's for a quick lunch. Then maybe looking at the stores on *Cinco de Mayo*.

About five she headed for the Carolo for some coffee before returning to her apartment for the evening. Entering, she saw the second table free and sat at it. She looked around and saw there were few people there. She expected it would be more crowded soon since many Mexicans had a snack about that time before heading homeward for a much more substantial meal in the evening, at about eight. She ordered a *café Americano*.

Almost as soon as she had been served, one of her students, Roberto, the one who sat in the far corner in the back, entered, saw her, and approached.

"Hi, Teacher," he said. "May I join you?"

She said yes and he sat down, keeping his plastic briefcase full of books and papers in his lap. He looked at what she was drinking and ordered the same from the waitress.

Roberto was definitely adult, very handsome, and looked (as a man) on a social level equal to Magali. That is to say that anyone who saw them could easily mistake them as a couple—he as her date, or beau, or whatever along that line. And he looked handsome enough for her to feel rather proud that he chose to sit with her at her table.

He asked her how she was getting along in Mexico, and she responded that everything was going well. He asked about her research, and soon she was talking about her findings at the various libraries she had come to know, especially that of the social sciences.

He asked her if she had seen the Lafragua. She said no, that she hadn't heard about that one yet. And that opened him to telling her about his favorite historical gem in Puebla.

"Ah, Lafragua is a library you must not miss. It might not have the books you need for your work, but it is a gem of antique books, worth seeing solely as a tourist attraction. The main library is in the Carolino. Its books are well protected, in glass-windowed, wood bookcases. But there is another Lafragua, rather a 'secret' one because it is not open to the public, and it has even greater treasures. It also is in the Carolino, but it is on the other side of the second patio, in the lower level, under the ground floor. Its entrance is near the office of the University Director of Libraries.

"Lafragua—at least the 'secret' library—is under the care of one of the most respected and honorable persons, acting as its librarian. His name is Don Romualdo, and we all call him 'Maestro,' though he doesn't really have that academic degree. Nor does he have the official position of 'Librarian.'

"In his 'secret' library are all the old books which have not yet been catalogued and not yet assigned a place on the library shelves. There, there are many very valuable antiques, many incunabula, or books made before 1501. There is a copy of Newton's Principia Mathematica, the first of the final compilation, published in Spain, printed in Italy.

"It is very hard to save these books. Even the Americans are a threat to their preservation."

"How are the Americans a threat?" said Magali. "I should think they would even give some financial support to protecting such valuable books."

"Ah, but you do not know what really happens when the Americans offer help," responded Roberto. "Let me tell you of one incident. Some years ago a famous librarian came from the U.S. to help organize the library along modern methods. As the new Director of the library, one of his principal policies was to rid the library of all books which were old and unconsulted. He and his minions were on the second floor of the library, throwing out to the patio below books which were more than ten years old and had not been consulted during the latest year. They threw out books which were from the 16th, 17th, 18th, and 19th century, and many valuable books from even the 20th century. It was an afternoon of light rain, and the books fell into a pile in the second patio of the Carolino. But Don Romualdo and several students began to collect the most valuable ones first, and then what others they could, as fast as they could, and get them to safety. The 'gringo' left while his minions continued to carry out his directives. And Don Romualdo's helpers continued to work below. It was well into the evening before all that was thrown away was gathered into the safety of the lower Lafragua. I know all of this for a fact. I am now one of Don Romualdo's helpers. This was many years ago, and we are still trying to catalogue those books and to store them in some permanent place of security. So much for help from the Americans."

"But that was terrible. That man must have been some nut. He must have had political connections to have gotten such a job," said Magali.

"Still, he got the job, and he performed his task as he did," acknowledged Roberto.

"But I don't want you to think I'm anti-American," he quickly added. "I'm not like many pseudo-communists you find in Mexico. Politics and economics do not really interest me, nor the pursuit of money and power. Such things cannot sway me from what is good in life, and most of the good things are free, or at least cheap. No, I'm more interested in real satisfactions like art, music, literature, and philosophy—and love."

More people were now entering the Carolo, and many greeted Roberto as they came by him. Finally some young female students came in and almost assaulted him. They sat at a table just inside the back room, and soon, after a few more exchanges of small talk with Magali, Roberto excused himself, saying he had some "school business" to talk about with the girls, and moved over to their table. Magali was ready to head for home, anyway, since it was now beginning to get dark and she wanted to get home while there was still a little bit of light. The sun set around six most of the year at Puebla's latitude. Also, the sun appeared to set more quickly and it appeared to get dark more quickly in Puebla than it did in the latitudes to which she was accustomed—in Massachusetts and Vermont.

10

FR. FLYNN

Magali usually went to the Villa Rica for her morning coffee break when she was near the ILE. If she got there about ten, she usually met and sat with Father Flynn. They always got into a prolonged discussion, usually conversing in English or French, but sometimes they spoke in Spanish, especially when others from the ILE sat with them.

She found it most interesting that the mood and subject of their conversation adapted itself naturally to the language they used. In French they were French people in a French world, with interests in things that interest the French: literature, the arts, philosophy. In English, it was another world—more cold, mechanical. In Spanish, more laid back, easy, almost carefree.

Also, how interesting that the Irish got along so easily with other peoples: James' father in Quebec, as well as James in Mexico. So, too, did the French and the Italians, unlike the English and other Germanic peoples, who always kept themselves aloof. In the States as in Mexico, as probably in all of Latin America, the French tended to disappear into the populous— except for a few places, like Quebec and Louisiana, where they are still somewhat self-isolated. She found that the Irish had some renown in Latin America; many national heroes at the time of the liberation from Spanish dominance were Irish.

As time went on, Magali learned more of Father Flynn's past, and it was not long before she felt she had the whole story—at least generally.

James' father, Michael Flynn, came from Ireland to Montreal, where he met Annette Maurois, a farm girl from Quebec who was working in an office there. They were married, and within the year James was born. Soon after—actually before James could walk—Annette's father died, following on her mother, and Annette, being the only child, inherited the farm. They moved to the farm and there James grew up, along with two younger brothers and a still younger sister. James learned French from his mother, their neighbors, and his schooling. He learned English from his father, though with it he caught some of his father's brogue.

When the time came, he went away to college, to Montreal and McGill, where he perfected both his French and his English. He soon took Orders, to his mother's delight; it appeared that his father was not so pleased, but he accepted it with grace.

James' younger brothers soon also left the farm and went away to school. They took up careers in business, and the third son, Kevin, moved to the U.S., to San Francisco, while the second son, Brian, stayed in Montreal. James' father then died, and that left his young sister, Mary, with her mother on the farm.

Mary soon married a neighbor, about three farms away, with whom she had grown up. He was Quebecois, and the couple set up their home on the farm with her mother. James' mother died a few years after her husband. The farm, then, returned to the French Quebecois. James' younger brothers meanwhile had sons, so the name endured, and James knew that his father would have been happy knowing that.

James eventually became a professor, and now here he was in Mexico, contributing who knows what to the advancement of man's knowledge.

Magali became an ever closer friend to Father Flynn, and one day he suggested that she not call him James anymore, which she gladly agreed to, since James to her was almost as formal as Father Flynn. He told her that his really close friends called him Jamie, the name he was called by his father as a child. His real name was Seamus, in Irish, but his father called him Jamie as the English form of it. Magali thought it was much better than Jim or Jimmy. She liked it the more as it reminded her of Errol Flynn (maybe a relative?), who was called Jamie in a movie he was in about pirates. He played a Scotsman, and a comrade, an Irishman, always called him Jamie.

It was the next day, Thursday, that she dropped into the Villa Rica about ten, and there was Fr. Flynn. In the course of their conversation she casually asked him how he was progressing with his study of the tunnels of Puebla, and he launched forth.

"The system of tunnels consists of several main routes and a few minor ones. The cathedral is the central point of the network. One route goes westward to the *Convento de San Agustín* and on to the *Cerro de San Juan*—which is now the *Colonia La Paz*. There is a branch in this tunnel, just west of the *Convento de San Agustín,* which connects northward to the Church of San Javier. A minor route goes from the Cathedral east to the present University and the Church of the Company. Another minor route goes northeastward to the *Casa de Las Muñecas*—just across the *Zócalo*—and then on to the old *Hospital de San Pedro*. And another minor one goes south to the *Convento del Carmen.*

"The main route of the whole system goes northward to the *Convento de Santo Domingo,* on to the *Convento de San Antonio,* then on to the Forts, *Loreto* and *Guadalupe*. It then loops southward to the *Convento de San Francisco*. From there it goes westward to connect with the tunnel northbound from the *Convento de Santo Domingo*. There is another connection at this point, which leads westward to the *Convento de Nuestra Señora de la Merced.*

"The construction of these tunnels did not all originate with the Cathedral. Many were probably begun from a particular church or convent—or fort—and eventually made a connection with another point in the net. And it is said that many private parties made connections to the system from their houses or businesses. Most of the principal tunnels are now cut off by later constructions or cave-ins. The construction of the sewer and drainage works in the 1930's brought about the closing of many of the main tunnels, and probably a good number of the private ones. And the reconstruction of private homes and businesses resulted in the closing of many entrances to the system, knowingly or unknowingly.

"The tunnels still exist in some places, though as a system they no longer work. Most of the pieces remaining, to which we have access, are those immediately adjacent to the buildings to which they connected. Some of these tunnels have been converted to other uses, such as those at the Churches of Carmen and La Merced, which have been converted into *osarios*.

"The date of construction of the tunnels can be inferred from the date of construction of the buildings to which they connected. The whole system was probably begun at the end of the Seventeenth or the beginning of the Eighteenth Century, so it was rather late in the construction of Puebla.

"I've been into some of them. There is little to learn from the experience, however. What I'm trying to do now is locate and enter the parts which have been closed off. There is a greater likelihood of finding something there—rather like exploring the pyramids of Egypt. I'm finding some entrances from private houses, but they usually go nowhere. I keep looking for others. I'm recording all this, of course, on a map, and the whole system is really immense—like a huge spider web of tunnels. I'm sure that at the time they were in use the authorities—civil, military, or church--didn't realize how big the system had grown, nor how many other people knew of the tunnels and were secretly using them."

And suddenly he stopped.

"Whoa . . . I've gotten carried away," he said, and took in a deep breath and sat silently for a while.

"Much too much detail for an answer to a simple question. You must forgive me my enthusiasm."

"No. It's all right," said Magali. "I'm interested in what you do. It sounds fascinating, and adventurous. As you say, like searching for buried treasure."

"Well not quite that," he said. "And we've talked enough. I've got to be moving on to some appointments. But, if you're really interested in it, I might take you to see some of the tunnels some time. Now, let's go; 'I've got places to be and people to see.' "

* * *

On Friday, just after nine, Fr. Flynn met Magali coming out of the ILE faculty room and said he had a treat for her in the afternoon if she could be free after two. She assented, and he said, "Okay. Meet me here at two."

She was there at ten till two, and there was Fr. Flynn, seated at a table, reading a book. He immediately got up, put the book in his locker and closed it, and said. "Let's go." They left the ILE, turned left and walked to the end of the block, where he hailed a taxi.

Settled in the back of the VW bug, Fr. Flynn told Magali he was taking her to see the *Alliance Française*, which he thought would be very important to her during her stay in Puebla. He said that she brought a taste for her own cultural baggage with her to Mexico, and that she would miss it at times, and that some of it included French things—the language, music, food. The *Alliance Française* could provide her with some of that, and she could rest there in a more or less familiar atmosphere whenever the conflict of the Mexican culture was getting too much for her.

The taxi headed for the *Boulevard Héroes del Cinco de Mayo*, turned right on that and proceeded toward the southern part of the city. They stopped at an old building, which appeared to be in good condition, a structure much like the ILE. It had an interior court like the ILE, and surrounding rooms on two levels. But it was very clean and well kept.

Magali followed Fr. Flynn to the main office and there he introduced her to the director, Olivier St. Jacques. He was of course older than Magali, but a little younger than Fr. Flynn. He was very handsome and elegantly dressed in a navy blazer and grey slacks, complete with a light blue shirt and a red paisley ascot. Not quite as tall as Fr. Flynn, but still tall, and very solid, though slim. He must have done very controlled weight exercises because he had muscles you could see in his form; yet, in no way did he appear muscle-bound. The girl students at the *Alliance* must really fall for him.

Olivier offered to take Magali for a tour while Fr. Flynn paid a short visit to the library. After the tour they would meet again in the cafe of the *Alliance*, where they would also meet Olivier's wife, Marie.

The tour did not take a long time, and it was most interesting to Magali because it showed her how, with money and taste, these old buildings of Puebla could be made really beautiful.

Olivier first took Magali to the second floor, where the classrooms were located. The building had an interior court like that of the ILE, but it was tiled with large squares, about a foot and a half square, of a dark red, almost burgandy, color. A broad stairway at the rear of the court led up to the second floor, and a walkway went around the court, separating it from the classrooms. A wrought iron railing lined the side of the walkway overlooking the court—the same design of railing and banisters as that on the stairs.

The classrooms had wood floors, like the ILE, but these were clean and shiny, well waxed and polished. The rooms were all clean, including the blackboards, and there were erasers and yellow chalk in the trays under each blackboard. What luxury! There were regular school desks in some rooms, all lined up properly. In others there were large tables, with padded chairs positioned around them. These latter rooms were probably for the more advanced classes. The curriculum included basic French language classes for beginners, French conversation and literature as a second stage, and French culture and history for a third.

Olivier and Magali attracted the attention of the students as they walked the tour, many of the girls in twos and threes stopping to huddle and giggle.

Back to the first floor, Olivier showed Magali an audio laboratory for perfecting one's pronunciation; a French TV room, using tapes from France; a really nice library, with tables and chairs for studying, as well as some big easy chairs for reading; a small bookstore which sold a limited amount of school supplies (paper and pens) and some French books and magazines (Magali had to make a special mental note on the magazines). On the first floor also were various administration offices, which they did not bother to visit. And on the other side of the court from the offices was the cafe.

Magali was not sure if it was her becoming acclimatized to the Mexican way of life, or something left over from her mother's heritage (French) or from her student life in Boston, but she suddenly felt a kind of warm glow, knowing they were going to sit a while and rest, and enjoy some good coffee among friends in a most pleasing ambience which she could already divine from what she could see of the cafe through the wide, open doors and the students seated or walking about, laughing quietly, or talking seriously—of their studies, their lives, or their loves.

Olivier led her in and over to where Fr. Flynn was sitting at a table with a quite beautiful woman: Olivier's wife, Marie. Magali thought France did well in sending two such beautiful specimens to advertise their nation. As Olivier and Magali neared the table, Fr. Flynn immediately stood up and pulled a chair back for Magali. She accepted it and Fr Flynn helped push it in to the table as she sat down on it. Olivier introduced Marie. Fr. Flynn took orders for coffee. Magali asked for a Cappuccino. Fr. Flynn also suggested some French pastries, for which the cafe had a certain reputation. Magali said, "Certainly. Yes!" In fact, she insisted on going with Fr. Flynn to select some, and to look over what the cafe also had to offer in the way of food. The pastries were first class, and she had a problem selecting a few only. The food, as she should have expected at a student facility, was limited to some sandwiches and local munchies.

For almost two hours they sat in the cafe, talking and watching the students and visitors. They were interrupted several times when people came from the office to have brief, whispered conversations with Olivier. It appeared that they asked him what to do about something, and he quickly gave them some short explanation or command, and the interruption resulted as only a short pause in his participation in the conversation, which went on without him.

It turned out that Marie taught French not at the *Alliance* but at the FALE, the Faculty of Foreign Languages of the UPA. This was just down the street from the Carolo, so Magali could look forward to visiting with Marie in the Carolo, having coffee there. Marie was a gem of a woman, and she hadn't allowed her beauty to interfere with her person. She really cultivated an intellectual career: not a public career like a teacher, but an interior career, much like the medieval monks in contemplative monasteries— though she cultivated a study of herself and the real world, rather like what is done in the eastern religions. Marie had to go to the *Alliance* office at one time while they sat there, and Magali was surprised to see that besides having a beautiful face, she also had a fantastic body. She could imagine the effect Marie had on the male students at the FALE, and on the male members of the faculty. Olivier, on the other hand, though he might be coveted by many a young, or not so young, lass, had something good to hang on to, and surely would not risk losing Marie. Magali could see this, and the small chance she or anyone had with Olivier. And Magali already felt a friend to Marie and somewhat protective of her. Besides, she had her own François, or at least she thought she still had him—but he was back in Boston and represented quite a catch himself.

11

PAUL'S THING

Paul was in his thirties with dark and slightly wavy hair, intense looking eyes. He had a well trimmed black beard and bright white teeth, which appeared all the more white when shining through the surrounding black of the beard. He was of average height, lean, and strong without being overly muscular. He was always very well dressed, even in his most casual clothes. In sum, he presented to Magali and to others the look of a very healthy and virile young male.

He was well aware of the effect he had on the opposite sex and took great care in his appearance. In this he showed good taste and wisdom. In other things he had his failings—as much or more than ordinary men, he thought. He was in Mexico because of one failing; he had gotten a young girl pregnant in San Diego, a girl he definitely did not want to marry. He had been a fool indeed to play around with her, but, he rationalized, that was an error of youth. Still, it had its results. Faced with a disastrous social situation in the at that time still small Mexican-American community in which he lived, he opted for the easy (for him) way out and moved to Puebla, Mexico, where he had some sympathetic and protective relatives: two uncles and a brother.

Once in Puebla, his luck began to change. With his degree (B.A.) from the University of California (at San Diego), his having been born and raised in the U.S., and his family being Mexican, from Puebla, it was easy for him to obtain a position with the UPA, teaching English. And this gave him the life he really enjoyed. As a half-time professor he only had to teach two classes a week: one three-hour class and one two-hour class. He usually had these classes in the morning. Sometimes he managed to get them scheduled for the same hour: one on MTW, and the other TTh. In the worse situation, when the hours were not too close together—one early, at 8:00, and the other late, at 12:00—he still was done with classes by one o'clock in the afternoon. This gave him plenty of time to have lunch and prepare for his real day.

His position in the University helped him greatly. It gave him some class, put him on a social level well above that of the common herd. It also provided him with a never ending stream of new young girls. And in Mexico he didn't have to worry too much about any "accidents." Medical facilities were available, and it was a country designed for the *"macho."* His position also provided him with contacts for his non-academic life.

And what was this "non-academic" life? It was a life of many adventures. In this life women and sex did not enter. It was solely directed at his own cultural betterment and his own economic enrichment. He was in and out of countless business deals, sometimes to a profit, and sometimes with a small loss (he always was careful to keep participation with his own money to a minimum, preferring small participations in many deals, with their concomitant contacts). He attended cultural and academic events where he hoped to meet the "right" people, but he was not adverse to engaging socially or in business with any lower class where he saw a chance of a profit. He maintained a "democratic" attitude toward people, something he learned in the U.S. with its upwardly mobile social structure. He thought Mexico was becoming in that sense more like the U.S., and he didn't want to be left out of the momentum wherever he could participate in it. He had dreams of being a "tycoon," and if it meant getting there through doing many small deals, he would do them and try to keep moving upward and outward. One would have to say that his many activities at least exhibited variety. There was nothing he would not consider, and he enjoyed every adventure to the full.

Teaching English at the ILE was not without its own benefits. As an attractive young male he had many opportunities with young female students. He felt and feels sure that they are not tempting him in an effort to get good grades, though he had once in a while suspected it. He rather thought it was because he was so handsome, so *macho*, so gracious with them. He did not, however, allow any seriousness in these affairs. And he changed girls quite often and did not try to hide anything, so that the other girls would know that he was merely dallying with them, having fun—innocent fun. This term he is devoting a lot of time to one student, Carmelita, a pretty and petite, but shy, girl who is taking Magali's English class. She also works for the ILE as a student doing "social service." But he still keeps his relations with her on a fun level.

His regular girl-friend is Susan Martin, a teacher at the nearby American University (*Universidad Americana*, or UA), a private university in a rural setting to the north of Puebla. She is American, in her twenties, and he has a special relationship with her. He thinks he is on a level with her, but she thinks he is a little below her, and not to be taken seriously. It works for a really nice deal for him. She wants some fun out of her time in Mexico, and enjoys sex with him, but she also enjoys him as an elegant escort at all kinds of social functions. They get to depend upon each other as if they were a formerly married couple, now separated, and still great friends, not above reliving their former intimacy on occasion. This certainly was great for Paul's swinging lifestyle.

Paul had fallen in love with Magali as soon as he saw her. Although he never demonstrated his feelings for her openly (he knew that Magali was more or less engaged), he thought that perhaps the distance would cool relations between her and her fiancé, and, with time, she would come to accept him. He tried to avoid being accepted just as a good friend.

Paul and Magali met on occasion in and about the ILE. They also sometimes shared coffee at the Villa Rica, usually with others from the ILE. So it was that on Thursday, about ten, Magali entered the Villa Rica and there were Paul, Fr. Flynn, Hans, and Charley in a vigorous conversation in English. They usually spoke Spanish out of respect for other Mexicans, especially for the owners of the Villa Rica. Hearing them speaking English perked up Magali's interest in and curiosity about their conversation.

Charley, in the appropriate location, got up when she entered
and grabbed a neighboring chair for her. The conversation did
not pause. Magali sat, ordered coffee when the owner came over,
and remained out of the talk, just listening, while she tried to
catch up on what they all were saying.

They were talking about the Jesuits. And it looked like Fr.
Flynn was cornered, and on the defensive.

"That's just a bunch of fairy tales, legends. Urban
legends—like the 20 foot long crocodiles growing in the sewers
of New York City. They just aren't really there," Fr. Flynn was
saying. "Likewise, there's no gold in the tunnels."

Charley: Sometimes such legends have a grain of truth in them.
When the Jesuits were suppressed in the mid-1700's, it's said and
believed that they hid lots of gold and books and records in the
tunnels.

Fr. Flynn: Nonsense! There was no gold; the Fathers used all of
the income they had from donations for the education of the
Spanish young and the native Mexicans. The books, what there
were of them, are either in the Lafragua library or in the
Biblioteca Polifaxiana. Or they were destroyed in the turmoil of
those times.

Hans: But you can't tell me that old Juan Polifax did not have lots
of wealth. He wasn't a bishop for nothing, and I've heard that he
ruled with an iron hand. He must have had a lot that he hid over
the years.

Charley: And what of the French? When they lost in the Battle of
Puebla, on the *Cinco de Mayo* in 1862? They are said to have
hidden lots of French gold in the tunnels that connected with the
Forts. It's also said that the officer in charge and the men who
hid the gold were later, as a unit, wiped out in another battle, in
Mexico, and with them went the secret of where they hid the gold
because the French did not let the secret out to anyone else in
their forces. When the French came back to Puebla, they hunted
for the gold but could not find it.

Hans: The French were not the only ones who hid gold in the tunnels. Think of all the local merchants and men of wealth. What do you think they did with their wealth in all of the troubled times in Mexico's history?

Charley; Yes, before the French there was the invasion of the Americans, in the Mexican War of 1848. They went so far as to occupy Mexico City. And there's the revolution of 1910. What about that?

Hans: And just recently. they say, a house was torn down in Puebla and within one of the walls they found a lot of hidden gold coins. And the house had an entrance to the tunnels, but the tunnel appeared to have caved in, for it was filled with lots of debris.

In all of this Paul didn't say much, but he asked many questions: What was that? What about . . . ? When . . . ? Who . . . ? Where . . . ? He appeared to be acting like a moderator, or a secretary, taking minutes. In fact he was taking notes, scribbling on a pad every once in a while. Especially when he had asked a question and gotten an answer, he quickly wrote it down on his pad.

Fr. Flynn: But nobody has ever found gold or anything else of value in a real tunnel.

Charley: Well you Jesuits are still in the thick of it here in Puebla. You know, you were just too good at what you did. You created a near monopoly on the one thing that always has value: education. And you made many people and institutions jealous of you. You invited your troubles with your success. But I have to hand it to you; you stick by your guns, so to speak. You still have lots of universities and other schools all over the place, especially in the U.S. and Canada. You, yourself, are a prime example of the Jesuit force.

[All sat in silence for a while.]

Charley: So tell me, Father, . . . [Pauses, smiling.] What have you found so far?

Fr. Flynn: I haven't found anything! I'm still trying to map where the tunnels went, where they were connected. Most of the system has been destroyed completely, or the tunnels and their connections have been plugged, filled in. I'm trying to discover and describe what went on at the time of their construction and use, as a part of Jesuit history in Puebla; that's all. I'm not looking for anything. And I don't believe there is anything to be found.

Come Sunday, Magali was at *Los Sapos*, seated at what was becoming her regular table, at her regular time, more or less, under the red canopy at *Los Gatos*. Her waiter knew her well by then and hurried over to take her order. It was, as usual, for a Sidral. So, there she sat, watching the show. The people getting ready for the fair of antiques and the first future customers beginning to arrive and to begin nosing about the stalls and displays being set up.

Magali was adapting well to the Mexican way and was now as laid-back as any as she watched over the fair. Almost passive, watching the change in color in her vision. Suddenly she awoke from her enchantment as she thought she saw Paul enter the scene on the far side, directly in front of her, and walk hurriedly through the crowd now forming near where the old ladies were firing up their pots of food.

But she knew it wasn't he, and she wondered why she had thought so. Maybe some premonition of something to do with him?

She finished her Sidral, paid the waiter, and began her tour of the fair. Of course, the same people were displaying the same things, or things like them, and she now knew which had the things in which she was interested. She never tired of looking at the books, and sometimes she found some good ones—to keep, adding them to her growing library, or merely to read. And she was always on the lookout for some good Talavera pieces, at the right price, to add to her kitchen.

She made the circuit to *7 Oriente* and turned to do the east side of the plaza. As she came to the eating area, she was surprised by Paul coming out from the "Gallery," almost colliding with her before he stopped and recognized her.

The "Gallery," so-called, was not an art gallery, though there was one within it. It was rather like the *Gallerias* of Milan, but not nearly so grand. Those of Milan were a huge structure, like a U.S. shopping mall. This was only a small building, not even as large as the ILE. It had a metal roll-up front, not ten yards wide. Inside, the first part of the building was open, now the site of display for a number of items of antique furniture. To the right was a small shop whose left wall was the outside front wall of the building. It sold objects of art: mostly knickknacks, some dishes and glassware, and a few small statues and paintings, not too antique—more like art deco than anything, probably from the 1930's or 1940's. To the left, behind the area now covered by the furniture, was a store that called itself an art gallery and it had for sale a number of paintings, large and small, many modern. In the center was a hallway which extended straight backward through the building. It had small shops on both sides and one at the end. These sold a mix of art objects and antiques. Magali did not know if it was from the hallway or from the art gallery in the front that the place derived its name, but that's what the people called it. There was no sign anywhere confirming the fact.

"Magali!" Paul said. "What a surprise. And what brings you here to *Los Sapos?*"

"A surprise for me, too. I never expected to see you here."

Both were silent for a moment while they recovered their breaths.

"I come here almost every Sunday," ventured Magali, "partly to shop for things for my apartment. Partly just to see the fair and to get a bit of recreation."

"How nice! But strange I've never see you. I have a shop here. Would you like to see it?"

"Yes, Where is it?"

"It's here, inside the Gallery," he said, taking her by the arm and turning her to usher her in to the Gallery. He led her almost to the back of the hallway, stopping at a small store on the right, just two stores short of the hallway's end.

"Here we are," he said. "Not such a great thing, but it's mine."

It was small. Not much more than a bedroom inside. The walls were almost covered with bookshelves. On them were all manner and all sizes of old books. Some were no larger than a popular paperback, but well bound in old leather. Others looked like huge old ledgers, about the size of a tabloid newspaper, also in heavy leather-like bindings.

Scattered about were small religious statues, like those seen in churches. There were also religious images in bas-relief, which also looked like they had been removed from an old church. And there were many old paintings, mostly also of a religious subject, in huge, ornately carved wood (or something that looked like wood) frames, many painted gold. The paintings were both small (about letter-size; some less) and large (some were about four by six feet or so). Many were stacked against one wall, where they could be flipped for viewing.

"Wow!" said Magali. "Amazing! Are all of these valuable?"

"Some are; some aren't," responded Paul. "The good books, or paintings, or such, are sold for that value. The others are sold for decoration. It's not a bad small business."

"Do you sell a lot?"

"Quite well. Most of it is for export. I send them to a dealer friend in San Diego. There are a lot of people in southern California who are building new homes in the suburbs of L.A. and San Diego in the Spanish style, and who lap up old relics for decorating their homes with the real thing."

"You must know a lot about antiques."

"No, not really. I'm just a beginner. Just learning the trade."

"That's why you were asking so many questions the other day in the Villa Rica?"

"Knowledge about antiques is the best thing to have in the trade. I try to get it wherever I can. It's not just knowledge of the thing, the object. Of course it's good to know about the crafts of art, how paintings, and books, and statues, and furniture are made. But more important is knowledge of those who made them, and some history of the things made and the times in which they were made. Therein lies the romance of antiques—and their real value."

"How so?"

"Well, let's say we are offered a painting. We see the thing and can determine how it was made, with what materials. The kind of material gives it one kind of value. We see how it was made and we can determine from that something of when and where. We see a basic quality in its work. And we can decide that it is well done and has a value. But many were made in that area and at that time; and, 'So what?'

"If we know who did it. And if that person did others, and if he was famous, and if his works command high prices in the market, we have a different valuation of the thing.

"Many people painted at the time of Rembrandt, but a painting by Rembrandt is the one with the high value. Knowing about him, his history, is what gives his work such high value. And Picasso. He can create trash and it has a high value. Fame is part of it, but fame itself is just widely spread knowledge. That's why I ask questions. And as I gather answers, my knowledge of artists, their works, and their histories increases. And my chances at placing a correct value on an object—and a higher value when I sell it—is my only assurance of success in the antiques business."

"But, while you're here," continued Paul, "I was just going out for some refreshment. Could I invite you? There's a really nice cafe here. I'm sure you'd enjoy it. I know the people, so I'm sure we can get a table with only a short wait."

Magali assented and Paul led her out and over to *Los Gatos*. The waiter saw them coming. Before they got there a table was just being vacated, and the waiter waved off a group heading for it, indicating that it was not free, but reserved.

Paul and Magali approached the waiter, and Paul and the waiter embraced one another, exchanging greetings, and the waiter moved over to hold a chair back for Magali. They sat down. Paul ordered a beer, and Magali a Sidral.

12

THE EXPLORERS CLUB

On Monday Magali checked into the ILE faculty lounge about nine, said good mornings to the ladies there, looked over the bulletin board (nothing of importance posted), and since she was already prepared for her class (which didn't start until eleven), left the lounge and headed for the ILE library. On her way she was thinking how having a whole program for the term set up for the class, she really didn't have to do any daily preparing. All she had to do was to keep the record of the class' progress. She even had her tests for each week all ready to duplicate, and a few short pop-quizzes ready to throw in on occasion to keep her students on their toes.

Before she made it to the library, she ran into Fr. Flynn coming through the main entrance of the ILE. He altered his course slightly to intercept her and suggested they take themselves to the Villa Rica.

"Just needed to rest a while in friendly company before starting the week," said Fr. Flynn, now seated in the Villa Rica with Magali, as the owner hurried over to them.

"Two good, large Cappuccinos," said Fr. Flynn. And to Magali, "I think I need a good, big coffee to start today."

"What's wrong?" queried Magali. "Have a bad weekend?"

"No. It was all right. But I have a lot of work to do this week, and I guess I'm just procrastinating a bit before getting into it. We really were created, you know, to simply enjoy life—in a lovely garden, no work, no worries."

"So they tell us," said Magali. And after a moment of silence she couldn't help but say, "So tell me, Father, . . . What have you found so far?"

"Touché!" returned Fr. Flynn.

"Well," he went on, "I haven't found anything. As I told Charley, I'm really not looking. At the present time I've been doing mostly library research: going through old books and records; collecting what references to the tunnels I could find. I've got a big map of the city on which I plot what I find of the system. I've got a little one here, showing the general layout."

He stopped to rummage through his briefcase until he came out with a letter size paper which he set down before Magali. Thereon was an inked pattern of lines and some small squares in the form of a general map of the tunnel system in Puebla. The squares were identified as churches or convents or hospitals. The river San Francisco was identified, coursing through the middle of the city, generally from north to south (it had long since ceased to be a feature of Puebla's landscape, having been enclosed in a large storm sewer in the 1930's). The two Forts, Loreto and Guadalupe, were also plotted there in their appropriate locations.

"The solid lines are known major tunnels," said Fr. Flynn. "The zigzags in the lines show where they've been closed. The dashed lines show where we know there were tunnels, but we're not sure they're still there, or can be entered and are passable. The dotted lines are where we think there are major tunnels, but we don't know that they're physically there, if they ever were. The little red lines are where there are private tunnels or private connections to the major tunnel system."

"There are a lot of those. Have you been into many of them?"

"No. Actually, into very few. Most of them are closed. And many promising entrances turn out to be red herrings. For example, I had already checked out the house Hans talked about—the house where the gold coins were found within a wall. There *was* what appeared to be a tunnel connection, but further exploration by the workers there found that it went nowhere. It turned out to be what they call a vault. A structure like a tunnel, extended underground a little, but dead-ended. They were used to hide in during problems in the city: revolutions and such. Their entrances from the houses were well camouflaged. And in some cases the vaults in turn had hidden within their walls secret doors to where the owners hid certain treasures—like gold and jewels and money. But nobody has ever found anything left in any of the vaults which have been discovered in old buildings. Not to say that someone might not find some treasure in such vaults some day."

"The tunnels you can get into from the few of these entrances that are still open," he continued, "are so clogged in parts that I hesitate to try to enter them. The fact is I'm a bit too tall to try to negotiate the tunnels. The Spanish were really kind of short by modern standards. And the doors you encounter in the tunnels are really small. Most are only about four feet high, and so narrow that only one person can pass through at one time. The people probably had to crouch to get through them, and there was probably someone waiting on the other side with a sword or club in case some undesirable tried to come through. The one thing the tunnel construction proves is that no one tried to hide any large furniture or such down there. What I need for that part of the discovery process is a crew of cave spelunkers."

"Well," said Magali, "in the States you'd get grad students to do the dirty work. Why don't you get students here to do it? Free student labor! Slaves, they call them at some western universities. There are probably a lot of *macho* students who would see it as an adventure. Maybe you could make a club: The Explorers Club of Puebla."

"Hey," Fr. Flynn almost shouted. "That's a great idea." Then, more calmly, "We would have to have some kind of organization of the work anyway. A club is the perfect form for it. Meetings, progress, achievements, celebrations. Go out to a dinner. Great! Hey, nobody said we couldn't have fun in our work. The Explorers Club of Puebla. Perfect name for it. Implies more than it is. Could even develop into a permanent institution for the field study of Puebla. And it need not be limited to males. I can see some young ladies participating."

"Does that mean I can be a member?" asked Magali.
"Magali, you're a Charter Member."

By then, the middle of September, Magali had settled into a
kind of routine of living in Mexico. Sunday mornings she usually
went to *Los Sapos* and the flower market, and then had lunch at
McDonald's on the *Zócalo*. During the week she prepared her own
meals at home, but she sometimes had lunch out, sampling new
things to eat at a number of different restaurants. She always liked
to explore.

Coffee breaks, which were an important institution in
Mexico, were usually taken at the Villa Rica or at the Carolo. She
preferred the Carolo, on Avenida Camacho, because of the
student and faculty atmosphere. There she occasionally met other
foreign faculty who taught at the nearby Faculty of Foreign
Languages, including, on occasion, her new friend Marie St.
Jacques. There was a bookstore next to the Carolo in which she
loved to browse. And the Church of the Company was also
nearby, where she would go for a quiet moment.

She slowly got to know the people who frequented the
Carolo, many of them teachers, but many also advanced students
or graduates who were in the art or theater world. She often saw
one of her students there, Roberto, the young man who sat in a
corner in the back and who loved antique books (as did, it turned
out, Paul).

He showed promise as a student, though not in her English
class. He appeared intelligent to the extreme; he just appeared to
be not applying himself to his studies. This might be explained by
how she saw him in the Carolo. He was always sitting at a table
with other students, usually girls, and rather nice looking girls at
that. Sometimes he was sitting with only one girl; but too many
times it was a different girl.

The next day, Tuesday, Magali dropped into the Carolo
shortly after three in the afternoon for some coffee and found a
table near the entrance. She settled in and looked around, and
there was Roberto, seated with five very nice looking girls.
Presently they all rose to leave, and Roberto was left alone. He

looked over at Magali, gathered his things, got up, and came over
to her table.

"Hi, teacher," he said, cheerfully.

"Hello," Magali replied.

"May I sit with you."

"Of course."

He sat down, placing his things on one of the empty chairs
at the table. "I have just been with some friends. They are going
to the library. I have to go home soon, to study."

"I know that you are a *pasante,*" Magali said, "that you have
finished all of your course work for your degree, but in what
field, exactly, are you studying?"

"I am in psychology," he replied, rather proudly.

"That must be interesting," said Magali. "And what do you
study within the field of psychology?"

"The field of psychology *is* very interesting. And I am
studying a very interesting part of it. It is that part called, in
Spanish, *onéirica.*"

"*Onéirica?* What is that?"

"It is a very difficult and complicated subject. Do you really
want to know?"

"Yes," replied Magali. "I'm always interested in learning of
something new."

"Well. I shall try to give you a simple lesson. But I shall have
to do it in Spanish because you know my English is not so good."

"Go right ahead," said Magali. "It might be for me a good
lesson in Spanish, too."

He switched to Spanish, and the lesson commenced.

"*Onéirica* refers to dreams. The Greek word for dream is
onéiros, like the word for work is *téchnos. Onéirica* refers to dreams
like *técnica* refers to work, as a general term. Technology is the
study of work, and oneirology is the study of dreams. But what I
want to study is not really dreams: not *onéiros* but *onéirica.*

"That part of psychology I want to study deals with our
knowledge and how we act. As you know, all living things act,
and they act according to their knowledge.

"We have many kinds of knowledge; the classic three are
sensory, intuitive, and reflective. In more modern times we

discover that we also have temporal, spatial, and processal knowledge. We also have what might be called tacit knowledge, and knowledge from reflection which is structured as words, which can be called explicit knowledge—this, whether it has been voiced aloud or merely mused over in the mind.

"Most of our knowledge is tacit. We have it, but we are not really aware of it. Tacit knowledge includes sensory and intuitive knowledge. We know heat when we feel it, and a rose when we see it. It also includes that knowledge with which we control our body's movements. We know how to walk, though we are not aware of all the muscle motions we must do to walk from here to somewhere. We breathe and our hearts beat without our having to occupy our conscious minds with doing these things. These things are sometimes referred to as a kind of animal knowledge.

"Almost all of our tacit knowledge deals with our being in a material world. It is natural to us, and it usually makes us do the wise act. In this relationship the more knowledge we have, the better and more wisely we can act. Tacit knowledge is usually true, though we can be fooled into misinterpreting what we experience.

"Explicit knowledge, however, is different. This knowledge is symbolized. Its form is in words, or mathematical symbols, or musical notation, or some other semiotic device. But it also exists in the mind as ideas of these symbols when we reflect on something while using these ideas. Such as talking to oneself in the mind. Explicit knowledge in the form of real thing symbols, outside the mind, such as printed words or maps or mathematical formulas, can be examined and proved. Such is scientific knowledge: what is said describing the world. We can study this symbolized knowledge, reflect on it, debate it, restructure it, and even expand or extend it. We can also create it; and with it we can make mistakes—or tell lies.

"Anyway, these ideas are what we understand as the basic ideas of knowledge. Now, *onéirica!*

"*Onéirica* refers to dreams, as dreams are a form of knowledge. At least, we know our dreams—if we can remember them after we wake up. But what appears to happen in dreams is not real. Knowledge of dreams is knowledge of an unreal world.

It should not, normally, be used to guide our actions in the real world.

"Tacit knowledge informs us of the real world. With it we form a mental model of the real world and how it works. We use this model to design our actions. We know how any action would affect this model, and from a knowledge of the change brought about in the model we can anticipate what the action would produce in the real world. And thereby we have an idea of the success or failure the action would have in achieving our desires. All this we do without consciously laboring at it.

"Explicit knowledge, especially scientific knowledge, can modify our understanding of the world and our mental model of it. The more and better understanding of the world we have—made better through scientific, explicit, knowledge—the more likely our actions will fulfill or realize our desires.

"Any explicit knowledge can change our knowledge of, or our model of, the real world. *Onéirica*, as a doctrine of study, postulates that, like dreams, knowledge of an unreal world can also change our view of and our actions in the real world. It is this unreal, this non-material, world and the way it affects our actions that *onéirica*, 'the doctrine of the unreal,' seeks to study.

"Such unreal, non-material (spiritual, or hypothetical, if you wish) worlds *do* affect us. These are created by men, through the creations of religions and politics, as well as other cultural structures, organizations, and institutions. Ways of doing work—that is, *técnica*—affect our view of the world. Ways of doing commerce, social values, family relations, even natural things, such as seasons and weather, take on oneiric significance and power when they are coopted by religions or political powers.

"Take the case of a soldier of the U.S. in 1942. The Japanese are the enemy and Chinese are allies. In 1952 the Chinese are the enemy and the Japanese are allies. The soldier has not changed, but his life has; and all because of politics. So, too, the life of a Christian changes when he is 'born-again.' Both politics and religions are constantly changing, affected by economic opportunity and advances in knowledge. And they will continue to change, as will the lives of those who are governed oneirically by these phantom systems.

"And oneiric things not only affect us now. They have affected humans since there were humans. And they shall continue to affect us until we can more truly understand them and come to dominate and control them."

"Wow!" said Magali. "You overwhelm me. I'm glad I'm studying something as simple as language."

"But," he said, "language is a semiotic system. It is a product of a society, a culture, created and designed to serve that society. It is structured by and filled with all the real and unreal ideas we carry about with us. The very meanings of words refer to what our beliefs are; and our beliefs, especially those relating to oneiric fields of knowledge, are sometimes very unreal, and false. Our knowledge of reality is dependent on experience, and our experience is interpreted in accordance with our view of the world, and much of that view is shaped by the premises of an oneiric idea of the world. A true study of any language should include in its description all the things that go to guide us in discerning the interpretation of the words that form it, and the strange oneiric powers that many words have, and the special meanings they entail in our use of those words and in our use of the language itself in our daily lives."

"We believe our knowledge." he continued, "comes from our experience. But even in the best of situations most good knowledge, that based on a true interpretation of experience, is only of the quality of opinion. It is like statistics. We believe in probability. If we see a lion doing damage to a person, we come to believe that any lion will do damage to any person, so that if we see a lion in the streets, we seek sheltering protection. In most cases that is not a bad way of appraising the world. In reality, then, there is very little in the real world that we really know from our own sensory experience. Science helps us through directly discovering and proving true knowledge, and in providing through the dissemination of its findings—really the experiences of others—a second-hand experience which we can use just about as well. That is a boon from semiotic systems, provided we are not deluded by them, for they can lie as easily as inform. We should remember that not all that we are given as scientific truth is true. Much is full of mistakes, with wrong conclusions. Much is lies—whether to support religious or political power or to deprive us of our money (as in advertising). And much is based on a wrong idea of reality or a bad interpretation of experience. Remember Socrates' story of the cave!"

After class the next day Magali went down to the ILE faculty lounge to put the collection of books she was using in the class into her locker in the lounge. There she met Fr. Flynn, who asked her how it was going. She said it was going rather well, and he asked her where she was going at that moment. She responded that she was going to go to McDonald's on the *Zócalo* for lunch.

"McDonald's?" Fr. Flynn exclaimed.

"Yes," said Magali.

"Then, it's true what they say about Americans and fast food?"

"This is different. You don't know how good it is until you've tried it."

"Well, if it's so good, maybe I should join you, if that's all right."

"You'd be quite welcome. And I'm sure you will enjoy it. But I take a rather long time at it. It's not really *fast* food for me."

"I'll try it, anyway," said Fr. Flynn. "But first, would you like to go with me to the Cathedral for a moment? It's just across the way. I've got something I want to show you." And in almost a whisper, "A tunnel."

"Fine," said Magali. "And then we go to McDonald's and I can show you how to enjoy American fast food in a continental manner."

And with that they left the ILE lounge and the ILE and headed westward toward *Cinco de Mayo* and the Cathedral.

They entered the Cathedral through the north side and at the back of the church proper. Fr. Flynn went directly to an office where he talked with a man who must have been some kind of porter. The man got some keys and came out with Fr. Flynn, and they all proceeded to a stairway which led below.

At the bottom and along a long hallway they came to a door which the porter unlocked. Through that, they went along another hallway, not so long as the first, and to another door, which the porter also opened. They entered a room, not too big, and facing them on the opposing wall was another door, which the porter also proceeded to open. Behind this door, near the far side of the room, there was a metal railing or fence, looking like wrought iron, it was so dark grey in color, and it had a gate with a huge lock as for a prison door. The porter withdrew from his pocket a large, ancient looking key and began to open the gate lock.

"Quite a difficult thing to enter from the legal way, isn't it?" Father Flynn asked to Magali. "And, I guess. from the other side it must be as difficult to get out of."

The porter said he would wait for Fr. Flynn to complete his task (whatever that was).

Fr. Flynn entered through the gate and motioned to Magali to follow him, which she gingerly did. Before him, against the opposing wall, about eight feet away, was another door, with a wooden bar across it. Fr. Flynn lifted the bar and shifted a support up under it. He then opened the door, pulling on it, and it appeared to be quite heavy since he moved it so very slowly. It surely was a thick and heavy wood door, thought Magali. And it was, made of wood planks about three inches thick, with at least two inch boards laid across these main planks, all bolted together.

Inside, it was vaulted, about seven or eight feet high, and smelled stuffy. The walls were of the dark volcanic stone with which the Cathedral and most of the sidewalks of Puebla were constructed, and that didn't help in illuminating the interior of the tunnel, for this was indeed a tunnel. Inside, about twelve feet or more, was a small door in the opposing wall, about five feet high and three feet wide. Fr. Flynn opened the door. The door itself was ancient but it had a door knob of rather modern construction, with no lock. Inside of this door it was definitely dark, and smelled of mold. Fr. Flynn moved a switch which was on the wall to his right and turned on a light: a naked bulb and socket hanging from some wires on the ceiling. The ceiling was only about six feet high, and Fr. Flynn could not stand all the way up inside the tunnel.

"This is it," said Fr. Flynn. "This tunnel goes across the *Zócalo* to the *Casa de las Muñecas*. Unfortunately, you can't get there this way because the central part is caved in. And there's no use in trying to fix it because, what with the traffic around the *Zócalo* and the *temblores* and earthquakes the area experiences, any repairs you wanted to do would probably not last very long."

They stood looking out into the darkness for a while. Magali finally asked, "Are they all like this?"

"Most are like this, or worse," said Fr. Flynn. "But I'm sure that some spelunkers could find a way even through this. It would be a bit risky though."

"Well, I might go through some passable tunnels, but for the rest I'll do paperwork for the club," said Magali. "I'm adventurous, but maybe not that much."

They turned to make their way back, Fr. Flynn turning out the light and closing the doors. The porter closed and locked the metal gate and the outer door, and followed Magali and Fr. Flynn out into the hallway. Fr. Flynn offered him his thanks, and he and Magali proceeded to leave the Cathedral while the porter locked the other doors behind them.

They crossed the *Zócalo* and headed for McDonald's. Magali led the way in. She asked for a simple hamburger, a regular order of fries, and a vanilla shake, suggesting to Fr. Flynn that he get the same. He did, but asked for a chocolate shake. They paid their respective bills, took their trays, stopping to get some straws and napkins from a stand on the way, and went out of the restaurant to sit at a table on the sidewalk in front, under the arcade, to watch the crowds as if on the Champs Elysées or the Via Venetto.

It was late, nearing two in the afternoon, and though the stores were closed for lunch, there were still many people walking about. Only one other outside table was occupied. Next door three tables of tourists were still lunching at the Royal hotel. They were both hungry so without talk they devoted themselves to their food.

Fr. Flynn was the first to speak, and he said, "Hey. This is a pretty good hamburger. Most unexpected. Real meat. And the french fries are not greasy like they are in Canada."

"I thought you'd like it," said Magali. "The french fries are really tasty. I could almost make a meal out of them alone. They must cook them in a special oil. I should find out what it is."

"Absolutely delicious," said Fr. Flynn. "I commend you on your taste."

"The shake, I'm sorry to say, is like in the U.S., as it probably is in Canada, too. A bit artificial. They say it's mostly soy. In the U.S. McDonald's doesn't call them milk shakes. Probably because there's no *milk* in them. But they're still good—and refreshing."

They quickly finished their hamburgers, took a little more time with their fries and shakes, and soon were left sipping occasionally at their shakes while they watched the passing parade. Fr. Flynn eventually took out a cigar and lit it. They both relaxed, talking a little, but mostly just watching for another hour the world of Puebla and its central square on a lazy, sunny, and warm September afternoon.

13

LAFRAGUA

"La Biblioteca José María Lafragua . . . tiene como antecedentes las disposiciones que hiciera Don Melchor de Covarrubias y Cervantes, benefactor principal del Colegio del Espíritu Santo, más tarde Colegio del Estado. . . .
"En la introducción a su testamento, Covarrubias y Cervantes insistió en que el Colegio debería adquirir una 'librería de libros . . . , para los estudiantes, lectores E Predicadores,' que ningún rector podría vender o enajenar y que debían adquirirse con los bienes de la fundación, señala el historiador Efrain Castro Morales en su **Breve Historia de la Universidad de Puebla.***"* [1]

"La Biblioteca del Colegio del Estado, antes de abrir sus puertas al público, ya existía desde 1874, en el interior del plantel, para uso exclusivo de los alumnos. Veamos la siguiente acta: 'En la ciudad de Puebla de Zaragoza, a los cinco días del mes de mayo de 1874, se reunieron en este salón el ciudadano Gobernador del Estado Ignacio Romero Vargas, el C. Director del Colegio Pedro J. Sentíes, los ciudadanos catedráticos de este establecimiento y algunos empleados de la Federación y del Estado con el objeto de inaugurar solemnemente esta Biblioteca.' . . .

"La Biblioteca [La Fragua] se inauguró [el 16 de setiembre de 1885] con 6,000 volúmenes que fueron de los jesuítas y que, por lo mismo, eran propiedad del Establecimiento, a ellos se unieron 2,300 volúmenes que legó el Sr. Licenciado D. José María Lafragua, quien en la cláusula undécima del testamento que otorgó en México, el día seis de marzo de 1871, dice: 'Dejo veinticinco porciento al Colegio Carolino, hoy del Estado de Puebla,

---

[1] Alfonso Yáñez Delgado, "Librería de libros...para los estudiantes, lectores E Predicadores," **Universidad**, Año V, Num. 24, 3 de Octubre de 1985, p. 3.

precisamente para libros de su Biblioteca. En consecuencia, los libros que existen entre mis bienes y que no sean relativos a América, se entregarán por su precio íntegro al expresado Colegio en abono del veinticinco porciento referido, de cuyo importe se deducirán los libros relativos a América, los cuales se entregarán a la Biblioteca Nacional de México.'

"*Según los datos que hubimos, hojeando los expedientes de la Secretaría del Plantel, el 8 de noviembre de 1877, se hizo cargo de la Biblioteca el Sr. Lic. Ramón Gómez Daza, a quien suplió, desde el 24 de ese mes hasta el 15 de enero de 1881, en que tomó posesión el Sr. Lic. Nicolás Meléndez, erudito histiógrafo . . .*

"El Sr. Lic. Meléndez se entregó, desde luego, a la bien difícil tarea de clasificar los libros que a su cuidado se encomendaron, . . .

"Para prevenir, con todo cuidado, la apertura de la Biblioteca, se le envió a su Director el siguiente oficio:

'El Presidente del Colegio, teniendo en consideración que V., como Bibliotecario del Establecimiento, debe ocuparse por ahora, de los trabajos relativos a la inauguración de la nueva Biblioteca, que debe verificarse el próximo día 16 de Setiembre, se ha servido disponer, que no permita V. la entrada a dicha Biblioteca a los alumnos o personas extrañas al Establecimiento, sino es con orden escrita de la Presidencia.—Lo que comunico a V. para su cumplimiento.—Lib. y Const.–Puebla de Zaragoza, Julio 3 de 1885 —J. M. Carreto. —Srio.' . . .

"A la biblioteca se le puso el nombre de C. Lic. José María Lafragua, polígrafo eminente, a cuya munificiencia se debe, en mucho la grandeza bibliográfica de élla.

"El Sr. Lic. Nicolás Meléndez se cesó en sus labores como Bibliotecario del Colegio, en 1892. Le sucedió el Sr. Lic. Francisco Barrientos, de quien dice el maestro D. Jenaro Ponce: '. . . se empeñó en difundir entre los lectores el amor a la lectura de la Historia, de preferencia a la de la novela.' . . . en este caso, el Sr. Lic. Francisco Barrientos aplicó, sabiamente, el gran precepto de Horacio: 'Omne tulit punctum qui miscuit utile dulci, lectorem delectando pariterque monendo.' " [2]

---

[2]*Delfino C. Moreno, "Noticia Histórica de la Biblioteca 'Lafragua', de la Universidad de Puebla,"* **Revista de la Universidad de Puebla.** *Año I, Num. 3, Noviembre de 1943, pp. 67-71.*

14

DON ROMUALDO'S LAFRAGUA

The first time Magali met Don Romualdo was at the Carolo. She was having coffee with Roberto when he suddenly got up and approached a nearby table where an older man had just sat down.

"Buenos, Don Romualdo," he said respectfully to the older man. sitting there in a white lab coat.

"Buenos, Roberto," replied the man, rubbing his right hand on his lab coat and then firmly shaking it with the young man in a gesture of friendship. They exchanged a few words and then looked both in the direction of Magali. The older man got up and they came toward Magali's table.

"Please, Don Romualdo," said Roberto. "I would like you to meet Miss Magali Smith, from Boston."

"Es un placer, señorita," he said. "I have heard a lot about you at the University."

"Please sit down with us," invited Magali. "I have also heard a great deal about you from Roberto. He has the greatest admiration and respect for all the work you have been doing at the Lafragua Library."

"Lafragua is my life, *señorita.*"

"Please call me Magali."

Don Romualdo sat down and ordered a *café con leche* from the waitress that came toward them.

Turning again to Magali, Don Romualdo said, in very good English, "I have heard much about you. You have visited many of the University's libraries, but not yet Lafragua. Many talk of what you are doing, your research, but I do not know the details of exactly what it is. What *are* you investigating here in Puebla."

"Well," said Magali, continuing in English, "I'm looking at the old churches and many old books about the colonial times, trying to study the Spanish language and its relation to the churches, to the people, and how it incorporated their religious life and beliefs—how the churches show, if they do, their involvement in the language, or how they might have altered the language, enriched it. It's not easy to explain, probably because I don't know what I'll find, or, indeed, if I find anything of interest. Here in Puebla I'll just be doing a monograph. Later they'll determine back in Boston if there's anything in it worth expanding into a dissertation for the doctorate. I guess this is serving as a field study and as the basis for a preliminary examination to candidacy for the doctoral degree."

"That does sound interesting," said Don Romualdo. "It will surely be a difficult work. I'm sure you will find much of interest, but I agree that you might not find anything that your professors in the United States will accept as meeting *their* needs—*your* need for a dissertation topic."

Roberto: I, too, find it interesting. I have always found language itself most interesting. Remember, Teacher, our conversation about *onéirica.* Language is probably the greatest key to any society or culture. In fact, it might be used to identify a culture. We speak the same language? We belong to the same culture! Even within a culture there are sub-cultures that differ according to language. The *jerga* (slang) of youths within their own gang; jokes shared and known only to the insiders. And the jargon of professionals which becomes an esoteric language—the better to establish an economic monopoly for the initiated few. And the power that priests give to special words to instill fear in those they wish to dominate—the *holy* name of God. In the end, Peirce appears to have been right with his pragmatism: The purpose of language is to make the hearer think as the speaker wishes him to think, and to govern his behavior accordingly.

Don Romualdo: One thing is certain, language is a key to many things. I, myself, have learned much of other cultures through the reading of books. And I had to learn several new languages in order to be able to read many of them.

Roberto: It is too bad we have lost so much of the languages of past cultures. We might have learned much of their way of life from their languages alone. Even in our own culture much of colonial Mexican life is forgotten and unknown by us. Maybe in your studies you *can* discover much of value. Maybe contribute to methods in archeology. I think, maybe yes.

Don Romualdo: Hmmm. What Roberto has said is true. But, fortunately, you have much of the old language still available to you, in old books. And, of course, the churches have other symbols for you: their plaques, statues, pictures, the buildings themselves. Your study can at least explore many cultural treasures for their meanings. There is sure to be much there that you can discover.

Magali: There is actually even too much to explore. I have to narrow my search to investigating those sources which can provide me with useful information. My time is really quite limited. A year is a very short time for a study such as I am trying to do. A lifetime could be spent on it. I have to find the really good books, and the really good physical evidence in the churches and convents. That's the real problem. To carry out a fruitful and efficient investigation with the resources I have or can get, in the time I will have for it.

Roberto: Spoken like a true American. The efficiency of a machine.

Magali: Yes, but when you have to do something, the really smart person will do it with the least work and in such a way as to produce the greatest results. Who cares what ideology or technology is used in accomplishing the task. The job is to get it done, and done well, with good results.

Don Romualdo: Well, we have here at the University a lot of old books that you can look over.

Magali: That is what I spend most of my free time at the University doing. I've been to a score of small libraries all over. But I still haven't been to Lafragua . . . nor to your own Lafragua.

Don Romualdo: Well, I should like to invite you to visit my part of Lafragua. At your convenience, of course.

Magali: Is that really possible? I have been told that only the part of the library opened to the general public can be visited. The other—

Don Romualdo: The other is available to scholars, book lovers, and friends.

Magali: I'm flattered. Thank you very much. I've been curious about your library since I heard of it.

Don Romualdo: Well, you are a book lover, and, I hope, a friend.

Roberto was now sipping his coffee in silence, very pleased to see how the two were getting along.

A group of students suddenly invaded El Carolo, talking and laughing, pushing chairs around, and grabbing the few tables still unoccupied.

"Ah," said Don Romualdo, "classes are over. It's time I return to my work." Then, looking at Magali: "Are you, by any chance, available now, *señorita?* . . . Magali?"

She got up immediately, opened her *mochila* and took a few pesos out of a small leather *monedero*, putting them on the table, enough to cover the bill for herself and Don Romualdo.

"I am," she said.

"Me too," said Roberto. And he also put money on the table, enough to cover his share of the bill, plus the *propina* (the tip).

The three of them went out into the street, through the crowd of young people.

"Permiso," said Roberto, who went in front. *"Permiso."*

They crossed the plaza, entered the Carolino by the main door, passing through the inspection of the door guards, who openly admired Magali as she walked by, and went into the main entrance hall which was filled with people hurrying either from a class or to a class or on some other mission which called for them to hurry. This was one of the few times during the day that a Mexican was seen to hurry (the high altitude of the city did not generally encourage such activity). From the main entrance hall they went through a side archway to the first patio, then along an arcade and into the second patio. Crossing this patio, they entered a door to a stairway which led down to the administrative offices of Lafragua. Don Romualdo walked toward a small *pórtico* on the side of the hall at the bottom of the stairway and opened its old fashioned lock with a huge key that he took out of his pocket.

"Pasen, por favor," said Don Romualdo. "My budget is almost nonexistent, except for the help of my friends." He motioned them inward to a large room lined with a series of metallic shelves partially covered with books of all sizes and shapes. Some of the books were neatly arranged in rows on the shelves, some were in small stacks. Others were piled up on small tables here and there. They all looked very old and in a poor state of preservation. There was one huge table (it must have been forty feet long and six or eight feet wide; or maybe it was more than one table, grouped together) covered with old books in one great disarray. Most of these truly looked ancient, as Magali could discern from their bindings. Some were bound in leather, some in what appeared to be a heavy paper or board. The pages in most had not been trimmed, their irregular edges suggesting that someone had probably torn apart by hand the sheets forming the signatures. She could see the titles on some of the books, and the typography looked like something out of pirate stories.

Don Romualdo showed Magali around his domain. The tables where his assistants would sit, their books in neat stacks. The tables where work yet to be assigned was waiting, some books neatly stacked, others like they were just tossed there or put in any space which could support them. And finally the one huge table (or tables), where the books looked as if they had no friends, had been unkindly discarded as if they were trash.

"*Aquí,*" said Don Romualdo to Magali. "This is the result of a 'modernization' project of one of your compatriots."

"Oh!" said Magali. "I heard about that. Roberto told me all about it. It's hard to believe that anyone could be allowed to do . . . this. I guess that as an American I should apologize for what he did. It does make me a bit ashamed, . . . as an American. But, of course, there are bad ones in every group."

She began to look over some of the books—open one, examine a few pages, move on to another. "What a great number of books you have here, and such a variety of sizes and bindings. And of such interesting subject matter."

"And we don't even know what we have," added Don Romualdo. "This table has not yet been sorted and catalogued. We haven't even seen, really, what it is we have. We might have some treasures there which will shock us in their discovery."

"This is amazing. What a job you have with this. And what discoveries you can look forward to. As for my own work, though, I've got to come back and get your help in finding what is in Lafragua—the main library, not your section. And after I finish with that, I would be truly grateful if you could show me what books you have here that might help me—even if I have to wear plastic gloves and be watched by armed guards when I read them."

"I would be glad to offer you any assistance I can," said Don Romualdo. "Plastic gloves might be necessary, but I think armed guards would not."

"Can I contact you through Roberto? He is in my English class, so I see him three times a week."

"I think that would be a good arrangement at this time," said Don Romualdo.

"Good," said Magali. "Now, I have to go. I have my own class soon. And I cannot thank you enough for your showing me your special part of the library (I won't tell anybody)." And to Roberto, "You'd better hurry, too. You've got the same class in an hour."

Roberto said his goodbye to Magali; he would stay a while longer because he and Don Romualdo had some things to talk over. He promised he would help arrange with Don Romualdo for her coming back soon to Lafragua.

After Magali had left, Roberto turned to Don Romualdo and said, "You can trust Magali. She is one of us . . . in spirit."

"Is she, now?" said Don Romualdo. His black, intense eyes looked directly into the soft eyes of the young man.

"I wanted you very much to meet her, Don Romualdo. I believe she can be of great help to us," said Roberto. "I have not told her any secrets . . . except that you could use some help in a special project. I was going to bring her to you this week-end. But this is great. Now, you have met her, and she you. Now—?"

"Now," said Don Romualdo, "she has gone back to her duties, and I have to go back to mine. But . . . we will talk of this again. Very soon. I promise."

15

LOS LIBROS

"La Biblioteca [Lafragua], que tiene un acervo aproximado de cien mil obras, principalmente de los siglos XVI al XIX, se ha conformado con libros del Colegio del Espíritu Santo, de los conventos suprimidos por las Leyes de Reforma, del Colegio del Estado, de las bibliotecas del doctor Rafael Serrano y del licenciado Rafael Isunza, de la Colección Lafragua, de la Escuela de Medicina de Puebla y del Antiguo Colegio de Abogados." [1]

Entre los manuscritos más importantes está el "Archivo Jesuita" donde se tratan asuntos en su mayoría relativos a la Compañía de Jesús, antes y después de su expulsión. Las marcas de fuego en los cantos de numerosos volúmenes que se encuentra por miles, nos indican sus orígenes en los conventos de San Agustín, Sto. Domingo, San Antonio, San Luis, del Carmen, de la Merced, y muchos más que enriquecen nuestra biblioteca.

". . . abunda en obras que tratan de Historia Patria, contiene interesantes manuscritos . . . Entre lo más notable que posee se encuentran, 'Arte y Vocabulario de la Lengua Matlazinga' por el P. Diego de Basalenque, . . . Autógrafos de don José María Morelos y correspondencia de los insurgentes, causa, original, del Dr. Fray Servando Teresa de Mier, comenzada en 1794 y concluída en 1818, Incunables de gran valía y manuscritos interesantísimos de la Edad Media. Por lo que toca a la obra del P. Basalenque, según la autorizada opinión del Dr. Nicolás León, polígrafo que honra a las Letras Nacionales, sólo hay dos ejemplares, uno en la Biblioteca de Nueva York, y el que tiene esta Biblioteca, . . ." [2]

---

[1] Alba Judith Iriba Castro, "La Biblioteca Lafragua, Hacia su Segundo Centenario," **Universidad**, Año V, Num. 24, 3 de Octubre de 1985, P. 7.

[2] Delfino C. Moreno, "Noticia histórica de la Biblioteca 'Lafragua', de la Universidad de Puebla," **Revista de la Universidad de Puebla**, Año I, Num. 3, Noviembre de 1943, pp. 77-78.

Otras obras que contiene la Biblioteca incluye obras de Santo Tomás de Aquino; trabajos de Erasmo de Rotterdam; **Titulos y méritos de los sres. Covarrubias,** *1a. edición, Madrid, Juan Pablo Martyrrizo, 1629;* **La cuarta parte del Abecederio espiritual y ley de Amor,** *1566; y el incunable* **Manuel du Libraire et de l'Amateur de Livres,** *por Jacques Charles Brunet, 1473.*

Una de las joyas es un **Breviario Romano** *anterior a la imprenta, escrito en latín y en pequeñas letras góticas, con capítulos de color de gran belleza.*

Se recibieron en 1920 45,196 volúmenes, las que estaban amontonadas "en un salón anexo, al cual, según consta en el Archivo, le llamaron, impropiamente, bodega, . . . Estábamos [el director Delfino C. Moreno y otros] en ese salón, en los trajines propios de una biblioteca, cuando nos soprendió el sabio Dr. Nicolás León, maestro en asuntos biblioteconómicos y nos dijo: 'Está usted en el glorioso polvo de las bibliotecas.' " [3]

"Durante la dirección de Esparza Soriano son numerosas las sustracciones y pérdidas de libros, entre éllos, la **Opera Medicinalia,** *de Francisco Bravo, incunable mexicano, impreso en 1570, que al salir a la venta en Nueva York, es recuperado afortunadamente por gestiones del doctor Ignacio Chávez, del licenciado Gustavo Díaz Ordaz, entonces funcionario de Gobernación y del doctor Manuel Santillana Santillana, rector . . .*

"La sustracción de la **Opera Medicinalia** *descubre otras, y esto motiva que Esparza Soriano presente su renuncia como director en 1957 y sólo le es aceptada hasta el 29 de setiembre de 1958, mientras se hacen trámites para la recuperación del incunable mexicano.*

"Por las sustracciones, Esparza Soriano es encarcelado; no obstante el 20 de Febrero de 1959, desde la cárcel de San Juan de Dios, pide permiso para ausentarse como profesor, pero cinco meses más tarde, el Consejo Universitario lo destituye públicamente como catedrático. . . .

. . . "A la sustracción maquinada, en la administración de Esparza Soriano, se suma el abandono de joyas bibliográficas que por varios años merecieron el cuidado de otros directores. El robo de los libros se intensifica al grado que entre algunos empleados despedidos era frecuente decir: 'Vamos con Chava.' Esto significaba que el anticuario Salvador Macías Contreros, dueño de un bazar . . . , frente al Jardín de Los Sapos, adquiría las sustracciones

---

[3] *Ibid., p. 75.*

bibliográficas que se hacían a la biblioteca . . . La gente, irónicamente llamaba a este bazar 'sucursal de la biblioteca Lafragua.'

"*En diciembre de 1970, los consejeros universitarios doctor Marco Antonio Rojas y profesor Alfonso Vélez Pliego, denuncian ante la Procuraduría General del Estado, la sustracción de los libros impresos en 1741 y 1753, propiedad de la biblioteca Lafragua.*

"*Se trata de los libros* **Tractatus Theologicus**, *del padre Franciso Suárez, impreso en 1741 y del* **Clypeus Theologicae Thomisticae**, *del padre Joannes Baptista, impreso en 1753.*

"*Tras la denuncia, la policía localiza ocho libros más, todos de teología y pertenecientes a la biblioteca universitaria. También se encuentra un recibo de compraventa a nombre de un empleado del Departamento de Bibliotecas . . ." [4]*

A la historia de la sustracción de libros a través de los tiempos, se sumaban muchos otros hurtos, hechos en forma de órdenes dadas directamente por altos funcionarios del Consejo de la universidad o notables personalidades de gran influencia política, no registrados; sin tener en cuenta la desaparición progresiva de preciosos volúmenes a manos de maestros, alumnos y visitantes. Ya que no había un registro completo y oficial de todos los volúmenes, y ya que Lafragua no estaba dotada de ningún dispositivo de seguridad o control, estos robos eran no sólo factibles sino en extremo fáciles.

---

[4] *Alfonso Yáñez Delgado, "Librería de libros...para los estudiantes, lectores E Predicadores,"* **Universidad**, *Año V, Num. 24, 3 de Octubre de 1985, p. 5.*

16

EX-LIBRIS

Don Romualdo, *"el Maestro,"* had formed a small and secret group that he had baptized "Ex-Libris." The group, whose members had been chosen and interviewed with great caution, taking into consideration not only moral values but also the skills necessary for the work, included Roberto among them.

The task of the organization was the preservation of the many ancient and valuable books and *incunabula* which had been transferred from the official Lafragua to the studio of the Master (although the most famous had remained in view of the authorities). The books were there catalogued, cleaned, dusted with borax, and then delivered to the Master, who deposited them, very carefully wrapped with a special acid-free paper and plastic and sealed with plastic tape, in wooden boxes. The boxes were placed in a special room whose entrance was only from within Don Romualdo's own office in his section of Lafragua, and whose only key was kept by Don Romualdo.

The idea was to protect the books from theft by students and foreign visitors, and from the covetousness of some of the directors. This was to be accomplished by taking the books out of circulation under the pretext of their being "restored." Since the books remained within the property of the University, and could be taken out of their sanctuary at whatever moment, the plan presented no legal problems. And, since there were no complete lists of the works, there always existed the possibility that no one would ask for them. The solution was temporary, while a greater plan was being readied to take them to the National Library in

Mexico City. All were aware of this second, final stage that assured, definitively, the preservation of a patrimony of incalculable value. But the details of this final stage had not yet been, at that time, discussed.

The meetings of Ex-Libris took place each month on the fourth Thursday at 9:00 in the morning. In it they discussed the work to be done during the next month at Lafragua: what kind of books were to be catalogued, of what subjects, of what historic dates, and so forth.

At the meeting of Thursday, September 22nd, one of the members had brought a magazine that contained an article about past robberies from Lafragua, and Don Romualdo took it, a bit distractedly, and began to read from it:

> *Durante la dirección de Esparza Soriano son numerosas las sustracciones y pérdidas de libros, entre éllos, la* **Opera Medicinalia**, *de Francisco Bravo, . . .*

Had not Don Romualdo read these things time and time again? And, nevertheless, was not each time like the first? Each time he was more and more convinced that he was the one called upon to right this crime against humanity: a knight in shining armor, to the rescue.

Not wanting to disturb the Master in his reading, the group members were talking in low voices of diverse things: the attack on an employee of McDonald's as a crazy protest against the American capitalists, and other local *"noticias."*

"Excuse me," said Don Romualdo, regaining control of the group and the meeting. "Although I am perfectly up to date on the situation of the robbing of books from Lafragua, it always surprises me and makes me indignant. Of course, it is because of this situation, that we all know so well, that we are all here as the society Ex-Libris. But now," said Don Romualdo. "Now, we must get on with the business of our meeting."

Each one of the members of Ex-Libris had in his charge a collection of books on which he was working. Ernesto, leading off the role call, began to report on his work, reading his list of books:

De Las Cosas Maravillosas Del Mundo. Iul Solino. Traducido por Christobal de las Casas. Sevilla: Alonso Eseriuano, 1573;

Los Cinco Libros Primeros de la Crónica General de España, que recopila el Maestro Floria de Ocapo, coronista del Rey nuestro señor, por mandado de su Magestad. Camora: Juan Iñiguez de Lequierica, 1578;

Vindicias Históricas por la Inocencia de Fr. Gerónimo Savonarola. Fr. Jacinto Segura. Valencia: Antonio Balle, 1735;

Crónica del Señor Rey Don Juan, segundo de este nombre, en Castilla y en León, compilada por el noble caballero Fernan Perez de Guzman. Valencia: Benito Monfort, 1779;

Exposición del Libro de Job. Obra Pósthuma del Padre Maestro Fr. Luis de León, de la Orden de N.P.S. Agustín, Cathedrático de Escritura de la Universidad de Salamanca. Madrid: Pedro Marin, 1779;

Compendio de la Historia de la Filosofía. Compuesto en Portugues por el P.D. Teodoro Almeida, de la Congregación del Oratorio de San Felipe Neri de Lisboa, Traducido en Castellano por D.J.H. 1787;

Grammaire Egyptienne, ou Principes Généraux de L'Ecriture Sacrée Egyptienne. Champollion le Jeune. Paris: Didot Frères, 1836.

Lucinda Vargas Mendoza entered into the office of the Director of Libraries, Lic. Fernandez Acosta, and stood in the center of the large and dark room (the Director not having arrived yet), thinking.

She was doing her Social Service through working for the Lafragua Library. This was work that all students had to do, working a few hours per day in some department or faculty to help defray the expenses of the University. The UPA was a State school and charged no tuition, the only required payments by the students being a nominal sum for registration and what was individually required for the purchase of books—and a term of Social Service.

She liked the work in the library. She had a small cubicle in a corner of the reception area of the Director of Libraries, and except for Don Romualdo (who also had his office there, but only came for one or two hours in the early morning) she was alone and undisturbed most of the time and could study or dedicate the greater part of her four hours each morning to what most interested her, which was to spy for the Rector.

The Rector, in the medieval structure of the University of Puebla of the Angels, was an independent power. She had heard of his circle of supporters, groups of people from all social levels dependent on him for work or favors, and his army of informants and spies that covered the vast organization of one of the most important universities of the country. She could see he sought to attract the attention, and favor, of higher political authorities in Mexico by having the University gain national and international fame. He supported programs for computing and for English that would put it in a position competing with other large Latin-American universities. Above all, he avoided political problems with the Governmental Party.

Shortly after she had begun her Social Service term at the library, Lucinda had accepted with pleasure an invitation from one of the minor officials of the Rectory to a special meeting. She and other students, all girls, met in one of the large staff meeting rooms and this official explained that they were all invited to join a group of "friends" of the Rector (formed at the behest of none other than the Secretary of the Rector, Lic. Manolo Fabregas Ruiz) which would assist the Rector's efforts at improving and developing the University by observing those with whom they worked in their Social Service positions and informing on possible thefts of University property or mismanagement of funds or materials, as well as to relay any rumors or gossiping against the "Supreme Chief."

Lucinda had earned her admittance to this group through her having been responsible for the firing of Sra. González—the former assistant librarian—who had insisted that Lucinda work more at her job. She even criticized her wearing tight dresses and high heels and decidedly too much make-up for a young girl (she was—Lucinda was certain—just jealous of her young figure). She also stopped her going out to get coffee in the mornings, which Lucinda had done mostly in order to gossip with her student companions; and she stopped her making calls on the office telephone. Lucinda looked at the desk, now vacant, of her former co-worker, smiling maliciously.

She had discovered, by chance, that Sra. González was not a Mrs., had never been married, but had had an illegitimate son for whom she wanted to gain a post in the administration. That this situation was in no way uncommon in the real world of intrigues and passions was no excuse. But Lucinda supported her denouncement with the accusation of having heard Sra. González express her contempt for certain superiors, for their lack of culture and failings in spelling, among which was the very Director of Libraries—which was true, since that position had been filled, like most of them, by reason of political influence rather than technical qualification. To cover appearances, the poor woman was informed that her position with the University had been terminated as of that very day for reasons that had to do with "morals and good manners."

Lucinda remembered the scene: the woman returning from the office of the Director wiping her eyes with a handkerchief, black stains of eye shadow on her eyelids; hurriedly gathering up the photograph of her son in its silver frame, her papers, and various documents; taking off her uniform and grabbing her purse; quickly leaving the office without saying anything.

It had been a day of intense celebration for Lucinda, who in that manner had had her revenge on the "old boss." She had immediately thereafter gone out to have coffee and celebrate her success with her friends. More than anything, a sensation of power flowed through her. She felt, suddenly, important.

And now—now she had someone even more juicy to work on: Don Romualdo.

Don Romualdo, who hardly looked at her, who hardly noted her presence, who despised her, who asked her for the newspaper and had her serve him a cup of coffee every morning, like she was a servant.

She had the feeling that he was mixed up in something important, and if she could expose him in it, she would surely gain the special approval of the Rector. She already saw herself, admitted to the office of the Rectory, waiting for the Rector to call her. And the Rector coming out to call her personally. He invites her to enter. He has her sit on one of those marvelous dark leather sofas, so soft, so comfortable. He talks with her, Lucinda, friendly and interestedly.

One of her girlfriends had been called once to the Rectory, when the Rector was absent, and one of the Rector's student assistants who was her friend showed her the Rector's immense and luxuriously furnished office, the massive desk in the back, the beautiful painting of Don Melchor de Covarrubias hanging on the wall, the various tables and chairs where he attended visitors . . . the velvet curtains, the crystal chandeliers, the rugs—so thick, so velvety—that were like walking on a cushion . . . even the telephone, white and gold, and the adornments of heavy bronze and crystal on the tables . . . and she had told all her fellow employees of the marvels of that place that only a few privileged persons knew.

Don Romualdo arrived, interrupting her dreams of glory.

"A cup of coffee, Lucinda! What? You haven't prepared it yet?"

She hurried to the automatic coffee maker, rinsed it in the bathroom, put in the filter and four teaspoons of coffee, filled it with water, and plugged it in.

"*Sí, Señor Director,* right away . . . it will be ready in a moment," she responded, submissively. Don Romualdo would have felt worried indeed if he had noted the mocking semi-smile on her face. But this day he had more important things in mind. Much more important things.

17

MAGALI GETS INVOLVED

Paul and Fr. Flynn were seated at a table in the Villa Rica having coffee when Magali entered shortly after ten, having just come from checking in at the ILE as she did each Monday morning in deference to the ladies on the faculty. She went to them and asked if she could join them and was accepted with an almost overflowing welcome.

"Well," proffered Paul. "How goes your shopping?"

"Shopping?" responded Magali.

"At *Los Sapos*," said Paul. And, turning to Fr. Flynn, "Magali is a fan of *Los Sapos*."

"Oh! Oh!" said Fr. Flynn. "Be careful with buying anything from this guy. He's a sharp dealer (you notice I didn't say 'crook' outright)."

"Hey!" cried Paul.

"Actually, Magali," said Fr. Flynn. "He's really one of the few trustworthy dealers in *Los Sapos*. I was just joking."

"You know about his shop, then," said Magali.

"Oh, yes," said Fr. Flynn. "Paul is one of the new Mexicans. A budding entrepreneur in the style of the Yankee carpet-bagger, or should I say of the reformed hippie. Independent, and a go-getter. All the virtues of the newly respected capitalist. None of your socialist nonsense with him. He's going to be somebody, make something of himself."

"We all do what we can," said Paul, adopting a mask of humility.

"How *is* your business doing?" asked Magali.

"It's okay," responded Paul. "Rather slow, but it still gives a profit. And you know what the old jew said: You can't go broke making a profit."

"So what else is knew?" continued Magali.

"We were just talking," said Fr. Flynn, "about Halloween. One of those confusing aspects of Mexico. The original Halloween was called in English: All Hallow's E'en. Which meant the evening before a feast of an all holy something, in this case such being All Saints' Day. It is Halloween in modern times in the U.S. and Canada. The older Mexicans, on the other hand, celebrate the 'Day of the Dead' instead of All Souls' Day, coming after All Saints' Day. And the modern Mexicans are being swamped with the sale of Halloween paraphernalia from the U.S. and are fighting it, trying to preserve their Day of the Dead."

"Well," said Paul. "The Catholics took the day from some other people, so why shouldn't the Americans take it from them? And the Mexicans keep their Day of the Dead? After all, holidays are for the people celebrating and the merchants making money."

"I'll agree with half of that," put in Fr. Flynn.

"It really doesn't matter to anyone, anyway," said Paul. "I think the protest against Halloween has more to to with not buying more American, waste I'll say rather than goods, than it does with preserving a supposed old Mexican custom. And it *does* give to us Mexicans another Holiday which we would not have otherwise."

"You can see how we waste our time," said Fr. Flynn. "And what's new with you, Magali."

That afternoon, just after three, Magali was sitting in the Carolo, having coffee alone at a table, when in came Roberto and Don Romualdo. Roberto headed straight for Magali and asked if they could join her. Magali of course said yes, and Roberto and Don Romualdo pulled out chairs and sat down, ordering coffee from the girl who rushed over to them when they had finished being seated and adjusting their chairs.

Magali waited for them to be served and to take a first sip of their coffees.

Don Romualdo began, asking her how she was coming with her investigations. Magali knew that in Puebla 'investigation' meant 'research,' as a researcher at the University was called in Spanish an *"investigador."*

Magali told Don Romualdo of her research efforts. She found a book about the *Historia de la Iglesia en México,* which gave a good overall view of the Church—all about the Jesuits and Franciscans, the expulsions and disenfranchisments, the confiscations of Church goods and properties—a book about church architecture, and one about the churches in Puebla. She, of course, was just exploring the general scope of the subject matter at this time, not going yet into too much detail.

Don Romualdo suggested she check a book about local legends, saying, "Language is changed by the people who use it, and in the field of religion the beliefs and customs of the people were sometimes more important in such change than the teachings of the Church." He told her about some private libraries, and about certain professors who had their own collections in their offices—books that were purchased by, and were technically the property of, the University. Magali, meanwhile, had taken out a pad and was taking everything down.

Don Romualdo poured out more information and suggestions, and Magali took it all down in her note pad. They discussed language and old books, their authors, and the times in which they wrote. All of this was in Spanish, and Roberto sat through it all, listening to their exchanges. He noticed that as their conversation wore on, Magali appeared to mimic Don Romualdo, and in the mimicing her Spanish was improving—her pronunciation, her choice of words. He noted how that was the way a child learns language, and here Magali was unconsiously doing the same.

Soon the conversation had turned and they were talking about Don Romualdo's problems. His huge pile of uncatalogued books on the large table in his Lafragua. And suddenly it came. Magali had suggested that she might join his volunteers for at least a few hours a week. She was sure she could spare them, somehow. She suggested that, though she really knew nothing about the preservation of old books, she could help in the sorting of the books on the large table. She could sort them by size, by bindings. It shouldn't take much intelligence to do that. She could collect together Volumes I, II, III where they existed, put together those of similar bindings or size, where in some cases they would be from the same publisher. Others could later do the important sorting—by author or subject matter. And she could put in a few minutes at a time at it without disturbing his other assistants, or even an hour or so when she could spare it. It could go quite well, and she thought it could be fun. Don Romualdo said her offer was most generous, and he would consider it and see if something could be worked out.

And then they had to leave. They had been at it for more than an hour and had consumed three cups of coffee each. They said goodbyes, and as Magali walked off toward her apartment, she realized how it was true that much of the work of the University was done in cafes—outside the regular work environment with its coercive demands—in cafes, consuming good Mexican coffee, where one could participate in earnest, for the love of the work, the discussions, negotiations.

On Tuesday Magali arrived about nine to the ILE, early for a Tuesday. Fr. Flynn was sitting in the faculty lounge. She checked the bulletin board for anything new, while Fr. Flynn approached her back. He said in a low voice into her ear that he had something to talk to her about, and they both left the lounge and stopped near the center of the court. Fr. Flynn said he had two new members to the club, and that they were going to explore a tunnel in the afternoon. Would Magali like to go along to see what it's like. She thought she wouldn't like to, but she couldn't resist and said, yes, she would.

Fr. Flynn said it would probably be a little dirty so she had better wear proper clothing. He suggested jeans, to protect the legs; a long-sleeved shirt; a light jacket if she had an old one, probably a wind-breaker. Magali stopped him, got out a pen and some paper, and said she had better take some notes. When she got those items noted on the paper, Fr. Flynn continued with: a cap, even a baseball cap would do; work gloves or gardening gloves if she had some; a bandana or large kerchief or scarf because it might get dusty; a flashlight, two would be better; and anything else she might think would be needed. They were going to meet at three in the Villa Rica.

Magali arrived exactly on time with the equipment she could bring. She brought two two-celled flashlights and a penlight in her pocket. She wore jeans and a long-sleeved cotton shirt. No jacket; no gloves; but yes, both baseball cap and an old but still presentable scarf.

Fr. Flynn and the two boys were already seated at a table having coffee. Magali sat down and ordered one for herself. Fr. Flynn introduced the two boys to Magali and suggested they tell her something about themselves, and Magali could do the same.

The first was a young Irish-American named Kevin Murphy. It was a wonder Fr. Flynn found him in Puebla, because he was perfect for the job. He was only twenty-two years old, about five foot eleven, reddish brown hair, a typical young American boy. He had just graduated that year from Georgia Tech in civil engineering. He said he wanted to work as an ex-pat.

"What's an ex-pat," asked Magali.

Kevin explained it meant "ex-patriot" and applied to anyone who worked in a foreign country. His father was one for many years. He worked at building a road in Peru, in the Amazon area, as well as roads in Arabia and Thailand. The pay was very good and one had lots of leave time to do some travelling. And you got to work on some really fantastic projects.

Kevin was at the UPA for a year to study Spanish for his future career. At the same time he taught a course called "English for Engineers." He got the usual thousand dollars a month for the teaching, which was more than enough for him. He figured he was really a student there; the teaching was for him just another course he was taking, for in it he learned a lot of Spanish for engineers.

The other boy was Mexican, from Cuetzalan, a town in the mountains in the northeast part of the State of Puebla. He said it was quite a tourist spot and that Magali should try to go to see it.

His name was José Hurtado, but he went by the knickname of "Pepe." He was a *pasante* in civil engineering at the UPA. He was still trying to get either a thesis or a project approved for his degree. He was twenty-three, and about the same size and build as Kevin, and they both looked a good pair of young men. Father Flynn knew both of the boys, but this was the first time they had met each other. They were certainly well chosen for the club.

In the way of equipment they brought each a pick, a flashlight, and suitable clothing. In addition, Kevin brought a folding shovel (it looked like war surplus), and a coil of nylon rope no more than a quarter, or at the most three-eights, of an inch in diameter. The rope was not too long, probably about 25 or 50 feet—so it appeared to Magali.

Magali told the boys about herself, her education at Boston University, and her current project in Puebla.

They talked some more about the club and finished their coffees. Both of the boys were eager to get started. Fr. Flynn said the tunnel they were going to investigate was the one that led north from the Cathedral toward the *Convento de Santo Domingo*. And with that they got up, gathered their gear, and left to begin the first club "exploration."

On the next day at the end of Magali's class, after the students had left, Roberto, who had stayed behind, came up to Magali's desk, where she was still putting her books and papers into her briefcase, and said he had to talk with her. He suggested a small cafe on *4 Norte,* which was on the way to her apartment anyway, and she agreed with that, finished her packing, and went with him. In the cafe Roberto found them a table a bit back and to one side, somewhat private, and ordered two coffees.

"So," said Magali. "What's the big problem?"

"No problem," responded Roberto. "I talked with Don Romualdo and now I have to ask you if you were serious about joining those who are helping him with the books."

"Yes, of course."

"Well, I have to ask because it's not just any work. It's very important work, and, in a certain way, very dangerous work. Not for the people doing it," he quickly added. "For the books. They could be damaged or, worse still, stolen. Don Romualdo cannot let just anyone into his area."

"I can see that. I understand."

"In order to maintain some sort of control over the work, and those who are helping him with it, he has created a kind of society of his helpers. A secret society. He calls it 'Ex-Libris.' It has its own rules, such as they are. You have to swear an oath. A very serious oath.

"It's not a bad thing. The work is important. And the members are all really nice—all students, so always some leave and new ones come.

"You can see that new members must be well chosen. They are normally selected from among friends and acquaintances. Then they are screened to see if they are really suited for the work and trustworthy. After that the members vote on whether or not to admit them to the society. If approved, they are invited to join, and if they accept, they are admitted."

"I can see that."

"Well, we have talked about you. In your case Don Romualdo has decided in your favor. And if he decides, there is no vote of the membership. It remains only for you to accept."

"You mean I'm invited to join?"

"Yes. If you want to. I have to respond this afternoon to Don Romualdo so he can gather the members for your admittance."

"Well, I do want to. I accept. I'm honored."

"Great! We shall have a meeting tomorrow at 10:00 in Don Romualdo's Lafragua. Nothing fancy. Come as you are, as they say. Normally we have our meetings on the fourth Thursday of the month, at nine in the morning at Don Romualdo's Lafragua. We had the regular meeting for September last week. This is a special meeting. The next regular monthly meeting won't be until October the 27th. We usually just talk over the work we have to schedule. Don Romualdo will probably give you a free reign with your work until you know enough about the preservation process to get involved in it. It will be great having you with us. So, tomorrow at 10:00."

Magali went home for lunch, feeling elated and excited. She looked forward to exploring among the books in Don Romualdo's Lafragua. Who knows what might be there? She was interested in the books not for her own project, but for the joy of examining them, like a little girl playing with old necklaces and brooches, like they were pirate treasure.

She arrived before nine at the main iron gate to Don Romualdo's Lafragua, which had been left open. When she entered, Don Romualdo himself came forward to bring her upstairs, to the back of a sort of mezzanine. Under a very high-mounted, semi-opaque window, like those in half basements in the States, were seven other people, seated around a long wooden table.

"*Bueno, bueno,*" said Don Romualdo. At that moment Roberto entered and joined them, and after a few niceties had been exchanged all around, the Master addressed the group.

"I have called you today to introduce to you a new member of our little group—chosen especially by me."

"But, Magali, before you accept to be part of our . . . conspiracy," said Don Romualdo, looking to see the reaction of Magali at this word, "let me explain completely what our society is all about. And, if you decide not to join us, we trust we can we count on your discretion concerning our existence and our work?"

"Of course!" protested Magali. "Of course!"

She sat in the chair that was offered to her, to one side. A brilliant yellow light glowed at the window, and then descended into the room, forming a pale, warm, and golden, little round stain over the surface of the wooden table. And the sound of voices and images of color came through, as people, probably students, moved about in the patio above.

"*Bien,*" approved *El Maestro*. "I don't know how much Roberto has told you, but it doesn't matter. You are aware of the fact that books have been and are stolen, every year, from our precious library. But maybe you are not aware that these thefts come, many times, under names such as 'official expropriations,' 'gifts,' and others, and are ordered by the same library higher authorities who are supposed to be protecting a precious and fragile national patrimony. During my whole life's work at Lafragua, I have had to accept a situation that I, alone, could not fight. Any protest from me would have been taken as a disobedience to a superior authority. I would not only loose my position here, but the books would be left to the mercy of anyone—lost forever."

He poured water from a bottle of Junghans into a glass which, sitting on the table in front of him, reflected the light from the window into a rainbow of color. This hit Magali's hair, producing a wave of iridescent sparkle. The men at the table looked at Magali. She blushed. *El Maestro* continued.

"On the other hand, the authorities have left me to myself to do a work that nobody cared to undertake. During my fifty-odd years with the University, I have acquired the reputation of a scholar and a decent worker. I do a job that nobody wants to do. I am paid a pittance to do it, and I do not interfere with the administration or get into any political activities. I am the perfect non-entity to perform a non-job." He stopped the protests of the group. "Please, I know I am among friends—the real value of this job resides in its anonymity. I am free to do as I please. And, during the years and months and weeks and long, long hours working with the books, I elaborated a plan to save them. A plan so simple and yet so sound . . . a master plan."

He waited to see the impact of this statement on Magali, then continued. He had gotten up, and was now nervously pacing the small area in front the table where his helpers sat.

"There is no inventory of the books, nor classification system, nor any other method of proper library technique, except for my own list and my own inventory, which I keep in a secret drawer in my desk. I alone have the key to this drawer. I alone know it exists. And my group: the group of people I put together and organized to clean, classify, and—put away—some of the most precious, older, and unique books of Lafragua. Books that belong as a patrimony not only to Mexico, but to the whole human race."

His eyes were now shining, and Magali felt a chill along her spine. She had a sense of unreality, like when she was a kid, and her mother took her to an old Boris Karlof movie. Unreality and almost fear. Don Romualdo continued, but Roberto noticed the uneasiness of Magali and touched her hand in a friendly and supporting gesture.

"We are gathered here, this morning, to welcome Miss Magali Smith, if she accepts us, as a new member of our group. Magali, you will have, no doubt, questions. Please don't hesitate to ask."

"Maestro, you said 'put away.' What do you mean?"

He smiled, a warm, paternal smile, to Magali.

"Of course. What I mean is into a safe and secure place, in this same building. Each of the members has a number of books to take care of: clean, classify, wrap in special paper and plastic, and then put in a wooden box, which will be placed in that secret place known only to me. But, don't worry. There is a letter that, in case something happens to me, will give directions as to how to find this cache. A separate copy of this letter is addressed to each of you—and I will also make a copy for Magali. And you will have to swear, Magali, on the Bible, under penalty of losing your soul, like the other members of our Ex-Libris group, that you will not open that letter nor divulge the location of the secret place until after you are sure that I am dead. So the ultimate security lies with each and every member of Ex-Libris.

"Any more questions?"

Magali said no, and Don Romualdo gave Roberto the order to arrange for her taking the oath. which would make her one of the group.

"... *so pena de la salvación de mi alma.*"

18

THE REMINGTON AFFAIR

The sun was shining and the sky was a solid, deep blue by the time Paul turned into the *Jardín de los Sapos* that Sunday morning. He felt good. People were scurrying about, carrying wares to their various places within the open air market, and arranging them on the tables or on the mats spread to occupy their territory.

He walked through the vendors to his own shop, opened his three locks, and entered, thinking to arrange his own space better for whatever visitors might be curious enough to venture in. But, thinking again, he left things as they were and decided to first have a drink at *Los Gatos*. Locking the door again, with only one lock this time since he would be back soon, he began threading his way back through the market toward the cafe.

At that early hour there were several empty tables and he sat at one and ordered coffee. He sat watching the milling crowd. most of them assistants to vendors, still bringing various things from nearby stores or vehicles to their display areas. Magali was not there yet. He sat alone—just sat and stared about him as the fair was being made ready.

He sat for at least some twenty minutes, nursing his coffee and idly looking at the movement of the people at the fair, now with the first customers of the day arriving. Suddenly his vision became focussed on one spot—a reflex action—and he became alert to a strange figure of something being set up almost in front of him. Midway across the plaza, between the west and the east sides, there was a low wall, just south of a small stairway of about three steps which led from the west half of the plaza down to the east half, leading from the cafe area toward the area where the old ladies had their cooking pots and fires and some tables for those who ate the *chalupas* and such that they prepared. On that wall, on the end by the steps, some people were arranging something for display. Something very heavy, dark, and of irregular shape. He had to see what it was. He called the waiter, paid his bill, and went over to the wall, moving slowly, looking at other things laid out for display along his way. He tried not to look interested in his destination.

He managed to walk by it first, descending the steps to the east side and looking at several of the displays in that area near *5 Oriente*. Then he meandered in his way toward the steps again and went up them right next to the wall. He looked at the object on his way up, and stopped just as he passed it, turned ninety degrees and looked back at it. He then turned fully about to face the object, and stood observing it for a while. Then he went closer to get a good look and began examining it.

It was a bronze statue, a casting. It was on a bronze base, and the base was fixed onto a piece of green marble. The base was like a rounded trapezoid. The marble was about two inches thick, and the base was about an inch and a quarter or so. The statue was of four American cowboys on horses in full gallop. They were brandishing guns and ropes. He examined closely the base itself, and on it there was affixed a small copper nameplate which said, "Coming Through the Rye," and under that the name of the artist, Frederick Remington.

Frederick Remington. It sounded familiar. He'd better check this out carefully.

He went on around the plaza to the south, looking at other displays, trying to appear nonchalant. He rounded the plaza on the south and moved toward his own shop. He went in, as if nothing had happened. Once inside he quickly found a book on art and looked through the index for Frederick Remington. There he was, an American painter and sculptor specializing in scenes of the Old West. He had actually lived in the West, which probably accounted for his having it as his subject matter. He found another book on Western art and under the works of Frederick

Remington he looked for the statue he had just seen, and there it was: "Coming Through the Rye." There was a small picture of it, and yes, it was the same. Maybe he had found something. He tried to not get excited. But it was hard to contain himself. Maybe he *had* found something. He quickly read all there was in the book on Frederick Remington and his art.

He finished with the other books in his shop just before noon but hadn't found anything more on Remington or on the statue. He locked up his shop and headed for Sanborn's, in the center of the city, just a block from the *Zócalo*. There he explored the books they had on sale, checking all of the art books, and even checking the art magazines in their magazine section. In some he found some ads for Remington statues or paintings, but no prices. If you have to ask the price, you can't afford to buy, he thought. But from both books and magazines he found no new information. Now well past the hour of one, he decided to get a sandwich for lunch in the restaurant. Sanborn's had a fairly good restaurant, but a bit pricey for most Mexicans. He didn't care. He was more concerned about his health at that instant; he knew he had to keep with good nutrition in his new undertaking. Good health was good business, especially in times of stress. And he now felt stress. As to the cost: He would consider it as a business cost, chargeable to his Remington Adventure.

Back to *Los Sapos,* and the statue was still there. Paul made another round of the exhibits in the plaza before arriving again in front of the statue. He stood for a while looking at it. He once more approached it and examined the nameplate, the signature, and the bronze base.

Only after a minute or two of this did he stand back a bit, look it over generally, and then approach the woman who was apparently the owner—or the dealer. He asked her what was she asking for it.

"Four thousand pesos," she replied.

At the current rate of exchange that was more than a thousand dollars. He mentally calculated it and came to about one thousand two hundred. He thought for a while. About right for a Mexican sale. But what would it be in the States? And if it is an authentic Remington, it surely must be much more than that.

He asked her if she could give him the address of her shop, so that he could visit her, perhaps, before the next Sunday fair, and she gave it to him. It turned out to be just down *5 Oriente* about half a block. He thanked her and continued moving through the display, as if his stopping there was just a pause in his shopping tour of the fair, but still giving her hope that he would be visiting her shop soon.

On Monday, just after his class ending at noon, Paul called a dealer friend in San Diego and asked him to find a dealer, probably in L.A., who could handle a Frederick Remington statue. He called back after five and his friend had the information he wanted. He had a dealer in L.A. who actually specialized in Remington statues and paintings. Paul took down the name, address, and phone number and said he would call the L.A. dealer in the morning, profusely thanking his friend and acknowledging to him his debt and his eternal gratitude.

Magali had not gone to *Los Sapos* on Sunday because she was exploring another tunnel with Kevin and Pepe. Fr. Flynn did not participate, it being Sunday and he felt he should not be doing anything like work on that day. The boys were in agreement about Sunday. They didn't mind Fr. Flynn not being there because that gave them more freedom for their own spelunking. Magali had found the first day's exploration not too appealing. Her task had been holding the flashlight and dragging along the gear not actually carried by the boys, passing one thing or another to them as they called for it. The work was very dusty. The times she went since then were just as bad. She went through mud and water in one of the tunnels, and that was a bit scary. Then she began to have her bad dreams again, dreams of being lost in an ancient tunnel, which she thought was from her childhood in the convent school in France. She decided Sunday night to quit active participation in the exploration.

On Monday she checked in at the faculty lounge and asked for Fr. Flynn. The teachers there told her he had gone out for coffee somewhere. Magali thanked them and headed out to the Villa Rica. And there was Fr. Flynn, sitting alone with a large Cappuccino.

"Hello, Fr. Flynn," said Magali.

"Hello, Magali," responded Fr. Flynn.

"Just the man I was looking for," began Magali.

And she told him of her dreams and the tunnels as being the cause of their reoccurrence. She said she should quit active participation in exploring the tunnels. But she did want to remain in the Club. She could help with the paperwork involved—the record keeping, the map making, anything needed other than going down again into the tunnels. Besides, the boys were doing quite well by themselves. She could help, maybe, in finding a replacement. Maybe a young man who could do the work and who knew something about the city.

Fr. Flynn tried to reassure her in her problem. He was sure everything was for the best. Anyway, the tunnels were no place for a scholar like herself. And God knew there was certainly some need in the paper end of the task. He could use help in getting all his notes and other research together, but he didn't want to use her as a research assistant. She had her own research to do. But handle the findings from the tunnel explorations? Yes, she could help with that. Finding one's way through the maze was important, but the fact of getting from one entrance to another was only part of it. There were many side entrances encountered along the way. It might work out to be an advantage if Magali, as an outsider, could get the information, including measurements and descriptions, from the boys, or whoever else got into the Club and helped with the explorations. She could approach the whole exploration in a detached, methodical manner, thereby assuring an unbiased but critical recording and evaluation of the experiences gathered in the explorations. Yes, it could be quite an improvement in the organization of the Club's operations. By all means, she should quit the tunnel work and start organizing the paper work.

"But now, join me with a Cappuccino," said Fr. Flynn. "And how about some pastries? My treat."

L.A. was Pacific Time while Puebla was Central, so Paul had to wait again on Tuesday until his class ended at noon to call the dealer about the Remington. By then it was after ten in L.A., a reasonable hour to expect the dealer to be in his office, or at least someone there to talk to.

He got the dealer himself and told him of his discovery, describing as best he could the statue, the stone base, the nameplate, and the signature. He asked how much it was worth.

"Probably two-fifty," said the dealer.

"Two hundred and fifty?" exclaimed Paul. "Dollars?"

"Oh, no," said the dealer. "I'm sorry. We speak in thousands. It would be two hundred and fifty thousand—dollars. And of course I would charge a commission for placing it."

"Of course," said Paul. "And how much would that be?"

"Somewhere between fifteen and twenty percent. It would be higher if I got a better price."

It all seemed too good to Paul, and he said he could agree to that.

The dealer asked him if he could take some pictures and measurements of the statue and send them to him. Paul agreed, and said he would call him when he sent the pictures so that he could be on the look-out for them.

In a great mood, almost dancing, Paul went for lunch.

Paul had a date that evening with Sue, to take her to a piano concert at the American University. He was in an exceptionally good mood for seeing her and put on his best dark suit for the occasion. It was always great to go well dressed to these social things, and Sue always looked a great addition to his appearance. He drove his Vocho to her apartment, arriving early, and took her out to dinner before the concert. The university was way out near Cholula, so he had to time everything well, eating in Puebla and then driving out to the university.

The concert was piano—Chopin and Mozart. All very well done, but not what he was used to in San Diego and Los Angeles. Still, he could not complain, and he did his duty applauding.

After the concert he took Sue to her apartment and, of course, went up with her. She went directly into the bedroom and put away the stole she had wrapped herself in against the chill of the autumn evening. Paul sat down on the couch in the living room. She had a nice two bedroom apartment, with a living room and a separate study for her school work—what would be a den for a man like Paul. She came into the living room and offered a drink, to which Paul readily accepted, with the suggestion of a snifter of cognac. She went to the kitchen, got the bottle and poured two snifters, and brought them into the living room, giving one to Paul. She sat with him on the sofa and took a sip of her cognac.

"So. What's new in the antique trade?" she asked.

"Nothing much," replied Paul. "Everything as usual. Nothing to get excited about."

"Nothing?" pursued Sue.

"No." repeated Paul.

"Come on," said Sue. "I know you. You've been nervous and fidgety since the start of the evening. You couldn't sit still in the concert. Something's up."

"Well, not really up. But there is a possibility. Nothing definite. Maybe nothing in the end. I'm still exploring it."

"Must be something good, the way you've been acting. Tell me about it."

Paul took another sip of his cognac and placed the snifter on the cocktail table in front of the sofa. Sue took another sip from hers but kept it, looking at Paul, expectantly, like a good listener. Paul sat a moment in silence, warming to his subject. He looked at her, smiled, and began.

"I was at *Los Sapos* Sunday and saw what might turn out to be something of some value. But I haven't really determined that yet. It was a bronze statue which might be by Frederick Remington. It was called 'Coming Through The Rye.' Four cowboys on horse, coming at full gallop, waving pistols and quirts. They were affixed to a bronze base, and that was mounted on a piece of green marble.

"I've made contact with a dealer in L.A. to sell it in the States. He wants pictures and measurements of it, which I shall see about getting tomorrow. If all works out, it should get a very good price in the U.S. Of course, that's a big *if*, but I'm hopeful. For good or bad I have to go through the routine of checking it out and arranging for the deal with L.A. That's enjoyable in itself, so nothing much is really lost in going through the motions. And there is always the possibility of a successful operation. I guess that's what has got me somewhat fidgety."

"It sounds pretty good," said Sue, "but be careful. Don't get too hopeful for success; it might lead to a terrible let down if it doesn't go through. You know there are an awfully lot of reproductions of Remingtons floating around. To find a good one is rare. Probably even more rare is finding a good one in Mexico. The odds for that must be really high. Don't hurt yourself."

"Don't worry," responded Paul. "I approach antiques with a wary mind. I learned while working in the trade in San Diego to be very ordered and systematic. I worked under a very good teacher—a jew, even. The whole thing is part merchandising and part detective mystery. One has to be part historian and part craftsman. Add to that, scientist. A very methodical experimental research type scientist. That's the way I go about it. After the truth and value are established with respect to an object, only then does the trader enter in and one has to begin to control greed and expectation with barter skills, with acting and dissembling. I know odds can be great, but so can the payoff."

"Some advice!" said Sue. "Your odds are like those of winning the lottery."

"If you like long odds and big payoffs," she added, "why don't you go down into the tunnels of Puebla, and under and around the churches? You know, I'm sure, about *El Sol de Puebla,* the Sun of Puebla, the gold monstrance?"

"No," answered Paul.

"Well. It's not Aztec gold. It was made by the local Mexicans around where the Spaniards put the city of Puebla. They collected their private gold, the earrings and bracelets of their wives and children, the small necklaces, and made from that a solid gold monstrance for the church and presented it to the Jesuits of Puebla. The legend says it shone like the sun, hence its name. When the Jesuits got kicked out of Mexico in the 1700's, it disappeared. Find that! It's probably worth millions!"

* * *

"*Después de la caída del sol, el 24 de junio de 1767, reunió el Virrey Marqués de Croix en su Palacio a la Real Audiencia, al Arzobispo D. Francisco Antonio de Lorenza, y a otros funcionarios, a una Junta secreta.*

" *En élla expuso haber recibido órden del señor D. Carlos III, que entonces regía las Españas, para el extrañamiento de la Compañía de Jesús de sus dominios, pidiéndoles su parecer sobre el modo de darle cabal y debido cumplimiento. En seguida les presentó el pliego, en que se les comunicaba la real disposición que había recibido de la Corte, por conducto del primer Ministro Conde de Aranda, bajo tres cubiertas, o sobres, cada cual con su sello. En el primero, únicamente constaba la persona a quien se dirigía. Sobre el segundo se leía: Pena de la vida, no abriréis este pliego hasta el 24 de junio a la caída de la tarde.*'

"*Cuando se abrió el pliego, se encontraron instrucciones sobre el arresto de los religiosos jesuitas, y los nombres de los indivíduos que debían llevar a cabo la comisión, asi como otros pormenores para su exito.*

"*Los miembros de la Junta entonces procedieron a abrir el último pliego, en la cual se encontró lo siguiente:*

" *'Os revisto de toda mi autoridad y de todo mi poder para que se mande la expatriación de los Padres Jesuitas de Puebla.*'

"*Los Padres, advertidos por los fieles quienes tenían algunas personas de confianza en el servicio de la casa del Arzobispo, se apresuraron a salvaguardar algunos preciosos pergaminos y otros teseros en receptores construídos en los pasillos secretos que unían la biblioteca del convento y la iglesia de la Concepción, y cuya situación estaba escondida y secreta, y era sólo de conocimiento de algunos de los Padres quienes habían jurado no dar jamás a conocerla, so pena de la salvación de sus almas.*

"*Mientras tanto, procedieron a confiscar, por la Corona Española, los bienes temporales de los jesuitas, incluyendo sus bibliotecas.*" [1]

---

[1] From private notes of Dr. José Manuel Guerra.

19

DON ROMUALDO'S STORY

About nine on Wednesday Paul went to the shop of the statue seller. Fortunately she was in, and he asked to see the statue again. He explained that he might have a buyer for it, but his client, being out of town, asked him to send him some pictures of it first, so he asked if he could take some pictures of the statue to send to his client. She said yes, and called a man she had helping her around the shop, which included a court and some other rooms which were some kind of work areas. It appeared that she also had an operation of making pots and wrought iron things. The man and Paul lifted the statue from where it sat in a corner and on the floor of a window area displaying onto the street. They set it on a kind of counter separating the window area from the shop's entrance area. The door for this was just inside the main entranceway to the building.

Paul looked over the statue very carefully, noting the condition of its various parts and taking overall measures with a tape rule. When he had finished, he thanked the woman very much and asked if he could come about the same hour the next morning to take the pictures, to which she assented. He offered to help the man move the statue back into its corner. The woman, however, said to leave it there. He said thank you again and wished her a good day.

He went to a photo shop on the *Calle Cinco de Mayo*, where next door there was a long-established cafe. He bought two rolls of 35mm color film with which to take the pictures. He then went into the cafe for a cup of coffee and to rest up a bit before his eleven o'clock class.

That Thursday there was a meeting of Ex-Libris, on the third Thursday this month instead of the fourth because of the holidays at the end of the month—All Saints Day and All Souls Day, the latter of these celebrated in Mexico as the Day of the Dead; and, for some, the American Halloween, which some thought was replacing the Day of the Dead, though they were actually two very different celebrations and on different days, the one on October 31st, and the other on November 2nd.

Magali liked her work at Lafragua. She came to know through the old books she examined some of the flavor of life in that old Mexico of the books. She also enjoyed many conversations with Don Romualdo and came to really sympathize with his cause. Over time Magali came to know the inner Don Romualdo, and his story.

Don Romualdo had begun to work in Lafragua at the age of fourteen. When a small boy he had demonstrated a passion for reading and a love of books. He was accustomed to go the library of the University to help Master Rodriguez to dust the old parchment volumes, those with fire brands on their spines, which had come from the treasures of the convents that had been confiscated by Benito Juárez after his Revolution, his "War of the Reform."

When the time came to enter the *Prepa* (the preparatory school), Master Rodriguez, who suffered in his breathing and was at an advanced age, retired, and Don Romualdo assumed the position of Librarian Assistant, which, in those times, only required that he spend a few hours in the library putting books back on the shelves and watching to see that none were stolen.

There was no system for cataloging the books, and since no one watched either the entrance or the exit, it was of course very easy to steal them (not counting the "official" requisitions). Don Romualdo eventually finished his studies for *Licenciado* in the evening school and retained his position *sin título* as librarian assistant of the Lafragua.

Since there weren't sufficient funds to support a real librarian (there never is for those projects which are really important but not politically desirable), the Director of Libraries was happy to leave everything to Don Romualdo, paying him a meager salary and giving him no assistance in materials or employees.

Don Romualdo saw his life's dream realized: he was alone, in charge of a treasure of incalculable value whose importance very few knew. He employed most of his time and effort in trying to organize a system to catalogue his precious volumes; but much of his time, especially the nights, was also dedicated to reading. He read everything that fell within his sight. He even read in foreign languages that he did not at first understand, and in that way he learned Latin, French, English, and Russian. He acquired an extraordinary knowledge of esoteric subjects, especially of calligraphy and typography. Little by little the exterior world ceased to exist for him.

Though he was young and not bad looking, he declined all invitations to go out with the other young men of his age to the bars and cafes where they gathered. His mother was always worried about his misogynous tendencies, but, in the end, she gave up and accepted a situation that, at any rate, she could not change.

Don Romualdo (they all called him Don, in spite of his youth) gained the respect of the successive Directors of Libraries; and since he kept what was called "a low profile," and never asked for funds, except in extreme cases (such as after a particularly strong earthquake when many of the book cases were destroyed and the beams in the library ceiling had to be reinforced to prevent their caving in), and never for himself, the Administration left him alone in his position, in which, being one of those semi-official and little known posts, no one was interested anyway.

It was he who undertook the establishment of a time period for study of the books in the library, and got it stipulated that no book more than 100 years old could be taken out of the library. It was he who began, with a lot of work and personal effort, the transfer of certain precious books from the public Library to his private work area (with authorization of the Director), and the cataloging of volumes, first by order of age, and later by language and by subject. The director of Lafragua was aware that Don Romualdo worked during his own time in his private work area on the restoration of certain books, and he was given complete liberty in that since he was held by all in great esteem (so long as he complied with the administrative work rules, and did not collect overtime pay).

Don Romualdo did not trust foreigners (he had had a terrible experience with that consultant librarian from the U.S. who began to throw out all old books—those more than ten years old—to the patio, where they remained exposed to the elements until Don Romualdo and a group of students managed to rescue them). But after working for a while with Magali, they became friends. He had found in her one with whom he could communicate his preoccupation for the preservation of his books, as well as one schooled in languages and ancient texts who helped him in his translations, and an expert in calligraphy; and she in him, a friend.

Again early in the morning (for him) about nine, Paul showed up on Thursday at the statue owner's shop to take pictures of the statue. The same man was there and he had placed a table in the court, in the shade, on which to set the statue. Paul helped him to move the statue out to the table. They turned it so that the front could get the best light, though still subdued under the roof-like extension which came out from the area between the first and second floors on one side of the court. Paul got his camera and equipment out and made ready to take the pictures. It was an old camera, an Exakta single lens reflex. He had to use a hand-held light meter to gauge the time for each shot, each being of a different angle and sometimes at a different distance. It was an old fashioned way of doing things, but it gave great results.

Paul took the film immediately to the photo shop on the *Calle Cinco de Mayo* and asked that the pictures be made as soon as possible, with three prints of each. Then he went next door to the cafe for a coffee before going to the ILE and his class. Things were going well so far, so he thought.

* * *

On Sunday Magali was at *Los Sapos* again, things getting back to their normal routine. She had made the rounds of the displays early in the morning and sat at a table at *Los Gatos*, having her Sidral, watching what had come to be the regular show of Sunday morning. She took it slow-and-easy that day, glad to be out of going through dirty tunnels. She was now getting settled into her work of keeping and organizing records for the Club and it was going well. She had been right to quit the tunnels. It was no work for a woman. It wasn't that she wasn't up to the work. She had a good body, with good muscles, though on the slim side. She wasn't a P.E. major, but she was a good and active swimmer, and if she had to do something physical, she felt she could do it as well as anyone. But she felt more comfortable with books, with words and writing. It probably came from her having been a student almost all her life. Grade school, high school, college, an M.A., and now she was trying for a Ph.D. Her life had been a life with words and she liked it that way. Let the men have the action.

She had been sitting there for a little more than a half hour, watching the development of the fair and reflecting on her present situation, when Roberto came by and joined her at her table. He ordered a beer and she ordered another Sidral. He asked her how things were going and what she had been up to. They talked of Ex-Libris, and soon Magali had let slip about her work with Fr. Flynn and the tunnels. It was then that she got the idea of Roberto taking her place in the active work of the Club. She told him of her involvement, of her quitting the exploration part, and her now being secretary and record keeper for the Club. She suggested maybe he might want to replace her. She told him of Kevin and Pepe. She told him of the fun of exploring. Roberto had tried on occasion to interrupt her, but he saw that her enthusiasm about what she and the others were doing would not permit it. Finally she stopped, and he said "Okay."

"What?" she asked.

"Okay. I'll try it."

"You will?" she let out, more in surprise than anything.

They both sat quietly for a second, and then Roberto asked, "What do I do?"

"Oh," said Magali. "I . . . I guess I should talk to Fr. Flynn. I know he'll want you. Then I'll get back to you. I'll probably see him tomorrow. I might have something to tell you by class time. I'm sure it will be okay. You'll like the Club."

Meanwhile, Paul had come to his shop. After arranging things therein for a while, he left, locking all three locks, and began walking about *Los Sapos*. Of course he gravitated toward the Remington statue, which was in the same place—on the wall near the steps at the north end of the *Jardín*. The *Café Los Gatos* was also at that end and, inevitably, Paul saw Magali and Roberto and wandered nonchalantly over to join them.

Paul knew of Roberto, but he had never been introduced. Magali did the honors, mentioning that Roberto was one of her students. They began to talk, and soon Magali asked Paul what he thought of the Remington statue, adding that she saw him looking at it.

"It looks pretty good," said Paul, "but I don't know that it's genuine."

Magali responded by talking about Frederick Remington's life in the West and his paintings, drawings, and sculptures. She appeared to know quite a lot about Remington.

"One problem with Remington," she said, "is that he was probably too good. Because of that, many people, to this day, have copied his style. There are many paintings and statues that look just like the work he did."

"That one over there," she added, "is, of course, one of his more famous ones, 'Coming Through the Rye.' A good copy. You know there's another just like it in the lobby of the Hotel San Leonardo?"

20

ROBERTO JOINS THE CLUB

Monday morning Magali checked in at about nine to the faculty lounge of the ILE, paid her respects to the ladies, and looked over the bulletin board. Nothing on it of interest to her, she said her farewells as best she could and hurried out of the lounge and out of the ILE and over to the Villa Rica. Inside, as she had hoped, was Fr. Flynn, enjoying a Danish and a large Cappuccino.

"Again, just the one I wanted to see," said Magali as she placed her briefcase on one chair and pulled another back and sat on it.

"I have a replacement," she announced, ". . . for me . . . for the Club."

A waiter came over to get her order, the owner being occupied in the kitchen. Magali asked for the same that Fr. Flynn was having, and turned to Fr. Flynn to explain her last remark. She told him about Roberto, her student. She told him of his size and stamina, his studies and interests, and her own respect for him. She didn't tell him about Ex-Libris.

Fr. Flynn responded with, "It sounds good to me. We can use anyone we can find with strong arms and a strong back. And your recommendation is enough."

Her coffee and Danish arrived and Magali took a good bite of the Danish and had to wait until she had consumed it before she could say her thanks to Fr. Flynn for Roberto's acceptance.

"By the way," he said, "I'm calling for a meeting of the Club tomorrow at 3:00 p.m. We can meet in a second floor classroom at the ILE. I've got one reserved: Room 110, near the back. We'll go over our progress so far and our plan of work. I've found the mention of a more-or-less major private tunnel in an old book, and I want to find it and get into it. We'll have to mark it on our maps and be sure not to miss it when we get to where it's supposed to connect with the system. If you could get Roberto to come, it would be a good time to orient him to what we're doing, and for him to meet us all—especially Kevin and Pepe. I've already informed them and they'll be there. You see, I've also been wanting to see you. After the meeting we might retreat to a cafe for the equivalent of high tea."

They passed the rest of their morning coffee-to-get-started break discussing unimportant things while Magali sat nervously, yearning to tell Roberto the news. They parted before ten and Magali, not having an office of her own, went to read in the Social Sciences Library.

At her eleven o'clock class she waited outside the classroom, looking over the railing into the court below, until Roberto came. She met him outside the door and gave him the news: He was accepted into the Club. She also told him about the meeting of the Club on the next day, at 3:00 p.m., in room 110 of the ILE. She added that she would also be there, and so would Fr, Flynn, and Kevin and Pepe, the two active "explorers."

Paul, meanwhile, picked up the developed film and printed pictures at about ten that morning, and then went into the cafe next door to look them over and to have a coffee before his eleven o'clock class at the ILE. He found a table and sat, with his back to the wall. Looking around, he noticed that almost the same people came to the cafe at that hour of the morning. He ordered a *café Americano*, and while the waitress was fetching it, he looked over the prints.

They all looked good. He selected a set of six and placed them in a padded manila envelope he had already prepared to send to the dealer in Los Angeles. In it also went a letter he had prepared for the dealer. He marveled at how well ordered and prepared he was in doing all the necessary steps in this project.

He sealed the envelope and put that into a special DHL envelope for sending the pictures to the States. He couldn't trust the postal service with this kind of *envío*. After he had finished his coffee and paid his bill, with the customary *propina*, he took the envelope with him in his Vocho to the DHL office near the *Colonia La Paz*, where he sent it out as a letter with photographs, of no commercial value. From there he went to the ILE for his class.

When the class had ended, Paul went to the post office on *4 Norte* and from their public service phone called the dealer in L.A. He told the dealer he had taken the pictures and that they were on route to him via DHL. The dealer said that that was all very well, and that he would review the pictures and that Paul should call him back again at the end of the month.

"By the way," he added, "I don't know if I told you to check the foundry marks."

"Foundry marks?" exclaimed Paul. "No. You never said anything to me about foundry marks."

"Well," said the dealer, "I should have told you. On all of Remington's authentic castings there are foundry marks on the bottom of the base. That's the chief indication that the piece is probably genuine. 'Roman Bronze Works, N.Y.' is inscribed into the underside of the base, together with a casting number. There are thousands of surmoulages around, all of course counterfeits of the original castings. Check for these marks. If there is a number, let me know of it when you call back at the end of the month."

The next day, again at nine, Paul was at the shop of the statue owner, asking for a last look at the statue. The same man helped him to take it out to the table again, and helped to hold it tilted while Paul examined the underside of the base. It was a heavy statue and base, and Paul took a long time exploring every hidden part of the base. Finally, however, he had to let the man set the statue down. He could find no foundry marks. He thanked him and helped him to carry the statue again into the shop. He thanked the lady and said he had all of the information he was asked to obtain, and that he should get a response from his client by the end of the month, not too far away.

Paul then went to the Hotel San Leonardo to have a look at that statue. It was almost exactly like the one of *Los Sapos*. But its base was slightly different, not so large in area, and a slightly differently shaped trapezoid, but not too different. The horses and men were of exactly the same size as far as he could tell. It definitely looked like the same statue.

The statue was mounted on a bronze base, but that was not on a green marble nor any other stone base. It sat on a glass coffee table in the lobby of the hotel. This made it easy to look underneath the statue without tilting it or otherwise manhandling it. Paul managed to even lie on the floor with his head under the coffee table to look at its underside. He could move it and turn it on the table as needed. And he had a flashlight with him to give him good light for his examination. But this statue also was without foundry marks.

He left the hotel in spirits not as high as they were when the morning started. Two strike-outs. In the end, it appeared, they both must be copies. Not too far from the Carolo, he went there for some coffee and to collect his thoughts and get reanimated before his morning class. It looked like his great discovery had not panned out. But he was still alive, and he had gotten some more experience along the way. It might not have been such profitable experience in terms of results, but it was of some value in his having tried something new. Who knows? There might be something even more valuable than a Remington out there waiting to be discovered.

The Explorers Club of Puebla met at 3:00 p.m. in Room 110 on the second floor (American custom) at the ILE. Fr. Flynn was already there when Magali arrived promptly at three. Roberto arrived just after three and Magali introduced him to Fr. Flynn. The two went to a couple of chairs near one corner of the room and began to talk between themselves. Magali remained outside of the classroom, looking over the railing at the entrance to the court, watching for Kevin and Pepe.

Two other young men arrived, whom Magali did not know, and came up the stairs and toward her. They were looking at the door numbers of the rooms as they passed. They walked right by Magali and stopped at Room 110 and entered. Seeing Fr. Flynn in the corner with Roberto, they sat in two chairs along the wall opposite the door. When Fr. Flynn and Roberto were through, Fr. Flynn got up and went to the two new men. Roberto came out to where Magali was and stood with her, looking at the entrance to the ILE.

Roberto didn't say anything, and before he could, Kevin and Pepe came into the court, went to the stairs and up to where Magali and Roberto were. They were greeted by Magali, but neither they nor Roberto exchanged words. They all went into the classroom, Kevin and Pepe leading the way.

Kevin and Pepe grabbed some chairs in the front of what would otherwise be the class. Magali and Roberto took some chairs to their left. Fr. Flynn took the teacher's chair at the head of the classroom, on the other side of a small table. He suggested the others should grab some chairs and group themselves around the table, which they all did.

"Well," began Fr. Flynn (in Spanish). "We have some new members to the club which we should welcome, but let me start with presenting the old members. Ladies first, Miss Magali Smith, from the United States, who is here at the UPA teaching English at the ILE and doing some research for her Doctorate at Boston University. She of course already has her Master's. Then the men. Kevin Murphy is the *gringo*. He is teaching a course in 'English for Engineers,' and is studying Spanish. Kevin has just this past June received his Civil Engineering degree at Georgia Tech in the U.S. His buddy is José Hurtado, whom we call Pepe, Pepe is from Cuetzalan, and is a *pasante* in Civil Engineering at the UPA.

"Now for the new members. To Pepe's right is Tomás Llanos, from Puebla, and he too is a *pasante* in Civil Engineering at the UPA. His companion is Francisco Urrieta, whom we should call Paco. Paco is also from Puebla and is a history student at the UPA, in his third year, for whatever that means. On the left of Kevin is Magali's companion, or should I say *protegé*. He is Roberto Aguilar. Roberto is an intellectual compared to you others, a *pasante* in Psychology at the UPA. He also is a student of Magali's at the ILE. He tells me it is his third year at taking the course, not because he couldn't handle it, but because too many intervening opportunities got in the way of ever completing it and getting a grade. He says he takes it just to keep a hand in at being a student. As you *pasantes* in Mexico know, finally getting to be a *Licenciado* is many times a matter of political connections, or of just finding a professor who will take the time to read your thesis. This is just some side information that Paco probably should be aware of as he continues his years at the UPA. I should add that Roberto has several seasons of field archeology, so at least he is not new to the world of digging. And he is now the eldest of all the members, not counting myself. We don't really know Magali's age.

"Before we get to the main part of our meeting, I should like to propose some organization for our work. The two men Kevin and Pepe are already working as an exploration team, mostly digging their way through some tunnels we are studying. Kevin is the most educated, he having already received his Civil Engineering degree, and he is of course already teaching at the University. Pepe, however, is the eldest, and knows Spanish as his native language. Pepe, therefore has been acting as chief of exploration, and he has had to prepare all of the reports which go to Magali, our chief mapmaker, record keeper, and general Club Secretary and Treasurer, though we have as yet no treasure. I think Roberto should join with Kevin and Pepe. They can acquaint him with how they have been doing it so far, and he can add his experiences to their method.

"We can then form a second team, made up of Tomás and Paco. I think Tomás should be the team leader, since he is the elder and a *pasante* at the UPA. If it would be better to have Paco as leader, they may change after a spell of digging with Tomás in the lead. Kevin and Pepe have worked out who would be leader without any guidance from me, Tomás and Paco may choose to do the same after having had some experience of digging in the tunnels.

"I should say that Roberto has already told me that he has no ambition to be a leader. And, of course, Magali has a desk job that is enough to keep her busy.

"Now, as to the main task of the meeting. We shall try to go over our progress so far and our plan of future work.

"Wait, one more thing: Let's try to have a regular club
meeting every month, say every third Wednesday. I'll have this
room reserved for this time—3:00 p.m.—every third Wednesday
of the month, unless something comes up. In which case I shall
try to notify everyone. No meeting for December; that's
Christmas Holiday time!"

And so the meeting continued until about six, when they all
decided to repair to a cafe.

On Sunday Magali was again at *Los Sapos*, this time
somewhat after the fair was practically well underway, about ten
in the morning. Still she found a table free at *Los Gatos* and sat
and ordered a Sidral. Almost as soon as she was served some
people arrived and sat at two nearby empty tables. They were
regulars most Sundays, and appeared to be a rather jovial crowd.
One was always the center of attention, and she learned after a
few Sundays that he was a popular radio disk jockey. She was told
that he even had on many occasions played classical music on his
program, which was usually of current popular recordings, both
Mexican and the many being imported from the U.S.

Today this group came specially dressed. They wore black
jeans or trousers or skirts, and black T-shirts. But the T-shirts had
printed on their fronts the white bones of skeletons. It didn't take
long for Magali to realize that it was for the Day of the Dead,
which was coming soon. Monday was the 31st, the American
Halloween. Tuesday was All Saints Day, and Wednesday would be
All Souls Day, which in Mexico was celebrated as the Day of the
Dead. Between Halloween and the Mexican Day of the Dead, the
latter appeared the more gruesome. She had noted the skeleton in
many objects of folk art and had wondered about it. And she
knew of the Aztec practice of eating their sacrificial victims, of
even fattening captives for the sacrifice. Surely, the Day of the
Dead must be much, much older than Halloween. But, she
thought again, the Aztecs only go back a few hundred years
before the Conquest of Mexico, which would be about the year
1300 or 1200. In Europe that was only the end of the Dark Ages.
They were coming out of the bad time in Europe, while in

Mexico one might say they were only going into it. And the Christian (Catholic) religion was already more than a thousand years old at that time. The Christians won in being earlier, but the Mexicans won in being more primitive. Strange world, thought Magali.

Monday was Halloween, or "Holy Evening," the evening before All Saints Day. Tuesday was All Saints Day, a Holy Day. A high feast day for those of the Catholic religion, to celebrate all those who had made it. But it was Wednesday that was the holiday. Wednesday was All Souls Day, a day for the lower classes, for those poor dead souls who didn't quite make it on the first try. True, they would eventually get there (to Heaven). Eventually. Well, they did have an entire eternity in which to realize their goal, and they were assured of ultimately realizing it, though for how long they might be able to enjoy it when they finally got there was not stipulated in the guarantee. On earth the day was at least something to partially assuage the future disappointments of all those who would surely fall into the class for All Souls Day instead of All Saints Day. And it was politically a fine day to award something to the working classes. A day off to rest, though many there were in Mexico who would not be paid for this day off, so they might not enjoy it so much.

Monday was also the last day of the month of October and Paul had to call the art dealer in Los Angeles. He did not look forward to it. He was sure his luck was not holding out on this one. His Remington must be a copy.

Nevertheless, at about fifteen after twelve he picked up the phone in his apartment and put the call through. The dealer himself answered and Paul duly reported to him, saying he had checked for foundry marks and there were none.

"Yes," said the dealer. "I know that. I've since been in touch with a contact in New York who is an expert on Remington. He's told me that all the numbers for that casting are accounted for. Every owner is registered with him, and he keeps tract of all exchanges. So, yours has to be a copy. I'm sorry. For myself, too, since I had already two buyers who were interested in it. Well, that's how things turn out sometimes."

Paul acknowledged the facts, thanking the dealer for all the efforts he put into the sale, and saying if he ever came across another such object, a good one, he would certainly give the dealer first crack at it.

Hanging up, Paul felt as low as he thought he possibly could. And then, he smiled, thinking that he knew when he called that his Remington was a copy. Why should he now feel disappointed? He had gone through all that for the last few days. Ever since he saw the statue in San Leonardo. Anyway, there surely would be many other things coming his way and some of them would be good. That was how the antique trade was.

So, slowly, he made ready to go out for lunch somewhere, and then to go to his shop in *Los Sapos* for another day, maybe another adventure.

21

ROBERTO'S PROJECT

It was Tuesday, the eighth, before Magali again saw Fr. Flynn, and it was at the Villa Rica after ten. Paul was sitting with Fr. Flynn; they were just finishing their coffees of the morning. Magali pulled back a chair and sat down, ordering a *café Americano* from the waiter who came quickly over to her.

"Long time no see," she said to Paul.

"I've been around; just busy," said Paul.

"So. What have you been up to?" asked Magali.

"Oh, a little bit of antique business. Nothing worth reporting on. Things are slow this time of the year. Should pick up a bit as we near Christmas," ventured Paul, not too enthusiastically.

"Did you see the Remington in the Hotel San Leonardo?"

"Yes. It, too, looks like a copy. Though both it and the one at *Los Sapos* are pretty good copies."

Magali switched to Fr. Flynn. "I hear from Pepe that Roberto is working out rather well in the tunnels."

"Yes," said Fr. Flynn. Then, "I'm sorry, Magali, but I am going to have to leave you all now. I have a meeting with a visiting priest before getting ready for my class in the afternoon."

Paul joined in with, "I shall have to go also. Things to do."

Then, Magali: "Is it something I said?"

"No. No." replied both of them at once.

"I know. I'm just kidding," allowed Magali. "You all go to what you have to do. I'll get back on schedule by tomorrow and we can start anew."

Fr. Flynn and Paul gathered up their books and papers and left, while Magali finished her coffee alone.

Two days later Magali was having coffee late in the afternoon, about five, at the Carolo, when Roberto came in and joined her at her table.

"Hello, Teacher," Roberto greeted.

"Hello, Roberto," replied Magali. *"Qué onda?"*

"Nothing much," offered Roberto.

The waitress came over and Roberto ordered a large *café Americano.*

"You don't look so cheerful," ventured Magali. "Did something bad happen?"

"Well, as a matter of fact, yes," responded Roberto, "but it's a long story."

"So," continued Magali, "Tell me about it."

"Remember I told you about *onéirica?*"

"Yes."

"Well. I almost had a dream-of-a-project with which to develop my ideas and methods. I almost had an opportunity to study oneiric effects in the past—in archeological times. I and some other students developed a project to study an archeological site. The group included an archeologist, an architect, a physician, a sociologist, and a psychologist (myself). My part was to study the oneiric structures and systems they had and how these affected the way they lived. Most of the evidence for this would come from their architecture, and from whatever symbols we could find. We would look at tools, clothing, food, methods and utensils for food preparation and preservation, crops, medicines, illnesses, burial practices, and such other things we might find there. We would try to look at a complete culture at the site. A comprehensive view, as well as an analytic examination. The project would open a whole new field of study and investigation. It would especially be, for me, a chance to see how oneiric ideas and systems affect real, material life of a people in a particular place.

"It all seemed so great. But then we had to present it to those-that-be for permission and funding. And there is where we enfronted [sic] reality. We presented our proposal to the archaeological people—those of the State government—for permission to study the sight. We also presented the project to the historical commission of the State for funding. We made three such presentations to both groups. And we were turned down, rejected. The archeological people didn't want unqualified people digging in the site, and they and the historical people didn't want this approach to the ruins and their artifacts. They considered our proposed studies of the ancient ideas as disrespectful of the ancient peoples, or of being inconsistent with the policies and customs of our Mexican culture and society. They just didn't want to consider new ideas or new approaches to understanding things. They just rejected us."

"That's too bad," said Magali. "What will you do now?"

"Well, with that project, nothing. There might be another opportunity some day. But, I see now that my pursuing *onéirica*, as I want to develop it, will be to go against the established professors and *their* view of science. They will allow of no new thinking."

"That is usually their attitude toward students. It's a rare professor who can recognize anything new and good from a student. You'll just have to wait until you get your degree before you can present new ideas." This was the best that Magali could offer him, and she felt it was not nearly enough for how he felt about his project's rejection. She, too, felt badly about the rejection. She thought his ideas of *onéirica* were, in her words, "sensational." She could see how they would open whole new worlds of understanding, and new fields of investigation. But—she too was just a student.

Then the bomb fell.

"I think," said Roberto, "I shall have to drop your class."

"Why would you have to do that?" asked Magali.

"I have to adjust my ideas now. I have to pull back on the things I wanted to do. I have to do as in the military, regroup my resources and prepare a counter attack, if such is possible. At any rate, I can't apply myself to studies right now. It's best to drop the class. I can always take it again, maybe next year. I'll still be a student at the UPA. At least until I get my degree. I should probably work on a thesis topic and finish the degree and move on into the real world. As a matter of fact, I have a new job I shall be starting next week. I had not even been thinking about it, my mind on our project. It's with a psychologist in *el centro* of Puebla. I will be counseling the 'wayward youth' of the rich. There are a good number of people in Puebla who consider themselves rich, and who have what we call 'problem children.' It's not a job I would prefer, but it will pay some money, and I can do it without much effort. And for that I *am* 'qualified.' "

At *Los Sapos* they were getting ready that Sunday for a really beautiful day, the sun shining brightly, the sky a deep blue. About eleven Paul closed up his little shop and wandered over to *Los Gatos* for some coffee. He found a table free and sat, having it all to himself for about twenty minutes, which was rather good fortune for him, since he wanted to relax and just watch the crowd. He was in no mood for company. But just about then Roberto came by, saw him, and came over to join him. He sat beside him—the two facing the same general direction—so he, too, could watch the fair. He ordered a beer, Paul another coffee.

"You don't look too cheerful," said Paul (in Spanish). "Everything going all right?"

"*Así. Así,*" said Roberto. "The fact is I just had a big letdown, but I'll survive."

"What happened?"

"I was in a group developing a great field project in archeology and other fields. It was rejected for funding. Same old problem: lack of connections."

"That's not so bad," shot back Paul. "I just lost a million pesos. Well, not really lost it: didn't get it."

"Lost the lottery?" offered Roberto.

"No. I almost found a great antique worth 250,000 U.S. dollars, but it was just a copy. Happens quite often in the antique trade."

"I also dropped Magali's class," added Roberto.

"So," put in Paul, "another year as a student?"

"Of course," said Roberto. "It's enough to make a man want to quit altogether. Why is it that the old will not let the young progress? Are they jealous of youth? What is one to do?"

"Well one can always get drunk. Or, better yet, there's always girls," offered Paul.

"Girls?" said Roberto. "There are always girls. But there are few really good ideas, and they are precious. With them you can build understanding. And with them you can appreciate and enjoy life. And they need never die, but can be passed on to others. And they can grow to provide larger ideas and deeper understanding, and they can give birth to new ideas."

"Good ideas are a dime a dozen," said Paul. "It's putting them to work and getting a profit from them that makes them worth anything."

Monday morning found Paul in the Carolo having coffee with a young girl student. She had to leave for a class, and as soon as she walked out the entrance, in walked Roberto. Seeing Paul alone at a table, he went to join him.

Roberto greeted Paul, pulled back a chair opposite him, and sat down, ordering a *café Americano* from the waitress who quickly came over to him.

"So," began Paul. "Any new ideas?"

"I see you do not forget anything," responded Roberto. "That is good. I do have something, at least new to you. I've been thinking about you since yesterday and I have come to the conclusion that I might be involved in something that would be of interest to you."

"What? I'm at least ready to listen to anything," said Paul.

"You are an educated man. You are a professor at the UPA, and though I know many are low moral types, I think you are not one of them. In fact, I have heard many good things about you, and about your dealing in the antiques field.

"I also know that you deal in many old books, but you deal honestly in them. Perhaps you might be of help to us in a project we are involved in with respect to old books."

"I'm listening," said Paul.

"What I tell you must be held in confidence."

"I can keep a secret."

"This is a very important thing, and it must be protected."

"I said I can keep a secret."

And so Roberto proceeded to tell Paul about Ex-Libris and what it was doing, seeking to invite Paul to participate in the work. He told him everything Paul would need to know in order to understand its purpose and to come to a decision about joining them. And when he had finished, Paul responded:

"Okay, '*so pena de mi alma.*' "

Magali, shortly after returning to her apartment that evening, received a phone call. That did not happen often and she wondered who it could be and what it must be about as she walked over to it and lifted the handset from the cradle. It was François. He was coming for Christmas.

On Wednesday, just before Paul's 11:00 class, Roberto met him coming into the ILE and told him that he had had a talk with Don Romualdo and that Paul was acceptable as a member for Ex-Libris. His induction as a member would be in the meeting of Thursday, November 24th. It would be in Don Romualdo's area of the Lafragua Library at 10:00 in the morning. Roberto could meet him in the Carolo to take him in. Paul thanked him for the good news and said he would be at the Carolo at 9:30 or before, having coffee and preparing himself for the induction.

Sunday, November the 20th, was a special holiday. It was a celebration of the Anniversary of the Mexican Revolution. Magali looked forward to *Los Sapos,* but first she went to the *Zócalo* to see what was going on there. Many of the people there were dressed in what might be called native Mexican dress, though in Puebla that was nothing very unique. Except for the women, who wore very decorated skirts. The men wore their usual Sunday best. For the more common people this meant a white shirt—something like the Cuban *Guayabera*—and some regular, dark colored trousers. All of the children going to the Cathedral were so dressed, especially the girls in their decorated skirts and ribboned hair.

Los Sapos had extra decorations in the trees and over the stores bordering the *Jardín*. She got a table at *Los Gatos* and sat to watch the show. Paul showed up shortly after she arrived and joined her. About fifteen minutes later Roberto came by and also stopped at their table. The two men were drinking beers; Magali had her usual Sidral. It was an especially happy morning there, the three of them watching the Sunday fair.

Then it was Thursday, November 24th, the fourth Thursday in November, Thanksgiving Day in the United States. It was the same as any other day in Mexico. Magali went to the Villa Rica about 9:30, but no one was there—that is, neither Fr. Flynn nor Paul. And she never saw Roberto there; she usually met him at the Carolo. He had dropped his class, and who knows where he was or where he was going now. She drank her coffee alone and then went toward the Carolino for the Thursday meeting of Ex-Libris. She walked slowly; there was no hurry.

Just after 9:30, Paul entered the Carolo for a morning coffee. About 9:40 Roberto entered, saw Paul, and sat at his table. Together they discussed the coming induction of Paul into Ex-Libris. And Roberto had something else to discuss with Paul—also a secret thing. About five to ten they paid their checks and left to Don Romualdo's Lafragua for the meeting.

The meeting of Ex-Libris went smoothly. Roberto presented Paul for induction and all of the members agreed to accept him. He took the vow of secrecy and was in. He was very proper in his behavior, very quiet and humble. Magali thought it rather strange to see him so formal in everything. Not the go-getter she normally saw. But soon the induction was finished, discussions of the coming work were conducted, and assignments of a few new tasks were made. The meeting ended and they were all free to go about whatever they had to do.

Magali congratulated Paul and welcomed him to their organization. She said she never thought Paul would want to be in such a work-oriented group. He said he was not afraid of work and he liked learning more about old books.

Then Roberto said to Magali that she had to come to lunch to celebrate, to which she agreed. He suggested going to a place he was sure she had never been to before, a really good Mexican restaurant. Paul already knew about it and he had agreed. The lunch would be on them.

They left the Carolino and walked toward the *Boulevard Héroes del Cinco de Mayo,* as if to find a taxi. But they crossed the boulevard and walked westward a bit, then crossed a street marginal to the boulevard and entered a house on the corner. The sign outside said *Puente de Analjo.*

The house was of the old Spanish type, with a small court in the center and rooms around it, and stairs just beyond the main entrance leading up to the second floor. In this case they were wide stairs to the right of the entrance, and very well carpeted. The court had been converted to a patio bar, with small tables and chairs distributed about a central fountain. Very elegant. The rooms around the court had been converted into a series of display areas for native crafts and such. There were dishes and cups and things of Talavera; things of onyx, some chess sets and some checkers pieces together with boards of the same stone; pots of various kinds and sizes; lamps; clothes; small furniture; even silverware and some jewelry. They made the politely obligatory tour of the rooms, looking at everything, but buying nothing.

Paul had disappeared about the middle of the tour, and reappeared near the end. When they had finished and had come out to the court, Paul said their table was ready and they should go now upstairs.

So up they went. At the top a waiter came over to them to lead them to a far corner table, set for the three of them. They sat at a good sized, round table, in comfortable, though antique, arm chairs. The entire atmosphere was antique, and very elegant—first class. Heavy, carved banisters; large portraits of old colonial Dons on the walls; some tapestries; and the walls themselves exhibiting some water stains here and there in their paper covering, especially in the corners near the ceiling. The ceiling itself was of a decorated metal.

After they were all seated, a waiter began to pour a dark red wine into their wine glasses while another placed menus in heavy leather folders on the table for each of them. The waiters then left, and Roberto lifted his glass to offer a toast.

"*Salud,*" he said, "And Happy Thanksgiving."

"We are," he continued in English, "so thankful to have you here with us in Mexico. Our little *gringa,* who is so beautiful, so lovely, and so nice—and she has a brain. Happy Thanksgiving, Magali."

"Hear! Hear!" said Paul, in a somewhat English accent.

The following week was the last week of the term. Classes ended on Friday and exams would start on the following Monday. Magali's English class would have a small exam because she had given the students numerous quizzes throughout the term which would count for a major part of their grade if they passed them. If they didn't do so well on them, they could still get a good grade out of the course if they got a good grade on the final exam. She had no students who were in danger of failing the course. Actually they had not only done rather well in the last quiz, but many, though they had started out with low showings, had improved continuously throughout the course. And she had talked Roberto into taking the final exam and getting his grade, instead of just dropping it and losing all of the work he had put into it for almost the full time of the course. What were a week or two of absences?

The few in the business course were taking it for practical purposes, and they would all be given passing grades. They, also, had improved in a continuous manner throughout the course. They might not know English like a native, but they had certainly acquired a lot of knowledge of business terms and phrases, and a feeling for the mechanics of business as practiced at least in the United States and in international trade.

And so by Wednesday of the exam week Magali was pleased to give everyone their passing grades, some high and some not too high, and they were free until the next term in the next year.

Christmas was coming and the time of *Posadas*, a kind of Christmas party traditional to Mexico, was at hand. Many students were returning to their homes in nearby towns. Some were going back into the mountains of the State of Puebla, to their small and picturesque villages. Magali was going to get ready for a trip back to Springfield, Massachusetts—to her own home, the home of her parents. But first, she was going to take a small vacation with François in Mexico.

Before exam week started, Magali got her tickets for her visit to the States. Then she began to arrange for the arrival of François: first, a night at the *Hotel Catedral* in Mexico City on the day he arrived; then, a week-end at a small resort type hotel in the city of Veracruz.

On Thursday, the 15th, Magali received her last pay of the year. She also received her Christmas bonus, her *Aguinaldo*, which was one and a half times her monthly pay. She had had to stand in the pay line for a long time, seeing friends in the line in front of her paid from an armored car parked in the court and walking away with thick envelopes of money. When she received her pay, she marvelled at having so much money. True, it was pesos, but the sheer size of the material made her feel like she was rich. When she found a pocket of her coat large enough to hold it all, she stuffed it in and left the court of the ILE and went straight to the bank to change most of it to U.S. dollars. They were not nearly as much as the pesos. In fact, thinking about it, she would actually be receiving poverty level wages if it were in the States. In Mexico, however, she was in the comfortable class.

The next day, Friday, was the last work day before the Christmas vacation, but Magali had already finished with her classes and had turned in the grades to the ILE, and was free until next year. This gave her all morning to get ready to go to Mexico City to receive François. She cleaned up the apartment, and had an early light lunch. By noon she was in a taxi and headed for the CAPU to catch a bus to the D.F. and the airport. She did not want to be late for the arrival of François.

22

FRANÇOIS VISITS

On Friday, December 16th, at 10:04 in the morning, François left Boston, Massachusetts, on flight 2032 and, after a stop at Dallas/Fort Worth, arrived at 5:00 p.m. at International Airport in Mexico City, Mexico.

It was raining. The City of Mexico was dark, wet, and cold. After having his tourist visa passed by immigration and clearing customs (he got a green light), he went toward the exit of the (still under construction) international section of the airport. It was a large, impersonal, and cold hall, probably like all large international airports are now, so different from the old one which was full of color, boutiques, and a more leisurely people. There was now a crowd of anxious people looking for their relatives and friends, and tour representatives and limo drivers who were holding up cardboards with printed names.

Magali was waiting for him, pressed against the railing. She felt her heart beating fast to see him advancing, with quick, rapid steps, searching for her with his gaze. "Ah," she thought, "how did I manage to live without him all this time?" They embraced with a quiet intensity, without saying anything, in a sweet and strong movement that drew them gradually together until there was no space between their bodies. They could feel through the clothes the warmth of the skin, the beat of the blood, the bones. They left the airport thus entwined, she barely reaching François' shoulder, almost incapable of breathing.

They went to the windows of the *taxis autorizados* and got a ticket to the area of their destination, the cost prepaid in accordance with a standard estimated distance. There were several taxis parked along a side road at the south exit of the airport, and immediately the chauffeur at the head of the line came to them and, after a polite *"Bienvenidos"* to Mexico, took their ticket, opened the door for Magali, and helped François put the luggage in the trunk of his old, but very well kept, Chevy. In Mexico people, especially the ones that made a living with a car, took loving care of their vehicles. They not only kept them in good working condition by doing the necessary minor repairs themselves, but they adorned the interior with religious images, sometimes curtains on the side, pictures of their children, baby shoes, and several items of *bric-à-brac* that made them feel at home. François was fascinated.

The taxi exited the airport area and headed toward the *Periférico* at a very fast but controlled speed. When the chauffeur entered the "Peri" (as they called it in the *Distrito Federal*) without signals, merging quickly onto the very busy highway, François nervously grabbed the seat with both hands while Magali laughed. "I was scared the first time, too," she said. "But then I realized they don't follow our American driving rules. They go by different codes—eye contact, hand signals. And, really, there are very few accidents, considering the amount of traffic there is and the speed at which it moves. They travel very fast, and there are an incredible number of cars on the road in the D.F."

After about twenty five minutes the chauffeur took an exit and entered the streets of the central area of the city. François regarded the old, colonial style buildings, the streets bordered with old rubber trees, and the vendors on every corner under plastic, very colorful tents, with their *tortillas* and their enormous pots of *menudo* (meats and sauces) that produced such delicious smells.

"I'm hungry," said François.

"Lunch time here is at 3:00 p.m. This is coffee and snacks time. Dinner is not until 8:00 p.m., but," she said, looking at the discouraged face of the young man, "for Americans, there is McDonald's and Pizza Hut, and they serve at any time. Anyway, by the time we arrive, it will be dinner time. This is a big city."

"Ah, bon," said François.

About twenty minutes later they arrived in the area of the *Zócalo*. The *Zócalo* is the old center of this capital city, a very large square (a little like the Vatican City's *Piazza di San Pietro*), totally bare, with the Cathedral on one side, the *Palacio de Gobierno* on the Cathedral's left, and the *Municipalidad* facing it. On the side to the right of the Cathedral there were stores under *portales* (an arcade), which gave the square a very European, old world, atmosphere. At the corner of the *Zócalo* to the left of the Cathedral, uncovered by the removal of damaged buildings from a recent earthquake, were ruins of the Aztec City. The Cathedral was built on top of the foundation of an Aztec temple, from which came the name *Zócalo*, which means pedestal or foundation. The Cathedral was gradually sinking on its own foundations, and works were being undertaken to keep it up and to restore the building to an even keel.

The taxi turned off of *República Argentina* and entered to the right on *González Obregon*, went around the block to the left and stopped on the street parallel to Obregon, called *Donceles*, in the middle of the block, at their *Hotel Catedral.* The hotel was an old, Spanish looking building that had been recently remodelled to attract the foreign tourist trade. It was lovely inside, and very *acogedor*. They took their luggage—with the help of a valet that came running from the hotel—and gave the taxi driver a *propina*. By the time they registered and entered their room (a large, comfortable, old-fashioned looking room, with solid wooden Spanish furniture and a huge double bed), put their still packed suitcases aside, and refreshed themselves, it was time for dinner.

They decided to have dinner at the hotel—Magali's suggestion.

The meal included *sopa de calabaza, carne asada con arroz, ensalada,* and *flan* for dessert, followed by an excellent *espresso.* The meat was spicy, flavored with chili and coriander; the rice was like a "Spanish Rice," with onions and tomatoes, accompanied by a green sauce. And they brought, instead of bread, a basket full of steamy *tortillas* covered with a white napkin.

They drank beer—which goes very well with Mexican food. François enjoyed his first really Mexican meal, asking lots of questions of Magali about the condiments and the nature of the food.

When dinner was over, they went out for a walk to the *Zócalo*. The city—contrary to American cities which are dead after five o'clock—was full of people, lights, noises, colors, smokes, and smells. There were young couples of the working class—native girls with long braided black hair, young men dressed up in jeans, white shirts, and light jackets like windbreakers—walking hand in hand or kissing in the dark corners of the buildings along the street; groups of noisy American tourists talking very loudly, laughing, carrying backpacks or with their waists wrapped in "bananas;" families with young children, coming or going to dinner or for ice cream; and a variety of police, military, and other assorted authorities strolling along with friends and family, smoking, or carrying little children. It was a happy atmosphere and François felt immediately the attraction the city and the country offered to foreign people. Mexico City had an atmosphere, a real atmosphere, free of the artificiality of the big American urban centers.

They got to the *Zócalo* and stopped at *La Catedral.* The Mexico City Cathedral had been built on the ruins of an Aztec temple centuries ago, and now it was sinking. Magali showed François the pendulum that was hanging in the middle of the atrium, indicating the angle at which the Cathedral was off of level. They both admired the baroque work on the wood ornament of the main altar, the sombre oils hanging on the walls, and all the grandiose and rich tradition that had made of that particular church a work of art.

They left there and Magali took François to see a little of the Aztec ruins, at the left side at the Cathedral, between the church and *El Colegio de San Ildefonso.* The *Zócalo* was full of vendors that sold everything from Chicklets, religious stamps, silver necklaces, and hand made sandals to Japanese electronic games and ghetto blasters, and native ornaments and clothing. François was shocked to see huge rats, larger than squirrels, rooming freely among the vendors and the people.

"Magali", said François, "are those really rats?"

"Yes" she said. "When I first saw them I thought they were some kind of Mexican pets," she laughed. "But, don't worry, they are very tame. They are well fed and never attack people."

"Uhh," said François. *"Alons, viens,"* and he led her away from the crowd.

Before they returned to the hotel, Magali and François stopped at an outdoor cafe overlooking the *Zócalo* and were immediately approached by a very attentive waiter.

"Qué les traigo, señores?"

François ordered a Margarita, and Magali a Sombrero (Khalua with cream). He lighted a cigarette, which he put aside when the waiter brought the drinks. They both started immediately to sip at them, but slowly and contentedly.

"I understand a little bit better your adventure," said François. "This country has an undeniable charm."

He took her hand and kissed it, in the way that only French men can do.

"It's about time we went back," he said after they finished their drinks.

She knew what was on his mind, because her mind was longing too.

They got up at seven, and after showering and getting dressed, they went for breakfast at the hotel's restaurant. It was, even at that early hour, full of noisy tourists, talking about their plans for the day, maps and schedules in their hands.

Magali and François sat at a corner table, and had coffee, *pan dulce,* papaya and pineapple, orange juice, and scrambled eggs.

They left the hotel after breakfast, taking a taxi to the TAPO, the bus station, where they took the ADO bus to Veracruz. First class Mexican busses were quite different from those stereotypes of the movies. And they were surprisingly inexpensive. The TAPO was a station that served bus lines going east from Mexico City. The service was great, a bus leaving every twenty minutes to Puebla, every half hour to Veracruz. Tickets were issued at the ticket seller's window by computer, and you could pick out your seat from a seating plan of the bus on a computer screen that the seller would show to you. And the busses were air conditioned and had restrooms on board.

There was a short line of people waiting to get on: an American (no doubt a professor) with a pile of suitcases and cardboard boxes tied with twine; followed by a blonde girl, extremely thin, her uncombed and unwashed hair covering her eyes, carrying a baby. A boy of three years, very blond, followed her, holding on to her skirt. Two Mexican women of a certain age—very elegant, in suits and silk blouses, gloves, and leather suitcases—looked sideways at the *gringa*, exchanging significant glances.

François got the luggage loaded and received the luggage check from an employee of the line, a short, heavy man with dark eyes and bright rodent-like teeth. They got onto the bus, François giving his ticket to the conductor (or was it the driver?), keeping a stub. They easily located their seats by number as in a theatre.

Outside the city, and now having passed the toll gate (the hostess had meanwhile brought very bad but hot coffee), from a VCR they started to show a movie on the television monitors.

It was another bad American movie. Class D or less in quality. Unfortunately, on many bus trips that Magali took they showed these same kinds of movies: of the poorest taste, many even obscene, movies that they surely couldn't show in the States. It seemed that Hollywood also made this kind of movie, and dumped them onto foreign countries where they probably could not be understood, and certainly where no one could complain.

An older man once explained to Magali about the A,B,C,D classification for movies they used to use in the States. The A movie was for a really good one. The B was a fairly good movie, but far from being in the top rank. The C movie was passable. One never recommended it to a friend. It was, however, enjoyable, and no one left the theatre disappointed. It did it's job of entertaining, and that was that. The D movie was a bad story, bad actors and acting, bad filming—just all around bad. The now current "x" classification did not exist. Such movies were forbidden to make or to distribute.

He said the first "western" to make it into the A class was
"My Darling Clementine." That was a classic. Almost all westerns
prior to that were C, or at worse D. There must have been few
"D's" because not much was demanded of the western. He told
me of the Saturday matinees of older times. For ten cents one
would see a cartoon, a serial, a western, a newsreel, a C movie, a
short subject, and a B or A movie. That must have been some
bargain. Now it costs an arm and a leg to see a movie that is so
violent or vulgar one leaves the theater feeling cheated.

They said Ronald Reagan was a B movie actor. But his acting
must have been on the D level, or at best, on occasion, up to the
C level. Magali could only remember one B movie in which he
played; in that he was a U.S. Cavalry officer. Error Flynn was the
star (he was a real Irishman; Reagan was so "Irish" they called
him "Dutch"). Reagan was hardly a supporting actor, though he
did have some speaking lines. They said of him that at least he
could read his lines. That was true. He showed it in the "I paid
for this microphone" scene he did in a presidential campaign
debate. Of course the scene was rigged—stolen from an old
movie about a man running for governor in some State. But that's
the modern politician. They have no original thoughts, so they
mouth the statements of others. And then the media is instructed
to make them famous for it. For the media it's "good copy,"
"more papers sold," or "higher TV ratings." And with the ever
greater number of unthinking "Simpsons" in the U.S. now, it's
easier and easier to do that. The quality of presidents descends
ever lower and the modern politician at any level in the U.S.
becomes at best "a mediocre crook."

Magali blocked the movie from her attention and she and
François looked out of the window and talked.

The mountains began to appear in the distance, covered with
pines and eucalypti, and the fields along the road were covered
with flowers (yellow and pale pink). The recent rains had covered
the mountains with a humid and cool blanket of air. The land
displayed a patchwork cultivation of corn and other crops of
different tones, from dark green to a golden green, semi-covered
by the fog that the soil exhaled.

The volcano Popocatépetl suddenly appeared in the distance, majestic and imposing, covered with white snow and crowned with a thick white *fumarola*. It had an almost perfect cone, painted dramatically against the sky of turquoise: every bit *"Un gran señor,"* as they say in Puebla.

"Que c'est beau!" exclaimed François. They remained contemplating the landscape, the mountains covered with pines, the road snaking between the hills. Finally all those turns and the altitude had a hypnotic affect on the pair. Both were tired. Magali sought refuge in the arms of François and soon fell asleep.

François continued looking out the window. They went over the pass and began a descent toward Puebla. The area of trees ended and cultivated land filled the view. Again fields of corn. Then an urbanized area, and past that (was that Puebla?) they were again into open fields, now mostly truck gardening. The climate must have changed to desert; cacti were more visible and trees were only seen as if they had been planted in their locations.

They crossed a great distance of flat, dry land—but land cultivated, probably by irrigation. Then they began to wind through hills, covered with trees and shrub. They continued to descend, passing fast running small streams, and fields of corn and tuna. Along the way were many bee hives, and then more palm trees. The vegetation was becoming definitely tropical. And then there were large fields of grass, like for cattle. Many were also covered with large trees, spreading their branches out to provide fantastic shade beneath. These were regularly spaced, like an orchard, but spaced far apart: they were huge trees. He later learned that they were mango trees—so many mangos!

More huts began to appear along the road, then small groupings of houses, like hamlets or small villages. And then they were suddenly entering into Veracruz. They arrived at 4:30, a seven hour trip.

They took a taxi from the bus station to their hotel: an old, one-time luxurious vacation hotel for Mexican families. Called the *Hotel La Playa*, it was now rated as a one star inn, but it had big rooms, and the atmosphere was very appealing to Magali and

François. Tropical flowers, even in winter. Just beyond the lobby was a large patio with a central fountain and outdoor seating around ornate low "coffee" tables. Huge ceiling fans turned throughout the lobby area and corridors.

They registered, and once in the room, Magali immediately changed into her swimming suit, grabbed a towel, and went down and across the street to the beach. François hurriedly got himself ready and followed her. The water (Gulf of Mexico) was cloudy and the sand gray, but the feeling of the ocean on her skin while she swam was wonderful. Out of the water, she sat and breathed in the sea air. It was then she noticed how full of oxygen it was, and she realized she was down to sea level again. She inhaled again, slowly and deeply, savoring the tropical sea air—the smell of many flowers, the taste of salt.

After the swim they returned to the hotel, showered and changed, and grabbed a cab to the center of the city, to the *Zócalo*. On Saturday or Sunday evenings there occasionally was dancing in the *Zócalo* by one of the schools of the *Danzón*, the regional dance of Veracruz, brought from Cuba a long time ago. Magali and François planned to eat at the *Zócalo*, and there see the show, which the lady at the hotel desk said would be on this evening.

There were several restaurants under an arcade along one side of the *Zócalo*, and from there one had good seats for the show. They had arrived just after six, and there were still seats available for the evening meal, but one could see that the area was beginning to become crowded, and there were lots of tourists milling about. François led Magali through the crowd and to two good seats at one of the restaurants. They settled down to enjoy a very leisurely meal until the dancers should arrive.

There was another show to entertain the two while they ate. Small groups of musicians walked in turn by the arcade, playing on their instruments (guitars and marimbas for the most part). They played quite well, and they collected offerings from the tourists sitting under or in front of the arcade, either drinking or dining. Some tourists made special requests. Then the musicians would move on and another group would approach, like a continuing parade. One did not have to give, and it could be seen that there were more than enough that gave. Also passing before those at the arcade tables were a number of merchants of trinkets, and a goodly few beggars. Magali and François were two tables removed from the front so they could devote their time to eating.

There was a festive air in the *Zócalo*. The Cathedral, across the plaza from the arcade, had the main door facing the street which ran by the *Zócalo* open and many women went in an out, passing along the street, or around the corner and along the side of the church facing the *Zócalo*. Meanwhile a heavy traffic of cars and busses slowly went along the street. Much of the traffic, of vehicles and of people, was a trailing part of the evening rush hour. But in the Cathedral they were also having confessions in preparation for the coming Sunday.

The *Danzón* was a traditional dance in Veracruz. More than that, it was an art. Something the people of the region were proud of, and something many from other parts of Mexico (and of the world) came to see and applaud. Suddenly there was a hush all over the *Zócalo* area: the dancers are due to arrive.

More people gather in the plaza; musicians take their place on one side of a cordoned off square, wait by their instruments, occasionally sounding some notes; everybody is watching the long corridor for the entrance of the school—tonight, the principal school of the city, the most famous in Mexico. Finally, the dancers start to exit from under a dark portico just beyond the plaza, led by an older man and a middle-aged woman. She is tall and lean and has a Spanish look, hair in a tight chignon over the neck and a gardenia over the ear. She wears a tight, dark suit, a white lace blouse, and high heels. Her lips are red and she wears heavy makeup—like a ballet dancer. The man has grey hair, a moustache, and dark eyes; wears a tuxedo and patent leather shoes.

Older men wearing crisp, white *guayabera* shirts, pressed linen trousers, and shiny patent leather shoes then lead out women clothed in immaculate white dresses. They are followed by several very young and very pretty girls in white dresses. The dresses are very tight from the waist up, with ample skirts covering lace pettycoats, silk stockings, and shapely legs. Many are children, both boys and girls, aged eight to eighteen. When the music starts, the young dance with the adults, and after the first piece, which is a demonstration dance for advanced students only, with each other.

A master of ceremonies masterminds the almost continuous music and the dancing goes on. Couples look solemn enough to be attending a funeral, though under a frozen torso and poker face legs and hips gyrate to the beat. When the music stops, between songs, the men look bored while the women fan themselves nonchalantly. Only the novice hints at exertion or enjoyment. The dance is all the more passionate for this icy repression.

After the schools have completed their show, the dancing is open and the students dance with the public—young boys with old ladies, and very old men with beautiful little and graceful girls. The mood is not casual or light, but solemn. Nobody smiles or talks, but the bodies sway to a rhythm that comes from ancient times in Andalucía in Spain and from very old rites. There is a mixture of sensuous movement and precise steps. Even foreigners are tolerated and danced with, provided they observe the greatest of solemnity.

It's hard to keep the flicker of a smile from one's face while surrounded by such an orgy of rhythm, but it's an evening which shouldn't be missed.

Magali and François enjoyed the dancers and the music as long as they could, and when they began to feel too tired and too sleepy, they left to find a taxi and returned to the hotel. The long trip, the soothing sea swim, the food and drink, and the *Danzón* were too much for them. They showered and went to bed and almost instantly fell asleep.

Early Sunday morning Magali got up and put on her swimming suit and beach jacket. She left François sleeping and went out of the hotel and across the street to the beach for an early morning swim. To her there was almost nothing better than an early morning swim. She loved to have the beach all to herself, no people, just herself and the sea.

When she came back to the hotel, François was already up and dressed for the day. Magali took a quick shower and readied herself, and they both went down to check out the hotel breakfast.

It was a buffet. And what a buffet! Everything was there. Fruits of all kinds: melon, grapes, papaya, mango, even apples and pears. Pastries of all kinds, breads and rolls. Juices, at least four kinds, including the ever present orange juice. Even American pancakes and waffles. And small boxes of American cereals. They got plates and joined the line.

After that, feeling quite stuffed, they went upstairs again to finish preparations for the day. They were going again to the *Zócalo*, because that was the center of the city and where the action would be. And there was the cathedral, and it was a Sunday morning. They got a taxi and were dropped at the *Zócalo*, just past the cathedral. But they were looking for the *Café de La Parroquia*.

The Cathedral of Veracruz, also known as *La Parroquia* (meaning the parish church), is located facing a major street of the city called *Independencia*, and across the street, facing it, is the *Café de La Parroquia*, where you should forget the idea of sightseeing altogether.

Here, in heady confusion under spasmodically whirling fans, the exuberant atmosphere makes eating an optional extra. Between eight and nine in the morning businessmen and politicians uniformly dressed in *guayabera* shirts sit in wicker chairs under the porticals and have impassioned discussions over glasses of coffee. The tiled walls and mosaic floor of the cafe resound to the tinkle of glasses being tapped to attract the attention of flurried waiters. Finally a waiter arrives, an inch of coffee is poured into each glass, and a steaming kettle pours frothy milk from a great height into the glasses below.

Inside the cafe, shoes are being cleaned and lottery tickets sold to old-timers sitting at regular tables reading *Dictamen*—the local newspaper, the oldest in the republic. Outside, small military bands and groups of marimba players move through the tables under the porticals, apparently trying to drown out one another with sound.

Very young kids with very old faces circulate among the tables, asking for money, or trying to sell candy, matches, souvenirs. A couple of old ladies with baskets of mangos peddle their merchandise, and the sellers of phoney coral necklaces put a match under the beads to prove that they are real, but they do so in such a way that would not allow the heat to melt the plastic.

The aroma of the coffee, the strong smell of cigars—many made in one of the oldest cigar factories in Mexico, the one that used to provide (according to the stories) cigars to Fidel Castro; the strong perfume of the young Mexican girls, dressed up in colorful, long skirts and lacy, white cotton blouses hanging loose off their shoulders; the gardenias in full bloom mingled with the salty scent of the sea—always present: it is all almost unbearable, like the warm smell of the tropical rain forest. A constant traffic of cars and buses flows by, spreading the smell of their exhausts among the people. The ones on the side of the cafe and the ones walking or standing or crouching by the massive, grey walls of the cathedral, separated by the busy street, form two different crowds: one peddling vice and pleasure, the other prayer and salvation—both trying to survive in a crazy, mixed-up marketplace.

The Zócalo itself is to the side of the modest cathedral. Porticals across the plaza are filled with tables where, day and evening, sea-weary sailors swill beer cheek by jowl with exquisitely made-up transvestites. Russians converse in faltering Spanish with Swedes. Ten different music groups play at the same time, and all around are Mexican couples who burst into spontaneous, hip-swinging dance.

It was a Sunday, and if there were businessmen and politicians present, they had to mix now with tourists and church-goers and citizens of the city who came on a Sunday to do what they could not do during the week.

From the Zócalo, Magali and François went to see the port area, which they were told was easily within walking distance. They passed along the cathedral side, and continued to an open area in front of the Fort Real Felipe. Before them was a long quay, and on the quay was a building which housed a long line of shops selling tourist objects, and arts and crafts. It was hot. They moved along the row of shops, examining casually what was offered. Magali stopped at one in which coral necklaces and other objects were exhibited, made of both red and black coral. The

vendor lighted a candle under one of them to show how genuine
it was. *"Mira, señorita, no es plástico, es coral verdadero, compare!"*

Magali approached closer, admiring a black coral necklace.

"Cuánto?" asked François.

"Cien pesos, señor."

"Cien? No. No—"

"Para Ud., sesenta—"

"Le doy cinquenta, y es un buen precio."

Magali smiled at François' Spanish and his bargaining
technique. She accepted the present that he put around her neck,
enjoying the contact of his hands on her skin.

"Merci," she said, simply.

They moved further and soon came to the end of the
building housing the shops. There was a small space at the end of
the quay, and there tied to the pier was a huge American warship.
It didn't look like a destroyer or battleship as Magali had seen in
old movies of the Second World War. It was boxy, looking more
like a cargo ship, but it was huge. François suggested it might be a
guided missile cruiser, it was so big. Or it might have been a
frigate or something else. He, too, said it certainly didn't look like
the warships he was used to seeing. So the Navy was in town!
There surely would be lots of American sailors at the *Zócalo* this
evening.

François said they should go back to the *Zócalo* for lunch, so
they meandered slowly back on the side of the quay where the
shops were, and where there was a wide, paved area, watching the
street vendors along the way. One of them had some plastic
airplanes of an ingenious design. It was made of a kind of
styrofoam, like in packing, but of thin sheets. One put the two
pieces of which it was composed into the form of plane body and
wing, attached a string to it, and flew it like a kite. It was
beautiful.

A little further on they came to a vendor of what Magali
called the "taca, taca," a toy boat that moved under power from a
lighted candle within it. She had seen it and liked it in Puebla, and
she was delighted to see it here in Veracruz. Such a toy should be
widely available. She felt pride for the free enterprise in Mexico,
though she was not Mexican nor any part of free enterprise.

After lunch, again at the *Zócalo*, they caught a cab back to the hotel, where they went to their rooms for a *siesta*. They needed the rest. But about three o'clock Magali got up and dressed for the beach. She slipped quietly out and went across the street for an afternoon swim. She couldn't keep away from the water, so close at hand.

François was still asleep when Magali returned to the room. She quietly went into the bathroom for a shower. The noise of the shower, however, woke François, and when Magali came out, he was sitting in his robe by the window, looking out at the flowers in the garden, waiting for his turn to clean up for the evening. They both packed for leaving the next day. But they were going to spend their last evening in Veracruz at the night club across the street. They were told that the food was really good, and that they had a band and a dance floor. They decided to "dress" for dinner and do it up right.

The club was indeed nice. It was very tropical in decor. It had a high peaked roof of bamboo poles and thatch. Inside, it had rattan chairs, and though the tables were of some Formica-like tops, they were framed with rattan sides to keep the look of noble materials.

And the band was terrific. Magali grew up with a cosmopolitan outlook and had learned to dance very well both American style (square dance, polka, waltz, foxtrot, etc.) and Latin style (Samba, Rumba, Bolero, Mambo, Meringue, and the Cha-Cha-Cha). She was surprised on discovering that François could also dance Latin style very well. The band played all the latest from Cuba, and played as well as any band she could remember—Pérez Prado, included. By the time they went back to their hotel they were so tired they undressed, crawled into bed, and fell to sleep in each other's arms.

The two tired tourists got up early the next morning and had breakfast at the hotel, the buffet so rich in its offerings that they had to take special care to not eat too much. They took a taxi to the bus terminal in time to catch the mid-morning ADO bus to Puebla.

In Puebla they went directly to her apartment. It wasn't very much, and Magali was not very proud of it, but François thought it was cute. He liked the Bohemian style, probably because he, also, had spent most of his life as a student. They went out to a nearby restaurant for a light evening meal and returned to shower and go to bed. They lay late just talking about things, and then, with a long day ahead for François, they called it quits and went to sleep.

The next day, Tuesday, December 20, they got up early and had coffee and some rolls that Magali had bought the evening before, preparing for this event. They both got into the cab that would take François to the CAPU to take the *Estrella Roja* bus directly to the International Airport in the *Distrito Federal.* He was going to France for Christmas with his family.

Wednesday, December 21, Magali got up to a smell of sulfur in the air. She looked out at the city and saw it covered in grey, under a grey sky. Early in the a.m. the Popo had erupted. She went out onto her small balcony to see the floor covered with grey dust. Even the plants were covered with grey dust. The street and the cars were covered with grey dust.

She finished the morning packing for her own Christmas vacation in the U.S. After lunch she took a *siesta,* she was so tired. Maybe because of the high altitude. She spent the evening arranging things for during her absence and after her return—actually just messing about with things. She was too tired to read. Later in the evening, well after the banks had closed, it was announced by radio that the peso would be allowed to float. The Popo goes up; the peso goes down: truly *un país tropical.*

23

CHRISTMAS

Thursday the Christmas holidays officially began. Magali spent the morning packing to go to the States. She had arranged with Amanda to have lunch in Puebla. Amanda was still her best friend, at least her best female friend. With her, Magali confided all her troubles and triumphs. They were almost like school girls in their confidences and outlook. But they enjoyed it.

They met in the Sanborn's in the center of the city, in a lobby area for the restaurant, where they have some comfortable chairs and a sofa in a somewhat isolated area with a bit of privacy in its separation from the rest of the store and from the entrance to the restaurant itself. They decided to have lunch there in Sanborn's, and there at the table they exchanged Christmas presents and gossip. Amanda of course succeeded in Magali's business English class with a good grade. And she was going to sign up for the class for the second term also. So they could look forward to having a way to see each other, and to have a late tea or a light lunch with each other from time to time. And to arrange outings on Saturdays when Victor didn't come home from Mexico City, as they had done in the previous term.

The next day, early, Magali took a taxi to the CAPU and caught the *Estrella Roja* to the airport in Mexico. From there she went to Miami, where she changed to a plane to Hartford-Springfield, where her mother and father were waiting for her. She had a happy homecoming, the great adventuress returning to tell tall tales to her young brothers. But she thought too much of François, and at times became distracted from what was going on around her. Her mother noticed it and tried to keep the boys from pressuring Magali too much to be involved in what they were doing.

And so a normal American Christmas passed for her in Springfield, Mass. There were presents under the tree on Christmas morning, and a turkey for Christmas dinner. In the afternoon Magali met with some of her childhood girl friends and had to tell them some of what she was doing in Puebla, Mexico. They were all in a state of awe. They had all been to Boston, and one had been to New York City, but that was the extent of it. Only Magali had ever actually gone out of the country—not counting her early childhood in France.

On Friday she was ready to return again to Puebla, having been gone only a week: it went so quickly. She took the plane at Hartford-Springfield, following the same route she had come. In the afternoon she arrived at the D.F. and took the *Estrella Roja* bus back to Puebla. By seven-thirty she was in Puebla and on her way by taxi to her own apartment. It was the same as she had left it, and she felt so miserable that she showered and went to bed, trying hard to fall quickly asleep.

The next day was Saturday, the last day of December and of the year. What would she do?

All of her school friends were gone, and she didn't want to impose on those she referred to as "city friends," those not connected with the University. She got up and got dressed and went out to find a place to eat breakfast, or at least get some coffee.

She started with coffee at a small cafe-restaurant just a block from her apartment on *4 Norte*. Then she walked toward the *Zócalo,* going first to the *Calle Cinco de Mayo* and following that southward, looking at the stores along the way. She turned at *2 Oriente* and went to Sanborn's to look at what they had in magazines and books in English. From there she went back to the *Calle Cinco de Mayo* to look at the stores in the rest of that street before reaching the *Zócalo.* She ended her trek at McDonald's and stopped for lunch.

She returned to her apartment and lay down on the bed to rest a while, but as soon as she had gotten comfortable the phone rang. It was Marie St. Jacques. After some preliminary niceties, she told Magali about a New Year's Eve party they were having at the *Alliance Française*, and asked Magali if she wanted to come. She added that there would be French champagne. Magali of course accepted and said she would be there in her finest. Well, something good turned up! Now she began to feel better. She immediately turned to her wardrobe and began searching for something to wear. New Year's Eve with the French, and drinking French champagne at that.

Magali awoke the next morning at what she thought was an ungodly early hour. The phone was ringing. Somewhat angrily, but accepting her fate, she answered it. It was François. He had called from France to wish her a Happy New Year.

She showered and dressed, and went out for some coffee, if she could find a place open. It was by then eleven in the morning, and there were numerous places open, it not being so early as Magali had thought. She went to the Villa Rica and had breakfast there, wishing a happy and prosperous New Year to Ramón, the owner. Then she walked over to *Los Sapos*, it being Sunday. She went immediately to a table at *Los Gatos* and ordered a Sidral, and there she sat watching the already well underway show of the market. By then she felt she was back home again. A new year, a new adventure.

24

COURSES START AGAIN

It was Monday, January 9, the first day of classes in the new term. Magali looked out on the grey street: the pavement, the cars, the grass—even the plants on the balcony—were still covered with grey dust (though not as thick as when the Popo had first erupted). But the Popo had continued from time to time to send out to its neighbors a reminder to say it was still there, alive and well.

She checked in at the ILE and greeted the ladies, expressing wishes for a good year for them. She had already gotten her class assignments from the administration the previous week. She had the same classes at the same times and in the same rooms. This term was just part two of the same courses. Amanda was signed up for the business course, and Magali's regular students were back for the English literature course—except for Roberto.

Magali left the ILE and went over to the Villa Rica. There was Fr. Flynn, already seated and sipping on a Cappuccino. Magali pulled out a chair and sat with him. It seemed like forever since she had last seen him—a few days before the end of the term when she said goodbye to him. He was heading for the D.F. to take a plane to Montreal to report to his Jesuit superiors at McGill and to spend a Christmas back in the folds of his order: his old room (his cell?), and his fellow members of the cloth.

They talked about the new environment in Puebla. The Popo's grey ash was everywhere, and the mountain made rumbles now and then and belched a white or grey cloud every so often.

But most important was the new economic situation. The peso was beginning to stabilize, but at about seven to the dollar. That made the peso only half as valuable as it had been. And that meant that the pesos the teachers were paid, though the same in number, would be worth only half as much. Changed into dollars, their salaries had been cut in half. It would be a bit harder going for the rest of the year. Less money to pay for any trips to the States or to Canada. And less spending money in Puebla; the prices of things had already begun to be adjusted to the new value of the peso. It looked like a rather bleak second term in Puebla. They could only hope that the University would adjust their salaries to compensate for the monetary devaluation.

They talked also about the Club and the new period of exploration. Fr. Flynn was keen on moving forward with all dispatch. It was winter in Puebla, and that meant it was dry. No rain, and more than likely less flooding in the tunnels. He wanted to get as much done as he could, and as soon as possible. And he had to finish before the term ended because he had to finish his paperwork before returning to Canada. It had been a good two years, but it would soon be over. He told Magali that she had better think of her own schedule of work because it would also soon be the end of her year. This she knew. And she, too, thought she had better make the most of her remaining time.

* * *

Puebla, Pue., Mexico
February 6

Dearest Mama,

Just a short note.
I finally went to see the butterflies.
No, its not a joke. And there were millions of
them. The Monarch butterfly (Danaus Plexippus
Linneo) comes from Canada and the U.S.A. to beautiful
Michoacan, Mexico, to spend a long honeymoon (from
November to March) and then go back north. Talking
about honeymoons and vacations: this beautiful insect
travels 4,000 km and eats almost exclusively
Asclepias—plants that contain a poison (to which they
are immune) which gives them a particular pigmentation
and keeps away the predators. These butterflies live 9
months, while most species live only 24 hours.
I travelled from Mexico City to Zitacuaro, and
from there to Angangueo. where the Butterfly sanctuary
is located in the midst of a forest of pine trees and
mountain flowers at 3,300 meters above sea level in the
majestic Sierra Madre. The sky is blue and the sun
shines through the branches that bend with their cargo
of colorful, winged insects. The spectacle is awesome.
We on the tour started on a very steep uphill path
among cascading monarchs that fell, drunken with light
and lust, from the tall trees. The tourists—mostly
Americans, a few English, and some Germans—clicked
their cameras nonstop while the insects made love. I put
myself in front of a fat woman from Tennessee that was
using a whole roll of film on a couple of insects that
were mating at her feet.
"Madam", I said. "Don't you think you are being a
little indiscreet? After all, how would you like to have a
bunch of insects taking pictures of you and your

husband on your wedding night?" She looked at me in disbelief, totally upset.

"Well!" she said. "Well!"

The husband, a corpulent farmer with a cowboy hat, grinned at me, took his wife by the arm, and said, "Come on, Honey. We have a while to go." He started to walk in front of me, holding his outraged wife by the arm. Then he turned his head and touched his hat with the tip of his fingers.

There were also some elderly people that could barely walk—even one with a wooden leg. And, of course, the *"prepa"* (high school) students on the tour, with a teacher herding them and cautioning them to be quiet.

And there is the sound. If you stay perfectly still, away from the crowd of tourists, you can hear it, like the murmur of a river, or a stream. It's the movement of hundreds of thousands of wings lightly fanning the air, pulsating in the rising heat, knitting a silk *sarape*, orange and black.

The tour took an hour, with frequent stops to rest and breathe because the altitude and the heat made it very difficult to climb. On the way back we went on a horse to where the trucks were parked—even though it barely looked like a horse, more like a mutation between a donkey and a mule. Mine was the scrungiest of all: a small, skinny, brown thing that had, nevertheless, a very firm step going downhill. We came to a stream covered entirely by butterflies drinking water, and the kid who led the horse by a rope stopped to move away the insects. I was curious.

"Por qué quitas las mariposas, niño?"

He looked at me like the dumb tourist I was.

"Pos pa' que Lupita no los pise, seño," he told me. At this point, the little horse took independent action and jumped over the stream so suddenly that I almost fell among the cacti.

We got to our truck (a homemade contraption, like a pick-up, except the box in the back was made with shaky wood, and you had to hold on to it for dear life through dust and bumps on the winding, perilous road). The jovial Pancho Sombrero driver was waiting for us with a Tecate in one hand and some little light blue plastic masks in the other that we had to put over our faces for the return trip.

We started the descent: a young Mexican couple, joking and kissing (the man gave me a tangerine saying, very slowly, about the same way the Americans talk to Mexicans and other foreigners in the States, *"Es una fruta, señora, le hará bien."*), a girl with a baby sleeping in her arms, and two healthy German girls, giggling.

Half-way down we were stopped by a rope, held on both sides of the road by a group of *bandidos*. The driver had to pay a toll to them to go by. He paid without complaining. When I asked him how the police permitted that, he said, *"El Capitán* send them, *señorita,"* and laughed. It certainly is a tropical country.

Your loving daughter,

Magali

25

ARMANDO

Lic. Armando Alarcón de Medina was a Mexican professor: 5 ft. 11 in., medium build, with long, only slightly wavy black hair the length of his shoulder, moustache, soft brown eyes, and a sensuous smile. He was always dressed with European flare and discreet elegance. He spoke fluently French, English, and Portuguese, was single and in his late forties, and was what in France would be called a *vieux garçon*. He held the post at the UPA of *Coordinador de la Facultad de Lenguas Estranjeras* [FALE], the head of the Department of Foreign Languages. He was popular among the female students at the University, and he was notorious for his affairs with the wives of several married professors and administrators, which had more than once gotten him into trouble. It was even rumored that he had some very young boy friends. He was a most charming and interesting man.

Magali met him during a French teachers conference in Mexico City, which was held on Tuesday, February 7, in the famous *Palacio de San Ildefonso,* two blocks from the *Zócalo.* Magali was not teaching French, but because of her background she was encouraged by the French teachers at the ILE to attend the conference. She had shown a lot of interest in the event when it was first posted—on Monday, just the day before the conference—in the teachers' room, and Paul suggested that she immediately talk to the Director about attending the conference. Being new, he said, she was sure to get permission to attend.

As usual, these events were never ready on time. When she arrived in the capital (she had taken the ADO bus to the TAPO station, then the metro to the *Zócalo*) and was directed by a very polite guard to the place of meeting, people were just starting to put the tables out in the patio and to arrange materials amid mingling professors, a fluster of students running around, and older organizers shouting orders. It was already almost 10:00 and the conference was supposed to start by then. Magali decided she was going for a Cappuccino. She had noticed an outdoor cafe nearby, and she found a seat at a square wooden table, outside. There were a couple of older tourists—Americans by the look of their clothing—at the next table, and a man, seated with his back to her, at another one. She could only see a formal, blue jacket and the long, shiny, dark hair with a few silver streaks covering his neck and curving at the touch of his collar. She noticed the blue-white smoke gently rising from a cigarette held between his fingers, and she instantly admired the shape of the long, strong, but delicately shaped, hands. They were a man's hands, but also, she thought, a poet's, maybe an artist's.

The *mozo* arrived and she ordered a Cappuccino, and the man at the table instantly turned around to look at her. Their eyes met.

"Disculpe," he said. "I didn't mean to . . . It's your accent."

She smiled, noticing the interest in the man's eyes, and was flattered.

The American couple had asked for the check and were leaving; the woman was big—very fat, dressed in tight, pink slacks and a T-shirt, white with red stripes. She bumped Magali's chair when she got up. Magali's coffee spilled on the table. The woman apologized profusely, shaking her dyed blondish curls in Magali's face, then left, hurriedly catching up with her husband.

The man with the long hair, still at his table, got up and approached Magali, calling to the waiter. *"Mozo, venga aquí, por favor. Traiga un trapo para limpiar la mesa de la señorita. Y otro Cappuccino."* Then, to Magali: "May I offer you my table? At least it's clean."

Even when his last words were lost in the noise of a bus going by—the traffic had increased noticeably since Magali had arrived, and everybody was honking loudly—she understood the gesture and could almost read his lips, and she moved to the chair opposite to his.

"May I introduce myself?" he said, rather than asked. "My name is Armando Alarcón de Medina. I am a professor from the *Universidad de Puebla.*"

"*Yo también,*" responded Magali. "*Me llamo* Magali, Magali Smith."

"Ah," he smiled. "That Magali!"

She looked at him, questioningly.

"I'm sorry!" he said. "It's just that, well, everybody knows about the beautiful new American *profesora.*" Then: "That means that you are attending the conference? How wonderful! I, too!"

The conversation evolved to an exploration of themes of the University, teaching in a foreign country, and, of course, the conference.

"I was also early," he remarked. "But, you know—"

"Yes, I know," she interposed, smiling. "*Es un país tropical.*"

Their laughter was mixed with the loud sounds of the street, the vendors of Lottery tickets, Chiclets, and souvenirs; the people going by; and the traffic; and then it was dispersed, like church bells, into the deep blue sky.

After the first session of the conference, which was only a welcoming ceremony, there was a one hour lunch break. Sandwiches were provided in the building patio, but Armando approached Magali and asked her if she wanted to go out for lunch.

"*Encantada,*" she said.

He took her by the arm in a friendly, familiar way.

"I know this little place right by the *Plaza de los Escribanos,*" he said and, noticing the puzzled look in Magali's face, he added, "In the old times—and even now—there is a group of people called *escribanos* that make a living writing letters for the people that can't read or write. They gathered with wooden boards, sitting on the ground, in this area, under the *portales,* writing letters by hand, with pen and ink. Now they have little wooden tables and a typewriter, but the business is the same. —and it's right around the corner."

They walked a couple of blocks, and at the bend of a corner there it was: an old Spanish looking church and a little plaza, surrounded by *portales,* under which a bunch of men of different ages and all dressed in the same style—blue pants, button-down shirts and ties, some with a *chamarra,* and wearing dress shoes—were sitting by small tables and old fashioned typewriters. They were surrounded by men and women, *campesinos,* dressed in regional clothes, some barefooted. At one side of the plaza there was a row of small restaurants and *taquerías.* Armando guided her to the second one, called *"La Margarita."* It was a small, ancient looking place, with heavy, wooden tables covered with colorful tablecloths. There were fresh flowers on each table, and two *mozos* were waiting at the door, offering the couple a hand written menu. There were ceramic pots hanging on the walls, and pictures of a town in the mountains.

"Pásenle, señores. Tenemos un 'menú corrido' especial hoy . . . Muy bueno."

"Corrido is a full luncheon menu, what you would call in the States the 'Special of the Day,' " explained Armando. They looked in and saw that it was dark and empty (lunch hour in Mexico starts after 2:00 p.m.), so they took an outside table where they could observe the colorful crowd on the plaza, the children playing, and the gathering of people waiting patiently for the *escribanos* to finish their messages to their families and friends.

The menu of the *corrido* consisted of *flor de calabaza* soup, white rice, *aji de ternera,* and *flan* as dessert. The waiter first brought a steaming little basket full of *tortillas* and two Corona beers to the couple. Magali was enjoying herself. Armando was an easy man to talk with; he spoke in an educated, gentle voice, but the girl did notice an undercurrent of strong feelings under all that politeness and casual chatting. She was used to being admired by men, but she still felt flattered.

They finished eating but had to return to the conference, so there was just a little time for an *espresso.*

Somehow Boston and François were in another country, in another age, in another world.

* * *

Later that evening, after the last session—a particularly stupid and boring one, lead by a French teacher who insisted that *"argot"* should be integrated into the language being taught—Armando and Magali went back to the *Hotel Catedral,* where all the attendants to the conference were staying. There was a happy atmosphere of teachers at the bar, both Mexican and French, all speaking French, and little groups were forming of teachers from the same universities or institutions. Armando and Magali joined the group from Puebla, which consisted of less than a dozen teachers, including a middle-aged Mexican man and wife, and they exchanged comments and appraisals of the event. After a while they all went to dinner at the hotel's restaurant. After dinner was finished, Armando asked the Mexican couple if they were interested in going out somewhere. They said no, they were going to turn in, they were tired. Armando turned to Magali and asked her if she wanted to go out, to see the city by night. She agreed happily, under the malicious stares of the other professors.

"I'll pick you up at eight," said Armando, in English.

Magali walked up to her room on the second floor and took out of her suitcase her best dress, a white satin, very simple dress, with a straight skirt and a generous *decolleté* that enhanced the curves of her well shaped shoulders and her young bosom. She had brought it "just in case," and it was good that she did. She put on high heel shoes (which she wore only for special occasions) and a single string of pearls. Her hair was left loose and fell, wavy and shining, on her back. She looked approvingly at herself in the dresser's mirror and smiled. She looked very beautiful, indeed: young, and excited, like a girl on her first date. "Well," she thought, "it must be all this Latin atmosphere!"

Armando was waiting for her at the bottom of the stairs, looking very handsome in a dark suit, white shirt, and a green and blue French-looking tie. He was smoking, and Magali had the sudden impression of being in an old black-and-white movie, a Cesar Romero movie. She laughed. She felt she hadn't been on a real date since high school. Her affair with François had been something quite different: a serious, involved thing from the very beginning. This was fun.

Armando looked up and saw her coming down. He stood there, just looking at her. "She is so beautiful," he thought. "So alive."

They went to a night club; they slow-danced and drank champagne. When they came back to the hotel, he kissed her, and she knew, in that instant, that she wanted him.

But she said good night, like a lady, and closed the door of her room. "The rules are different here," she thought. "I know that we American girls have a bad reputation in Mexico, and I don't want to give him the wrong impression. I really like him. And I'd better be good: after all, this is only our first date."

Armando stood for a moment in front of the closed door and smiled to himself. He knew the rules, too. And, after all, it was men such as he that had created the rules. He was the master of the game.

Coming back to Puebla, Magali avoided sitting with Armando, as several of the teachers of her university were also traveling in the 9:00 a.m. bus. She went directly back home and called François. She knew he didn't have any classes on Wednesday.

"Hello," he answered.

He just woke up, thought Magali. She was struck by a sudden feeling of longing, and jealousy. Was he alone?

"C'est moi, Magali."

"Magali!" He sounded alert now, and excited. "Magali," he repeated.

"I miss you," the girl said. She hadn't realized how much she did, really, miss him. Only a few weeks had passed but they seemed like years—in another life. She fought the tears that were already rolling down her cheeks. They exchanged the usual trivialities.

"I wish—" the girl said, finally.

"Yes, I know. But, *écoute, petite.* Time goes really fast, and I will come to see you during the school vacation."

She was about to tell him about Armando, but what was there to tell? When she hung up, she found herself feeling much better. François still loved her. The rest of the world could disappear; François loved her.

She didn't see Armando until a meeting on Thursday morning of teachers from the ILE and the FALE at a room in the FALE. They were sitting far from each other. Gossip was a way of life among teachers and students, and she was notorious enough—for her beauty and her background, and for the simple fact that she was American. She didn't want to add anything that would make her more vulnerable among the staff.

As usual, the meeting involved administrative matters—coordination of the two arms of the UPA that were concerned with the teaching of foreign languages, and some new programs which were to be incorporated into the curricula of the two institutions. When it was finished, Armando approached Magali.

"How about a nice cup of coffee?" he suggested. "I don't know about your schedule, but my first class is two hours from now."

"I don't have any this morning," she said, smiling. She could feel the attraction of the man as a tangible force, touching her body as an embrace. They went to Sanborn's—an Americanized combination cafe, restaurant, drugstore, and bookstore—a few blocks away, just a block north of the *Zócalo*.

Sanborn's chief attraction was its book section, well stocked with American, French, and Spanish magazines and books, but also attractive was the section offering toiletries, chocolates, and gifts and souvenirs.

The restaurant part was decorated with Mexican flare for the tourists, but it had the latest in modern cooking and serving equipment, clean bathrooms, and air conditioning for the summer. The waitresses wore a stylish Mexican costume, very colorful, and one of them approached with a very large menu. She was a pretty girl, with big brown eyes which immediately flirted with

Armando. Magali noticed that, and felt flattered to be in the company of such a handsome man.

"*Café, solamente,*" said Magali, and Armando asked "*Dos cafés con crema.*" *Crema* was what they called evaporated milk, used for all types of coffee in Puebla. The waitress smiled, picked up the menu, and gracefully left. Armando offered a cigarette to Magali.

"*No fumo, gracias,*" she responded. "Now, tell me about yourself."

"I'm single," said Armando, "and I live with my mother."

"Oops!" thought Magali. "He must have seen that I'm interested." Armando immediately realized her confusion. Like Magali, he was also accustomed to the admiration and interest of the opposite sex.

The cafe was buzzing now with the sounds of the many conversations, in English as well as Spanish, from the many people who had suddenly entered and sat at the tables. It must be that time of the morning. There was a group of Canadians at a nearby table talking in French. And a little further away there was a table of German tourists.

The waitress brought the coffees, a separate container with steaming milk, and a basketfull of sweet rolls.

"Have you tried the *pan dulce* here? It's excellent, and freshly made each morning." He was making conversation, and the girl was grateful. They discussed some of the problems of the University, the lack of materials and books. Magali said she was planning on visiting the American Embassy in Mexico City to see what kind of programs and materials they had available to support the teaching of English.

"When are you going?" Armando asked casually, sipping his coffee.

"Next week. Tuesday," said Magali.

It was a date.

That Sunday Roberto was sitting about ten o'clock at a table at *Los Gatos* in the plaza of *Los Sapos.* He was sipping at a *Negra Modelo* beer, enjoying its rich dark body, watching the passing parade at the fair. Magali was nowhere to be seen, probably not even there. Roberto enjoyed being alone at times, and this was one.

Nevertheless, it wasn't meant to be. Paul came by and sat with him. He, too, ordered a *Negra Modelo*.

"Nice of you to come by just at my ten o'clock break time," said Paul.

"So happy to be of service!" replied Roberto.

"What's new?"

"Nothing much, and you?"

"How's the big wide world treating you, now that you're no longer a student?"

"Actually, the same as always. I'm always a student."

"What are you doing now?"

At that, Roberto took a long drink of his beer and sat silent for a moment. Then he said, "I'm working downtown in a psychologist's office. I *am* a *pasante* you know."

"Hey," said Paul. quickly. "I meant no disrespect. I was just being friendly, asking about your welfare."

"I know," responded Roberto. "But I really am working at a psychologist's office. I'm doing family counseling, for families with problem children. I'm a sort of specialist on spoiled rich kids. And it seems all of the newly rich young families in Puebla have such kids."

"It's a situation," he continued, "where the newly rich parents are having trouble adapting to a special role they are assuming in our modern society. It goes with their new station in life. Everyone at that social level *must* have such problems with their children. Its part of the structure of our modern culture. There's nothing they can do but come to see us, and pay.

"What is interesting to me in this is that as a psychologist, I can see through what the sociologist can only describe.

"The work is easy, and it pays me well."

"Anything," said Paul, "to keep body and soul together. But apart from that and Ex-Libris (sorry, I didn't mean to say that so loudly), what else are you up to? Any new girls? Any really fantastic adventures?"

"Yes," said Roberto. "I've been getting dirty underneath the city. Been helping Fr. Flynn's exploring the tunnels."

"You're helping Fr. Flynn in the tunnels? Did you find anything?"

"No, of course not," said Roberto. "He's got this Explorers Club of Puebla doing the work. He keeps the records. Or rather, Magali keeps the map and related records. I'm on one of two teams. The other has two boys; mine has three. I'm the last to join, and the others are more experienced in the stuff than I am. Engineering students. I'm actually just helping them. The third wheel on the bicycle."

"Hey," said Roberto, suddenly. "I've got an idea. How about you joining us. We two could form a new team. I've learned enough to be your leader. We could have some fun. Maybe find some gold or something. They say there's a lot down there, though I haven't seen anything of any. Come on, join us. What do you say?"

"Sounds interesting," said Paul. "It does offer some possibilities. And it could be fun. Okay, I'll try it for a while. What do I do?"

"Leave everything to me. I'll talk to Fr. Flynn and get back to you. In the meantime, let's have two more beers."

26

PAUL JOINS THE CLUB

The day had come, February 14th, for Magali to go to the
D.F. and the American Embassy. The ADO bus was half empty
and stopped to pick up a female passenger shortly after getting on
the highway. The women—a Mexican, middle aged, dressed in an
ample black skirt and a very tight cotton top, and carrying a
covered basket—was heavily made up and wearing long, silver
earrings in a double loop. Carrying such extra passengers was, of
course, forbidden, but in Mexico the law is written but hardly
ever enforced. One Mexican saying was, *"La ley se obedece, pero no se
comple."*

The driver—a robust Mexican male, clean shaven, wearing
sun glasses and a blue uniform consisting of slacks, leather jacket
(hung to one side of the driver's seat, on a hook), and a white,
stiffly starched shirt, greeted the woman.

"Hola, Lupe! Cómo estás?"

She laboriously climbed up the two large steps and sat on the
seat reserved for any visiting driver. *"Pues, no tan mal, Javier, y tú?"*
She turned on the switch of a small, portable radio. *"Un poco de
música?"* [Radios were not allowed on the bus.]

"Andale, Lupe," he said, looking at her in the mirror. Some
ranchero songs invaded the few passengers' privacy.

As long as it was not that phony rap music, imported from
the States, Magali didn't care. She was looking forward to the visit
to the Embassy, and to meeting Armando. They were getting
close to the Popo, and she noted the gray, heavy, thick *fumarola*.
The volcano is acting up again, she noted. And she was suddenly

overcome by the memory of François, of when he came to see her, and of his awe of and interest in the volcano and the landscape. She could feel him at her side—even when she was sitting all by herself—and it gave her a pang of sorrow. As she was in the second row close to the driver, she tried to follow his conversation with the woman. He was telling her about another friend of his, also an ADO driver, who was held up by bandidos.

"Fué en el turno de noche. Había un camión en la carretera, y antorchas encendidas en el camino; y un hombre se puso en medio y lo hizo señal de parar. Tenía un pañuelo en la cara. Dentro del camión [in Mexico they called a bus a *camión*] *de mi amigo se levantó de su asiento una mujer, que también cubrió su cara con un pañuelo, y tenía una pistola. Dice mi amigo que podía sentir el calor y el perfume de su cuerpo; era joven, y debía ser hermosa, con largo pelo negro cayendo sobre los hombros. Pudo ver sus piernas, de la rodilla para abajo, y los vió lindas y firmes, y las manos, que sostenía la pistola, eran blancas y delicadas.*

"Mi amigo paró su camión de golpe, y los pasajeros comenzaron a gritar, las mujeres a llorar y pedir ayuda. La mujer se volvió hacia ellos, amenazándolos: 'Cállense o les va a costar!' Tenía una voz fuerte, pero agradable, no chillona como muchas. Dice mi amigo que le dió ganas de tocarla, pero tenía los brazos en alto.

" 'Saquen sus carteras ahora mismo, y no traten de esconder nada, o los mato,' dijo ella. Lloriqueando, *las mujeres deshacieron los nudos del pañuelo con los pesos guardados para el mercado en la capital, y un par de turistas sacaron sus carteras del bolsillo.*

" 'Please, don't take our passports,' *les rogaran.*

"La mujer sacó los billetes de las carteras, tomó dólares y pesos, los puso en su bolsa, y comenzó a caminar hacia la portezuela del camión. Mi amigo la miró pasar a su lado, muy cerca, miró la espalda. los hombros graciosos, la delgada cintura, la cadera ondulante, y no pudo aguantarse. Dice que se puso bruscamente de pié y la cogió por detrás. Ella, sorprendida, dejó caer la pistola. Mi amigo cerró de prisa la puerta del camión, y sacó el pañuelo de la cara de la bandida. Era tan hermosa como él se la había imaginado, y más. El la sujetó con fuerza, ya que élla se debatía como una potranca salvaje, y la besó violentamente en la boca."

"Y luego?" asked Lupe.

"Luego . . . pues que te cuente él," the chauffeur laughed. *"El hecho es que se volvió héroe. Los pasajeros aplaudieron, la mujer se deslizó al*

suelo como una muñeca de trapo, sin fuerzas. Y él, muy fiero, arrancó el camión."

"Y que pasó con la bandida?"

"Eso," said the chauffeur, *"Eso es otra historia."*

Magali smiled. "Wow!" she thought. "There is a lot of living to do in Mexico." Suddenly she felt better, and looked forward again to her new adventure.

After arriving at the TAPO, again amazed at the number of people that were moving around, arriving or departing, eating at the numerous stands in the circular bus station, peddling, or simply waiting for their buses to depart—to say the least, a colorful and noisy crowd—she took a taxi to the American Embassy, next to the famous Maria Isabel Hotel and near the *Zona Rosa,* a very popular tourist area.

She was poorly impressed by [shocked at the sight of] the ominous appearance of the American Embassy, an ugly, gray, cement building, more like a prison than an embassy: the iron gates, the black armed guards, and the fact she had to show her passport through the gate before they would open it and admit her. She then had to go through several security gates and have her appointment confirmed. She was given a "VISITOR" tag, and then had to wait for someone from the International Education Department to come down and lead her up to their offices. She was conducted to a small office, through guarded doors, and finally to a secretary that motioned her to sit and wait to be called. After a half hour her name was called, and she indicated she had an appointment with the Director of the International Education Department. She was conducted to another office and another secretary, and was motioned to wait again. Finally, she was introduced into a still smaller office, with metal furniture, and there a middle aged women with dyed blonde hair and curls, and an overly made up face and wrinkles, looking a lot like any other American housewife, asked her to take a seat in front of her desk. The desk was cluttered with files and papers and appeared completely disorganized.

"Anita Woodbury," she introduced herself. She at least had a nice smile.

"Magali Smith, teacher at . . . in Puebla."

"Puebla? Lovely city. Lots of colonial buildings and beautiful churches," she exclaimed. "I visited there last year. What can I do for you?"

"Well, I would like to know what kind of help, in materials and programs, we can obtain from your department."

"As a mater of fact, quite a lot! But usually, nobody asks for it. There aren't many Americans that come to teach in Puebla. Some Germans, other Latin Americans, Canadians. I'll be more than happy to help."

Magali was feeling much better now, and her hopes of contributing to the University and to her students were that much nearer to reality.

She was still feeling the enthusiasm from her interview when she met Armando waiting for her outside in the street. He listened to her tale of it with great attention, participating in conversation, asking questions, and generally showing interest.

"Sorry," said Magali. "I think I am going on and on like a school girl!"

"Not at all," he said, pressing her arm gently. They were walking toward the *Zona Rosa* and the restaurant area. It was past two o'clock and the luncheon crowd was already invading the outdoor cafes and restaurants.

"Where would you like to eat?" he asked. "We have a variety of restaurants, of every nationality, and some of them are very good."

They were walking in front of *"Le Jardin,"* a cute, small French restaurant with outdoor tables under red and blue awnings, It looked intimate and inviting.

"Here! This looks nice and cozy," she said.

Two waiters came immediately out and one led them to a table next to the *pasaje* (the former street had been closed and replaced by a paved, winding way, flanked here and there by large potted greenery). Restaurants lined both sides of the way, and one could sit and watch the people go by as they did on the Via Venetto in Rome, except that here there were no autos, only pedestrians. The table was small, covered with a white tablecloth, a fresh rose in a small vase in the middle of it. Very appropriately, they were playing *"La vie en rose"* from somewhere within the restaurant. The waiter, who looked French, was young and handsome, and he looked directly at Magali with his bright eyes.

"*Mademoiselle,*" he said. "*Voulez-vous, peut-être, un verre de vin?*"

"*Oui,*" responded Armando, and added, "*Et pour moi aussi.*" Then, addressing Magali, "*Rouge?*"

"*No. Un Chablis, s'il vous plait.*"

Armando ordered that, and the same for himself. The waiter came back promptly with two glasses of wine and a basket of freshly made baguettes.

"*A votre santé,*" said Armando.

"*A la votre,*" smiled Magali.

Almost all of the tables were very soon taken, some by Americans, others by Germans. There was an international atmosphere in the restaurant, and in the passageway outside. People were chatting and laughing, but not in the loud manner Magali so often was met with in the States.

Armando took out a cigarette from a silver case and offered one to Magali, who declined it.

"You are not in America anymore," he said. "Nothing to worry about here. Everybody smokes—even the Americans."

She took the offered cigarette, and the light he also offered, which he did by grasping her hand in his, retaining it for a time. Magali smiled. She recognized the European technique.

"Nothing to worry about?" she laughed.

The waiter approached with the menu. They were proving a very interesting couple, he thought. "*Eh Bien—*"

"*Monsieur, Mademoiselle,* are your ready to order?"

Lunch finished with *Crêpes Suzette* and a small glass of Napoleon brandy. Armando left a generous *pourboire* and helped Magali out of her chair. They walked down to the next cross street on which the native market was located, and when they got to it, they entered a crowded hall full of very small, cramped, one-close-to-the-other stands whose owners were inviting them to buy this and that. Magali admired the silver crafts, earrings and bracelets, the colorful pots, the beautiful hand-embroidered rugs, and some white, lacy gowns. Armando didn't offer to buy any of the objects, and she was grateful for that. She would've felt very disappointed if he had.

After a while she felt tired, and Armando took her to a nearby cafe where they sat, rested, and had a Cappuccino. Finally, he asked, "Are you engaged?"

The question was direct, and she liked that, too.

"I have a boyfriend, in Boston."

He didn't pursue the subject, and she didn't inquire about his love life. It didn't matter.

And then she remembered. Today was February 14, St. Valentine's Day, *"El Día de los Enamorados."*

That same day in Puebla, Roberto approached the faculty lounge at the ILE. Inside was Fr. Flynn, sitting at a table, reading.

"Good Morning Fr. Flynn," said Roberto. "I was looking for you. I looked in on Monday, but you were not here. I thank God I find you here today. I wanted to talk to you about the Club."

Fr. Flynn suggested they continue at the Villa Rica, just down the street, and they left the ILE.

Seated at a table in the Villa Rica, Fr. Flynn ordered a *café Americano*, and Roberto asked that he be brought the same.

"So," said Fr. Flynn. "What's up? Things going well in the tunnels, or do you have a problem?"

"Yes and no," said Roberto. "Things are going well enough, though I feel that my part is not too important. But what I wanted to talk to you about is the possibility of accepting a new member to the Club."

"Go ahead, I'm listening."

"I've talked with a possible new member, a man that you already know quite well. It's Paul García, a teacher at the ILE."

"Yes, I know Paul very well."

"I was talking about my part in the exploration work, and found myself suggesting that he join us. He has some experience in exploring, as a hobby, caves in the Southwest of the U.S., especially many in the State of New Mexico. He is interested in joining us. I said I would talk to you about it."

"That sounds all right. Now, what's this about your part in the tunnels?"

"Well, I think I've had quite a bit of experience now in the tunnels. I've learned much from Kevin and Pepe. But most of what I do is pass tools. Either Kevin is cutting way and Pepe and I pass tools, or Pepe is cutting and Kevin and I pass tools. I feel like I'm a third wheel on a bicycle."

After a pause, Roberto continued, "I was thinking I could form a new team with Paul. It would then be Kevin and Pepe; Tomás and Paco; and myself and Paul. With three teams we could do more, and I could be put to better use. What do you think of that?"

Fr. Flynn replied, "I think it's a good idea. Working with Paul as a new team would accellerate the project. I know Paul, and I believe he would fit in very well. Why don't you tell him he is more than welcome to join us in our work. But you should do it as soon as possible. You know that there is the regular monthly meeting tomorrow. Three in the afternoon. Room 110 of the ILE. Please, bring Paul to the meeting and we'll put him right to work."

Roberto wasted no time in telling Paul when he met him at the Carolo in the afternoon.

On Wednesday afternoon both Roberto and Paul were early in Room 110 of the ILE. All of the other members of the Club came in before three, so the meeting got under way immediately.

First item was Fr. Flynn introducing Paul, welcoming him as a new member, and saying that he was aware that at least half of the members already knew Paul quite well, and that the other half probably knew him better.

When the Club got down to business, Fr. Flynn suggested a reorganization of members and duties. From then on, he said, there would be three working teams in the tunnel. Pepe and Kevin would continue as one; Tomás and Paco would be another.

Roberto and Paul would form the third team. As to duties, the teams of Pepe and of Tomás would continue in the major tunnels. They would be the "engineer" teams, and would continue doing that that they were already doing so well. Roberto and Paul, as a new team, would concentrate on exploring and documenting the side connections to the major tunnels. For purposes of identification: all major tunnels would be those that connect the Forts and the principal religious institutions, such as convents and churches, as well as government buildings. Side connections would be the many minor tunnels that connect with private businesses, homes, and other such minor establishments. All of the members of course agreed with his proposal.

Then came Magali and her maps. Fr. Flynn announced that Magali, who was maintaining the general map of the tunnel system and all notes pertaining to its branches and connections, would now work on this main map as well as on five new section maps. These would be the following:

1. West Branch - *Catedral* to *Cerro San Juan.*
2. North Branch - *Catedral* to *Convento de San Antonio.*
3. South Branch - *Catedral* to *Convento del Carmen.*
4. Lateral Branch - *Convento de Nuestra Señora de La Merced* to *Convento de San Francisco.*
5. East Side - *Convento de San Antonio* to *Los Fuertes* to *Convento de San Francisco.*

Copies of the section maps would be smaller and much handier in the field. Where necessary, they could be cut into smaller pieces for use in the tunnels themselves. The "engineer" teams were especially in favor of this development.

A few other things were discussed, but they managed to finish everything within an hour and were glad to break off earlier than usual, having the latter part of the afternoon free for private affairs.

After the meeting Paul and Roberto went themselves to the Carolo. They sat at a table and ordered coffee and pastries.

Roberto congratulated Paul, and Paul thanked Roberto for getting him into the Club. Paul said he had been thinking all of the previous evening about the Club, and he had come to the conclusion that it could be a move of greater possibilities than he had first thought. As Roberto had suggested, there might be gold in the tunnels—somewhere. Paul thought there might also be books. Not necessarily books stolen from Lafragua or from some other library. Books that nobody even knew about. Books that were hidden, and those that hid them had either forgotten about them or they had met with an inability to retrieve them. They might even have met with their deaths before being able to retrieve them. And, yes, there could be gold. The French gold. Supposedly lost because the officers had been killed before they could tell anybody where it was hidden. Think of the possiblities. It would be our own side project. It need not interfere with Fr. Flynn's project. It would be our own little conspiracy.

27

TEACHING AT THE FALE

On Friday the 17th, mid-morning, Magali was sitting at her usual table in the Carolo for a coffee break when she spotted Marie St. Jacques come in. She was looking about as if she was looking for someone special. Magali got her attention and invited her to sit at her table.

"I was looking for you," said Marie breathlessly. "But a coffee would be very welcomed!"

There was the familiar, noisy crowd in the cafe—smoking, talking, and laughing. The morning was still cool and pleasant outside, but it was already getting warm inside.

"I have a proposition for you—from Armando," said Marie. Then, looking at the expression on Magali's face, she corrected: "Work! Armando needs a substitute teacher for an English literature class, Tuesday and Thursday from 10:00 to 11:00 in the morning. Are you available?"

Magali smiled. Marie's English was good, but there were some things in the language, like "proposition" and "available", that were special in the culture, and you had to be in the know to really be aware of their double significance.

"Sure," she said. She loved teaching, and even when she already had a full schedule, she was happy to help—and she knew Armando would be grateful. They spent the rest of about a half hour gossiping and making arrangements for Magali's taking the class. Here, again, a teacher had suddenly departed, leaving the students abandoned.

* * *

Her first meeting of the class was on Tuesday, the 21st, not really giving her much time to prepare for it. She went early to Armando's office at the FALE to check in and to get any papers or forms or special instructions she would need. She especially wanted to chat with the secretary there to find out what she could about the class, the former teacher, and anything unique about teaching in the FALE.

The class met in a room on the first floor, to the left. There were seventeen students, all majoring in English. None were yet *pasantes.*

When it appeared that everyone had arrived, she opened the class introducing herself and explaining that she was taking over the class for the rest of the term. She took the role from the list of students she received at the FALE office; everyone was present. She conversed briefly with whoever was willing to talk and learned that most in the class were studying to become teachers—teachers of English, at that. Her students were to be the future teachers of English for Mexico. She had better take great care with these.

The first problem came when one of the students offered the suggestion—more like a demand—that since they were to have a new teacher, they should have a new book also. And he was immediately supported by most of the class vocally agreeing with him.

Magali asked if anyone had any suggestions for a new book.

A young man in the back spoke up, saying that he had a good book he was reading at that time and it would probably be a good one for the class.

Asked what it was, he said, "A book by Rex Stout, called *Homicide Trinity.*" This brought on a few laughs. He added that the first story in the book was about the right length, some seventy pages, and it was called "Eeny Meeny Murder Moe." This brought on some more laughs.

Magali looked over the class in silence and, after a short pause, said, "Okay."

"Okay. As teachers of a language, it is not enough to merely be proficient in the language: to understand what is said when you hear it; to be able to speak it and make yourself understood by others; to read it and to write in it. You have to understand the rules which govern it. Not just grammar and syntax. Not just spelling. You have to know it and to be able to explain it as idiom: a special relation of the language to the culture of those who use it. So you have to know also some of the culture of the U.S., and of Britain, and Australia and New Zealand, and other places where English or some form of it is a native language. And many countries now have English as a national language, India for one, while for others have it is a second language, Russia for one, and China for another. And people from these and other countries are writing books in English. And the English they right is not the same as that spoken on the streets of New York.

"Not having been raised in the U.S. (whose language we shall use as model), it will be hard for you to understand many things about the language. You will have to work doubly hard at understanding what you read and hear. You will have to be attentive to everything, to the smallest details of the construction of utterances. Even the situation in which an utterance is made, and who makes it, and to whom, and how it is made, will affect its meaning and how it is to be comprehended. Like detectives, you will have to observe every clue. So, maybe it's just as well to examine a detective story as a means of learning a language.

"Okay. Make copies of the story for the class. And have them ready and distributed by the next meeting, on Thursday."

Magali then began to go through the same kind of examination of the students she had developed with her ILE class. She first had them take the same written quiz. Then she asked each of them some questions, in English, trying to determine how well they could both hear and speak in the language. And for the rest of the class period she tried to engage as many as possible in a free discussion of the political situation between the United States and China.

* * *

Class dismissed, Magali gathered up her papers and prepared to leave, but in walked Armando. He invited her for coffee at the Carolo and she gladly accepted.

Seated at a table and sipping two Cappuccinos, they blended well with the students and professors in the Carolo at that time of the day. Many were clearly preparing to eat lunch; others were having coffee, indicating that they had planned for lunch elsewhere and later.

Armando said, "Well, welcome to the academic side of language learning. How did it go?"

"So far so good," replied Magali. "They're about the same as my class at the ILE. Most know very little of the language."

"And," said Armando, "they are to be the future teachers of English in Mexico's schools."

"I know," said Magali, rather sadly.

"Anyway," said Armando, "thanks for taking the job!"

28

SEARCHING, SEARCHING

It was Wednesday, March 1st, and in the middle of the afternoon Roberto and Paul were down into the tunnels again. It was now two weeks that they had spent working in the tunnels, exploring side connections and making notes on their construction, their locations on the main tunnels, to what they connected, and their probable use or purpose. So far they had not found anything of significance, either for Fr. Flynn's project or for their own purposes. All of the connections they had so far explored were from private houses, and who knows what purposes they served?

Roberto was disgruntled and expressed it in no uncertain terms. Paul tried to cheer him up.

"Look, we are doing two things that are definitely beneficial: First, we are helping Fr. Flynn and his study project—mapping the tunnel system, and helping him in describing the part it played in the history of Puebla; second, we are looking for treasure—for our own profit. Success in either makes it all worth while, so let's get on with it and stop complaining. Think of the riches that we might find."

It didn't placate Roberto much, but he continued plodding along in the work.

About an hour later they were exploring a side tunnel off of the western part of the Lateral Branch, that part east of the *La Merced* church. The side branch went northward for a while and then ended. It appeared to go nowhere and to have no other connections. On the way back from the end wall Paul stopped to look at a portion of the east side of the tunnel.

"Hey, do you see something strange here?" he asked Roberto.

"No."

"Look at these stones. They are all lined up pretty even. And they're all about the same size. Look at the mortar, so even. But then look at this stone to the right. It doesn't appear to have any mortar."

Looking closely, Roberto saw what was meant. They examined it all very closely. Then Paul noted that there was a small hole in the mortarless stone. It was like a small slit. Paul got out a probe from his tool bag. The probe was one he used in his office for various pickings at his typewriter and other machines. It was about a twelve inch rod with a kind of knurled handle in the middle. Both ends were pointed, but one was bent at right angles to the rod itself, making a side pick about a half inch in length.

Paul stuck the probe into the small slit in the stone. He wiggled it around, much like he was picking a lock, and got it caught in one side. He pulled to extract it. The stone started to come out instead of the probe. Paul continued to tug at the probe and the stone moved out further. He pulled the stone almost completely out of the wall. On the lower side of the stone there was fixed a metal plate with a lower surface of raised rails. These were probably what the stone slid on. This base had a side to the right that protruded to underneath the adjoining stone. Its edge was angled so that it protruded more towards the back of the stone. That part of the metal base had a long slit in it which ran parallel with the right edge of the stone. When the stone appeared to be completely out of the wall, Paul's pulling went to the right as the right edge of the metal base was caught on something and the stone was made to pivot to the right. A large open space was exposed where the stone had rested in the wall.

Paul reached his hand in while Roberto stood in awe, watching.

He found a chain, and moving his hand along the chain came to a metal knob. Wiggling this to find out how it moved, if it did, he tried to pull it upward, like pulling a nail. It came up. It was a spike, and it was probably like a pin, holding something in place. He pulled it all the way out and lay it down, still within the space in the wall.

Paul then tried to move the door. It would not go in, but it did respond some to being pushed and then rebounding outward. He tried his probe on some rough parts of the stones and they moved a little. He went back to his tool pack and got out a small crowbar. Roberto got out his and they both started to pry at the edges of what they thought was a door. The side to the right moved outward, and soon they got a good grip on it and pulled the door completely open.

Their light showed a clean tunnel behind the door. By then it was after five, so Paul suggested they close the door again, but not too tightly, and go get something to eat, coming back afterward to finish this exploration. It looked like they might be on to something and they had better allow a block of an hour or two to explore it well.

They went back to the *La Merced* church, where they had entered the tunnel, and sought the nearest cafe or restaurant where they could get a light meal. They took their time eating, letting it get well dark before they returned to the work.

Of the few people in the church at that hour, nobody bothered seeing them as they walked with their tool bags to the room to the side of the main altar where the entrance to the tunnels was. Soon they were back where they had left off and had the secret door open again.

In the new tunnel Paul checked the walls around the door and discovered, as he had suspected, a similar mortarless stone to the left of the doorway. He pulled that stone out and could see all the way through to the tunnel through which they had come. He went back and pushed in the stone on the other side, and then he pulled the door closed. He reached into the exposed open space, found the spike, and placed it in its hole to lock the door again.

They were now in the hands of the Gods. They could get out again, if they weren't dead. But no one knew where they were, nor how to come to their aid. This gave their venture the risk needed to get their juices really flowing. They were off—to wherever the tunnel led.

The tunnel went a short distance and then made a left turn, to the north, parallel with the side tunnel they had been exploring. This tunnel went quite a way and ended at a stone wall. There were no indications of any side tunnels to it in all its transit, but a good examination of the wall at the end indicated that it might be a secret door. They finally found the key stone, on the right, but the mortar ways appeared to have been filled in, probably with nothing more than dirt. A little scraping proved that to be the case. They found the slit and inserted the probe. Soon they had the key stone out, the spike pulled, and the door open.

They were in a small room, a room of a house or building. To the right was a stairway, a winding stairway, which led up to a small door. Quietly pushing the small door open, they found themselves in a small chapel. They moved around, listening carefully for any noise, any indication of inhabitants. All was quiet. They found the door of the chapel and went out, into a gardened courtyard. They could see what appeared to be the main building of the complex in which they were, and some larger buildings nearby. Some church spires also rose not very far away, but they were surely not part of where they were.

Roberto nudged Paul and whispered, "I know this place. It's the *Convento de Santa Monica.*"

The Convent of Santa Monica was founded in 1606 as a cloistered convent and served for the secure lodging of the wives of noble Spanish women when their husbands had to be away. It later served to house the daughters of noble families while they—the daughters—were supposedly on trips to Europe. This was usually for short periods only, usually of only nine or ten months. Those less patrician spent the time serving as novices in the convent. The convent was closed by the reform laws of Benito Juárez in 1857, but it secretly continued in its services until 1935, when it was discovered, publicly, that it was still very much in operation. During the period in which it did not exist, a normal looking house provided a front for the convent. The public entrance to the convent was through what was thought to be a cupboard in the dining room of the house. Other passages were afforded by moving wall panels and bookcases. A secret exit to the street was available from a secret room in the chapel.

Paul and Roberto went back into the chapel, where Roberto said there was supposed to be a secret door to the street. They soon found another small room with that secret door. They tried it and it did open to the street. So, back they went to the room with the tunnel entrance, locked its secret door from the inside, and then went back to the door to the street and went out. They walked to the corner of *Cinco de Mayo* and parted, each going to his own home—tired, but finally with some satisfaction from their work. The future looked quite a bit brighter for both of them.

Magali, meanwhile, was having an increasingly complicated and burdensome cross to bear. She now had two English literature classes, though they were well organized and ran smoothly. The new one, which she now referred to as her teacher's English class, was getting to be fun. She had to explain such diverse things as the meaning and origin of "Eeny Meeny," the titles and powers of officers in the New York Police Department, and such word contributions to the English language in New York as "schlampick." Still, she could see that the students were learning English, as well as learning that English, as any language, was a complicated system of social behavior. And English in America was an especially live and constantly changing system. The approach to the study of English she gave to them was being avariciously adopted. The story was easy to follow, but the language was becoming a rich and revealing world for them. They revelled in picking apart the smallest clue. The whole class was in danger of becoming a class in culture rather than a class in language. She wondered if that was bad.

Her other literature class was going so smoothly that it presented almost no problems. The business class required the most attention. The literature classes were for young people who were getting an education. They were being exposed to life, and getting some experience which would be a basis for a later understanding of how things worked and what was important. The business class students, on the other hand, were adults, and they wanted to learn. They were paying for their lessons, and they wanted to take away something that they could apply in their

work or their lives. It was a serious thing for them, and Magali
felt that she should do her best to make them understand the
things she tried to teach them, and be able to use that knowledge
in the real world. Because of this she made a special effort in
preparing for her business class.

On top of her classes she had the Ex-Libris work for Don
Romualdo, which she enjoyed and felt was beneficial. She also
managed to pick up some bits of knowledge from the old books
which helped her in her own research—the most important thing
she had to do. Her work for Fr. Flynn, on the maps of the
tunnels, didn't contribute much to her own project, but she didn't
mind doing it, and it did help Fr. Flynn. Still, all told, there were a
lot of things to do, and she thought at times she was becoming
too involved.

All of this should have kept her from temptation. But there
was Armando. She couldn't keep away from him, anytime he
wanted her. And she knew she had to give lots of time to her
work, to the various things she had committed herself to. She also
had to keep their relationship from becoming too evident, from
becoming so known that it became a subject of gossip. A hard
thing to do in Puebla. But she tried to keep the whole thing from
getting out of hand.

Armando, himself, had his own problems. Though not much
was known about him and Magali, his liaisons with others were
notorious. Many a time he ran into problems in the University
because of his dallying with the wives of an important professor
or administrator. Some of them had even threatened violence, but
he managed always to extract himself, usually by simply breaking
off his relations with the wife. But there was always one or more
willing to step into the lost place. It wasn't for nothing that he
was known as "swinging" Armando.

Tuesday was Mardi Gras, Fat Tuesday, the last opportunity
to have a good time and eat and drink to the full before the
period of Lent: a period of fasting and generally not enjoying life.

When she saw Armando on Monday in the Carolo, before
her ILE class, she got him aside and told him she had received an
invitation from Marie St. Jacques for the Mardi Gras party at the
Alliance Française. She knew that he had also been invited and she

she wanted to go with him. But she had some conditions. They would go together, but each would dance with others at the party. They might dance once or twice together, but she wanted everyone to see that he was only escorting her to the party; he didn't have her to himself at the party. Then he would take her home, as any escorting gentleman should. That way they could have a good time without creating any scandal.

He agreed. Things went well with Magali and her work, even with Armando's diverting her at times from what she knew she should be doing. About a month later, on the sixth, she was having coffee with Armando in the Carolo, and broke to him her plans for the Easter vacation. The last day of work before the vacation was the next day, Friday, so this was kind of a last minute bit of news. She had been invited to go to Veracruz with the ladies of the ILE. She had accepted. They were going for two weeks to a resort hotel up the coast from the city. Magali had accepted for several reasons. One was that she wanted to improve her relations with the ladies. The other was that she felt she needed a kind of retreat. Two weeks with only women, and in a hotel out in the middle of nowhere, would provide her with some peace and quiet for a change, and a kind of penance for the way she had been living of late. She needed to clean up her life and her thinking. The year was passing, and she had not too much time to finish the research she had come to Mexico to do. Maybe after Easter she could get back at it with renewed vigor.

On Friday many of the ILE were already taking off on their vacation. Magali had to wait until Monday to board with the ladies of the ILE a chartered bus for their outing to Veracruz. The trip was like the one in "Night of the Iguana." She thought that that movie had finally come to life, except that this time it was in Spanish, and the religion was Catholic, And there was no beautiful young girl—unless it was she. Anyway, there was no handsome Richard Burton, nor anyone remotely like him.

The hotel they came to was an old one but in good condition. The service was quite adequate. The rooms were small but well furnished and clean. There were some Mexican families staying there. Magali had a small private room, which was good. She couldn't imagine sharing one with any of the other teachers.

And they were probably also happy that none of them had to share a room with her.

The hotel was on the beach, and Magali took long solo walks along it. The beach was a pebble beach. Rocks of the hills formed a stairway, descending by steps to the murky waters of the Gulf of Mexico. Magali reached an area that was bordered by a cyclone fence and barbed-wire, and she saw there a military post on the top of a rocky place overlooking the sea. She was curious. The fence was torn in many places. She went through a hole at one spot and climbed to the military post. It was a narrow adobe hut with one small window space—no glass or shades—and the Mexican flag flying from the top of the structure. Seeing her approach, a boy in a green uniform came out.

"*Está prohibido entrar, señorita,*" he said. But his dark eyes were admiring Magali's figure, head to foot.

"*Lo siento. Vengo del hotel. Por qué no se puede entrar . . . y qué es ésto?*"

"*Los Indios Verdes, señorita,*"

And then Magali understood. Of course. The nuclear power plant. That's what was polluting the ocean and killing the sea life. All those dead fish she had just seen on the beach back there.

The boy walked her out of the premises through a rickety gate which opened to the area outside of the fence, and from there, looking down from her higher elevation, she could see the "nukes" stretching out below. It was a messy array of plain and ugly buildings with a huge cylindrical cone in the middle. As she neared the beach again, from behind a rock a huge and very old iguana came and stood for a moment looking at her, superbly indifferent to her presence, as though she were a creature that could not possibly be of any importance to it, and then slowly proceeded to move on its way, down toward the ocean. She felt very sad as she hurriedly walked back to the hotel.

On Easter Magali and all of the ladies put on their Sunday best and went to Mass in the nearby village. It was a small and very old church, but it was beautiful. The local people also came in their very best clothes. The local dress appeared to be, for the men, white *guayabera* style shirts and white trousers. The women wore skirts of different colors, some very gay and some simply white. It was a festive church going, and outside in the small plaza were sellers of balloons, flowers, and ices and other treats. It was what she could call a typical Mexican Easter, like in the movies.

On Friday the vacation officially ended, and all of the ladies boarded again a chartered bus to take them back to Puebla. On the road the chauffeur put on *"Como agua para chocolate,"* a considerably better movie than usual. This was surprising but appreciated. Magali was very happy when she finally arrived back home. She looked forward to *Los Sapos* on Sunday. Maybe she could find some renewal there.

29

GOLD

It was Sunday, the last day of April, and Magali was established at a table in *Los Sapos*. She had been sitting there for quite a while—she was on her second Sidral—when Paul came along and sat with her.

Paul had fallen in love with Magali on the first day he saw her. She was American, young, very well built, and well educated. A perfect catch for him. True, Sue was also of almost the same type. Maybe that should have told him something about the kind of women he was naturally attracted to. Paul knew Magali had a fiancé in the States, and he had always thought that after enough time she would forget her fiancé and turn to him. But that hadn't happened. So now they were just good friends. But to Paul, Magali was a bit more than a friend. She had evolved from a possible sex partner to a charming person who was somewhat vulnerable in a foreign country. He had had that experience in the U.S., and in Mexico, so he could empathize with her. In the end she had come under his protection, he felt, and he looked on her in that position and enjoyed it. He had become like a big brother to Magali. Besides, Sue could handle well all his other needs, and she didn't mind his occasional side ventures with young students. So they sat, two old friends, watching the passing parade at *Los Gatos*.

Suddenly, Paul pointed out a man he and Magali had seen many times in the Carolo. He looked like any professor. Paul called her attention to the fact that he sees him every time he goes to the Carolo.

"He is from a very old family in Puebla, a family which used to be quite rich and many of its members have held important political positions in the city's history. But that was long ago. Now it is not so rich. And this is the last son of the family. He has been unemployed for a long time. He now just hangs around the cafes. He can't find suitable work. I know that he has been offered various positions, even here at the University, but he has rejected all of the offers. It is a sad case."

"You're right," said Magali. "Every time I've come with you for coffee he's been there. And that's almost the whole school year. That's a long time to be without work."

And then she thought that the big city of Puebla was really just a small town where the fortunes and misfortunes of the people were all known by their neighbors.

But then she thought: If Paul sees him every time he goes to the Carolo, he also sees Paul. He must also think Paul has been unemployed for such a long time too. She looked at Paul and saw that he was trying to hide a smile. She got caught! She thought: stupid and gullible me! And then she also smiled. but for herself, not letting Paul know she had finally seen through his joke. She let him keep smiling, and smiled to herself at that.

Monday was May 1st, *El Día del Trabajo*, Labor Day for Mexico, and a general holiday. Armando came by Magali's apartment in the evening about seven. They were going out to dinner. Magali was dressed well but in a rather plain outfit. She didn't think it was right to dress too well on Labor Day, and they weren't going to any special place anyway.

They had a good dinner, but the conversation was mainly in the small talk class. She began to suspect that something was wrong. But they went home together and everything appeared to be normal.

In the morning Magali had hot coffee and sweet rolls waiting on the table for Armando. They had a leisurely breakfast. Then Armando let out the news.

"I'm afraid I have some bad news for me that I should tell you. It seems that I have rubbed certain officials at the University the wrong way. They are rewarding me with a grant to study abroad. I should be grateful for that. I can't tell you much about it, or who the officials are. Suffice it to say that they are in very high positions—one in particular. I am to go to Paris to study for a year at the Sarbonne. It doesn't sound too bad, but it's a way of nicely getting rid of me. I get this in return for my absence, and my silence. I shall be leaving at the end of May. So, we have somewhat less than a month. I cherish every moment of what I am fortunate to have remaining with you. I never want to hurt you."

Magali commenced her class Wednesday morning in the ILE a bit distractedly. In a certain way her mind could not get concentrated on Hemingway and his *Old Man and the Sea*. How could she explain to a group of young people—who except for one or two exceptions had never seen the sea—about the sensation of solitude of the old fisherman, the motivation of his lonely fight in the ocean with the sharks and with destiny? These ideas of Hemingway were absolutely foreign here in the midst of mountains and volcanos, and the culture so totally different.

It had been the same with the beautiful poems of Robert Frost. In a certain way she had also felt a stranger to that New England culture, although she understood well—more now than ever—the feelings of the author in his words. She, too, had made promises to herself, promises that she had made to her family, to her fiancé.

She took attendance. She was doing her work on automatic, which was rare for her. She always strove to be a good teacher, giving as much of herself as possible. But now she answered without enthusiasm the questions that the students asked. When the class had ended, she put her books and papers in her briefcase.

Armando was leaving.

About mid-afternoon Paul and Roberto were in the tunnels. Going down a side tunnel, they came to what looked like another secret door. It was, and they found the key stone and pulled the spike. With their crowbars they then opened the door. But it went nowhere. It opened to a space the size of an small alcove, as if someone had planned a tunnel but never had gotten started on it. The distance from the doorway to the facing wall was only about three feet.

They examined the facing wall and discovered another key stone, just off center, halfway up from the floor. They pulled it out and discovered behind the stone a wood box. There was no spike or chain. They took the box out. It measured a little over two feet long, more than a foot wide, and about eight or ten inches high. It must have, they thought, something valuable within it.

Thinking they had to get it secretly out of the tunnels, they decided to put everything back as it was and go out for a light afternoon meal and come back after dark. They could take it out by way of the Sta. Monica convent.

And this they did, and under cover of darkness they put the box into Paul's car, which they had parked near the convent during their break. They went to Paul's apartment, where they could safely open the box and see what was in it.

They put it on the table Paul used for dining, got out their tools, and carefully opened the box. The inside was lined with felt, and in a space within that they found a bundle of wrapped linen cloth. They took out the bundle and laid it on the table. They stood back a while to look at it. After catching their breaths, since both were excited in anticipation of uncovering their find, Paul reached over and began to unroll the content from the linen covering.

Inside was a gold monstrance. It must have been solid gold, it was so heavy. It was about two feet high and about ten inches side to side. The measurements were not in whole inches, nor in centimeters. It must be old—and very valuable. The gold was either cast or carved, with a surface of very minute flowers and leaves and vines. The cross was backed by a thick disk of solid gold, whose diameter extended to just beyond the arms of the cross. A small round place for the host occupied the center of the cross, with a closable cover of gold in the form of a ring, the central part being open for an unrestricted view of the host. The disk was also cast or carved, but as rays of light or flame being emitted by the host. The whole thing was absolutely clean and shown brightly in the room's light. A true work of beauty.

Now, what was it? Before Paul could tell of Sue's telling him of the *"Sol de Puebla"*, Roberto said: "It's the *Sol de Puebla.*" So much for mystery!

This, then, was the infamous "Sun of Puebla" that was lost in the tunnels, the gold monstrance made by the Indians of the area and presented to the Jesuits. That was back in the fifteen hundreds, just after the conquest of Mexico. It really must be worth a lot of money, they both thought.

What to do with it? Paul decided it should be kept right there in his apartment.

"No one knows about it, so it should be safe here," he said. "At least it would be safer here than in *Los Sapos.*"

Roberto had to agree. Paul went in to his bedroom and came back with a set of keys to his apartment and to the front door of the building. He gave them to Roberto and said, "Just in case."

Paul added that he would call a dealer he knew in Los Angeles, in the States, and arrange to sell it through him. They would split the money they got fifty-fifty. Roberto agreed. Paul said he would drive Roberto to his place. They would get together again as soon as he had arranged things with Los Angeles.

And so Paul drove Roberto home, and when they parted, Paul got out of the car and went around to Roberto's side and embraced him like they were old family.

About noon the next day Paul called the dealer he had found for the Remington statue and told him of his latest find. He told him of the "Sun of Puebla," giving him some of the history of the piece: how it was pure gold, made by the Indians of Mexico at the time of the conquest and given to the Jesuits, and how it was lost for many years and finally turned up. He described its general design. and gave the measurements he had taken of its size and weight, not leaving out details of the box and the linen wrap.

When he had finished, the dealer agreed to handle the trade, but he added that in view of its history and provenance, he would recommend a private sale to a private collector. He said he would start checking his contacts and would get back to him at his home number one evening—when he would more likely be there. If he should hear nothing soon, Paul could call him anytime for a report on progress.

The great holiday for Puebla came on Friday. May 5th, *Cinco de Mayo,* the anniversary of the Battle of Puebla, where the Mexicans defeated the French in 1862. There was to be a huge parade, with girls in the traditional costume of the *"China Poblana,"* a noble Chinese woman who was kidnapped by pirates and sold on the west coast of Mexico as a slave. She was purchased by a man from Puebla who brought her to the city. As with many a woman in history tied to a rich man, she did many charitable works for the poor and came to be regarded practically as a saint. She was eventually set free, and converted to Christianity. The parade was to go up the *Boulevard Héroes del Cinco de Mayo,* which passed not far from Magali's apartment. It would wind its way up and over the hill where the Forts were, where the original battle of *Cinco de Mayo* took place. Where the road goes over the hill, there is a monument to the battle in the middle of the road. Magali was out on the street waiting at 10:30, just across from the Church of San Francisco. The parade began to pass at about 11:20. It was a good parade. She spent the rest of the day working on her monograph, in which she was getting behind relative to her schedule.

On May 9, Tuesday, in the evening, Paul received a call from the dealer in Los Angeles. He told Paul that he had three buyers for the piece. He was now in the process of negotiating for the best price. All he could permit himself to say at this time was that the prices offered were very good.

* * *

Wednesday was another holiday in Mexico. It was Mother's Day, *Día de la Madre*. "What a civilized country," thought Magali. Then, thinking of her own country, and her own mother, she thought she should call her. So, early in the evening she picked up the phone in her apartment and put a call through to her mother.

30

PAUL'S BIG SALE

Thursday evening Paul received another call from the dealer in Los Angeles. He had made an acceptance of the best of the three offers to buy the *Sol de Puebla*. Six hundred thousand dollars, U.S., five hundred for Paul and one hundred for him as his fee. Paul was overjoyed, and thanked the dealer for his work. Paul said the fee was well worth it. Asked when he could deliver the piece, Paul said he could be on a plane Saturday to San Diego. He would call him from there and be available to meet with him at his convenience. The dealer said, okay, and that he would arrange the transfer for Sunday.

The next day was the end of courses in the ILE. Paul was especially kind to his students that day. He spent the afternoon getting a ticket to Tijuana and packing for a long week-end. He packed his "box" well padded with clothes of all kinds wrapped around it, and the whole mess in a small but solid American Tourister suitcase.

Saturday at four he was on his way to the CAPU to catch an *Estrella Roja* bus to Mexico City and the International Airport. He arrived in plenty of time, and since his flight was a domestic flight, only to Tijuana, he found himself surrounded by fellow Mexicans as waiting travellers. He got on the airplane, with two carry-ons, the one the small American Tourister and the other a soft duffle-bag type of bag with his overnight needs. He didn't need to take much because he was going to his father's home in San Diego.

Well before noon the plane was over Tijuana. He looked out the plane's window to see how the city had spread since he knew it as a boy. *"Maquiladores"* were everywhere, the new industry of Mexico since the NAFTA treaty, like residential urban sprawl in the States. You could almost distinguish the Mexican plants from the American ones: the Mexican ones looked dilapidated; the others looked new and well groomed, actually too good for the wages they paid those who worked in them.

They landed, and Paul grabbed his bags and went directly to where the taxis were and took one to the border crossing with the U.S. There he got in line to go through immigration and customs. He got through the Mexican part easily. At the American part he presented his American passport, saying he was working as a temporary professor at the University of Puebla, visiting his parents in San Diego for the short vacation between the regular and summer terms. They passed him without comment other than to wish him an enjoyable vacation in the U.S.

He walked through the border and toward a parking area on the U.S. side. There his father was waiting for him. Their embracing was a rather emotional one, especially since part of Paul's joy at being there was to get all the money he was expecting for what he was carrying without incident into the U.S.

They arrived at his old home and sat down to what his mother announced was a typical American dinner made especially for him. It was a meal of steak, French fries, pieces of fresh onions, tomatoes, and lettuce, hot sauce, and *tortillas*. Just like what he had grown up with as a boy in San Diego.

The next day was Sunday, and Paul and his father prepared for the trip to Los Angeles. Being Sunday, there was not too much traffic on the freeways, and they had a rather smooth trip into the city. They arrived at the dealer's shop before nine, as arranged, and entered with the box. The dealer was there and led them into a kind of living room with nicely upholstered easy chairs. Paul introduced himself and his father. The dealer asked Paul about the object, and Paul indicated the box he was carrying. Paul put it on a table along one wall and opened it. The dealer took out the linen bundle and unwrapped it. He lifted the monstrance and looked it all over, using a magnifying glass to examine parts of it. He finished with a big smile. He said, "What a beautiful piece of work." Then he carefully re-wrapped the monstrance and replaced the bundle into the box, closing it.

He invited Paul and his father to sit down and offered them some coffee. He went to his desk, a large wooden one, probably of mahogany or some other exotic wood, and he pressed a button underneath on the side where his large, leather covered chair was, In came three men who looked like gangsters. They were all dressed in suits and were very muscular. In a moment, almost behind them, a young woman came in bearing a tray with a silver coffee pot and some saucers and demi-tasse cups, and she was accompanied by another man, similarly dressed in a suit, but older and not so muscular. She served a cup for Paul, his father, and the dealer, whose name was French, Jean Luis, and placed them on a low coffee table in front of Paul's chair. It was good *espresso* coffee in the Italian style, complete with sugar cubes and tiny slices of lemon peel. The three men took positions around the room, their backs to the walls. They looked like they were ready to shoot anyone who entered or who tried to leave. Jean Louis came to a chair near Paul's and picked up his coffee. The other man took a chair to one side of the desk. Paul and Jean Luis talked, some about Paul's activities at the University and some about his antique dealings in Mexico.

In about ten minutes a bell sounded and Jean Luis went to his desk and pushed a button. One of the three men left and presently returned with three other men. One of the new men carried an attaché case. The oldest of the three, very well dressed, came to Jean Louis and they shook hands. Jean Louis led him over to where Paul was and introduced him to Paul. He then led him to the table on which the box had been placed. The older man motioned to the one with the attaché case and he brought it over to him and put it on the table. The older man opened the case. It was full of money. Jean Louis opened the box.

The man took out the linen bundle and unwrapped the monstrance, hefted it a little to examine its weight and solidity, then set it down on the table and stood back a bit to look at it. He then took a thread-counting magnifying glass out of his pocket, opened it, and applied it to an examination of the monstrance. He, too, looked at almost every part of the object, the underside, and inside the part that was for the host. Then he made a similarly minute examination of the box and the linen. When he had finished, he turned and smiled. He then re-wrapped the monstrance and returned the bundle to the box and closed it. He offered his hand to Jean Louis, who took it. He then pushed the attaché case over to Jean Louis, who gave the contents a cursory examination. Jean Louis motioned to the older of his men who came over and counted all of the money at an extremely fast pace. It was like in the movies. He just flipped through the bills with a few fingers of each hand. When he finished and indicated that it was all correct, Jean Louis took the case and went to a place behind his desk, slid back a panel in the wall, and opened a safe, putting the case inside. He then went back to the buyer and they shook hands again and exchanged a few words. Then the buyer took the box, and he and his two men left. That was it.

Jean Louis sent his men away and returned to his desk. He opened a drawer and took out a piece of paper. He gave it to Paul. It was a certified check for five hundred thousand dollars, made out to his name. Paul had been quiet throughout all of the proceedings. He was just too overawed to really contribute anything to it all. But he thanked the dealer for the check, taking it and shaking the dealer's hand.

"That," said Jean Louis, "is just my doing a good service to my clients. But, there are some in the government of our country who might want to call it the laundering of money. Anyway, it's clean money now."

They said their goodbyes, Paul promising to contact him again when he had another something of value. Paul and his father left, the check firmly in an inside pocket of Paul's sport jacket. Together they drove back to San Diego, his father constantly looking around and behind them, while Paul tried to assure him that no one but he himself could cash the check and they were both perfectly safe.

Monday was a holiday in Puebla: the feast of *San Isidro Labrador*, a day for the blessing of farm animals and new seeds for the crops. It helped to give Paul a long week-end in the U.S. Being a regular work day in the U.S., Paul was able to finish all of the things he had planned for this adventure. He went that morning to a stock broker friend he had in San Diego and arranged for the investment of his new fortune. They set up two mutual fund accounts, one for him and one for Roberto. The broker chose a tax-free municipal bond fund. They were old friends—since childhood—so Paul had complete trust in him. The funds would pay quarterly earnings of slightly over four percent. They arranged to have the interest earnings deposited in a local bank. Four percent of a $250,000 fund would give $10,000 per year, $2,500 per quarter. That would average out at more than $800 per month. They could expect a first earnings payout in July. It would be less than $2,500, since it was only May and, consequently, this quarter would be, for them, less than two months instead of the usual three. His broker friend gave Paul the papers to sign for the bank and the fund, and Paul signed his and also signed those for Roberto, as a combined account for now. He took another set of papers for Roberto with him to have Roberto sign them in Puebla, and Paul would have them sent back to his friend in San Diego. Everything was working out well.

The next day, early, he arrived at the border with his father, walked through, and took a taxi to the airport in Tijuana. He certainly had less to take back to Puebla, only the overnight duffle bag. But in his pocket were some very valuable papers. Quite an adventure.

He arrived in Mexico City just before noon and caught a waiting *Estrella Roja* bus for Puebla. Exams had already started at the University, but Paul had arranged for his students to take theirs on Wednesday. He looked for Roberto in the Carolo, and there he was, as they had arranged.

Roberto looked anxious, he must have drunk too many coffees while waiting that afternoon. But Paul was there at three, as he had anticipated. Roberto had been there waiting since two-thirty. Paul sat down at his table and they ordered two coffees. Roberto evidently didn't think he had had too many coffees already. Paul told him about the sale, as briefly as possible, and then about the accounts. He took out the papers for Roberto

to sign, which he did sign. Paul said he would be sending them to
the broker in San Diego by courier as soon as he possibly could.
And he would get back to Roberto when all of the papers and
such were cleared. Then Paul explained the arrangements with the
broker and the bank. Roberto could budget US$800 to live with
each month, but the money would be deposited quarterly, the first
deposit not coming until July, and Roberto would have to control
well his spending to keep it within his budget. He should not, by
any means, attract attention to his now having some money, an
independent income. And he should say nothing to anybody
about their adventure. It never happened.

   Magali, meanwhile, had arranged for the exams for her
classes. The first was to be for the class in English literature at the
FALE. It would be a short exam at the regular class hour on
Tuesday, at 10:00 in the morning. That same day she would give
the exam for the Business English class in the evening at its
regular hour, at 7:00 p.m. Finally the ILE class in English
literature would have theirs at 11:00 in the morning on
Wednesday, the regular time for their class meeting. It looked
easy, and she meant to make it so. By mid-week it would be all
over and she could get about her own research work again.

31

END OF THE SCHOOL YEAR

It was Sunday. Exams were half-way over. And it was the XIX Anniversary of *Los Sapos*. Magali could not wait to get there early and get a chair at a table at *Los Gatos*. She was sure there would be a lot of people there.

But at nine o'clock in the morning there were few people there. The owners of the various stores were opening their doors; those who normally occupied certain places were laying out or otherwise arranging their displays, and the various helpers were bringing out the merchandise to sell to those setting up the displays. Things looked much like any other Sunday at *Los Sapos*, except for the banner across *5 Oriente*, and some odd decorations in the trees in the plaza. Being there early, she ordered a coffee, and was brought a large cup of *café Americano*.

Soon enough people began to arrive. She next ordered a Sidral and continued to sit there, watching the show. It was as interesting as always. It had always had a soothing effect on Magali, taking her back to her summer trips to Italy and the south of France, to the outdoor cafes in even the smallest villages. It represented to her not only life, but civilization.

Towards eleven she was joined by Paul, and later by Roberto. They both looked happy. They ordered beers and sat with Magali for about a half hour, talking of different things and watching the people meandering through the plaza. They, too, enjoyed just sitting and watching the people.

* * *

Tuesday was the last day of exams. Magali was ready at noon to turn in to the ILE administration secretaries her papers for the English Literature class. Of course, all of her students passed with good grades. She also turned in the papers for the Business English class. That concluded, she walked over to the FALE and turned in the papers for her teacher's English Literature class, and they also passed with good grades. And Magali could feel proud of the grades for she thought they certainly earned them. She had had good students and they had joined in with her methods and come out of it all with an improved understanding of the English language. For what more could one ask?

Now she was through with it all. All done! Free! Now she could concentrate on her own research project, her monograph.

The following Tuesday was the 30th. She had a date with Armando. It was to be their last night before he had to leave for France. They went to a concert given in the Auditorium up where the Forts are. It was a beautiful night, a warm breeze blowing. Brahms. They played Brahms.

They walked down to Magali's poor apartment. Not the best and most romantic place. But Armando always said he liked it, and he showed no interest in going out to any club, such as they have in some of the hotels in Puebla, Nor did he want for anything, so he said, other than herself.

When they went to bed she had tears in her eyes. And he was probably the most tender and attentive to her then than he had ever been.

They awoke early and had a light, continental breakfast of *espresso* coffee and sweet rolls. Armando left her place, alone, in a taxi to his own apartment, and eventually to a plane from the D.F. for France.

Armando was gone.

On Monday, June 5, summer courses began at the ILE. Magali had no courses; she was allowed use the rest of her contracted time to finish her own research. Paul and Fr. Flynn,

and the ladies, did have summer courses to teach. Magali set to
work in ernest to get her research and monograph finished. But
she still put in some time with Ex-Libris and with Fr. Flynn's
tunnel project, keeping the records and the maps. These actually
gave her a break from the stress of trying to finish her own
project.

A month later she was done. She finished her monograph on
July 4th, Independence Day in the States. Of course that day was
not celebrated in Mexico. Maybe at the U.S. Embassy in the D.F.,
but even of that Magali could not be sure. She celebrated the
Fourth, and her finishing her research project, by going for lunch
to McDonald's at the *Zócalo*. There she sat outside with a
hamburger and fries and a vanilla shake. She watched the
movement along the street, and over in the central part of the
plaza, thinking that soon she would be leaving all of this. She
already began to miss it. She took a walk around the square, and
then walked back to her own apartment.

There she checked over her work. In separate boxes on the
table were the results. In one box were her notes from various
interviews. Another held her documentation. This consisted of
copies of the title pages of books she had used for citations, and
copies of the pages for which citations were made. This in case
there should arise any questions about the veracity of her work. In
one long box was her pride: a collection of 3x5 cards with her
"glossary" on them. Each word or phrase was on its own
card—sometimes on two or more, as many as were needed. Each
record had the word (or phrase), its definition, root or origin,
changes over the years, related words or phrases, and how it was
used in documents for each of its evolved meanings—or senses.
A final box held the manuscript of the monograph itself. And to
safeguard all that, she had some computer disks on which were
the records of her word-processing files and other files of her
notes, her interview writeups, and her glossary. These were in a
small box which she intended to carry back to Boston with her by
hand. The four boxes and the box of disks she placed in her
wardrobe. She also had copies of the disks packed in her
overnight bag, which also contained toiletries and such. The disks
were in sealed food storage bags, so that they were guarded from

water or other things that might get spilled or otherwise into her overnight bag.

The next day she felt good not having anything to do. She walked around the University area, in the *Pasaje Carolino*, like a tourist, looking at the people and the buildings. She went to *Los Sapos*, which was empty and without any evident commerce. She visited *El Parián* and the *Barrio del Artista*. She then came back to the *Avenida Avila Camacho* and walked to the *Zócalo*. She had lunch at McDonald's. On her way home she stopped at the Social Science Library and went in to read some magazines. This was the closest to a library like those in the States that she could find in Mexico. She passed most of the afternoon there and then went back to her apartment.

About five she went out again and walked to the University again and went into the Carolino for a nostalgic tour of the building, upstairs to the *Salon Barroco*. It was getting dark now, so she left the Carolino and walked to the *Zócalo* and entered McDonald's again for an evening meal. After her supper she walked up and down the *Calle Cinco de Mayo*, looking at the store windows. She stopped at a cafe near the corner of the *Avenida Avila Camacho* for a coffee and then walked homeward down that avenue toward the University again. It was now getting to be about 8:30. As she approached the *Pasaje Carolino*, she decided to stop for a late visit to the Church of the Company.

La puerta principal de la iglesia está rodeada de una reja de hierro forjado, que le dá aires de prisión. El gran pórtico de madera labrada (a la usanza española), que consta de una puerta principal, ovalada, y dos laterales, también ovaladas, pero más pequeñas, dá paso a un pequeño atrio, en el cual dos puertas laterales permiten acceso al templo. En la iglesia está la notable pintura, imagen de la Virgen del Pópulo, que era propiedad de San Francisco de Borja, quien le dedicó y regaló a este templo remitiéndola con el padre Mescruriali. Había otra imagen de la Virgen que, según la tradición, sus alhajas eran parte de la propiedad de la mujer de San Ignacio de Loyola, mujer que tuvo antes de que se convirtiera, y un San José llamado del milagro que costó 290 pesos y se compró para la casa de ejercicio del mismo local.

La iglesia de la Compañia estuvo un poco de tiempo cerrada, y cuando se volvió a abrir, en 1821, hizo los nuevos colaterales el canónigo Don

Cayetano Gallo, y las demás obras de ornato moderno las hicieron en 1838 el también canónigo don Joaquín Mellado y el P. don Ignacio Centurión. Al lado izquerdo, sobre la pared y junto al altar de la Virgen de Lourdes (un altar de mármol gris, muy sencillo, que contrasta con el elaborado vestido de tul amarillento y lentejuelas de la estatua), se distingue una pequeña puerta de madera, de forma oval y muy baja, no más de 95cm; que casi no se distingue por estar pintada del mismo color amarillo de los muros, siempre cerrada, y al otro lado, escondida detrás de una estatua, su gemela, también camuflada en la pared y sin cerradura o candado visible, pero firmemente cerrada.

Hay una placa en la pared al lado de las puertas exteriores de la iglesia que dice, "En el arco principal de este fachada, estuvo colgada por orden de la inquisición la cabeza de Don Antonio de Benavidez (El Tapado) falso visitador de España ejecutado el 12 de julio de 1684."

32

AFTER THE ADVENTURE

Magali awoke the morning of July 6 suffering from a kind of hangover consisting of a headache and nausea. She opened her eyes with some difficulty. "What a strange dream," she murmured. She looked up at the high ceiling of her enormous room, at the worm-eaten wood beams that crossed it, at the pictures of little angels with gold wings, and at the blue enterlaced flowers.

With some effort she lowered one leg from the bed, then the other. She sat up, supporting herself with her arms on the edges of the mattress. Feeling a little sick, she lay down again on the pillow, casting her gaze about her room.

How nice a hot shower would be now! She sighed. She got up and looked at herself in the wardrobe mirror. She was fully dressed. She took off her clothes, slipped into the shower, and began to soap up all over, trying to wash the cobwebs from her mind.

By the time she finished her shower and brushed her teeth, she felt she was back in place. She was in Puebla, Mexico, and it was morning. She checked the calendar on the wall, where she had religiously crossed out each day's date number as it passed. She was now a short-timer, and it was July 5. But that couldn't be true. She remembered the holiday, July 4th, and she was sure she had finished all of her research project on the 4th. She had packed the monograph and copies of all her supporting documents for taking back to Boston. She checked the bottom of the wardrobe. They were all there, each box marked as to its contents. She remembered doing nothing on the fifth: *il dolce far niente.* It must be the sixth of July. She needed a coffee.

Rather than make it in the apartment, where she knew it would be good, she decided to go out into the street, into what she knew would be the real world. She put on a summer short-sleeve blouse and a calf-length, full, cotton skirt, with a belt. Looking in the mirror, she thought she looked rather normal again. On the floor were the shoes she had worn the day before. She noted that the edges were stained with a green mud, now dry, which had fallen to the floor in pieces. Putting on a pair of sandals, she went out to the cafe near the corner and ordered a *café Americano.* They had pastries, so she picked out one that looked closest to a Danish. It turned out to be peach, and that was good. She asked the waitress the day's date.

"Jueves, el seis de julio."

Great! That meant there was only the one night to reconstruct in her memory. Now, what to do? Her work was done; she had the research and monograph she had come to do in Puebla. Classes had finished more than a month ago for her. Fr. Flynn was still here until August, as was Paul, both with summer classes. Roberto was also in town. But she didn't feel like talking to them, and they were hard to find now in the summer.

Amanda! She could always talk to Amanda. But should she go out to Cholula or ask her to come into the city? She could only call and ask. She finished her light breakfast—it was now about ten—and went back to her apartment to call Amanda. She got her and gave her a short summary of her adventure, as best she could remember it. Amanda said she would catch the next bus to Puebla and meet her in the Carolo.

Magali went to the Carolo to wait for Amanda. The cafe was always dark and full of students and smoke. She was sure the most powerful light bulb they used was no more then forty watts. But, contrary to the United States where it was now almost impossible to find a place to smoke, in Mexico there were no restrictions; it was still a country of freedom and the young people as well as the old consumed a great quantity of American cigarettes. Magali seated herself at the first table, which had a view of the street, and access to some fresh air. She asked for a

Cappuccino and a pastry. (In Puebla the Cappuccino was made with condensed milk. The result was not authentic, but it was consumable.) There she waited, passing the time watching the people walking by.

A little before noon Amanda arrived. She sat at Magali's table and, like a school girl, wanted to hear the whole thing again, but this time in detail. Magali suggested, because of the hour, they should get something to eat, at least a sandwich. They ordered from the waitress soups and sandwiches—and Cappuccinos. They were both hungry, though Magali, at least, had just had a light breakfast. So, ignoring the need and the anticipation of talk, they devoted themselves instead to their food. When they had finished their soups and *tortas* and the waitress had brought them two large mugs of Cappuccinos, they settled down to examining Magali's adventure, Amanda all attentive.

"In English!" said Magali, softly. "Well, it all started when—"

By 12:30 the story had ended. And before they could begin to analyze what had happened and what it all meant, into the Carolo came Roberto and Don Romualdo. They came directly to Magali and Amanda, and Roberto asked if they could sit with them. Magali said, "Of course."

Amanda had been a student of Magali's in an evening class, so Magali thought surely she didn't know Roberto. She introduced Roberto and Don Romualdo to Amanda, and her to them.

They exchanged some small talk while the waitress brought the two men some Cappuccinos. Roberto asked Magali how things were going and she replied that she had finished all her research and her monograph and it was all packed to take back to the U.S. and to BU. Now she only had to wait till the end of the month when her contract would be completed. "I'll still be able to help a little at Lafragua," she said.

"So what were you in such closeted conversation here about," pursued Roberto.

And Amanda let it out that Magali had just had the most unusual adventure the night before, in a tunnel under the Church of the Company. A really amazing adventure.

Magali was not too pleased about that, but she had thought of telling Roberto anyway.

"Well," said Roberto, "tell us all about it."

Magali was somewhat reticent, but after a short pause, and a sip of coffee, she began—repeating what she had just told to Amanda.

"I dropped into the Church of the Company last night about nine, before they closed, just to rest and meditate a bit. I found a secret door near the altar of the Virgin of Lourdes partially open. When they started to close the church, I opened it and went in, just to see what was there. It was a small room, with a table, a chair, and a bookcase against one wall. I started to leave, but the main door of the church was closed at exactly that time and the gust of air it made blew the door to the room closed. I couldn't open it again, no matter how I pushed against it. I was trapped—I thought. But I eventually discovered how to move the bookcase, and behind it was another door. I pushed open that door, with some effort—I fell down when it opened and hurt my knees, but I was okay. That door led into a tunnel. Not being able to get out by the door to the church, I had to follow the tunnel to find another way out. It went straight ahead. The walls and the floor were damp and mouldy, and slippery. After a short distance the tunnel started to go down as a kind of rampway. The floor was very slippery. I felt my way along the walls. It went downward for a long way. Then I reached a bottom, where the floor was rough but dry. It felt like it was dirt. I came to a wall and the tunnel turned to the right. I went that way for a fair distance and the tunnel then turned to the left. The floor was still rough, but harder, maybe stone. I went along that stretch for a long time. Then I hit with my foot the beginning of some steps. Not too many of them, but I didn't count them. I probably should have, but all I could think of was trying to get out. I went up the steps and continued going along the tunnel. In that part the floor was smooth, like paved or otherwise finished. The wall soon appeared to curve to the right. It curved slowly and for a long time. Then it was straight again. Then I could see at the end of the tunnel ahead a very weak light. I eventually came to a door. The light had been coming from beneath it. I banged on the door and called, and after a while it opened. A monk had opened it. He was in a brown habit, tied with a white cord. It had a hood. I saw a room with a lot of books in cases against the walls. There was a table with a lighted candle on it, and there were 'parchments,' and a feathered quill pen in an ink bottle—like in a dream or an old movie. Then I must have fainted. I woke up in the Church of the Company, in a pew near the altar of the Virgin of Lourdes, like it had never happened and I had fallen asleep in the pew and dreamed it all. Outside I looked at my watch and it was 5:30. I grabbed a taxi and went home."

"Quite a story," said Roberto. "What do you think, *Maestro?*"

Don Romualdo looked very concerned. He suggested they take a look at this secret door in the church. "But, first," he said, "I should go back to my office and get some things which might aid us." They finished their coffees, paid their bills, and left the Carolo and went to the Carolino. At the foot of the huge stairway leading to the second floor, Don Romualdo suggested that Magali accompany him to his office and that Roberto and Amanda wait there in the Carolino. It wouldn't take very long.

Don Romualdo and Magali went to the second patio with its cut stone fountain—in which there was never any water (except that left over from a rain, during the season, yellow and dirty)—and its statue of the Marques de Covarrubias in whose hand a mischievous student had placed a cigarette.

They crossed the patio and went down the stone stairway on the southern side, toward the offices of the library, and crossed a large corridor whose walls contained old oil paintings which represented royal scenes of medieval personages painted in those somber and heavy tones that characterized the Spanish and European painters of those times.

Since Magali was a child, she had had a great sensitivity that had cost her many scoldings on the part of the nuns at *Sacré Coeur,* the exclusive French school where she spent two years—from age eight to age ten—when her father was sent by his company to one of its factories in France. A hard two years.

There, she could touch in the old walls the passage of time and the imprint of the life and emotions left by former occupants; sometimes she could almost feel them talk, laugh, sob.

Mère Virginie had told her, "Don't trust in those strange sensations. Watch out! In the time of the Inquisition they would have burned you at the stake." But Magali could not avoid it. She felt there in that corridor of the UPA the stamp of all the past lives break loose, surrounding her as in a cold embrace.

Entering through the iron barred gate, now open, and going down the four stone steps, they entered the Holy of Holies of the Master. The environment was damp and cold, and Magali shivered. Although she adored the familiar smell of old books, for some reason that darkness that surrounded her then, a presence, reminded her of her nocturnal adventure.

Don Romualdo went to his desk and took out a small flashlight and a plastic roll which probably was a small tool kit. Looking around to see if there were something else to be attended to, or something else needed, he apparently felt satisfied. They left his work area, and Don Romualdo closed the wrought iron gate and locked it with his ancient key and they proceeded down the corridor to leave.

Lucinda was entering at that moment to go to the administration offices and saluted Don Romualdo with great respect.

"Good afternoon, Master."

"Good afternoon, Lucinda. How are you?"

"Well, you know, Master."

She was a chubby girl, but pleasant looking, wore thick eyeglasses, mouth painted with dark red lipstick. She had on a dress which appeared more appropriate for an older girl, or for a young woman. She was in high heels, and her hair, black and lustrous, was gathered in a chignon at the nape of her neck. She was carrying a great quantity of newspapers.

"As you see, lots of work."

"That will keep you from temptation, girl."

She laughed, like a schoolgirl. Then she looked at Magali, shyly. "Good afternoon, *Maestra.*"

"Good afternoon, Lucinda," said Magali.

Hurriedly she entered into the office, closing the door, leaving a trace of scent—sweet, violet, strong—behind her, like the trail a snail leaves on the floor.

"I don't know," said Don Romualdo. "Lucinda worries me. Sometimes I think she's spying on me."

Don Romualdo and Magali went out to the patio and across it. They continued to the stairway where they joined again with Roberto and Amanda, and the four of them went on to the enormous entrance door, passed the security guards, and came out into the bright sun on the *Pasaje Carolino*. It was filled with students carrying back packs or book bags and talking animatedly, all hurrying to or from somewhere.

They made their way through the students and entered the Church of the Company. Mass was being said at the main altar, where an old, semi-bald priest in his green and gold vestment murmured a litany, his hands together and his head bowed. Magali noted that the changes brought about in the modern Catholic religion were hard for her. She was raised in the old Latin rites. The Mass was now said in Spanish, and the priest faced the faithful. But some things did not change: the candles and the flowers expelled a sweet-sour smell, and the smoke of incense from somewhere extended across the floor like a white, odorous fog.

Five or six women and an old Indian man dressed in his traditional suit of cotton (pants only to below the knees), *sarape*, and rubber sandals (made from old auto tires) were all kneeling in the middle of the aisle, answering the prayers aloud: "Lord, pray for us. Mother of God, pray for us sinners. Amen."

Magali crossed herself and went toward the north wall of the building. She stopped before an immense statue (the Saint with the Wild Eyes), pretending to pray. She made signs to the Master, who approached her.

"Show me!" said Don Romualdo in a low voice.

She moved toward one side of the statue, and going around it, to its back, she showed with a gesture the door on the wall, now firmly closed. Don Romualdo approached with caution, tried to push it, without success. He examined its edges, looking for marks, signs that it had been opened. Finally, kneeling on the floor, he passed his fingers over the tiles.

"Yes," he said. "This door has been opened. Recently. They don't begin to clean the Church until the afternoon. There is a fine dust of paint and plaster on the floor." He said no more. He motioned to his friends to leave, and they quietly moved toward the main door and left the church.

Pigeons, above, cooed to their young in the nests constructed in the corners and bends of the complicated adornments over the entrance. There were several Indian women with plastic containers full of water waiting just outside the door, within the area surrounded by the bars that in older times were constructed to protect the church from robbers. They were waiting patiently for the Mass to end, waiting for the priest to bless their containers (the blessed water had fame for curing illnesses and frightening off demons).

Outside, in the *Pasaje Carolino,* street vendors of religious pictures, *camotillos* (a traditional sweet made with sweet potato and sugar), baskets from Oaxaca, shirts in brilliant colors, craft objects, and candies cried their merchandise. A loud group of Canadian tourists in shorts, sweatshirts, bananas, and cameras poured into the court from the Hotel Hidalgo to await the bus that would take them on a tour of the city. Groups of youths moved about from one side to the other of the plaza, entering or leaving the University, laughing or talking. Some professors in suits and white shirts were heading to their classrooms, carrying leather attaché cases. The sky was blue—as usual.

"I think," said Don Romualdo, "we should continue this 'investigation.' Let us go to *La Flor de Puebla.* That cafe is not so frequented by those from the UPA." They walked to *La Flor de Puebla,* under the arcade at the *Zócalo.* Going past the Carolo, they ran into Paul coming out. Roberto grabbed him by the arm and dragged him along with them, the two forming the tail of the group. Roberto filled him in on the way. When they arrived at *La Flor de Puebla,* they found a table outside. Roberto ordered a Cappuccino; Don Romualdo, a *café Americano.* Magali and Amanda, as well as Paul, also ordered Cappuccinos.

After exchanging a few pleasantries in a tone of friendly conversation, Don Romualdo looked about at the group. The authority and intensity of his gaze made all, in an instant, quiet.

"Magali," said the Master, looking at the girl, who lowered her head and concentrated on her coffee, "has certainly had an extraordinary adventure."

"A priest?" asked Paul. "And his habit, it had a hood?"

"Come on," chided Roberto. "You're not going to suggest the famous 'Tapado,' the 'Hooded One?' "

Magali looked at him.

"Tapado?" she asked.

"Alvaro de Benavidez, El Tapado," said Don Romualdo. "No doubt you have read the inscription at the door of the Church of the Company. The one who passed for a visitador, a tax collector, from Spain and made the convents and parishes pay with gold and jewels their taxes to the King of Spain, depleting also in this way the private treasures of various high dignitaries of the local Court. Of course, he kept all that he collected for himself."

"And who," added Roberto, "betrayed by the wife of one of his victims—since he also visited the bed chambers of the ladies of the court to learn of the wealth and possessions of their husbands—ended being executed by the Inquisition."

"What a horrible story," said Amanda.

"Tell me," asked Roberto. "About the habit of the person you saw, what color was it?"

"Color? I think it was . . . brown, and it had a white cord. White—" she repeated, and remained in thought.

"Do you remember anything more?" inquired the Master.

Magali remained quiet, shook her head "no" and resumed drinking her coffee.

A mime stopped in front of the group's table, and getting himself behind a passerby, he followed him, imitating perfectly all his gestures without the person being aware of it, to the great delight of the clients of the cafe. Then he passed among the tables, extending a gloved hand. Paul put a few coins in his palm, and the mime made an exaggerated gesture of courtesy, in the old manner, and retreated.

A very small boy, of about five years, approached with a basket full of gum.

"*Cómpreme, seño,*" he said to Paul, who made a negative gesture with his head.

"Go on, kid, don't bother me. Get lost!" Paul spoke hard, and with impatience.

The little boy, accustomed to this kind of refusal, moved on to an American couple that was seated at a neighboring table, who immediately bought various packages, uttering expressions like "Poor child; so young. He already has to earn a living."

"Continue, please," urged Don Romualdo of Magali.

"I'm sorry . . . that's all." She looked at the Master, who leaned back in his chair, closing his eyes.

When Magali left she went with Amanda to the CAPU, where she got a bus back to Cholula. The rainy season was on them, and although it was only the beginning of July, it was beginning to get hot. On leaving the terminal, Magali looked at the sky—still blue. But the volcano La Malinche was beginning to cover itself with grey clouds like the veil of an old woman. The summer storms came from the direction of the La Malinche volcano, and the people of Puebla could forecast rain by watching the clouds and darkness build up on that mountain before moving over the city.

Magali sighed. She was anxious that the water eliminate the great quantities of dust that covered the city and refresh the atmosphere a bit. But the rain also presented its own problems—one being the streets becoming so flooded that it became difficult at times to cross the pavement from one side to the other. She took a taxi home.

After refreshing herself and changing clothes, Magali took her swimming bag and went to the Club Alfa for a late afternoon swim. She had learned of this club and its swimming pool in early June and had immediately gotten a membership. She loved to swim. There was something between her and water, a complicity that she had maintained from a fetal past. And the Club Alfa had an olympic pool, surrounded by trees, from the center of which on a clear morning she could see the peak of the Popo. She usually went early in the morning, at about 7:30, when there were few people—a couple of men of a certain age and a woman in a blue bathing cap that swam vigorously, and whose face she had never been able to get a glimpse of. That afternoon she felt tired and sore, and although it was hot out, she commenced to exercise with energy, to free herself from those black butterflies, those dark thoughts.

"What am I doing here, in this country which is not mine? I left our house in Massachusetts, with its painted white fence, its large old rooms, the wooden sliding doors, its walls papered with blue flowers, its air of New England; my roses, the grapevine that Don Luigi gave me, the one that he had with so much trouble brought from San Francisco; the security of home, my parents, my friend Vera. Autumn, the foliage, the maples turning into a luminous blaze of gold and red; the snow, the white snow, the crunch-crunch under my boots on the sidewalk in the cold, frosty morning. And Boston, BU, and François." François had asked her to marry him, but she was not ready to commit herself to one man, to a settled, ordinary life; what she wanted was freedom and adventure. Was that the reason for coming to Mexico—to Puebla? What had brought her here? "What am I doing here? From what am I running away?"

The water opened at her passage like a new rose. Some birds, flying by, tried to come too close to the surface. "Watch out, bird. You are going to finish like me, in a mess."

There were oranges on a tree near the pool, now almost ripe. The Popo was clearly visible in the blue sky. It no longer spit out ashes; now it was only vapor—rising at times straight up into the sky; at others, dropping downward, licking the slopes.

François. She was going to call him, to tell him everything. He, who was so sure of himself—of them both—could help her. She needed him, she needed him badly. "Oh well", she thought, "so much for women's lib."

She got out, shivering, covering herself rapidly with her blue towel. The sun was strong; it gave out a solid, intense heat. But the breeze on her wet skin made her feel cold. She went to the women's showers: very primitive; little cubicles of brick and a thin stream of warm water. One time, looking upwards, she saw in the metal showerhead's semi-green holes, showing themselves through the holes, the heads of ethereal and transparent worms that lived, without doubt, on the mold accumulated within the metal showerhead, and came out as miniature whales at times to breathe. She dressed quickly. It always smelled bad in there, behind the curtains of yellow, stained cotton, hanging from their plastic rings, never clean. She missed the cleanliness of her home: a pristine cleanliness, everything fresh, everything smelling of soap, wax, and freshly washed clothes.

On leaving, she bumped into a pile of trash on the corner (the trash and the rats). She took minibus #1, got down on *3 Poniente,* and walked eastward. But everything was still closed (they don't open the stores again in the afternoon until 3:30). She walked past San Agustín with its big, old, leprous walls, its unkempt garden. She once saw an old woman curled up there, and when she turned around to look at her again, she had disappeared. Now she felt the necessity to see François, to touch him, to smell him, to be with him. It was almost a year since she had left him. In the beginning everything was new, everything interesting; now she wanted to go back to her routine of kisses; she missed her man.

On arriving at the *Zócalo,* she went to the Cathedral. Being careful of the pigeons who were roosting above the entranceway, she went in to do her little round of inspection of the interior of the church.

"Why," François once asked her, "your passion for churches?"

"I could say," she had answered, "that it's a question of religion, but I would be lying. It means for me centuries of tradition, my roots buried in a world that I've lost, of which nothing remains other than certain memories transmitted by my spiritual DNA: smells, textures, colors, carpets, incense, organ music, Debussy, gold and silver vestments, and the High Masses of those times, when I was young; my mother who took me to the Santa Anna grade school, always so elegant, with her black silk dress and her two silver foxes wrapped around her white neck; and my father that played the violin and translated the Kyrie

Eleisons of Shubert and Ludwig Van. Generations on the part of my grandparents and great grandparents, on both my mother's and my father's side, all being baptized, making their first communion with warm and sweet-sour hosts, brides dressed in white with long veils of chiffon and lace. *Deus Profundis Ora Pro Nobis.* When I enter an old church, I touch the wood of the pews, look upward, and the windows transmit to me like a code of feelings and words, the features of a family that I never knew, in greens, violet blues, and sun beams. It's, in a way, me, a part of me. Without it I am incomplete—just a lonely being in a foreign world."

He had put his arms around her without speaking, and they stayed like that for a while together, filled with emotion, like touching an unknown dimension that was there, palpable, very much in reach, and they talked of things immortal and sacred.

33

COMPLICATIONS

On Friday morning the Carolo, the restaurant-cafe of the university crowd, next to the Neruda Library on the *Avenida Avila Camacho*, was full, as usual: students having coffee and discussing literature and philosophy, talking of studies and exams; or teachers gossiping, criticizing the administration, complaining of the little they earn while the "Americans" were hired with large salaries and "did nothing." Couples, hiding themselves at the farthest tables, were kissing in the corners.

Don Romualdo was early in the cafe. He was soon joined by Roberto and Amanda. Paul came a little later. They began talking about Magali's adventure, but in low voices, very seriously. Don Romualdo was cold and tense. His coffee steamed on the table in its large ceramic cup. His skin, more so than usual, seemed like an old parchment. His black eyes were very visible behind his glasses. Their gaze was almost turned off, dim as 20 watt light bulbs all used up. It is true that he almost never saw the sun, buried as he always was in his books in Lafragua.

"What is light? A wave or a particle? It is this duality of light that matters. Indeed, it is the perception of reality that matters, not the reality itself," said a white-bearded American professor at a nearby table to a group of students who listened to him with religious attention though they understood little of either his English or his science.

Magali arrived at the entrance, slim and young, and they all turned to look at her. Don Romualdo immediately got up, offering her a chair he had pulled back. She said good morning to him and to the others and asked for *café con leche* and a pastry. "Bring me also an orange juice—natural, please," she added.

At that moment Luis, one of Magali's former students, a boy with big, dark eyes and long black hair tied at the nape with a strip of leather, and wearing jeans, leather boots, and a multicolored vest which came from Chiapas and was in style at that time, entered the cafe, approached the table, and saluted respectfully the young teacher. *"Buenos días, Maestra."*

A young girl, slight in build but well shaped, also in jeans, and wearing a white cotton blouse, her mouth painted dark red, eye shadow on her eyelids, followed him at two paces distance. She stood behind the boy, smiling timidly.

"Buenos, Luis," said Magali. "How is everything going?"

"Well. But, if you have a few minutes, *Maestra,* I would like to speak with you . . . on a private matter."

"All right. If you can wait for a little while," said Magali with a smile. Luis assented and moved outside and to the left of the entrance where Magali could still see him.

The attraction that Magali exercised, not only as a foreigner and as a professor, but also as a beautiful woman, on some of her male students was not unknown to her. Having always been very attractive, she was accustomed to provoking a reaction in the opposite sex. It was, for her, something normal and expected, to which she gave no special attention, was hardly even aware of it—except if the reaction was expressed in a manner that went too far. In that case she defended herself very well, in words and in deed, having taken some courses in self defense in Boston.

Luis' girl was aware of the admiration of Luis for Magali, but said nothing. In the *machista* society of Mexico—although the female was accepted in literature, and there was a strong movement to recognize the female in various professions—the women occupied a secondary place in society and were always subject to the will of their fathers, brothers, boy friends, fiancés, or husbands.

Margarita, the waitress, who showed a very advanced pregnancy under the small apron of blue and white squares, brought the orange juice in a large glass. Magali, thanked her and asked her, as she always did these last few weeks, "How much to go?" while she began to drink the juice in small sips, deliciously savoring it. One could not compare it with that "reconstituted" juice, full of chemicals, from the U.S.

"Well, not much now, *Maestra,*" said the woman, moving herself with difficulty between the tables, her ankles swollen, and large black circles showing below her brown eyes.

"We have a sacred duty to protect our work," Don Romualdo was saying. "We are confronted with an unknown factor here and we have to decide on a plan of action. We really have to meet on this. How about this evening in my home? Say about seven? I can have some snacks and refreshments, enough to serve as a light supper."

They all agreed to the meeting. Don Romualdo gave them directions to his house. Paul offered to bring Magali, Amanda, and Roberto with him in his Vocho. Magali then began talking aside quietly with Paul, arranging for the time he would come by to pick her up. Having by then finished her pastry and coffee, she excused herself from the group, saying she had to do something important and would be back. Or, at any rate, she would see them all again at Don Romualdo's house that evening.

Luis was still waiting for Magali just outside the door. Magali apologized for making him wait, saying they were talking about something very important. Luis said it didn't matter, he had nothing to do at this hour. They walked slowly toward the *Pasaje Carolino.*

"So," said Magali, continuing in English, as Luis had spoken in the cafe, "what did you want to talk with me about?"

"*Maestra.* I am embarrassed to tell you this—but you know how much I respect you."

"Come on, Luis. Tell me."

"Well, I'm going out with a friend of Lucinda, who works at the Lafragua Library."

"Ah, . . . and is this pretty girl the one?"

"Yes. And I think that we shall become engaged very soon."

"Well, congratulations! She seems a very nice girl."

"*Maestra,* . . . what I wanted to tell you, is that . . . that Lucinda, who says she is a friend of my girl . . . is not to be trusted."

Magali remembered Don Romualdo: "Lucinda worries me. Sometimes I think she's spying on me."

Magali went from Luis to the ILE. She checked at the faculty lounge for any developments of interest to her; there were none. As she was leaving, passing by the administration, Inez came out and said that the Director wanted to see her. Inez was a woman of typical Mexican appearance (almost Indian); thick, dark hair gathered at the neck, nose slightly acquiline, high cheek bones, full lips, well formed figure, attractive. She was made up to perfection (the secretaries were paid very poorly but they had no qualms in taking on large debts with the "Avon Lady," which was quite successfully established in Mexico). Green eye shadow on the lids, mascara on the lashes, make-up base, and Coty Flaming Red "blush" lipstick. She wore the uniform of the UPA: tight skirt to just above the knees, tailored jacket, white blouse. On the majority of them it looked quite good, although the colors they had chosen—magenta and electric blue—did not go well with the dark matte skin of the girls.

Ana Luisa, seated at her desk, was doing, as she did each Friday, her manicure. She was soaking her hand in a coffee cup half full of hot water and detergent while a colleague painted the nails on the other hand with sure and expert brush strokes. There was a strong smell in the office of banana oil and enamel. And there was also a constant going and coming of students and professors, but this didn't disturb in the least the task of the girls. It surprised Magali a lot, this lack of professionalism, but she did not dare to judge these employees who had obtained their posts through friends and connections rather than abilities and skills—and besides, they earned much less than the minimum wage in the U.S. A compact "ghetto blaster" (easily obtained at the *Fayuca* for a very reasonable price), whose volume was set on high, provided some very loud Latin music.

Soon would come the seller of sandwiches, *chilaquiles*, and other snacks, carried in a lace covered basket: breakfast. At that time the secretaries would go to a small, dark, smelly room next to the bathroom to buy these wares and to eat. At midday various sellers of clothing, shoes, and books for children would invade the office. All was bought on credit, and although the payments were tiny, the usurious interests that were piled on made of such commerce a very lucrative business.

Ana Luisa's friend made a gesture to enter with the hand that held the brush, without raising her gaze, and Magali opened the heavy door to the Director's office and went in, closing the door behind her. The Director was signing a few papers, and he also made a sign, without looking at her, that she should sit. (Visual contact is one of the important rites of the Mexican culture—if you don't look a person in the eye, that person is of no importance. This is a thing to know when driving. To get another driver to allow you to move—such as change lane—in accordance with your hand or light signal, you must first gain eye contact with him. Then he will recognize you as a fellow human and allow you to do your maneuver.)

The director's personal "assistant," a tall, good looking boy dressed in a suit was sitting at his desk, writing something in a booklet. He raised his eyes, admired the figure of Magali, and returned to his task. Magali sat on a plush chair in front of the enormous, carved wood desk, which was covered with magazines, documents, and papers, while the smoke of a cigarette that rested in a beautiful Talavera ash tray rose in blue-white streams toward the ceiling.

Licenciado Manuel Rogriguez de Vásquez Plata sat in his specially made chair, wearing a grey gabardine suit, a pink shirt, and a dark Christian Dior tie. After a few minutes he raised his head.

"*Maestra*, I wanted to talk with you about your extra-curricular activities in the UPA."

She looked at him without answering. Ordinarily, if the Director called her, it was to assign her a new task: a translation, attending to visiting foreigners, or some such problem that he couldn't handle. Without responding, she waited.

"I refer to your work in Lafragua."

Magali did not respond, but her heart gave a jump in her chest. She had asked herself already, many times, when the situation of her activities in Lafragua would be told (as gossip, of course) to the Director.

"Work? Ah, you mean the 'research' that I'm doing."

"You are carrying out an investigation? I did not know that," responded the Director.

She smiled, coquettishly.

"After all, my contract does say 'Research Professor.' And I am here to work on my own project as well as attend to my teaching duties."

"Of course, of course." The man took an American cigarette from an open package on the desk. He offered the pack to Magali, who said "no" with her head. The boy jumped up to light it, then returned to his place and continued writing.

Inez knocked on the door and entered with a tray holding two cups of coffee, which she placed on the desk. Retrieving the folder with the signed letters, she quietly left the room without acknowledging Magali's presence. Her high heels clicked on the floor like castanets.

"As I indicated in my letter accepting this position, I'm documenting my dissertation on the churches and libraries of the city for my Doctorate from Boston University."

"Ah, but how interesting! Of course, you are free to carry out all the investigations you please and access the old books at our Lafragua. I am sure that Don Romualdo would give you all the assistance necessary."

"Don Romualdo has already been very cooperative and helpful to the extreme, Licenciado. But could I ask you what rumors are responsible for my being here?"

"Rumors?" The man laughed heartily, showing perfectly aligned white teeth, sharp like those of a wolf. "Surely you must appreciate, *chère* Magali, that your presence in this University has awakened . . . some, let us say—"

"Jealousy? Envy?"

"To say the least, yes. There are professors here that are not full time and are already working for the UPA for many years; and suddenly you come, full time, and are paid five times more than they."

"Doubtlessly, that is a problem of the system—not mine," argued Magali. "When they offered me the contract, I had no idea of the administrative problems of this important University."

"Yes, of course. Anyway, you need not worry about these things. But, I would appreciate your letting me know of whatever extra activities you might undertake related to the University . . . so as to avoid there arising any misunderstandings."

"Of course," replied Magali, courteously. Getting up, she said goodbye to the Director and left with her head high, without looking at the secretaries nor noting the malicious giggles she provoked in passing.

"*Alors,*" she thought. "Somebody is worried about what we are doing—and why. Very interesting. I must talk with Don Romualdo. I must put him on guard." Leaving the building, she was struck in the face by a sticky, overly sweet scent of violets and thought she saw a silhouette, half hidden in the entrance of a building just across the street from the entrance to the ILE, watching her. She shrugged her shoulders. "I'm getting neurotic." she said.

She returned to her apartment to eat something and to rest a bit. All this situation began to appear unreal, even ridiculous: secret passageways, hooded monks? "God, and this is the 20th Century," she said to herself. Her rigid American training converted this adventure into something not very probable. But her European background gave her an inclination to believe in things that were only illusions. In any case, she was on the road of adventure which would lead her—to what?

The sun was now hot, and the exhaust of the traffic and the smell of the steaming asphalt made the air suffocating. She went to the Boulevard to catch a breeze on her walk home and she stopped, as was her custom, on the corner where she was to turn northward, next to a vacant lot. Standing there, she heard a soft meow, and a tiny baby kitten, white with yellow stripes, came out of one of the bushes, staggering. The animals in Mexico suffer much more than the people. Many of the dogs are confined to the hot roofs, tied with heavy chains or thick ropes, and newly born cats are thrown away, sometimes onto vacant lots, in the middle of trash, to die. Without thinking, she bent to pick up the precious kitten, taking it into her hands and caressing it. "Poor little thing . . . I'll take you home. You need some milk." She put it into her book bag and continued her walk home.

When she arrived at her apartment, she opened the door to a surprise. The room had been searched. She found everything upset—the bed undone, her clothing thrown about. All her drawers had been emptied and their contents scattered everywhere. She covered her mouth so as not to scream, slammed the door with force, and ran to look for a telephone. And that, as anyone who has ever lived in Mexico knows, was no easy task. First, there were few public phones; and those that existed were most of the time out of service. She entered into a pharmacy and had to pay one peso to use their phone. She called Paul (who was a friend she considered best prepared, physically, to confront violent situations). She had to make several calls—to his shop, to the FALE, and finally to the ILE. He had a class at that time and they didn't want to fetch him, but Magali insisted it was an emergency and they finally called him to the phone. Paul said that she should wait right there, in the pharmacy, and not to move until he got there.

He arrived in his Vocho, after what appeared to Magali to be hours. He calmed her down, and the two returned to the apartment. Paul assured himself that there was no one outside observing them, and no intruder within. Then he cautiously entered, checked well the room to be certain that there was no one there, and, taking Magali by the hand, entered and closed the door behind them with the iron bolt. Magali sat on the undone bed. The mattress had been slit on the side, letting one see its insides of cactus wool.

She found her school papers and private letters intact in the drawer of the night table (the passport and the contract were in a safety deposit box in the bank, together with some travellers' checks). She checked the wardrobe and her research was all there in its boxes at the bottom, undisturbed, but covered with clothes that had formerly been on their hangers. Quickly looking around and checking for certain things which had a personal value, she found that nothing seemed to be missing.

Then she remembered her "baby," who was sleeping in the bottom of her book bag which she had left in her hurry to escape the apartment. It was on the floor. She picked up the bag and took out the kitten. Paul approached to look at it.

"And this?"

"It was abandoned. I—"

Magali started, suddenly, to cry. Paul approached her. "Come on. Come on. Calm yourself. It's all over."

She left the kitten in the center of the sheets and, hurriedly getting up, started to collect her clothes, stockings, a pair of shoes, tooth brush, paste, soap, shampoo, a small painted tin mirror, her alarm clock.

Paul helped her to rearrange the furniture, to replace what had been thrown from her dresser drawers, to pick up books and papers.

Magali said she wanted to call Amanda. She went to her phone and found it still connected and working. Amanda answered. Magali told her about the break-in, and Amanda said she should come and stay with her; it was dangerous and foolish to remain there. Magali agreed, and thanked her for the offer, and said she'd soon be there.

Then she thought she'd better call François. She put the call to his office at BU and he answered. Her luck was running well. She told François quickly of what was happening. He said he would catch the next plane to Mexico. She told him she was moving in with a girl friend for a while and gave him Amanda's number.

After she hung up, Paul said he would drive her now to Amanda's.

She put some clothes and some overnight things in a plastic bag and, assuring herself that there was no food left out, and that all was clean, she was ready to leave. She closed the door with key, though she knew that that would not keep her burglar out.

There was no doubt now that she had stumbled into something extremely dangerous. Paul took her to the house of Amanda.

Her friend, with her husband and her family, were seated at the table for supper. There was a porcelain bowl in the center, full of calabash flower soup that gave off an appetizing smell. They invited Magali and Paul to stay and eat. Magali waited for the meal to end and then related what had happened in the apartment. Victor thought that they were getting into a mess, and Amanda said that that was right, but that she thought they had to discover at least what was going on before they could have peace again. "We don't know what we should do because we don't know who the others are, what they are doing, or why."

"Perhaps it's a question of notifying the police," said Victor.

"You know what the police would do," put in Amanda. "Absolutely nothing. Especially in the case of a foreigner."

"I agree," said Paul. "They would say it's a case of another hysterical *gringa* looking for publicity."

"Well," said Magali. "This matter is getting quite ugly." In that moment the cat began to meow.

"What's that?" inquired Amanda.

Magali put her hand in the bag and took out the tiny animal, which was all rolled up, looking like a ball of yarn. The children immediately jumped at it. "Careful there, it's only a baby."

Angelica, Amanda's oldest daughter, who was now fifteen and was a very attractive young lady, went immediately to look for some milk in the kitchen.

"I'm sorry," said Magali. "I didn't have the heart to leave it abandoned in the street."

Her friend smiled. "There's always milk for one more," she said. "Don't you worry. Besides, it will grow up to take charge of the mice. And you will stay here, with us, until you feel safe to return to your own home."

Don Romualdo returned to his library—to the "glorious dust of the Library," as one of his predecessors had stated. He put on his white coat. "It's strange," he thought, "but eighty percent of the time we function on automatic. We get up; we brush our teeth; we don't even notice the flavor of the tooth paste; we put water on to boil; we make coffee." His forehead was furrowed; his posture stooped; his movements slow and studied, as if it cost him work to make the necessary gestures. He felt as if he had suddenly aged a hundred years.

He looked for his glasses at the bottom of one of the pockets of his uniform and clumsily put them on. He took out an old book from one of his secret, locked, hiding places. Before, only to touch the worn covers, to pass his fingers over the fire-mark on the spine, to open and smell the humid and yellow breath of the years would have given him profound pleasure. He would have felt, touching the fragile pages written with such love and illustrated by hand, transported to a kind of ecstasy, to a world in which time had lost its dimension. He would have been integrated into this past-present, forming part of it—the hand that touched the book and the book itself: a single thing, all amalgamated into a dust of stars, and himself within the patina of time, immortal, untouchable at his table of rustic wood, under the window of the vault (an arc, a meter thick) from which light filtered through a yellow pane which the rain washed from time to time. He would have felt totally happy. Now, it was only one routine more. The magic had disappeared.

"My God," he said aloud, "I'm so tired." He was reviewing the *Títulos y méritos de los sres. Covarrubias, Juan Pablo Matyrrizo, 1a. edición, Madrid: por los herederos de la viuda de P. de Madrigal, 1629*. The volume, 237 pages, 33.8 x 22.7 centimeters, contained nine water color portraits of the Covarrubias family, plus five birth certificates and the coat of arms of the family. But now the book was silent; there was no contact; the umbilical cord that tied it to the past was broken. He was alone. With an automatic gesture Don Romualdo took a handkerchief from a pocket of his pants and cleaned his glasses, which had begun to cloud.

Then, from the same pocket, he took out an antique watch and chain, of gold—his only jewel. Opening it carefully, he contemplated the photograph of a young girl with dark hair, with a large chignon on top of her head, dressed in the style of the last century: blouse with long sleeves and lace neck, cameo in the center. She had regular features—rather sharp, like those of a bird—straight nose, oval face, and very thin lips, stretched into a forced smile. The chin, pointed, gave her an unusual character.

"Maria-Esther, why did you go, why did you let him take you from my side? We would have been so happy. Look at me now.

I've allowed myself to be devoured by this monster of a library, but I never found in books the warmth of your child-like hands, Maria-Ester."

"*Feci quod potui,*" he murmured.

He wiped away a tear, carefully closed the watch, and put it again into the anonymous darkness of his pocket. "And now—*Les jeux son faits.* All is lost." With sudden determination he pounded the table hard with his fist.

"No!" he cried. "I shall not permit it. I've passed fifty years here, alone, fighting to protect—this. No one shall destroy my work, my life. *Causa victrix deis placuit, sed victa, Catoni.*"

With great care and extreme delicacy he closed the book, dusted its cover with a sweep of his hands, wiping them on his uniform, and went with it under his arm toward the rear of the library. He passed the section of antique parchments in Latin, went by that of French authors of the 14th century, and, careful to not step on the various saucers full of rat poison (of such a beautiful pink color), crossed under the last arc, going to an old bookcase that almost entirely covered the thick wall whose paint was peeling from the humidity.

34

AT DON ROMUALDO'S HOUSE

That evening, about seven, they met in the house of the Master. Don Romualdo lived with his mother (an old lady in her 80's, very nice, with white hair, short and well arranged, wearing eyeglasses with gold rims) in a small house of the colonial Mexican style on the outskirts of Puebla, close to Chipilo. Chipilo was a community of Italian immigrants, very private, that had dedicated itself for two or three generations to agriculture, and especially to husbandry. Their milk and milk products—cheeses and butter—were well appreciated and highly valued in Puebla as well as in the capital.

Paul picked up Roberto and then drove to Cholula to get Magali and Amanda. From there he went south to the Boulevard Atlixco, which was the old road (now replaced by a toll expressway) to Atlixco, and which would take them right by Chipilo.

They arrived shortly after 6:30. The little house of adobe with a roof of tiles, surrounded by bougainvillaea, roses, and fruit and eucalyptus trees, was most charming and was set in quite an extensive piece of land that comprised a small pond and a vegetable garden in the back. Some hens wandered loose, cackling happily, followed by a rooster who demonstrated his importance by sticking out his chest of bright and exquisite plumage. They parked in a driveway and approached the door to the house by a stone path. Don Romualdo was waiting for them with Kahlúa and coffee, and his mother had prepared a pastry. There were also small sandwiches on a side table in the living room, and some fruit juice punch.

"What tranquility you breathe here," commented Amanda.

"Not counting that you breathe," added Paul, always practical. Puebla already had a very high index of air pollution.

"Yes," added Magali. "Almost one year ago, when I first came to Puebla, there was only a third of the trucks and autos that there are now. And here in Puebla there are no regulations against the noxious emissions of the buses. When I asked a taxi driver why they didn't have fines for the busses that filled the city with smoke, he said to me: 'Fines? *Multas?* They have. You see, *Señorita*, the policeman stops one of those busses. The chauffeur of the bus gives him twenty pesos. That's the fine. And then both go on about their business. And everything's "fine." ' And he laughed."

"It's true," said the Master. "The city has grown much. And here in Mexico, unfortunately, the rules are made to be ignored. It is because of this that we decided, my mother and I, to buy this modest house in a green oasis of tranquility and peace."

After they had exchanged the customary courtesies and talked a little about the weather, the University, and horticulture, the old lady got up and made ready to retire from the room.

"You will excuse me," she said, "but at my age, although I appreciate visits very much, unfortunately I tire early."

They all rose to say good night. Magali kissed the woman on her wrinkled cheeks.

"Magali," she said. "Come. Accompany me a moment."

"Of course," replied Magali. The two women left, followed by the intense and worried look of Don Romualdo.

They went to her bed chamber, a room furnished in the Spanish style. There was a large mahogany bed with four posts; a dressing table from the end of the last century with an enormous oval mirror; and little bottles of perfume, an atomizer, a hand mirror, and an elaborate silver brush lying on the table cover of lace with crocheted borders. There also was a wicker rocking chair covered with comfortable cushions; two stuffed chairs upholstered in gold and coffee colored velvet; and an exquisite vase of Talavera holding some fresh peach-colored roses. The old lady noted Magali's look of admiration. "Talavera. Beautiful, no?"

"Yes. Do you know something of the history of this ceramic?"

"It was made here since the time of the viceroys; it came from a small town in Spain called 'Talavera de la Reina.' But, look. See that little book on one of the shelves, titled *Historia Compendiada del Estado de Puebla*? No, the other. That one! Look under '*INDUSTRIA DE LA TALAVERA*.'"

"'. . . *algunos de los primeros pobladores de la ciudad, originarios del arzobispado de Toledo, habrán sido los introductores de la noble industria.' Es de creerse que cualquier conocedor haya parado mientras en las buenas cualidades de las arcillas de los alrededores de la ciudad de Puebla; —Diego Antonio Bermúdez de Castro nos dá a saber que el barro utilizado por los alfareros provenía del rumbo de Totimehuacán, y muy en breve comenzaron a fabricarse platos, tazas, porrones, floreros, jarrones y azulejos. . . . la fama de los azulejos y la de la loza, nombrada desde entonces de* **talavera,** *se divulgó, y su consumo extendióse por toda la Nueva España. . . . La fecha de la aparición de la industria no ha podido aclararse, sólo coligiendo de los templos poblanos más antiguos adornados de azulejos, podría calcularse aproximadamente la segunda mitad del siglo XVI, tomando como punto de partida la iglesia de San Francisco, que data de 1567.*"[1]

"The favorite colors," added the old lady, "of the makers of Talavera are blue, green, and yellow. The finest ceramic has up to five layers, which you can appreciate in the admirable bricks of Acatepec with glazings in blue, purple, green, orange, and vermilion, not to mention the white enamel. Personally, I prefer the classic blue and white. But continue, please. Out loud. To read is a task for me. My eyes are tired."

"*Suelen ser de tres colores los azulejos del siglo XVIII, monocromos los de otras épocas. Hacían el esmalte o lustre fino con una arroba de plomo y seis de estaño; la loza corriente nada más llevaba dos de estaño, pintábanse las decoraciones con colores vitrificantes hechos de óxidos metálicos; pasaban, entonces, las piezas a un segundo fuego, para mezclar los colores con el lustre. . . . Donaldson [Eberlein] señala cuatro tipos definidos en la mayólica*

---

[1]*Enrique Cordero y T.,* **Historia Compendiada del Estado de Puebla,** *3 Tomos. (Puebla: Publicaciones del Grupo Literario "Bohemia Poblana", 1965), II: 226-27.*"

*mexicana; el hispano-morisco que duró hasta fines del siglo XVII; el de Talavera propiamente dicho que dominó durante todo el siglo XVIII, el chino que aparece en 1650 y el hispano-mexicano o poblano que comenzó a usarse en los albores del siglo XIX. Distinguían al primero los entrelaces, ojos y rollos peculiares del dibujo. El modelo de Talavera española suele presentar figuras de aves, cuadrúpedos y aún siluetas humanas en azul, con flores y follaje sobre fondo blanco; la mayólica mexicana que siguió tal modelo caracterízase por cierto punteado y rayado en azul hecho toscamente, pero de buen efecto a distancia, es acaso el tipo más común de **talavera** poblanas. La influencia del modelo chino se manifiesta en los asuntos, en el color azul más vivo y en la forma y contorno de las jarras, tinajas y cántaros, suelen estas vasijas 'presentar la figura de una pera invertida.' . . . La industria de la **talavera** en nuestro siglo, teniendo en consideración su importancia y fama de tiempos pretéritos, puede considerarse muerta; uno que otro magnate hace fabricar azulejos y artefactos, los que, ciertamente, no tienen ya la galanura de los antiguos." [2]*

Magali raised her eyes from her reading, scanning the room with a look while the old lady had her eyes half closed. She saw an antique high chest of drawers of carved wood, and lots of photographs on the wall, framed in mahogany, one of which showed a couple—a very attractive woman in a bride's gown with a long train, holding a bouquet of roses, and a young man in a military uniform, looking very serious. The old lady was resting on a small sofa next to the window, which was open and allowed a fresh and fragrant breeze to enter.

"My husband and I," she suddenly said, almost making Magali, who had thought the old woman was sleeping, jump from her chair. "The day of our wedding." Then she motioned with a gesture to various photographs of a very stern-looking boy, perfectly groomed, in a military style school uniform.

"My son. I am afraid that he did not have a happy childhood. An only son. His father was in the army. He raised him like a soldier, with the most strict discipline." She sighed.

"Is something wrong?" asked Magali.

"That's what I wanted to talk to you about, Magali. I know that you have a close relation with my son, and that he respects you very much."

---

[2]*Ibid., II: 228-31.*

"I also respect him, enormously."

"That's why I wanted to ask you if you have noted in him any changes lately."

"Changes?"

"I refer to . . . his paleness, his fatigue, his nervousness . . . and, something more, something that I can't quite identify but which worries me."

Magali approached the old lady, taking her hand.

"It is his work, you know. He is intensely involved with his activities at Lafragua."

"Involved? Yes. I ask myself—"

An owl commenced to let out the notes of a strange song in the dark. The old lady shivered.

"His father never pardoned his not wanting to take up a military career. He had trained him to be a soldier, almost since he could walk."

Magali, solicitously, took a *sarape* that was on the bed and put it around the old lady's shoulders.

"Thanks, child. You are so kind. Tell me, do you have a fiancé?"

Magali remained silent for a moment. "Fiancé? Yes. I have one—in Boston."

"And what are you doing here, then, girl? In my time a fiancé was all that a young girl wanted. Love, engagement, marriage, children, a family. Now . . . now girls have careers instead of children."

"Yes . . . we have changed much, and I don't know if for the better. Before, men treated us like ladies, they gave us a hand to get out of a car, they invited us to dinner, to the movie. We were cared for, protected. Now we have to pay our own way. And although professionally we have obtained some advantages, I always ask myself if all this feminist liberation is worth the pain."

A gust of wind blew the white cotton lace curtain from the window. Magali got up to close it. In doing so, she saw that outside the stars were shining in the dark and clear sky.

"Don't close it, girl. I love the breeze . . . and I can see the stars. But, go now. Your friends will think that I have kidnapped you."

Magali kissed the cheeks of the old woman again, and went out of the room, closing the door behind her.

When she returned, the men politely stood up.

"We were just talking about you," said Roberto.

The room was surrounded by bookshelves of antique wood. On the central wall was a fireplace where they had lit a fire which smelled marvelously of cedar. It was going into the second week of July, but in the highlands it was cool both at night and in the morning. The room was furnished with three leather sofas of natural color; a small table with a wood base and covered with glass on which were strewn academic journals; and a stereo phonograph in a corner, various records of classical music on a small stand at its side. There was also a small desk covered with books and various pamphlets; a couple of onyx ash trays; and a crystal lamp which emitted a diffuse, golden light. On the floor was a beautiful woolen rug with Mexican designs, thick and comfortable. In another corner was an enormous jug of Talavera.

It was a room of a professor, a scholar. A room comfortable with science and literature, with the peace of eternal truth. This night, however, the mood in the house was not so tranquil. The books remained silent on their shelves; the fire did not sparkle so happily; the light that came from the lamp was cold, almost sinister. Magali shivered. "Somebody is walking on my grave," she thought.

Don Romualdo got up and offered her a seat closer to the fire. "Sit here, Magali. If you are cold, I'll bring you a *sarape.*"

"No, thank you, Master. I'll be all right here. Go on, please. Don't let me interrupt you."

Don Romualdo brought her a steaming Talavera cup which smelled of good coffee.

"Thank you, Master. This is what I needed."

"Because of the adventure of Magali, we must now prepare an emergency plan," continued Roberto, looking at the girl, who blushed.

Roberto had lit a cigarette that Don Romualdo had offered him.

"I think that, to begin with, we should decide on dates and hours," said Paul.

"That is important," agreed Roberto, "but first we have to discuss an overall plan of action. That is, in case we find the place. And that it takes us to where we hope— In case of a meeting . . . with someone. What action to take? And, how shall we be received? We have to contemplate all the eventualities."

"Yes," said Paul. "Will we meet resistance? How many are there? Who are they? Will they be armed?"

"But," protested Magali, joining in though she didn't know all of just what they were talking about, "We are dealing with a monk. Or a person that looked like one."

"That doesn't seem very probable to me," responded Paul.

"Why not somebody—religious or not—just trying to save the precious books of the library?" argued Don Romualdo.

"You are a conscientious person, but without experience with the real world, my dear Master," said Paul. "In these times I do not consider it very probable that someone has an end so altruistic and so noble."

"I agree," said Roberto. "It is more probable that we are dealing with someone that has found a secret entrance to Lafragua through the passageways of the church, and who is gathering books as part of a big robbery. Who knows how many books are already in his hands, or even already outside the country?"

"But, why the disguise?" protested Magali. "It doesn't make sense. Why is there a need for a disguise?"

"A need? Yes, why a need? And if it is truly a religious—like the Templars and the Holy Grail—to whom, through the centuries, has the sacred task of protecting the books been transmitted? And by whom? By generations of what priests?" argued Don Romualdo, speaking directly to Magali.

There was a long pause while everyone considered quietly the facts. The owl, outside, continued sounding its funeral chant.

"That was my impression," said Magali, responding to the Master. "All of the room appeared outside of time, outside of this century, totally unreal, in another dimension. And, at the same time, there was something threatening in the scene that frightened me out of my wits. Unless I— Unless . . . I dreamed it."

"No, Magali," said Paul. "I don't think so. Of course we are all steeped in those stories of secret passageways and of monks and monasteries. But I do not think that you have invented all this. It would be too improbable, too ridiculous, and you are a sensible person. At least, I think so," he joked. "No. I think that all this must be a *mise-en-scène.*"

"For the benefit of whom?" protested Magali. "At the end of this passageway that nobody knows? To fool whom?" The group remained silent.

"Okay," said Paul. "There's only one thing to do: investigate. And the sooner, the better. There are so many stories of buried treasures in the secret passageways between the *Colegio del Espíritu Santo* and the Cathedral. The tunnel system ramifies so much, connecting almost all of the important churches and convents. If we go down there, we have to be prepared, dressed well, with boots, flashlights, tools. perhaps a revolver. My brother has one what he can loan us. I should say that Roberto and I have some experience through our helping Fr. Flynn in his explorations of the tunnels. And we have equipment. But Magali will have to go down there with us. I know she has been down in some tunnels, but we don't know the real conditions of where we are going, except for what Magali has told us. We shall have to take precautions that we don't get lost down there, or stuck there and forgotten."

"Listen to us," said Roberto. "It sounds like we're planning a coup out of a gothic novel—medieval, with hooded monks and hidden treasures."

"It is," responded Magali. "It's all about old books, and monks, and secret passageways . . . except that this is happening now, in this century. And lately I feel like I'm being watched, almost stalked."

There was a moment of silence, but this time it was not the passing of an angel.

35

ROBERTO'S GIRL

After returning to Cholula from Don Romualdo's, Amanda and Magali were talking on the small interior patio of the house. The sky was clear and there was a moon, as full as a Mexican silver medallion. The children had retired to sleep; Victor was working at the computer; and the little kitten was curled up at the feet of Magali. Magali sighed.

"I know who you're thinking of," said her friend.

"Yes. I really miss François. I feel so secure next to him, so protected, so complete."

"Girl, you're in love!"

"Well, yes. But I had to come to Mexico to realize it."

Just then the phone rang. It was François. He had a flight for Saturday—the same as at Christmas, but a different number: 1024. He would arrive at the D.F. at 5:00 p.m. It would take a little time to go through immigration and customs, but everything was in order and that should be completed quickly. He should be with her before six.

"Well, you'll have your François," said Amanda. "But, with all that's going on?"

"I know. And I didn't really tell him everything. He would worry too much."

"That's no good." said Amanda. "Tell him all. He's coming here to share in this adventure. After all, that's what love is all about, isn't it? Sharing."

Magali crossed her legs, and, in so doing, pushed the kitten who immediately complained, protesting with a loud meow. She stooped to get it up and put in on her lap, thinking.

"All this thing of the passageway, my nocturnal adventure, and— What were they looking for in my room? Who was it, and why?"

"Your anxiety is natural. All this has me nervous too. And I've got Victor with me."

"Yes, but he thinks we should forget it all."

"And it's possible that he's right. But do you realize what would happen? We would be the rest of our lives feeling sorry for having lost this unique, incredible opportunity, to have missed a fantastic adventure— to not have gotten to the end of—"

"The end of the mystery. That's what has me worried—the end."

"But think of it, Magali. How many people in the whole world have had or could have an opportunity as extraordinary as what you just had? It's just like a gothic novel, medieval, with hooded monks and hidden treasures."

"How romantic you are," said Magali. "But, you're right. I also would not rest easy if we didn't carry this to its proper end."

"To discover . . . to discover," Magali said to herself, "what is down there, who has the thread of this mystery, and then . . . to decide—if we are permitted a decision—what to do. Why, after all, do we have the right to intervene? We are penetrating into a world which to us is foreign: a world created by others centuries ago, hidden and forbidden. What reaction will our arrival provoke? And, if he—they—are protecting something sacred, we could destroy everything in our ignorance. (Don't discover America, Christopher. Return to Spain. Leave things as they are, virgin and pure. Ignorance is not always so terrible. Although there is much to say of the advantages of civilization, not everything is good.)"

She shivered.

"Are you cold?" asked Amanda. "It's probably better that we go in."

Magali wrapped the cat in some rags and put it inside its cardboard box.

"Why don't you go to bed, get some rest for tomorrow?"

"Yes. You're right. I'll better go to my room and get some rest. Good night, Amanda." She kissed her lightly on the cheek, and went into her room.

It was Saturday. Market day. Magali and Amanda took a minibus that went to the CAPU-Mercado Hidalgo, taking with them plastic shopping bags and money well hidden within their blouses. The Hidalgo Market is one of the largest and oldest in the city of Puebla, after that of La Victoria (which has had its beautiful iron work restored recently and been transformed into a "Mall"). They got down at the corner where they sell rustic wood furniture, simple but very useful and very cheap. They sold from the most simple piece to ones elaborated with colonial motifs, the latter heavy in the extreme and difficult to transport.

After that came the flower section: gladioli, roses, dahlias, carnations, violets, and a great many other varieties of ornamental plants—among which were bougainvillaea; rubber trees with their big leaves, oval shaped and shiny, of a clear and attractive green; and flowering laurels, pink in color. Roses did well in the region of Atlixco, famous for its flowers; they exported tons of them to Europe each year, and they had many of very pretty colors, from coral to dark red, yellow, purple, and combinations of white and pink, red and yellow, yellow and orange. The flowers produced a sweet and penetrating aroma that, mixed with the smoke of the *gorditas* (a kind of sandwich) and the *chalupas* of various nearby cooking fires, and with the bitter smell of the traffic with its black smoke from burning oil that poured forth from the old busses of the city, produced an almost nauseous effect.

Surrounding the market in an outer circle were a number of stands with awnings of colored plastic which displayed *fayuca* merchandise—that is, imported or smuggled (of very bad quality)—and among which roamed ambulant sellers of clothing.

After passing through all these merchants—the Indians with their braids and *huipiles* (a kind of veil that they wear on the head and shoulders like a shawl), carrying babies in their *sarapes*, farmers and ranchers with large straw hats, and farm laborers—one entered into the principal structure of the market.

The Hidalgo market is divided, though not formally, into various sections: meats, chicken, fruits and vegetables, dried vegetables, flowers and plants, and several areas that include everything from tools to herbs and witchcraft materials. The variety of foodstuffs is incredible. Here one can see what it means to be a country of great natural resources—in spite of the poverty of the majority of the population. For some Americans the display of whole pig heads, or of chickens hanging by their legs, head down, throat cut, still dripping blood, produced a cultural shock. Magali, being accustomed to the European ways, did not suffer so much, but she avoided looking at the dead animals. In the upper girders of the main market building there hung *piñatas* of every form and color, some representing animals and cartoon characters, others the traditional *piñatas* with the horns of bulls, both kinds with colored paper streamers dangling from them. Between one section and another one occasionally came upon a small shrine, with a statue or image of the Virgin of Guadalupe, or a cross, surrounded by lighted candles and flowers.

The heavy traffic within the market made walking difficult. It was comprised of carts transporting heavy boxes full of potatoes or other vegetables, and vendors of everything from avocados to plastic shopping bags, balls of yarn, aprons, baby clothes, toys, toilet paper, brooms, soaps and detergents, multicolored brushes, and feather dusters. Those in stands selling audio cassettes, pirated and of very poor quality copy (in Mexico everything was copied: books, magazines, courses, videos, films, music), put their rock-and-roll at full volume, their *Mariachis* enough to deafen, and their cumbias and salsas, with their irresistible rhythm, loud enough to make even the stones of the building's foundation dance. One had to choose among the many stands for those where prices were cheapest—tomatoes and vegetables, fruits and meat—and haggle in very loud tones, in order to be heard.

Magali and Amanda did not buy meat in the market because of the bad hygienic condition of the market itself, but they did purchase a large quantity of fruit: bananas, ripe pineapples, a whole watermelon, papayas, and oranges—of which there were

from those completely sweet to those most bitter and every flavor
in between. It was the season of mangos, and there were huge
orange and green piles of them of every type, which gave off a
penetrating and exotic odor.

When they had finished their shopping, they began to leave,
making their way toward the *Diagonal,* where they would find
another bus that would take them to near Magali's apartment.
They arrived at the door, Magali unlocked it, and they gingerly
opened it and looked in. It did not appear at that time as bad as
when Magali first saw it after the break-in. Paul had actually put it
in presentable order, most of her things having been picked up
and put back where they belonged. It didn't take long for the two
women to finish the task, and soon it looked like nothing had
happened. They settled down then to preparing a lunch from
some of the fresh things they had brought from the market.
Amanda stayed until one and then they left in a taxi for the
CAPU. Amanda took her bus to Cholula. Magali took the *Estrella
Roja* to the airport in the D.F.—to François.

That evening Roberto was with a girl from the University.
The two went for a walk to the *Zócalo.* It was seven, and many of
the employees that had just left their work were wandering in the
stores, looking at the merchandise displayed, or seated in the
cafes, sharing the day's news and socializing. The two made their
way to the *Oramus Café,* situated in the artists and students district
to the west of the center. The cafe-bookstore occupied the corner
of *5 Poniente* and *Reforma,* across from the *Restaurant Libanés.* Half
of the place was occupied by shelves of books, a counter, and a
cash register; the other half was a floor covered with round
wooden tables and chairs (a mix of *art déco* and French *fin-de-siècle*),
a small stage in the rear. On the week-ends there was music and
the reading of poetry. The owner was also a poet and was a
former professor of the UPA.

The cafe began to fill up with couples, small groups of
students of theater and music, and a few foreigners. This place
Roberto considered special. It was his sanctuary. Here he
communed with art.

They ordered soft drinks, and Roberto took the girl's hand, under the table. But she immediately retrieved it.

That evening there was a young man that played the guitar and recited some poems, quite bad ones, trying to make himself heard above the noise.

"So, what's wrong," said Roberto.

She answered, "I'm not ready to get married yet . . . nor are you. You're only a candidate for graduation. You have to graduate first."

"I know. But I've only a little to go."

"You'd have more time for study if you didn't occupy yourself so much with Lafragua."

"Shusst. That's a secret."

"And that, also, I don't like. It must be an idea of that American *profesora.*"

"My love. Don't tell my you are jealous of Magali!"

"Jealous? Hah! She doesn't even know how to dress. She doesn't even use make-up."

Roberto smiled. "Ah, I see."

"No. You don't see anything. You spend more time with her than you do with me!"

"You're a silly girl."

"Ah, really? Well, then let's go home. Right now." She quickly stood up. Her books fell to the floor. The boy who was singing stopped in the middle of a note, and everyone turned to look at the girl, who immediately blushed and recovered her books. She quickly left the cafe, followed by Roberto. He stopped her outside the door. He softly pushed her to one side, against the wall, and, cupping her face in his hands, he kissed her passionately.

"Silly," he whispered. "You know how much I adore you,"

The girl felt the body of Roberto next to hers, warm and strong, and she shivered. Strange and powerful sensations invaded her. She was afraid. She separated herself with a push.

"I don't want to wait," whispered Roberto. "I want you to be mine, all mine, now." He drew her to him again, violently.

An enormous black moth (those that appear in Puebla, as big as bats, around the cathedral and in the plazas at this time of the

year, and that, attracted by the lights of the lamp posts, burn their
wings and are found dead the following morning on the sidewalk)
flew by, suddenly, flapping wildly, and brushed the face of the girl
with its velvety wings, bringing from her a scream.

"It's bad luck," she cried. "The black moth . . . *quextehla* . . .
bad luck."

She began to sob, and pushing the boy to the side, she went,
running, toward a bus which she stopped in the middle of the
street. She got on, without turning her head.

Roberto was left standing, thinking.

"Bad luck," he whispered. Shrugging his shoulders, he
turned, reentered the cafe, and asked for a *tequila*.

36

FRANÇOIS ARRIVES

François arrived at the D.F. at 5:13 p.m. Magali was waiting for him at the exit for international passengers. The remodeling of the airport was almost completed and things were operating much smoother. There was a crowd waiting for arrivals. She saw François coming through the gates, and he quickly saw her. He was carrying two small suitcases. They met, walked free of the crowd. He set down the suitcases and they kissed.

They left the airport and went to take the Estrella Roja bus to Puebla. It was waiting outside, just on the other side of the roadway that ran by the airport exit doors (which roadway they crossed with great caution since there are no laws to protect pedestrians in Mexico).

Once seated on the bus, each one told the other what had happened during their most recent separation. Magali included her involvement with the tunnels and with the group of Lafragua, ending with her adventure in the secret passage.

"Mais, alors," exclaimed François. *"Quelle histoire!"*

When they arrived at Puebla, they got down from the bus, and François reclaimed the bags. Since he only had two, it was not necessary to use a porter, in spite of the insistence of the many who offered their services: *"Llevo sus maletas, seño. Por aquí, seño—"*

Magali approached the stand of the "authorized" taxis and bought two tickets for zone 3. They went to the outside area where they had to wait in another line and have their tickets stamped. At last it was their turn to board a taxi, and they got in. Magali gave the ticket to the driver and the direction of her own apartment. Now with François, she didn't have to be afraid of returning there.

When she got out her key to open the door, she saw another lock, a new shiny brass lock, in the door just above the old door lock. She unlocked the door with her old key and pushed on it. It opened. The new lock was an American night-latch type, the bolt held by the button which controlled it from the inside. Going in, she saw on the big round table a red ribbon in a bow. It went through a set of two keys, the keys to the new lock. Then she realized that Paul had had his cousin install the new lock in the afternoon and leave the keys for her there on the table. Good ol' Paul.

François deposited his bags in a corner. "Well," he said, "Everything looks in order now. What were they looking for? and who? and why?"

"I don't have any idea. All our plans were made out loud. We did nothing that would incriminate us or put us in any danger. Unless— Unless there is a spy among us. But no, no, that's not possible. We are all friends, almost since I arrived here, at the beginning of the school year. It sounds so melodramatic that I almost feel like laughing at it all. Except that—"

"I don't like this, *petite*. There must be some very powerful reasons for someone to have done this. And the police? Did you advise the authorities?"

"No. The police in this country are not that much to be trusted. And being a foreigner, any complaint could prove counterproductive."

"*Bon,*" said François. He approached the girl, drawing her gently into his arms. "Come on, you and I have some time to make up."

She went to the bed, arranged it a little, and began undressing. He approached to help her, kissing her tenderly. She curled up under the sheets, stretching like a cat.

"*Tu as l'air d'un petit chat, tu sais—*"

"You're right. I have always wanted . . . *me faire pousser une queu.*"

He laughed. *"Mais, quelle idée."* He bent down, taking the face of the girl in his hands. Making love was, for them, a habitual and easy rite. They were almost *"vieux époux."* Magali, having been raised in the U.S., learned to have the sexual freedom of the young girls of her time and did not give to their relation more than the natural and normal importance of the affair: "No strings attached." For his part, he, being French, also did not look on their relation as it is seen still in Mexico, where, in spite of the influence of the United States, sex was something of which one did not speak (except in the dark, or in the confessional), and was kept hidden by social and religious taboos.

In the morning, it being Sunday, they got up late. They had some coffee with some of the sweet rolls that François so liked and that Magali had bought. She told him they were going that morning to *Los Sapos,* where she would see her friends again and they could talk about her problem. After breakfast he showered in the small cubicle that she had surrounded with a pretty, plastic (translucent) sea-green curtain. She admired the well formed body of the man that without being athletic was muscular and attractive; his bearing; the head of long hair, now wet, stuck to the side of his face; the hands with long and fine fingers. For her, the hands were the most important part of a man. Many times she decided to not go out with someone who, although very handsome, had rough, stubby, or red hands. He got out of the shower, shaking himself like a Labrador dog, laughing. He had features of an intellectual, and clear eyes with an intense look. He dressed with the speed of one accustomed to a strict schedule: jeans, BU T-shirt, black leather jacket, tennis shoes. He caught the look of the girl, and she blushed. "Sorry," she said. "It just that it's been so long since I've seen you." He went to her and he passionately kissed her.

She got free of his arms. "I'm sorry," she said, "but we really should hurry."

"All right," he sighed. "Let's go. There is always the evening."

* * *

Don Romualdo was already waiting for them in the *Café Los Gatos* with its wrought iron tables and plastic tablecloths under a red canvas awning. The Master was sitting alone, drinking a cup of coffee. In spite of the fatigue that marked his features with dark lines, he looked very distinguished. He maintained his head high, with a very Spanish and very traditional look like in olden times. He arose on seeing the couple and grasped firmly the hand that François offered him.

"Je suis enchanté de faire votre connaissance," he said to the young man in perfect French.

François looked at him with admiration and responded, *"Moi aussi. Mais je ne savais pas que vous parliez français si bien."*

Magali smiled at her fiancé and kissed Don Romualdo on his wrinkled cheek.

"You're feeling well, Master?" she inquired, solicitously.

"You worry too much about me, girl. But, please, sit down."

He gave a sign to the waiter. Magali asked for a Sidral, François a dark beer. They brought him a *Negra Modelo*.

After exchanging a few words of general interest, Don Romualdo brought François up to date on the situation, talking to him in French, so that they would not be so easily understood by occupants at the neighboring tables.

"I passed all my life—all my life—trying to protect and save a patrimony that belongs not only to Puebla, or to Mexico, but to humanity," he concluded. "And now—"

It was as if a great cloud had passed over his face, a heavy cloud that made him stoop, shrink. Magali's heart ached to look at him.

"Mais no," said Magali. "We're here, we and the group, and we'll do something. It'll all come out okay."

The girl squeezed the hand of the old man that rested, like a dry and wrinkled branch, on the colored fruits painted on the tablecloth.

François looked at Magali, then at the Master.

"There's just one way to solve this problem," he said. "We have to discover the meaning of Magali's adventure as soon as possible. And I am on her side."

At that moment Paul arrived. He sat down and ordered a *Negra Modelo*. Magali introduced the two, Paul and François, to each other. And then, almost as if planned, Roberto arrived. He sat down and also ordered a *Negra Modelo*. And Magali introduced Roberto and François. François had almost finished his beer so he ordered another of the same, and Magali, not to be left out, ordered another Sidral.

Now they began to talk in earnest. Don Romualdo announced that François will be a new member of their group. Paul said he was welcome. He and Roberto had experience in the tunnels, but another able-bodied man could bolster their forces. They told Don Romualdo that they had it all planned out, and the tools for the task. They only needed him to get them into the church later in the night, probably after eleven. He said that was no problem. Then Paul suggested they carry out the operation on Tuesday, and that they have a final meeting to make sure they have covered everything before they go. That should probably be tomorrow in the afternoon, say about four, maybe in Don Romualdo's Lafragua. To this all agreed and Don Romualdo said he would meet them in the *Pasaje Carolino* at that hour and conduct them inside, since entrance at that hour was somewhat restricted by the guards. Paul said aside to Magali that if Amanda wanted to participate, he had a safe job for her to handle. Magali said she thought she might want to join them and promised to call her that afternoon or evening. Paul added that if she was in with them, she should come to the meeting tomorrow.

At that moment a small boy let two multicolored balloons escape from his inexperienced hands. They rose above the gay racket of *Los Sapos* towards the turquoise blue sky, up, up, till they were only two spots made golden by the sun and disappeared into space.

Magali and François went for lunch at VIPS. VIPS was a restaurant-bookstore-drugstore located downtown in one of the most interesting buildings of the city. Its facade and girdering was of ornamental iron, painted green. It was built by the French in 1793. It was also a meeting place for tourists and *gringos* of the city since it offered American breakfasts with bacon and eggs—although they added black beans and sauces to give it a Mexican touch. François asked for the American breakfast, and Magali asked for the continental: juice, sweet rolls, and coffee.

They sat at a round table next to the large front windows, which permitted them to observe the street, always full of people: on a Sunday, many tourists and few locals—mostly old men and women with children.

Magali was looking at the street, and suddenly she thought she recognized a figure that passed rapidly in front of the window. "Look! Isn't that—?"

François looked, but the man, in a black jacket and scarf, was just passing out of view. He then noted the nervousness of his fiancée. "Persecution complex?" he laughed. But she remained serious and worried.

A *gringa*—a teacher at the FALE—entered with her two boys of three and four years. The boys shouted and made a lot of noise, causing other occupants of the cafe to look at them, annoyed.

"I see," said François, "that there is a big difference—in behavior—between Mexican children and American. No offense, of course!"

"Of course not. I know that perfectly well. One admirable thing about this country is that children are seen but not heard."

The waitress approached with a tray and a large plate of bacon, two eggs, and beans; a bowl of green sauce (hot); and a glass of milk. She also brought two hot rolls that smelled delicious. For Magali there was a glass of papaya juice, coffee, and various sweet rolls.

"Mmm," said François. "I just noticed how hungry I am."

"*Tu as toujours faim, n'est-pas?*" joked Magali, and he lovingly pressed her hand.

François remained in thought. Magali finished her breakfast and accepted more coffee from the waitress who had graciously offered it. One of the pleasures of Mexico is the exquisite service that one receives, even in the most humble cafe or restaurant.

Magali looked at François with adoration.

"Il n'est qu'un grand garçon," she said to herself. *"Et je ne le laisserai pas s'en aller sans moi."*

Roberto returned to his room at *4 Poniente.* He lived in a *pensión,* in a dilapidated old building. His room was large and semi-furnished with a cot, a chair, and a small table. It had a water heater, a WC in a corner, a shower (similar to that of Magali), and some dying or almost dead geraniums in a couple of pots on a small balcony. The noises of the street invaded his privacy. But he was so tired at night that he had no problem in falling asleep. The *pensión* was close to the UPA and was economical. The food was not too bad, although there was a tendency to serve too much *tortillas* and beans, and little meat.

That night the heat was heavy, and he felt nervous. He could not sleep because of the humidity and the old odors of the building: the mold on the old paper on the walls, and the smell of the sewer that filtered through the nozzle of his shower. There was a pair of cats making love and meowing loudly on the roof. He got up, sweating, the sheets sticking to his body, and went in his shorts to the balcony in search of fresh air. He was anxious.

He could feel the presence of his current girl, her young body next to his, the salty tears rolling down her pale cheeks. He desired her, but, beyond that?

On the other hand, the adventure of Magali had put everyone in a state of excitation and anticipation, mixed with fear—that empty, nameless terror of the unknown. Until now his life had been very quiet. He studied, worked, made love with a variety of girls—some even worth the trouble—and once before had been in great danger of actually falling in love. His family lived near Cholula, quite accessible, but well outside of Puebla—which was perfect. His field of study had gotten him in with a group of bohemians, hypnotists, and just plain *locos* who were all very entertaining.

But now he suddenly had nostalgia for his farmer father—so correct, such a gentleman in the old Spanish style—and for the small ranch with its cows and horses and stupid cackling chickens. When he thought of his mother—still beautiful—a great blue sorrow clouded his vision. She was very formal; she still called her husband *Usted*. And she eternally wore a cotton apron with red and blue flowers, her long, now grey, hair gathered into a chignon on her neck. She was always cooking, or sewing, or cleaning. This week-end, perhaps, or the next, he would go to visit them. It would make them very happy since he hadn't gone home for quite some time.

He returned to the interior of his room and lay down, immediately falling asleep.

37

THE EXPLORATION

That Monday Magali left François at the Social Sciences Library, where he wanted to check out what they had, while she did some chores at the University.

First she checked in at the ILE, and then she went to the Villa Rica in the hopes of seeing Fr. Flynn. He was there, and she joined him at his table and asked for a Cappuccino. She asked him how things were going.

"Fine," he said. "We've stopped the explorations of the tunnels. I'll finish the study with the data we have already collected. Your maps are in good shape. You've been a life saver to me. And your idea of the Club was probably the best thing you could have done for me. I'll probably finish everything by the end of the month. That will leave August for corrections or filling any holes in the study. I should be able to rest a few weeks before my time to leave. And how is your work coming?"

"Mine," said Magali. "Mine's all done, boxed up and ready to take back to BU. So, this means that you don't need my help anymore?"

"You can always give my final draft a good read, give me a solid and critical review of it. And you can always share some coffee with me. Otherwise, you are free of me. Free to see a bit of Mexico as a tourist."

She did not tell Fr. Flynn of her adventure, nor of the new tunnel. She did not want to involve him in whatever it was. She did not want to compromise in any way his work, his research project.

When she left Fr. Flynn and the Villa Rica she went to rescue François from the Social Sciences Library. She found him in the office of the librarian, both in a lively conversation, in French. She came in and sat, waiting for them to finish, which took another twenty minutes. The librarian had helped Magali with her research, and was a good friend, and a very respected scholar in his own right. They had been discussing current French literature. Both were beyond Magali in their knowledge and their understanding of the subject. Still, after her greeting and farewell with the librarian, she managed to extricate François.

They turned toward the Carolino, but before they got there they took a turn to the right and headed to the *Zócalo*. She was taking him to lunch at her favorite Champs Elysées restaurant in Puebla: her McDonald's.

And that was a surprise to her cosmopolitan boy friend. After that, they went home to take a *siesta*.

At four o'clock in the afternoon the sun was striking the windows of the *Rectoría*, reflecting a thousand points of metallic light. The afternoon students were just leaving, the evening students arriving, and the two groups mixed in the *Pasaje Carolino* and circulated animatedly—talking and laughing, gravitating to the *tortilla* and *chalupa* stands (the Mexican version of "fast food") situated at the outside corners of the Carolino. There they gathered around the charcoal stoves on which were prepared the *tortillas*, the tables of the vendors covered with piles of calabash flowers, fresh cheese, and diced mushrooms, onions, tomatoes, and lettuce, while standing by was the enormous pot which contained the steaming beans.

A crowd of tourists conversed in loud voices, taking photographs of the Church and of the University. Some old women begged for alms; others remained curled in the shadow of the church, wrapped in their dark *sarapes*, eyes closed, one wrinkled hand outstretched to any passersby.

The meeting of the group was to be in Lafragua. Don Romualdo met them in the *pasaje* and went with them into the Carolino, getting them past the guards without questions.

François, who did not know the Carolino, remained in awe of the solidness and mass of the architecture. They went up the huge marble stairs of the main hall to where François could see the three main patios from above. On the way they went by the *Salón Barroco* which was open for an evening conference, and Don Romualdo took advantage of it to show that magnificent room to François.

He spoke, describing it, in the language he was more familiar with: "... *teniendo la rectoría el Dr. Juan Gonzalo, se restauró la capilla, ampliándola, y allí se instaló una galería denominada Salón Barroco. La modalidad artística es de procedencia árabe en el estilo barroco: la multitud de adornos, de 'arabescos'* ..."

They walked the immense halls with stone floors that once a week are washed with a mixture of water and muriatic acid (Magali had burned a few soles of her shoes from walking on them while they were being cleaned and still wet), viewing the height of the vaults decorated with figures in relief of angels and gold and blue flowers,

But most intriguing: the atmosphere that one breathed there was between the academic and the ecclesiastic, nourished with the patina of the centuries pressed into the walls and the rooms. For the occasion of the Annual Report of the Rector, a solemn date on which the University was honored with the visits of some high ranking national political authorities and representatives of various foreign embassies, the Committee of Press and Publicity had acquired enormous ceramic pots in which were planted young sheyrelle trees, adorning thus the austere severity of the building with their delicate green leaves, especially along the way from the main door to the *Salón Barroco*. Unfortunately, the trees were destined to a sad death since there was not sufficient light for them inside the building, nor were they adequately watered.

"This institution," explained the Master to François, "is 400 years old, built under the auspices of the Company of Jesus on the 9th of May in 1578, the date on which the Jesuits took residence in the city of Puebla and founded the House of the Company of Jesus, and, a year later, the College of San Gerónimo, both in houses belonging to the Canon Juan Vizcaino (now *3 Oriente*, number 406). It was the beginning of what is today the

Universidad de Puebla de Los Angeles. The religious disciples of Saint Ignatius Loyola had come to this city at the express wish of the *Cabildo* of the city to dedicate themselves totally to the task of education. Nine years after the arrival of the Jesuits, the merchant Melchor de Covarrubias gave part of his fortune for the building of a college. So, according to records of the 15th of April, 1587, with the assets given by Don Melchor de Covarrubias they founded the *Colegio del Espíritu Santo,* and they constructed the Church of the Company and the Carolino building."

"And who was Don Melchor de Covarrubias?" inquired François.

"Don Melchor de Covarrubias y Cervantes was the illegitimate son of Don Francisco Pastor de Valencia, who came from Spain among the first settlers in 1530. Covarrubias y Cervantes were the last names of his mother, *doña* Catalina, a descendent from a family of long lineage, known and esteemed in Spain. In that house were don Diego de Covarrubias, Bishop of Segovia, and other notable personages. The father of Don Melchor was a very renowned gentleman, with house and servants, arms and horses. Don Melchor was a native and neighbor of the city of Puebla. His parents wanted him to follow a church career, but he took the road of arms and business, achieving honors in the militia and great esteem in commerce. He gave 14,000 pesos to found the *Colegio del Espíritu Santo,* later called the Carolino, which was converted into a focus of humanism and science in the XVI, XVII and XVIII centuries and is now one of the largest and most important universities in Mexico."

They looked at the three interior patios and the immense classrooms that surrounded them, and then went down to the ground level to the Lafragua Library, which occupied what had been an old chapel on the north side of the second patio.

Don Romualdo then conducted them across the second patio to his private office, going down the stone steps that led to the administrative offices and the office of the Director, and entering by way of a small barred door into that other, secret Lafragua that was his place of work. He had arranged chairs for all around a cleared table.

* * *

"We have gathered here," solemnly said the Master, "to discuss the final details of our exploration plan."

There was an almost anxious silence in response to these words, and they all looked upward, trying to see the black angel who was soon to pounce upon them and devour them.

Paul broke it.

"Agreed," he said. "Let's ask the journalistic questions: what, who, when, where, how— To discover what, or who—"

"When?" said Don Romualdo. "At eleven tomorrow night. Where? Church of the Company. I shall have the keys to open the doors. That I have already arranged."

"As to my own participation," he continued. "I shall not go into the tunnel. My age and health. I shall stand guard within the church, waiting for your return. If there are problems, I shall advise the appropriate rescue authorities. We should have a time limit for your exploration."

"As you know," submitted Amanda timidly, "I also can't go with you. My husband, the children."

"Don't worry about that," said Paul, "You'll stay home. We need someone outside, to cover our rear, so to speak.

"We'll get started at eleven. We should be finished by one in the morning. That will give us two hours. If it is as short a distance as Magali indicated in her story, that should be plenty of time. After one o'clock you can assume that we've run into some trouble."

"Roberto and I," continued Paul, "have some experience in the tunnels, from helping Fr. Flynn with his research project. Magali has also had some experience there, though not as much we have. The core of the exploration crew should then be Roberto and myself. Magali will come along as a guide. François, who is at least able-bodied, may also come along. Don Romualdo will stay in the church until we come out. Amanda will stay at home, by her phone, until we have contacted her. If she is not contacted after the deadline, she will know that something has gone wrong.

"As for equipment, Roberto and I have complete sets of tools and clothing for the task.

"Magali and François— For clothing: each, some good boots, water proofed if possible, jeans or other hard, utility trousers, a long sleeve shirt, a light jacket, a kerchief for the neck, and a cap—like a baseball cap.

"In the way of equipment you should have basically a flashlight for each, and extra batteries; a rope, to take tied at the waist, to avoid anyone getting lost in the dark; and a bottle of water."

"And some bars of chocolate?" suggested François. Since all in the group looked at him with surprise, the young man explained: "Military field rations."

Magali looked at her fiancé: "I never knew, *chéri*, that you were in the army."

"There are many things that you don't know about me," he joked.

"Arms?" asked Paul.

"I don't think that that would be prudent," said Don Romualdo. "And if it is a matter of some religious person, or of someone who is passing as one, it doesn't seem that there is much danger of violence. But a Swiss knife is always a good idea. And a notebook for each member, and a pen. That may come in handy."

"*D'accord,*" said François.

"Perhaps a tank of oxygen?" suggested Amanda.

"An excellent idea, but not very practical," argued Don Romualdo. "It weighs a lot and, according to what Magali has told us, the distance from the access door to the room where she ended is really quite short."

"Anything more?" asked Paul.

"A camera," said Roberto. "With a flash. In case there is . . . evidence. And a compass and watches."

"One more thing," said Paul. "Have you thought of what we should do in case we encounter someone there?"

"That will be a situation that we will decide in the moment," said François. "It is impossible to foresee any action without having necessary basic information."

"But we are warned . . . and ready to act," concluded Roberto.

"Excellent," said Don Romualdo. "We'll meet at the Church of the Company tomorrow evening at eleven."

"I'm sorry to mention it," said Roberto, looking at Magali. "Rats?"

"You're right. There must be some, and perhaps they constitute a danger. A member of the group should take a spray to frighten them away. One of those sprays that they use for self-defense in large cities should be sufficient. They have some in the *Fayuca.*"

When the group left the Carolino, it had started to rain. It was now after five, time to go home and eat. Small rivulets were already forming in the streets, carrying away trash and mud, clogging the openings to the storm drainage, which produced flooding, which in turn made traffic difficult. Magali and François ran to take a taxi. Amanda carried an umbrella, and Roberto went with her to her car (with Victor working in the D.F., she had the car during the week, and for this occasion she had brought it to Puebla). Paul had his Vocho parked close by and offered to take Roberto to his room. They said good-bye with feelings of anticipation and fear, a whole gamut of human emotions that made them feel this evening, under the rain, particularly alive.

Magali got up at a reasonably late hour Tuesday. The stores weren't going to be open until mid-morning, anyway. They had a leisurely breakfast of coffee and rolls, and were out in the street by nine-thirty.

They went to several *ferreterías* (hardware stores), and some stores that looked like old-style American general stores, selling most everything, and it looked like to a rural clientele. They acquired two flashlights, batteries, shirts, some baseball caps, and two big red bandanas. Magali said tennis shoes were good enough for the tunnels. If it got too wet, you just got your feet soaked. It wouldn't kill you. (This was something she learned from an engineer who had done a lot of exploring in the Amazon jungle.) They both had light jackets, so there was another thing they didn't have to buy. They got a twenty foot, one-quarter inch diameter, nylon rope, which they cut into two pieces, one for each

of them. They also got two bottles of purified water, and some
chocolate bars for François.

When they had finished, they took their booty home, and
there they rested up a bit before returning to the street. It was
getting close to noon. It was lunch time and François insisted on
trying the typical *mole Poblano*, which made Magali smile with
tenderness.

"We are facing an adventure—a dangerous one—and you
think of eating?"

"*Petite*. It's called surviving. The older countries—Gallic,
Hispanic, Italian—survived during the war giving priority to the
basic necessities. Besides, I understand that *mole* is a specialty that
one should savor. And there's," he recited, "*mole de chipotle, mole de
cadera, de menudo, de tripita,* green or red, and—"

Magali smiled, then started to laugh. "I love how you
pronounce 'tgripitas.' "

"That's better," said François. "It's a long time since I've
seen you laugh. Let's go to the *Posada del Angel,* and we'll have an
unforgettable lunch."

"No, I will show you a place, close to *El Parián* that— You'll
see."

They went to *El Parián*, and walked through it. "This place is
fascinating," said François. "The jewel boxes of onyx, the silver
jewelry, the leather articles, the embroidered blouses, and the
sarapes—especially the puppets of bandits and old men."

"*Oh, comme tu es un enfant,*" smiled the girl. "But, now we're
here."

The restaurant was just across the corner from *El Parián*. It
was small but cozy. The walls were covered with tile of Talavera,
blue and white, and to one side a great steaming ceramic bowl
contained the specialty of the house. The tables were of wood,
painted green and covered with colored tablecloths, embroidered
by hand. In the center, a ceramic flower vase with paper flowers.
They sat at one of the tables close to a large window, and each
ordered a portion of *mole*.

The waitress, a pretty girl with long braids, dressed in the
typical dress of the *China Poblana* (skirt embroidered with red and
green spangles; a white cotton blouse, trimmed with lace, which
left the shoulders bare; hair worn in black and shining braids

entwined with colored ribbons) brought hot corn *tortillas* in a basket, and hot sauce. Later there arrived the plates of Talavera containing a quarter of roast chicken covered with *mole* and *ajonjolí.*

"Hmm," said François.

"Que ça a l'air delicieux! Mademoiselle . . . two Coronitas, please." The girl smiled to hear the French accent of the young man, adding a coquettish look that made him blush. Magali enjoyed herself.

"Come on, *mange, chéri."*

Now everything appeared normal, as if instead of preparing for a dangerous adventure, they were just tourists enjoying the city.

After lunch François insisted on going home for a *siesta.* And so they did, both of them getting some two hours' sleep, which they would need for their night's adventure.

They left the house again shortly after four and walked to Sanborn's for an evening meal. Then they checked out the newsstand section and looked over the latest in foreign magazines. Most were already several months old. François looked over the books they had, and not seeing anything of real interest, suggested they go home and to bed.

It was five-thirty when they returned to the apartment and began to prepare for the big adventure. It was a comfort to them that there would be two persons outside who knew of their plans and who would be ready to get help if they did not return within a certain time. But the prospect of returning to relive her adventure in the narrow and dark passages under the Church of the Company made Magali apprehensive. François recognized the fear and anxiety that she tried to hide, and, drawing her to him, he kissed her.

The night had fallen outside, and the sky was black as ink, lighted from time to time by blue lightning flashes.

"It will all be okay," he said. "You'll see."

They made love, and suddenly everything was marvelous and simple. The world had begun anew. They stayed a while, resting,

the head of Magali on the warm chest of her lover. The rain
continued its rhythmic tapping on the roof. The night was warm.
Inside the room the shadows advanced towards them like gentle
house dogs.

They got up at last and began to get dressed. Magali felt
tired, but the tension had passed. François was at her side. "How
easy everything is," she thought, "when we operate at the animal
level."

Each one carried a small plastic bag containing a bottle of
purified water, a first-aid kit, a flashlight and extra batteries, and a
pen and a pad of paper. François carried a camera with flash. Also
a Swiss knife. Both brought raincoats that they would leave in the
church with Don Romualdo.

They went out, securing the door, now with the two locks,
and grabbed a taxi. Inside the car Magali curled up in the arms of
her lover, wishing that time would stop there and that they would
never arrive at the Carolino. The rain made the traffic very
difficult, and there were areas in which they noted the streets
being flooded.

This is what the newspapers related the following day:

Se Inundó Centro Histórico

*Unas 300 personas y 30 vehículos quedaron atrapados en el
Centro Histórico de la ciudad, debido a que la lluvia que se
registró ayer provocó serias inundaciones por la falta de
mantenimiento en el sistema de drenaje y alcantarillado . . . los
torrenciales aguaceros de la tarde y el agua acumulada en las
calles que alcanzó en algunos casos hasta 2.20 metros de altura,
impidieron la circulación vehicular en el bulevar 5 de Mayo hasta
el entronque con el bulevar Valsequillo. Aunque no se reportaron
víctimas, la Cruz Roja Poblana atendió a unas 40 personas en
varios edificios. Cientos de personas se vieron imposibilitadas para
salir de los inmuebles debido al alto nivel del agua . . . por lo
menos 50 personas tuvieron que ser evacuadas entre la 5 y 7
Oriente y la misma suerte corrieron algunos alumnos de la UPA
que asistían a clases vespertinas en la Universidad.*

* * *

Roberto had returned to his room. He had no desire to eat. He felt too anxious with the prospect of the adventure. Everything would turn out all right. He took off his shirt and sat on the bed to remove his boots, when he felt rather than heard a timid knock on the door. He wondered who it could be at this hour. He opened it.

There stood his girl, looking at him from the depths of her black and humid pupils, her cheeks red, her wet hair stuck to the sides of her face, her blouse and skirt dripping water, placing in relief her firm breasts and the delicate curves of her hips.

Roberto remained for an instant immobile.

"You aren't going to ask me in?" she inquired.

"Yes. Pardon me. It's just that I—"

He took her by the arm and led her in.

He closed the door. She remained standing in the entranceway of the room, trembling. The water that streamed from her clothes extended on the floor in a liquid and circular pool.

They both remained there in the penumbra of the room for a few seconds, which appeared to be hours, when a clap of thunder made the girl suddenly seek refuge in the arms of the man.

They said no words. There was no time. The time had passed for words.

He gathered her in a movement in which his whole being was involved—tenderly, slowly, passionately, kissing her on the lips.

He was caressing the wet hair, licking the rain from her skin, from her eyes, from her neck, from her arms. She responded more by instinct that by experience. Almost without knowing how, they found themselves on the cot—he taking off her blouse, she helping him remove his boots. The body of the dark-skinned man and the clean whiteness of the girl formed a new and palpitant lightness-darkness. The sound of the thunder and the rain discreetly covered the moans of the lovers.

It was a brief and splendid encounter. It was after ten when they had finished. The bell of the Cathedral took them out of the privacy of their dreams. Roberto quickly dressed. She remained in the bed, covering her sweaty body with the sheet.

"Why do you get up?" she asked. "You're getting dressed? Where are you going?"

"I have to go out. I have to go to Lafragua. There is an important meeting."

"More important than I?"

"It's a compromise of honor," he responded. "I would never leave you if it was not for—"

"Honor?" She sat up in the bed. Her eyes shown in the darkness, like a cat. "And me? I don't count?"

He stopped in the middle of dressing and turned to look at her. "God," he thought, "what have I done? She's a child . . . only a child." He approached the bed; he sat next to her; he took her in his arms, caressing her.

"Those of our work group, in the library, have something very important to do. You shouldn't worry; everything will turn out all right. You'll see."

She freed herself from his embrace and, covering herself partly with the sheet, she jumped up.

"It's she, isn't it? The American. I thought that if I came here, that if . . . if I gave myself to you, you would forget her. It wasn't enough." She had gotten up and begun to get dressed, hurriedly, trying to fasten her bra—unsuccessfully. At last she covered her face with her hands and began to sob convulsively.

"Come on," he said. "Listen, silly. I love you." He was kissing her, tenderly now. "But this night . . . this night I have a mission I must complete. And you must trust me."

"A mission?"

"Yes. Please, don't ask me questions. I can't reveal the secret . . . to anybody. Come on. Finish getting dressed. Put on your shoes. We'll leave together. I'll take you home first, then— We'll see each other tomorrow ('if everything come's out okay,' he whispered to himself). We'll see each other tomorrow."

But she continued to cry, without knowing why. And a great and liquid sadness began to invade her, coming up from the feet, attacking her vital organs, stopping her breathing. At last, the tears stopped.

She sighed. Slowly, deliberately, she began to finish dressing. She arranged her hair, tying it in a chignon at her neck. She put on her tennis shoes and, without looking back, left with Roberto.

The only thing that remained in the room in memory of their encounter was a small puddle of water from the rain on the floor in the entrance, and two sheets, messed up and still warm on the bed.

In the atrium of the church, protected from the rain, Roberto was waiting, very impressive in his all black attire: jeans, water-tight leather boots, and jacket. Paul was similarly attired in black boots, jeans, and jacket. They both carried what look like gym bags, which held their tools. Don Romualdo was there conversing with them. Amanda had remained at her house, waiting by the telephone for news from the Master, ready to get help if necessary.

At the arrival of Magali and François, Don Romualdo opened the church door. The rain was now falling in torrents from the roofs and drains of the old houses and beat on the roof of the church like a hail of stones. Everyone had come with raincoats and umbrellas, which were left in the church—the raincoats on a pew and the umbrellas standing open in a corner. They went over to the secret door.

"It appears," said Don Romualdo, "that we shall probably have to force our way in here."

"No," said Paul. "Let's look it over first."

He examined closely all of the area around the line of the door's edge, but there was nothing. It all appeared like a smooth, blank wall. He checked the bottom, where there was a molding along the base of the wall. Where the right side line of the door touched the molding, there were two lines on it, about eight inches apart, each equidistant from the door line. The one on the right was at an angle; the one on the left was in the form of a semi-circle, its center toward the right. Paul got his tool bag and took out his probe. He looked at the piece of molding again, as if to make sure of what he was choosing to do, and then hooked one end of the probe under the molding of the end on the right and pulled on it slowly. He pulled it out ever so slowly, the other end pivoting as if on a pin, until he heard a click, at which he stopped, unable to pull any farther. The door had popped open.

"Just as I thought," said Paul. "It has a spring lock, opened by this molding as a lever. You see it pays to have seen a lot of old movies."

One by one they entered the first room, examining it carefully. There were no indications of it having been used, no signs of human presence. It was silent, dusty, and warm, but they all felt an atmosphere of oppression and threat.

"Evil. *El Mal,*" whispered Roberto, half joking.

Magali led them to the bookcase, which François and Roberto raised. They opened the door in the wall behind the bookcase, and there was the mouth of the tunnel, like a beast ready to devour them. They turned on their flashlights and entered.

"Come on," said Paul. The tunnel was humid, and the floor much more slippery than Magali had remembered. There were now actual seepages on the walls that made advancing difficult since they formed rivulets on the muddy floor of the passageway.

"Let's go carefully," said Roberto. "We must avoid falling since someone could get hurt."

"Listen," said Magali.

They all stopped. A dull and threatening sound made an echo against the walls. "It's only the rain," said Roberto. "Lets go on."

They advanced, descending, always more slowly, noting that there was already a lot of water on the floor which began to accumulate in the passageway. After a while the descent ended and they proceeded on a level. They soon came to a wall and the tunnel carried on to the left.

"I'm sure I went right," said Magali.

"You might have been mistaken," said Paul. "It clearly goes to the left. Let's follow this anyway, see where it leads."

In a very short distance it turned right. Magali said, "Something's wrong, I went for a long while and it turned left."

They continued going, downward, and into a water covered flooring.

After a few minutes Roberto slipped and fell against one of the sides of the passageway, making an opening in the wall on the right.

"What on earth?" said Roberto, withdrawing his mud-covered body from the opening. The group examined the hole in the wall with their flashlights.

"It's another passageway," said François. "Who knows where this leads?"

"Come on, we must continue moving forward," said Paul. "Otherwise we might get lost. There'll be another time to explore that way."

With even greater care they advanced.

"We should be close to the place," said Magali. "We should see the light."

"That is if there is a light," said Paul.

"In any case, we'll arrive sooner or later to the place where Magali entered the secret room," said François. "Look!"

The passageway had come to an end. There, where there should have been the entrance door to the room, there was only a solid wall. And the water was quite deep now.

"This can't be the place!" said Magali. "There was a door here."

François examined the wall.

"You're wrong, *petite*. There was never any door here. It's closed solidly with stones and cement."

The group was quiet, waiting for Paul or someone to come up with a new direction.

"Well," said Paul "I don't know if you've noticed, but the water is invading this passageway. We have to go back, before we drown here like— Sorry about that. This surely must be the wrong tunnel."

Suddenly they heard a loud bang, an explosion. Part of the roof of the tunnel began to fall in pieces. They continued in the retreat.

On coming to the place where they had made the new opening in the side, the group halted. The water was now up to their knees and penetrated the hole in the side forming a small rivulet of mud. It seemed, nevertheless, that the other tunnel was only recently becoming affected by the inundation, or at least was not receiving as much water.

"We have to take a decision. And do it rapidly," cried Roberto, trying to make himself heard over the noise of the in rushing water.

"You're right," said François. "It seems that we have no other option. By now our original tunnel must be almost completely inundated, if not destroyed."

They entered into the new tunnel, one after the other, each enlarging a little the opening—which was easy since the walls of the tunnel that they had left had been practically converted into mud. With great relief they saw that the new tunnel not only went upward to the right, but that the way was getting larger, permitting them to walk more comfortably, without bumping their heads on the ceiling. As they advanced, touching the walls, they also noted that these were solid, and almost dry.

A loud noise, followed by a sound that appeared to be a cataract, made them turn their heads toward the rear, where the ceiling had just fallen in, blocking completely any retreat.

"Well," said Roberto, "the only thing left is to go forward. Now the decision is made for us."

The group started the march again, in silence.

38

C'EST FINI

Amanda, next to the telephone, felt more and more nervous. The heavy rain outside, the flooding in the street, and something that bothered her, something insidious, in her mind, trying to open a way to her consciousness. Something strange, some detail that she had noted without realizing it.

"I'm very worried," she said to Victor—who had come home that afternoon, something in itself quite unusual. "It's been more than an hour since the group started the expedition. And there's no news."

"The Master hasn't called you? All this has always seemed crazy to me."

"Crazy? Crazy?"

She sat thinking. Her geraniums, in the window, were losing their petals, which, being red and mixed with the rain, fell on the sill like tears of blood.

Amanda shivered. "There's something. Something that I feel . . . something that is all wrong."

"Well. If you want to, let's go to the church. We'll leave the children with your mother. It will be difficult, because of the flooding. We'll take the car."

She looked at him with gratitude. "How well you understand me. And how good you are."

"Put on a raincoat and boots."

When they got to the city, they could move only slowly on the wet streets. The traffic was blocked in many places, and firemen began to come to the aid of the drivers of some autos who had gotten stopped in the middle of the flooded streets.

They finally parked and walked to the church. It was closed and dark. But on touching one section of the iron fence they noted that it was only pushed to and not locked. The section squeaked ominously on being opened. Suddenly Amanda screamed, covering her mouth, and grabbed the arm of Victor. There, illuminated amidst sinister yellow-black shadows, hanging from a rope around his neck, swung the body of Don Romualdo. He was hanging near the wall where there was a plaque with an inscription which said:

"In the main arch of this facade, was hung by order of the Inquisition the head of Don Antonio de Benavidez (the Hooded One) false inspector from Spain executed the 12 of July of 1684."

The authorities and the fire department having been called, as well as an ambulance, the church was soon filled with a heterogeneous and noisy group, all talking at the same time.

Amanda, who was suffering from shock, anguish, and cold, stood curled in the arms of Victor and barely answered with monosyllables the questions of the journalists. It was she who had informed the inspector of police that four professors had been trapped within the tunnel, whose entrance had been dynamited. She had already been interrogated by the authorities.

The police had discovered that a small amount of explosives had been placed within the entrance to a secret passageway to a tunnel under the church to close it. This, together with the rain, must have provoked an avalanche of stones and mud that formed a blockage in the tunnel and allowed little possibility of entrance from that direction.

The explosion had destroyed part of the north wall of the Church of the Company, that part where the secret room was, and had sealed the tunnel at that point. Any attempt to rescue the group of explorers, who might still be alive within the tunnels, was impossible from the church entrance.

The forensic medics had taken down the body of the Master, and took it to the morgue. The police launched an immediate investigation of the case. The Director of Lafragua and the Chief of Press and Public Relations of the UPA arrived a little later, alerted by the police.

A group of journalists immediately surrounded them.

"Señor Director," said a young man in jeans and jacket. "What can you tell us of the apparent suicide of one of the officers of your library?"

"We have no comments," the Director answered icily.

"Señor Director, did you know of the plans of the group of professors of the library to explore the subterranean passageways?"

"Of course," said the Director. "Nothing is done here without my knowledge and approval."

"But then," adventured timidly a young girl with glasses who worked for the newspaper of the UPA, "why were not precautions taken and the authorities alerted in case of problems?"

The Chief of Press of the University, a tall man, in a raincoat, still young, interrupted her severely, putting himself between her and the Director.

"We'll issue a written statement in the morning. Now we have to find the rest of this group."

Little by little the reporters began to disperse.

Amanda refused to leave the church, thinking of her friends and of Magali.

Victor, however, prodded by the Chief of Police to take her home, was ready to leave. He had promised that they would come to the *Prefectura* in the morning to sign a statement.

"But someone has to stay here. They have to find them," the woman sobbed.

At last, resigned, she left, wrapped in the arms of her husband, who almost had to carry her out. They walked to their car and made their way home.

The doors of the temple would be closed and sealed by the authorities until further notice.

The rain began to stop, and a cold and black wind ran through the *Pasaje Carolino,* shaking the branches of the trees of their load of water. The rain had stopped, but it still rained under the trees.

Meanwhile, Magali and her companions kept advancing in the other tunnel.

That tunnel, contrary to the first, had probably not been used for many years. It was filled with spiders' webs that now came apart from the water which began to filter through the walls. The floor, uneven and now becoming muddy, made the group's progress difficult. They continued the march, all quiet, each in his own secret world, perhaps remembering their lives, perhaps saying a silent goodbye to their loved ones.

Strange images went through the mind of Magali. One was of the big wooden confessional in the center of the church, located there like a historical monument, with its little round windows covered with glass, and a sign in gothic lettering in the middle, on which one read: *"Mancebo, a tí digo: Levántate. Y se levantó el que había estado muerto."*

And that of the frescos on the interior of the big dome, in pastels and gold, representing the Virgin surrounded by saints and angels, and in the center of which hung a big crystal chandelier that precisely at noon received the rays of the sun, reflected from somewhere outside, through a small hole in a side window, and scattered them in a thousand sparkles of aquatic colors, illuminating saints and demons, paintings and arabic designs, the living and the dead.

In silence they continued on their way. Suddenly, the passageway ended at a wall.

"Mais ça, alors," said François. They stopped a moment, indecisive about what they should do. "Well, it appears that we have to tear this down," he said.

Roberto made a quick examination of the wall. "I don't think so," he said. "Not when we have the 'Master of the Doors' with us."

Paul came forward and he, too, examined the wall. He found the key stone, got out his probe, and pulled it out. He then reached into the opened wall and extracted the spike.

After Paul and Roberto had found the doors to Santa Monica, they came across several more. At the first one after Santa Monica Paul noticed that about two feet above the floor there was a groove cut in the edge of the door. This was where he had gained a purchase with his crowbar to open the Santa Monica door. The groove was about an inch and a half high and cut to about half way through the edge of the door. Another such groove was cut just above that one, from the other side, also half way through, and it did not connect with the groove from the other side. At the interior ends of each groove there was a kind of irregular hole sunk into the stone of the door. Paul had reflected for quite a while on that, and then he realized what it was. It was like the interior of a lock. The key stone gave one access to the real lock: the spike. These grooves acted like key holes. There must be long keys that the monks pushed through the "key holes"—the grooves' ends, which appeared from the outside like slits—and turned. The key turned into the interior holes in the edges of the door. When they had been turned, they would catch on the edge of the interior hole and could pull the door open—or closed. No longer would they have to struggle with crowbars. Now they had a key stone where they could pull the spike, the lock itself, and a key hole, where they could insert a "key," turn it, and pull the door open or closed.

Paul had a key made for himself. It was really only a large lock pick. It was a steel rod, an eighth of an inch in diameter. One end was softened in a fire and about one inch of that end was bent at right angles to the rod. It was then put back into the fire and tempered. When it had cooled he had a strong rod with one inch of its end bent at a right angle: a giant lock pick. He had the other end pounded into a knob and that end of the "key" wound with rope and tape to form a handle with which to pull on. And all of this was possible because there still were blacksmiths in Mexico. Paul now had his "key" to all the secret doors they were discovering.

Roberto and Paul quickly had the door open. This door they pushed in. And they found themselves back in the tunnel through which they had entered. Water was running along the floor and into the passageway to the right. They pushed the door all the way open and were surprised to see that it pivoted to form a wall blocking the tunnel to the right. Very interesting, thought Paul.

Examination of the wall to the left betrayed it as another secret door. They soon had it opened, and it swung to the left and formed a wall where the other door had been. Now they had the original tunnel coming down to a wall in front and on the left, and a tunnel to the right. Just as Magali had said, the tunnel turned to the right.

This tunnel was dry and they quickly began to move through it. After a short distance it turned to the left, again as Magali had said. They went ahead for a distance and came to the steps. Not too many. Eight of them, Paul counted. He hopped up the steps, like a little boy, counting: "One, two, three, four, five, six, seven, eight." Roberto, not to be outdone: *"Uno, dos, tres, cuatro, cinco, seis, siete, ocho."* And then François: *"Un, deux, trois, quatre, cinq, six, sept, huit."* They were all acting like little boys, oblivious to the danger which they had anticipated lay before them. The tunnel soon began to curve to the right, in a long curve, and then headed straight toward a wall at the end. The wall turned out to be a door, the door to the secret room. No light coming from beneath it. After a bit of work with the crowbar, they had it open.

Inside they encountered a large room—a library full of bookcases and books, all in a good state of conservation. It had, in addition, an electric light, a table, on which there was a candle in its holder, and a pair of chairs. They all looked at Magali. She made an affirmative sign with her head. "Yes," she said. "This is the room."

Excited by the discovery, forgotten now the past danger, they began anxiously to explore the place. They found a jug of purified water and a couple of glasses, and all the signs of the room having been recently occupied.

There were a couple of antique parchments on the table. Also on the table was an old book, one of those with a firemark on the edge. It was left open to a page, one not in such good condition. And on the table was a parchment on which the page was being copied. Copied with an ink quite akin to the original ink. Paul gave it a closer look. It had been done with a feather quill, unmistakably. And there on the table were three such quills.

And a jar of ink, which was probably the ink the copyist had been using.

"It looks," said Paul, "like our mysterious monk is a copyist. He appears to have been engaged in restoring, or copying this old book. And a very good job he was doing."

"And here are others," said Roberto, "on this table, also in not such good condition."

"But what does all this mean?" asked François.

"Well," said Paul, "It appears that our monk was restoring, or copying, old books. I don't know for whom. Maybe to ship out of the country. Anyway, now the most important thing is to get out of here and communicate with Don Romualdo and with Amanda."

"Look!" exclaimed Magali suddenly. In a corner, hanging from a hook, was the dark woolen habit of a monk. Magali, on seeing it, let out a scream.

"What happened?" inquired Paul. They all turned to the young girl.

"Nothing . . . nothing. It's that—" She pointed with a trembling hand. "It's that—"

François approached the hook. He examined the habit with some care. "It's only a religious habit, *petite*. Without doubt that of the mysterious occupant of this room."

"No, it's not that. It's that . . . now I remember."

"What?" asked Paul.

"What I couldn't, what I wouldn't, remember. When I came to this room, I saw—"

They all waited expectantly for the revelation.

"I saw . . . a white lab coat, with brown smudges of dust about the pockets, hanging on that hook."

The three men remained in silence, looking from one to another, without understanding.

"And—" offered Roberto. "So?"

Magali got up, agitated, going to the corner and taking the habit down from the hook.

"Here was a white lab coat," she repeated. Then, noting the expression of the men, "No, I'm not crazy. Don't you understand?" She went anxiously to her fiancé. "François?"

He looked at her; then, "Bien sûr! The lab coat of . . . Don Romualdo."

"You mean to say that Don Romualdo and the monk are the same person?" said Paul.

"Yes."

Magali sat·down again on one of the chairs, and remained there, bent over, her head down like a punished child.

"I'm so tired," she whispered.

"Let's get out of here," suggested François. "We are all worn out, soaked to the skin, covered with mud. There'll be time for questions later."

Getting out resulted to be no problem. There was another door to the room and they opened it and found themselves in Don Romualdo's office. in his work area. The door had a bookcase affixed to it on the other side, which made it quite heavy, but it swung easily open. The bookcase made it so that the door could not easily be discerned from the office side. Roberto had keys to this work area and they easily got out and into the hallway leading to the outside. The outside door was, fortunately, unlocked, probably so the guards could inspect all the hallways during the night.

The main door of the Carolino was closed, but they found a telephone in the interior of the information area near the main door and called security. Two anxious guards, followed by several University and Municipal policemen, came to open for them, assaulting them with a multitude of questions.

"Please," said Paul, finally. "We are all quite exhausted. Let us go home. Tomorrow we can make the necessary statements."

Before they parted that night, the members of the exploration team decided to meet for breakfast on the following morning in the house of Amanda, and then to communicate with the authorities. Paul offered them all a ride, but François said he and Magali would walk home. It was only a short distance, and they were too wet and muddy to ride in his car. Roberto, however, accepted the offer and climbed in, mud and all.

* * *

Paul had called Amanda the night before, so she was expecting them when they all arrived the next morning at her house in Paul's Vocho. After embracing tenderly, Amanda led them all into the dining area and invited them all to sit with her at the dining table. Victor had left for work in the D.F. and the children were in school. After a good breakfast, and several cups of very hot coffee, seated comfortably around the table like a family, the group told Amanda of their adventures and received from her the latest news.

"So it was Don Romualdo!" remarked Paul at the end of his accounting, "He was the one who wanted to make sure that we would not come out alive from the tunnel, dynamiting the entrance and then committing suicide!" Then he looked at Magali.

"Yes," she said. "After more than fifty years acting as guardian of the treasures of Lafragua, impotent to protect them against the greed of officials, and slowly losing his mind, he forged a plan to put them safe from methodic and frequent pilfering and from those he saw as threatening. The first time that I came into the secret room, through the other door from the tunnel, which had probably been closed for quite a long time, I saw in the back of the room, hanging from a hook, the white lab coat. I think that that was what, more than anything, made me faint. The horrible realization of something that I couldn't understand or accept: the fact that the person in the monk's habit was, in reality, Don Romualdo. Why? I knew, in that same instant: he was crazy. And I wanted to obliterate that from my mind. I respected him, too much."

"A case of split personality," explained Roberto, the psychologist. "He was Don Romualdo the Librarian and at the same time the monk who watched over the patrimony of the Convent and copied the texts on parchments to assure their survival. After the explosion, confronted at last with reality, he realized that he had not only destroyed his friends but had put in danger the same books that he had tried to protect, so he committed suicide."

"The poor Master! What a magnificent madness!" said Amanda.

"There was something in him lately, in his look. A mixture of Quijotism and desperation," said Roberto.

"Nevertheless," said François, "we have to remember that he tried to kill us."

"He was in a frightening dilemma," continued Roberto. "His cause or his friends. For a fanatic like that, his cause is the motive of his very existence. Protecting it, he had to sacrifice the lives of his friends. That was his supreme sacrifice to his cause. And having done that, and knowing that as a result all of his work would be exposed and undone, he then had no reason to continue living. But I firmly believe that we should protect his memory. His suicide could be justified to the authorities by explaining that he felt responsible for having involved us in that plan and having been the cause of our deaths."

"And the dynamite placed in the entrance of the passageway?" argued Paul.

"Thinking that we were dead, he wanted the passageway to remain a secret from everyone," answered François.

"That makes some sense. And it's consistent with his whole life, dedicated to Lafragua," said Amanda. "I hope the authorities will accept our version. I'm sure that the University will support us. It's in the greater interest of everyone to convert Don Romualdo into a hero instead of exposing him as a crazy, mixed up murderer."

"And the books . . . the precious books to which he dedicated all his life . . . and his death? All that work we joined him in, because we believed in his cause. Will they continue to be stolen, abused, destroyed?" asked Roberto. "And what of our participation?"

"I think that we should keep secret the existence of our group Ex-Libris," said Magali.

"Under penalty of our souls?" inquired Paul.

"Under penalty of our souls!" swore all.

"Then, let's go to the *Prefectura* and get done with the fastidious legal proceedings," added Paul.

"I wonder," said Magali. *"Je me demande—* Do you know what day this is? Wednesday, the 12th of July."

They all looked at her, without understanding.

"The anniversary of the day on which was executed Antonio de Benavidez, *El Tapado.*"

François took her in his arms. *"Allons.* Let's go, *petite.* Let's go. *C'est fini.*"

That same afternoon the authorities of the UPA had released to the press a statement which said, in part: "With the approval of Don Romualdo, and the participation of three research professors and a visiting foreign professor, a small group carried out a discrete exploration of certain passageways that connected to Lafragua in order to determine if they did indeed connect with the interior of the library, and if they could be a means by which unauthorized entrance to the library could occur if such passageways were to be discovered by persons of few scruples, and were to be used to purloin books and other things of value from the library. Because of the inundations caused by the rain, and the consequent deterioration of the tunnels, the group become detoured in their exploration and temporarily lost in the passageways. Don Romualdo, faced with the apparent deaths of those who had helped him in this exploration, felt remorse to such extreme that his heart suffered from it and he died."

The statement ended by rendering posthumous honors to Don Romualdo for the uninterrupted work of his entire life in caring for and protecting those most valuable treasures of Lafragua.

"No one dies completely," said Magali, *"personne ne meure pas tout á fait.*"

39

C'EST LA VIE

Magali had made an appointment with the Rector for 11:00 on Thursday morning. She and François went to the Carolino before the appointed time and waited in the *antesala* to be called into his "presence." The Rector, in spite of the many machinations going on in his shadow, was a great head of a great university, and he used his powers to make it even better. He was truly a benefit to the UPA, to Puebla, and to Mexico.

When they were called, they went to the door to his office and one of his many assistants was waiting by the door to open it. Magali and François stepped in. The Rector was seated behind his enormous desk on the far side of his huge office, looking at some papers, and carrying on a discussion with his "advisors" there. He looked up, at Magali, and got up, brushing his people aside and came around the desk, walking toward Magali, saying, "Ah, Magali, Magali. You came."

He got to them and took her hand in both of his. Magali introduced François, her fiancé.

"Ah," he said, "the one from Boston University."

Then he switched from English to French, speaking with a decidedly Parisian accent. "Enchanted to meet you. You are a very fortunate man indeed."

Then to Magali, in English again: "You do me a great honor to come to say farewell to me. We have kept our eye on you here, and you have been a wonderful addition to the life of our University. It is sad that you have to leave us."

He praised Magali's handling of the "Lafragua affair." And
he remarked how sad was the death of Don Romualdo. "But," he
said, *"c'est la vie."*

In the afternoon, about three, Magali took François to the
Alliance Française. She took him there to see what they do there,
and so that she could make her farewells to her friends Olivier
and Marie St. Jacques. François enjoyed it, seeing the classrooms,
the library, the offices—and the cafe. They had good
Cappuccinos and good French pastries. And they passed a good
hour and some in French conversation.

Payday was Friday, the fourteenth. Monday was the start of a
two week vacation. Magali stood in line for the last time at the
UPA. They paid her for the first fifteen days of July and for the
last fifteen days as well, since the last fifteen were coincident with
the vacation. This pay also concluded her obligations under her
contract, which was till the end of July. She was actually free to
leave the country.

François was waiting for her outside of the ILE, and they
went directly to the bank to change her pesos for dollars, and to
buy some traveler's checks.

At 11:00 was Don Romualdo's funeral. Magali and François
went to Atlixco, to a cemetery on a small hill. There were a large
number of people there—his friends and colleagues at the UPA,
and a large number of people from an extended family. Magali
was amazed at the number of cousins, nephews, and nieces. All of
the members of Ex-Libris were in attendance, and they all
exchanged greetings and, in the case of Magali, goodbyes. They
said they probably would not continue in the work they had been
doing since Don Romualdo was no longer there to direct it. They
had no idea what would become of things, but they felt for sure
there would be someone put in charge of the books, hopefully
someone who would give them proper care and protection.

Magali saw Paul and Roberto there and talked with them for
a short while.

When she got the opportunity, Magali paid her respects to Don Romualdo's mother. But she was not sad. She said she had expected something like this for a long time, and she had already accepted the doom he was seeking for himself. *"Así es la vida,"* she said.

Magali left with that idea echoing in her mind.

At one o'clock Magali and François were having a late lunch at McDonald's on the *Zócalo*. The adventure was over. And both Magali and François were physically and mentally exhausted.

"Let's just get away from here," begged Magali. "I have a couple of weeks vacation. And I've received my last pay. Maybe we can go to some other place in Mexico."

"A better idea," said François. "Let's go to Boston."

"Okay. There's a travel agency around the corner," said Magali. "We can make reservations there. *Viens.*" She grabbed his arm and away they went. They turned the corner and walked a short way up *2 Norte*.

When they left the agency, they went to the *Aguirre Café*, which was nearby, for an *espresso*, and to plan their leaving. It was there that she remembered her commitment to Fr. Flynn. She explained her predicament to François, and they quickly finished their coffees and left to seek out the Father. They found him at the Villa Rica, alone at a table, reading some of his writing on the final paper. Magali sat with him, ordered another coffee for her and one for François, and began to explain her predicament. She explained that next week was the beginning of a vacation, and she was finished with her commitment to the University. Her contract ended on the 31st of July, and she had already received all of her pay. She was free to leave Mexico and return to the U.S. whenever she wanted to. She and François had already arranged to leave on Monday. Consequently she had to beg off on helping him with his final paper.

Fr. Flynn said that was all right, but what was this about an adventure in the tunnels that everyone was talking about? Magali told him of the affair, adding that she didn't go to him about it because she didn't want to involve him or to compromise his own work in the tunnels.

He said it wouldn't have affected his work. At least she had an adventure. He found no treasure, no secret rooms, no nothing—just tunnels. He had the dull academic adventure of describing the system, the origin of its various parts, and some of the uses on occasion of the tunnels in the history of Puebla and of Mexico. The most exciting part of it for him was his describing its use by the French in trying to escape with their gold. And they did get away with it. There was no gold to be found in the tunnels. (*But it had to be down there somewhere,* he thought.)

Saturday morning Magali and François had made arrangements to go out to see Amanda.

It was a sweet and sad meeting. They talked about Amanda's future studies and about Magali and François. Nobody said a word about the past adventure.

When François and Magali left, there were tears in Amanda's eyes. *"Hasta la vista,"* said Magali. "I leave with you my address in Boston. Come and see us!" But those words fell like feathers on the lovely blue tiled floor. Magali knew she would probably never see her friend again.

The rest of the day they spent finishing with the packing. They had an evening meal at home and went to bed early.

Sunday was to be Magali's last at *Los Sapos.* She and François toured all of the stands and displays, taking their time and looking for anything light enough in weight and valuable and desirable enough to take back with them to the U.S. They were tourists.

They ended up in an all too a short time at *Los Gatos.* The waiter had a table waiting for them. She would miss him.

He had brought her usual Sidral, and he took an order from François for a *Negra Modelo.*

About 10:30 Paul came to join them.

Paul was feeling exceptionally happy that morning. Maybe he had gotten a huge pay envelope. He ordered a beer and sat with them, watching the people pass by. He said he was going to his family in San Diego for the vacation. He asked Magali what they were going to do.

Magali told him about their plans to go back to the States. This was to be her last day in Puebla. She had been waiting for today to see him again and to say her farewell. The last few days were too filled to really accomplish anything.

She gave Paul her address in Boston, and asked him to keep in contact.

Just then Roberto arrived and joined them.

Roberto also looked very happy, in spite of the wild adventure they had just gone though. Paul asked what was new, and Roberto gladly responded.

He said he had met with a young professor who will guide and read his thesis for the *Licenciado*. They had come to an agreement on the subject, and it was to have a working title of "Psychological Varieties in Family Disorders."

Roberto explained, more to François than to Magali and Paul, that he had already been working with a firm in Puebla providing psychological counseling to juvenile patients, and sometimes to their parents—dealing with problems between members of the family, or problems with the children and their studies, or problems of juvenile delinquency—all very interesting, but it had not paid much money.

Roberto was going to associate himself with this professor in a new firm. His thesis would be published in fulfillment of the degree, but in a very limited quantity, and these would be distributed to a very few close friends. The publication of the thesis as a book, on the other hand, would give him some recognition as an expert in the field. Meanwhile he would rewrite the thesis as a manual for the treatment of family disorders. It will be used in the new firm, serving as a working manual to the many *pasantes* they will hire to do most of the counseling. They will use it much as physicians use drug manuals. They look up the disease and prescribe the drug and dosage the pharmaceutical company recommends. In the case of his new firm, the *pasantes* will diagnose the disorder and recommend the treatment according to the manual. Much like a pill or a shot of antibiotics. It will be assembly line work, but with some class. The new firm will seek clients even more wealthy. There are many rich families in Puebla, and they all have problems with their children.

Another great news item: through this professor he will have a contact with another professor in the D.F. This one is at UNAM. He will fix it so he can go to UNAM for a doctorate in psychology. This other professor in turn will establish and operate a branch of the firm in the D.F. There are even more potential clients in the D.F. who are rich.

Magali observed that that might not work out. Surely getting a Ph.D. must be more difficult than that. Connections can only do some much.

"You don't understand, Magali," replied Roberto. "We are a tropical country. Anything can happen in a tropical country, and usually does. Connections *do* count here. A cousin, a friend. Nothing is rigid. There are ways to get things done; there are many ways. Ways you or I have never, or I should say 'not yet,' dreamed of. Whatever a mind can imagine, and ingenuity can devise, can be done. Anything!"

Monday morning, at 6:00 a.m. (Magali had arranged for a "radio taxi" to come to pick them up), they took a last look at her apartment. Magali felt a pang of sadness. After all, it had been her home for almost a whole year.

She hadn't had too much to pack, and it had been easily done. She had given away most of her books to Amanda. She had the two suitcases she had brought with her to Mexico, which now contained what was left of her clothing and some Mexican outfits she had bought to bring back to the States. They also encased a few gold and silver presents she had bought for friends and family from a little old fashioned jewelry shop by the *Zócalo*. She had chosen a pendant of silver and black onyx for her mother (an Aztec Calendar) with a heavy silver chain, and several other brooches and bracelets for her friends, all with Mexican motifs. Her research and monograph were in a small American Tourister carry-on. One set of disks was in her handbag. The rest of her few possessions had been quickly thrown into another soft carry-on bag.

She opened the windows of her apartment and took a last look at the Popo, still smoking, still spreading, on occasion, more gray, oily ashes over the city. But the sun was rising, the sky turned suddenly blue, and Magali was filled with a sense of satisfaction and happiness.

They went out with their bags to wait in front of the door to the building for the taxi. But it was there waiting for them. Their bags were put in the trunk and they got in and the taxi headed for the CAPU where they would take the Estrella Roja bus to the airport in the D.F. They were going home.